Elizabeth Aston lives in Oxford and Lazio, Italy. She is married with a son and a daughter. *The Exploits and Adventures of Miss Alethea Darcy* is her second Regency novel. Her first, *Mr Darcy's Daughters*, is also available in Orion paperback.

The Exploits and Adventures of MISS ALETHEA DARCY

Elizabeth Aston

An Orion paperback

First published in Great Britain in 2004
by Orion
This paperback edition published in 2006
by Orion Books Ltd,
Orion House, 5 Upper St Martin's Lane,
London WC2H 9EA

1 3 5 7 9 10 8 6 4 2

A CIP catalogue record for this book is available from the British Library.

ISBN-13: 978-0-75-287737-2
ISBN-10: 0-75-287737-2

Typeset by Deltatype Ltd, Birkenhead, Merseyside

Printed in Great Britain by
Clays Ltd, St Ives plc

www.orionbooks.co.uk

For Paul

Prologue

The window slid up without a sound, with not a rattle nor squeak to break the silence of early morning. Alethea hitched a leg over the sill, leant down to pick up her bundle of clothes and swung the other leg over. Perching some fifteen feet above the ground, she glanced back into the bedchamber. The motionless figure on the bed was snoring quietly, an arm flung out over the covers, his hair ruffled. The remnants of a fire crackled as a burnt log broke and fell apart in a shower of sparks.

She eased herself down from the sill on to the branch of the magnolia tree espaliered against the red bricks of the house. The huge creamy flowers showed pale in the greyness of the early morning. She shut the window by tugging on the glazing bars, dropped the bundle, and began her descent.

A gentle scrunch on gravel as her feet touched the ground. A pounding heart, a catching of breath. Fear mingled with elation as she smelt the misty morning air and tasted freedom. She didn't pause to catch her breath or to think about what she was doing. There was not a moment to lose. She picked up her bundle and edged round the corner of the house.

No one stirred. No dog barked, no early-wakening servant called out to ask who was there. With swift, silent steps, she crossed the sweep, on to the lawn, running now alongside the driveway, visible to anyone who looked out from the rows of windows of the great house. No challenge rang out: no shouted demands for her to stop broke the dawn peace. The only sound was of birdsong, and, then, in a distant farmyard, a cock crowed.

Figgins was waiting beside the gate, her face tight with anxiety.

'What's there in that bundle, Miss Alethea? I thought you wasn't bringing anything with you.'

'Some clothes, and pray remember I'm no longer Miss, nor Alethea. Mr Hawkins, if you please. Mr Aloysius Hawkins, gentleman.'

They were walking briskly along the lane now, the huge wrought-iron gates behind them, the stately line of limes hiding them from any watching eyes. Only why should there be any watching eyes? How could anyone suspect that the dutiful obedient Mrs Napier should abscond before dawn, leaving husband, house and all behind her?

'I thought you didn't want to bring anything from there.'

'It's best that I'm thought to have left the house as a woman. If a blue gown is missing they will search for a woman in a blue gown, not a man. Now, tell me, where is the carriage?'

'I told them to wait at the corner.'

Alethea was striding along, relishing the freedom of trousers and boots, of stretching her legs instead of taking ladylike steps. She slowed as Figgins stumbled against a large stone.

'I can't be doing with these country lanes,' Figgins said. 'I don't know how folk put up with living in the wilds like this. It isn't natural, people were meant to live in cities.'

'This is hardly the wilds, we are a mere twenty-one miles from London.'

'Might as well be on the moon, for it's a different world out here and not one I fancy. It was so quiet waiting here for you, it fair gave me the creeps. And there was something up in the tree above my head making a dreadful hooting sound.'

'An owl.'

'Owls is unlucky.'

'Not this one.'

They were at the end of the lane. There, standing in the

mist rising from the warming ground, was a coach, with a postboy waiting by the two horses. As they approached, he went to the door of the carriage, and let down the step.

Alethea gave him a quick good morning, and then jumped in, followed by Figgins. Up went the step, the door was closed, the postboy swung himself into the saddle and clicked the horses into movement.

She had escaped.

PART ONE

Chapter One

'Do not trouble to deny that my brother is in,' said Lady Jerrold as she stepped over the threshold of the house in Milburn Street. 'This is not a social call, so, if he is still abed, I will wait for him in the breakfast parlour. Tell him I am here.'

The butler had no choice but to obey, and Lady Jerrold sat down to wait for Titus. It was so like him not to be up and about, it was all part and parcel of a life that lacked direction. Titus Mannigtree, in his sister's opinion, was a fortunate man. He was clever, well born, rich and handsome, had a splendid seat in the country, a fine house in Town, a numerous acquaintance and several close friends.

Yet there was no man more bitter in all London. A fine military career – promotion, mentioned in despatches, trusted by the Duke of Wellington – lay behind him, as did a political career – trust Titus to have been outspoken in the House upon matters that were much better left undisturbed. His mistress had abandoned him, and he had managed to alienate the king. It was time that he took himself in hand.

Lost in thought, Lady Jerrold didn't hear his footsteps, and she looked up, startled, to see him frowning at her from the doorway.

'What are you doing here?'

Her eyebrows rose, and she mockingly advised him to pour himself a cup of coffee and carve himself a slice of ham. 'For I am persuaded that this shortness of temper must be due to lack of sustenance, and that you will be restored to your usual sweet nature upon eating.'

He laughed. 'Cora, you've still got a tongue on you that

would make a viper weep. I don't know how Jerrold puts up with you, indeed I don't.'

'Jerrold loves me dearly, as you very well know, and he doesn't feel the sharp edge of my tongue since he genuinely does have sweetness of nature. Unlike you, Titus. Now, sit down, and I shall tell you why I have come and then I shall remove myself and you can finish your breakfast in peace. Meanwhile, you may pour me a cup of coffee.'

He felt the pot and rang the bell with angry vigour. 'It's stone cold. I keep a pack of servants in this house, eating their heads off, and the coffee's cold.'

'What this house needs is a mistress.'

'Oh, are you on that again? Well, I tell you, it needs no such thing.'

'Yes, it does. And I am sure that with Emily married to her Italian, you very much feel an emptiness in your life, a lack of congenial female company.'

'Mind your own affairs, Cora, and leave me to mind mine. Keep Emily out of this.'

'No, for it is Emily herself who asked me to help you.'

'Emily asked you? How dare she?'

'Emily is exceedingly fond of you, as you must know, close as you have been these five years or more.'

'Not fond enough to accept my hand when she was widowed.'

'She felt you were not the kind of man to make her a good husband. You are too restless, unsettled, angry with life.'

He gave a mirthless laugh. 'And that prinking musician is going to make her a good husband?'

His sister heard the bitterness beneath his angry words and saw a severe, shuttered look come over his face, a look that she knew all too well.

'Never mind Emily,' she said hastily. 'That is all in the past now, and you must consider the future. You grow no younger, and—'

'Thank you, I am not in my dotage, I believe, and I do not think five and thirty any great age.'

'Indeed, it is not. It is the age of maturity, when a man is at ease with himself, and has more to offer to a wife than at any other age.'

'The devil with your wives.' He brushed aside her protest at the strength of his language. 'Don't be missish, Cora, and don't pretend you don't hear a great deal worse any day of the week.'

'Not in the circles in which I move.'

'Then you're in dull company. I've no thought of a wife just at present, so you may save your breath. I have got a woman in my eye and my mind, though, and she is going to take up all my time and energy these next weeks and months. I shan't be satisfied until I have her home, where she belongs.'

'You're bringing a woman home? Here? A mistress? You cannot, it would never do.'

'Don't see why not, I could name you dozens of men who've done just that. Besides, she isn't that kind of a woman. You've got a vulgar mind, Cora, that's what it is, harping on mistresses and liaisons. What I'm talking about is beauty, a beauty the like of which you'll never find gracing your balls and routs and drums.'

'Who is she?' Lady Jerrold was all curiosity now, perched on the edge of her seat, leaning forward eagerly.

'Do you remember my going abroad with our father, years ago – you'd have been in the schoolroom? In the year two, during the Peace of Amiens?'

'I remember Papa going off to France, and Mama being in a dreadful state, for she insisted that Napoleon would start fighting again at any moment, and he would be swept away into a prison and never seen again, that was, if he didn't have his head lopped off. I don't recall that you went with him, however. I thought you were up at Oxford then.'

'He took me with him before I started at Oxford. He had no more expectation than Mama did of the peace holding, and he reckoned it might scupper any chance I might have of touring on the continent. He was right, too, it was several years before I was able to visit France again.'

'What has this to do with your beauty?'

'Only this, that while we were in Italy, our father bought a great many paintings. One of them was a Titian. A superb painting, one of his red-headed beauties, the most voluptuous creature.'

'One with no clothes on, I suppose from your raptures.'

'There is that, and her form is exquisite, but it is the face that enchants. Such eyes, such an expression, such a mouth.'

She was disconcerted by his enthusiasm. 'You speak like a lover.'

'Don't be a fool. This isn't some poetic nonsense about mooning over a picture. This is a missing painting, and it's mine, and I want it – her – back in my possession. Hanging on my wall, over the fireplace in the red drawing room at Beaumont. Or possibly on the stairs here. She's the only female I'm interested in right now, and pursuing her is going to take up all my time and energy. So if you've got a line of eligible females lined up for me to do the pretty to, you may dismiss them.'

Lady Jerrold flashed back at him. 'Eligible females, is it? The way you've been carrying on with Emily, there isn't a respectable mama in the town who'd let you anywhere near her daughter. You're dangerous, Titus. The best you can hope for now is a rich widow, and it so happens—'

'No.'

She knew that tone of voice. She rose to take her leave. 'I wish you joy of your picture hunt,' she said in a cold voice.

'Liar. You wish I may catch cold over it, and end up with lighter pockets and no picture.'

'Your pockets are quite deep enough to buy a Titian on your own account. I don't see why you have to make such a song and dance about this particular one.'

'Because it belonged to our father, it now belongs to me,

and I want it back. And, moreover, it transpires that the king has wind of it, wishes to add it to his collection, and I'm damned if I'll put up with his getting his pudgy hands on it.'

Cora had reached the door, but the savagery in his voice made her pause and turn round. She came back into the room and sat down by the window. 'Calm down, Titus, you are always telling me to be rational, now it is your turn. Why, if Papa bought this painting, is it not already at Beaumont?'

'The war intervened. Napoleon raised his ugly head above the parapet, and we were all at it again, up and down the countries of Europe, watering the fields with blood. It was impossible for our father to bring back many of the purchases he had made on that trip, it was a matter of getting ourselves back across the channel without being thrown into a French prison for the duration.'

'So there were other works of art that went missing.'

'Yes, but none so fine as the Titian.'

'Come 1812, why did Papa not go back to Italy and find the painting?'

'I have no idea.'

'And now it's reappeared, is that it? Have you papers to prove ownership? You may ask a good price, you know, from the king.'

'You don't understand. I, the owner of the painting, don't enter into these negotiations at all. George Warren has found out where it is, the dog, and intends to do a deal with whoever it is that has my painting in his possession. On the king's behalf. He will pocket a handsome commission from our fat monarch and walk away so much the richer.'

'Does he know the painting is yours?'

'Yes. It is well documented, the description he has given to the king matches in every detail.'

'If you are sure of your ground, then make the affair public, show how shabby Warren's behaviour is.'

'Much good that will do, the whole of London is used to Warren's shabby behaviour. And Warren's not the only one to behave shabbily, for I swear that the king himself knows that the painting belonged to our father.'

'Have you not antagonised the king enough?'

'It would give me great pleasure to annoy him further, and if I can do it by depriving him of a Titian for the royal collection, so much the better. It will be a good revenge to lay my hands on this Venus before Warren does, and bring it back to Beaumont, where it belongs.'

Lady Jerrold was somewhat relieved that her brother was not suffering from any Pygmalion tendencies, but she was alarmed to find him expressing such outright hostility to the king. However, it would never do to say so; once Titus had an idea fixed in his head, there was never any turning him away from his purpose.

'Do you know where it is?'

'No, but I'm damn well going to find out, if I have to put a posse of spies on Warren.'

'Just Bootle will do, I imagine, the man knows everything that goes on in London.'

Bootle was Titus's valet, a man of whom Cora heartily disapproved. She had to admit that he never gossiped about his master, but that was, in her eyes, his one redeeming feature.

She drew on her gloves. 'I imagine this means that you will be off abroad, or is the Titian perhaps hidden in some lonely castle in Scotland?'

'You read too many novels of the more sensational kind, Cora.'

'And you, my dear brother, are determined to live a life of the more sensational kind. You'll tweak the royal lion's nose once too often, and then you'll have to flee these shores for good.'

He bent his head to kiss her cheek. 'I hope my wicked nephews and nieces are in good health and spirits?'

'They are indeed, and wanting Uncle Titus to come and

play bears with them again. I told them that you are presently a bear with a sore head, and not in the mood for games.'

Bootle had known how it would be, when he brought his master the news that George Warren was on his way to Paris.

'The devil take him,' said Titus. 'He's off to get the picture. Well, he isn't going to find it as easy as he thinks. Bootle, start packing.'

Which Bootle already had, and he was quite pleased to do so. Maybe a journey abroad, for all its inconveniences, would shake some of the fidgets out of his master. He'd never known him to be so out of sorts for so long; Mrs Thruxton might have a lot to do with it, but there was more to it than that. Mr Manningtree was the kind of man who needed a purpose in life. His estates were in excellent order, and he wasn't one of your gentlemen farmers, happy to look after his crops and land. London society bored him and Bootle knew that his long sessions at Angelo's with the foils and his habit of walking wherever he went in town were merely a way of working off some of his energy.

Politics had seemed likely to take up a lot of his time and attention, but that hadn't worked out; that was the trouble with a man like Mr Manningtree, he was too clever and had too many ideas for those old dozers in the House of Commons. Yes, a trip abroad, sea air, the discomforts of travel, that would calm him down – if only for a while.

It might even rid him of this obsession with an old painting. Whatever had got into his master to get into such a passion about a picture? It was as though all his disappointment and rage had focused on the Titian, not to mention on Mr Warren – such a fuss about an Italian painting, it made no sense.

Chapter Two

'I took this chaise as far as Butley, like you wanted,' Figgins said. 'I told him we're changing there to the mail, going north.'

'Laying a false trail,' Alethea said, wrapping her cloak more closely about her.

'We've places on the stage that goes past at seven. When do you think they'll find you've gone and set up a hue and cry for you?'

Alethea yawned. 'Not till later than that. He'll sleep for hours yet, and I slipped some laudanum into the milk my maid brought me last thing – she always finishes up what I don't drink. She won't be up and about at her usual early hour.'

'Greedy creature, and more a wardress than a maid. Serve her right if she never wakes up.'

Alethea closed her eyes. Images of the life she had left behind her flashed in and out of her tired mind, tired because she hadn't slept a wink that night, nor for many nights before, and tired from the aching months of unhappiness.

How much she wished she could roll back time, undo those same months, and be as she was before her marriage: Miss Alethea Darcy, single and fancy free. Carefree.

Except that she hadn't been fancy free, that was the trouble. That was the reason for her precipitous rush into the married state. Marry in haste and repent at leisure, wasn't that how the saying went? How true, how very true, in her case. How could she have been so foolhardy? Even in the depths of her anguish, she might have known that Norris Napier was no fitting husband for her.

But then, she had felt that no man on earth would do, other than the one man she could not wed. And her pride, her cursed pride, had persuaded her that a marriage – any marriage – was the only way to deflect the pity and false sympathy and relish, even, of the polite world.

She didn't want to think about those dreadful days after the announcement of Penrose's engagement to Miss Gray, yet the memories would intrude: the nightmare journey back to Aubrey Square, the exquisite relief of reaching the privacy of her bedchamber, of lying wracked and exhausted across her bed, of Dawson, Lady Fanny's maid, coming in with brisk exhortations that belied the sympathy in her eyes and giving her a draught that sent her into a troubled, unhappy sleep.

Mr Fitzwilliam, tight-lipped, disapproving of her having so openly shown affection for Penrose, yet angry with the Youdalls for treating a member of his family in such a way.

Fanny, kind, understanding, sitting beside her and telling her of her own agonies as a girl when she wasn't allowed to marry the man she loved – 'He was so handsome and dashing, but he was poor and of no consequence or position, and I was an earl's daughter and had to remember my duty to my family, and make what they called a good marriage. I was wretched for weeks, and yet in the end I came back into my senses and began to enjoy life again, and then, when I met my dear Mr Fitzwilliam, I forgot all about that first love.'

Was that a consolation, that she might meet a man like Mr Fitzwilliam? Heaven forbid, and how could Fanny suggest that one would think for a moment of a Fitzwilliam when one was in love with Penrose.

'She's such a squab of a girl,' she exclaimed.

'Diana Gray? I don't care for her myself, and certainly in comparison to you . . . However, that is not what this marriage is about. It is about money and property and what an imperious mother thinks is best for her son. And you know, my dear, it is a weakness in Penrose that he should submit to his mother's will. People say he is a dutiful son; I say it is the behaviour of a milksop to marry a woman at your mother's behest when you are in love with another.'

Another storm of tears from Alethea: how could Fanny call Penrose a milksop?

'One's first love is always perfect until one meets one's second love,' said Fanny sadly.

Alethea didn't know just how much her cousin's heart went out to her. Fanny had expected the two of them to marry, believing them to be a finely matched pair. Her indignation at Penrose's behaviour, though, had to be shared with no one except Dawson, for Mr Fitzwilliam had decreed that the man's name was not to be mentioned under his roof, and Alethea refused to hear a word against him.

In return, Fanny insisted that Mr Fitzwilliam, though he might show kindness to Alethea, for he was a man of feeling beneath his rather conventional ways, was not to pity her. 'Believe me, my love, the one thing Alethea will not be able to bear is pity. She has her father's pride, and it will carry her through this setback, but she will not tolerate anyone who shows pity for her.'

'No, indeed, she will look down her nose at them, in that way she has.'

Fanny exclaimed at that. 'She does no such thing, she is always full of laughter and fun, what is this about looking down noses?'

'She's too like her father when something displeases her. Haughty, that's what she is. And even if she can put this affair behind her, she'd best learn to please a man, or she'll never get a husband.'

Fanny reported his words with some indignation to her friend Belinda Atcombe, who came to pay a morning call with the express intention of finding out the truth behind all the rumours that were flying about London.

'She has the Darcy pride, it is true, but she is as warm-hearted a creature as ever lived, and any man worth his salt would know it.'

'Warm-hearted or not, she's in trouble. Now, you know that you may trust me, Fanny,' said Belinda, smoothing her skirts as she sat down, 'for although I am a gossip to my fingertips, I also know how to be discreet when the need arises. Alethea is a connection of yours, I like her as well as pitying her from my heart. Young love – a first attachment I suppose? – yes, how well one remembers the anguish. I can be of great use in suppressing scandal, but I must have the full story.'

Fanny took a deep breath, and told her friend both what she knew, and what she suspected.

Belinda Atcombe gave a tsk of annoyance. 'Why ever did she fall for the worthless fellow? She is well rid of him, let me tell you.'

'They made such a handsome couple, it seemed a perfect match.'

'Nonsense. Alethea has far too much character and wit for a dolt like Penrose. It hardly takes a great intelligence to realise that he will live under his mother's thumb until she mercifully goes to her grave, and that he will meanwhile turn into just such another obstinate, narrow person as she is. His father was little better, the dullest man in Christendom. Is Alethea sighing and weeping about the house? Lord, how difficult girls are at that age. You could send her home to Pemberley, of course, if she's inconsolable, only that will merely fuel the gossip and spite. What do her parents say about it? Do they know how fond she has become of the young man?'

Fanny shook her head. 'I wrote to Lizzy, and said that Alethea greatly liked Penrose, but I didn't like to make too much of it.' She hesitated, then added, 'In truth, I do not think that Mr Darcy would be impressed by Penrose Youdall. '

'I am sure of it, and there are others who do not care for

him. I correspond with Hermione Wytton, who presently resides in Venice, you know, and she says that her son was dismayed to learn of his sister-in-law's attachment to Penrose.'

Alexander Wytton, Lady Hermione's eldest son, was married to Alethea's favourite sister, Camilla.

'Is he acquainted with young Youdall? I should not have thought they had much in common.'

'Enough, one gathers, for Alexander to despise him. I dare say he will think that Miss Gray is a better match for him.'

The two women spent a happy few minutes discussing the many shortcomings of that young lady, before Belinda Atcombe took a deep breath and said, 'That's all very well, but now we must consider what is to be done for Alethea to keep her good name.'

Alethea had plans of her own. Fanny had been right in saying that pity was what she most disliked, and she had no intention of showing her distress to an interested world. Summoning all her will, she forced her numb nerves into obedience, and went back into the social world that she had come to hate, armed with dignity, cool indifference and what a catty fellow debutante called that ridiculous Darcy haughtiness. She defied anyone to feel sorry for her, danced every dance at every ball, bought and wore new clothes, rode at the fashionable hour, said the right things at the right time and fooled virtually everyone except Fanny and Figgins.

Fanny's admiration for Alethea was beyond expression. 'She is behaving beautifully,' she told her husband.

'Cold-hearted, if you ask me,' said Mr Fitzwilliam.

Figgins had the worst of it, when Alethea let her guard down, allowing her maid to glimpse the depths of her misery and anger. Emotions cooled as time went by, into an indifference that Figgins found even more alarming. It was like the colour had gone out of Miss Alethea's life, she told Dawson, to which Dawson merely sniffed and said that the sooner the young lady was married and had a family to think about, the better. 'That Mr Napier will do well enough, he's showing her a good deal of attention, and he's a warm man, they say.'

Warm he might be, but Figgins hadn't taken to him, and she wondered just how much her mistress really liked him.

Had she been able to ask Alethea, and had Alethea told her the truth, she would have said that she was incapable of feeling any liking for any man, incapable of feeling anything very much at all. However, Napier was a great support to her at this time, encouraging her to play and sing. At first, there was nothing she less wanted to do; music would stir all the painful emotions she was so desperately fighting. He pointed out, in a civil, passing remark, that for her not to perform her music would arouse people's suspicions, and when, reluctantly, she went back to the keyboard she found that the music relieved her jangled spirit.

Tongues began to wag again. It seemed that Miss Alethea Darcy had not cared so very much for Penrose Youdall after all; she was heartless, no better than a flirt, flitting from one man to the next; Napier was a richer man, a better catch, but she'd never get him to the altar, scheming mamas had been after him for ever, and he had a mistress tucked away down in the country, so everyone said; it would be a good thing if she became engaged to Norris Napier, for it would lessen that smug Diana Gray's triumph no end; had they noticed Penrose Youdall's expression when he was watching Miss Alethea dance with Napier last night?

Belinda Atcombe conferred with Fanny. 'Is she really enamoured of Norris Napier? I know nothing against him, and yet I have a feeling . . .'

Fanny couldn't put into words why she, too, had a sense of unease about Napier. 'He has posted down to Derbyshire, to have an interview with Mr Darcy. The family are not well acquainted with the Napiers, they have asked Mr Fitzwilliam for his opinion.'

'Which is favourable, I suppose. Napier is a Tory, is he not?'

Fanny wanted to come to the defence of her husband, but could not. 'He says he finds Napier a very good kind of fellow.'

'Fitzwilliam never was a good judge of men, was he?' observed Belinda dispassionately. 'Men so often go by appearances and politics. Alethea has endured such unhappiness over Penrose, I should hate to see her make an unfortunate marriage.'

'There is the music, Alethea is so passionate about her music, it makes for a strong bond.'

'Strong enough, do you think? I doubt it. I think that Alethea had much better wait. At present, she imagines she will never truly care for another man as long as she lives, so what does it matter whom she marries? Delay matters if you can, Fanny, you will think of a way, I'm sure.'

Fanny had no opportunity. The date of the Youdall-Gray wedding became known and, within days, the Gazette carried the announcement of the forthcoming marriage of Miss Alethea Darcy, youngest daughter of Mr Darcy of Pemberley, Derbyshire, to Mr Norris Napier, of Tyrrwhit House, Hertfordshire.

Chapter Three

The stage was much less comfortable than the chaise, and Figgins was wedged between a clergyman of considerable girth and a burly merchant, both of them taking up more room than they'd paid for. Alethea was opposite, gazing down at her boots. Admiring the fine gloss Figgins had got on the gleaming Hessians? Figgins doubted it. Brooding, more likely.

Alethea looked up, glowered at the clergyman, whose face she seemed to have taken in dislike, and shut her eyes to blot him out.

Figgins sighed, and wriggled herself into a slightly more comfortable position. Well, Miss Alethea – never Mrs Napier to her – had plenty to brood about, the Lord knew. Her own mind, usually filled with the here and now, started to pick over the past, chewing over all that had happened to bring her and Miss Alethea to this rattling coach, on their way to London and then onwards to Dover and abroad.

Abroad!

Figgins knew about abroad; she had been abroad, and hadn't cared for it. Moreover, that had been a journey planned and undertaken in comfort with proper attendants and no sense of danger or urgency about it.

That had been before Miss Alethea's come-out, when her mistress hadn't known that men such as Norris Napier, rot his soul, existed. She, Figgins, could have told her what most men were like, but Miss Alethea had been bred up in a happy family, among good and honourable men; there was no reason for her to take any such cynical view of the opposite sex.

Well, she'd found out for herself the hard way, and Figgins

would have given a lot to spare her what she'd been through. What a mistake the marriage had been, and what a scrape it had landed them in. It was all very well to bowl across the countryside behind a team of galloping horses, but where would it end?

Still, if abroad was where Miss Alethea wanted to go, then she would need a companion, and who better than her one-time maid? Figgins still smarted under the contemptuous dismissal she had received from Miss Alethea's husband, on the very day of the wedding.

'That servant of yours is to be turned off,' he'd said, as though she was a piece of mouldy cheese to be thrown out for the stable cat. 'I'll have none but servants of my own choosing under my roof.'

And there had been Miss Alethea, arguing fit to bust, and she might as well have been addressing the statue in the square for all the notice he took of her. A right one he'd set to be her maid, too, a nasty, brutish kind of woman who had no proper notion of her work and was there to spy on Miss Alethea as much as to wait on her.

Lady Fanny had taken Figgins back into her household when she learned what had happened. 'I do hope he is not going to turn out to be a jealous man,' she had exclaimed. 'There is nothing more tiresome than a jealous husband.'

Jealous, well, that might be part of Napier's make-up, but it wasn't the worst of the man, not by a long chalk. She hadn't liked him, any more than she'd trusted that Mr Youdall, he who had broken Miss Alethea's heart, and had treated her so badly, bedding her and then wedding another.

Figgins had no time for men, no, nor for marriage. That was for fools, in her opinion. Look at her ma, seven children living and to be provided for, three dead before they were even born and four dead before they were five. What a way to spend your life! It was a miracle that Ma had survived, and what joy when she knew for sure she would have no more children. 'The happiest day of a woman's life, young Martha,' she had told her daughter. 'When you know the Lord isn't going to send you any more children.'

The Lord could have laid off his deliveries a long time before, Figgins thought. Much better not to marry, never to risk a pregnancy, not to put yourself at the mercy of a man and of a brood of children. She liked her little brothers and sisters well enough, and had done her duty by the children in the Fitzwilliams' nursery, but the happiest day of her own young life was when she left the infantry behind and was promoted to the different world of grown-up clothes and a mistress who was more of a friend than anything else.

She would never forget the look on Miss Alethea's face that day when they drove away from Lord and Lady Milton's house. Never. Stricken, that's what she was, and that's how she knew she'd be, from the moment she heard the news in the servants' quarters that Mr Youdall was to wed that Miss Gray, a pert, smug, disagreeable girl in her view, and one as deserved a husband as fickle as Mr Penrose Youdall would probably turn out to be.

Good riddance to him, or so she would have said if Miss Alethea hadn't ended up with a husband a thousand times worse. It made her want to cry, it really did, to see the come-down of Miss Alethea, from such a proud, independent girl to a shadow of herself, bruised in body and soul and driven to desperate measures that would make her an outcast from the world she'd been born to if it ever came out.

It was wicked, the way he'd been let get away with it, tormenting Miss Alethea like a little boy torturing an animal. Penning her up in that house, watching her, taking everything away from her, not allowing her to have her letters, or her jewellery or pin money of her own. And her so rich and bringing such a fortune to him. He had told her that she and everything she had owned now belonged to him and was his to do as he liked with.

Figgins had had to behave in a very underhand manner to get close to her mistress, which she had set about doing the very day she heard in a roundabout way that Miss Alethea was in deep trouble. She'd had that from Mrs Barcombe's maid, when Miss Alethea's eldest sister, Miss Letty as was, now married to the Reverend Mr Barcombe, had come with her husband to stay in Aubrey Square.

A sly, sneaky wench was Betty, one who listened at doors whenever she could, but this time Figgins was thankful that she had, otherwise how would she have heard that Miss Alethea, permitted a rare visit to her sister, had told her things about her married life that made even Betty's hair stand on end?

'You wouldn't believe it, Martha,' Betty had said. 'Sister or no sister, Mrs Napier had a hard time getting a few minutes alone with my mistress, for that husband of hers watches her like he's her gaoler.'

'Don't tell me so,' said Figgins.

'I do tell you so, indeed. He lays down the law like she's a child, tells her when to get up and when to retire, what gowns she may wear. He hands out her jewellery – her own jewellery that she had on her marriage – and she can only have the pieces he chooses for her to use. Then every bit of it is to be handed over and locked away in his strong box at night. He makes her sing, he loves to hear her sing, dreadful caterwauling I call it, but the gentry go for that kind of music, as you know. She can't sing what she wants, but must wait for him to say what she may play and sing. Her voice is going, she said to her sister, and my mistress says, a good thing too, high time to give up such interest in music now she is a married woman and she'll soon have her nursery to think about, and that will be an end to all the music nonsense.

'Then Mrs Napier comes right back at her and says she hopes there won't ever be no children, not the way Mr Napier is, and my mistress puts her fingers in her ears—'

'How do you know that?' Figgins had demanded. 'Being as how you had your ear pressed to the door, I never heard you had eyes that went round corners.'

'They were talking that loudly I didn't have to do no pressing. It's a big keyhole, and no key to it, so I took a look and saw her with her hands against her ears. Mrs Barcombe says, "I'm not listening to another word, I don't want to hear such things, you're making it up." Then she goes on about how wicked of her sister to invent such tales and how it's her duty, now she's a married woman, to obey her husband in all things.' Betty paused and wrinkled her nose. 'Not that it isn't a case of the pot and the kettle, for my mistress is one as likes to rule the roost in her own house, and the reverend knows better than to argue with her, not if he wants a quiet life.'

Trust Mrs Barcombe to take it all so priggishly. Figgins had never had much time for Miss Alethea's eldest sister. No, nor for the twins, who were next to her in age, a flighty pair they were, in her opinion, with never a thought for anyone except themselves.

Mr Barcombe was a pleasant enough gentleman, though; maybe it was a pity that Miss Alethea hadn't spoken to him. Mind you, given what Betty said, he might not have stood up against the strictures of his wife, even if he had believed Miss Alethea. Husbands and wives all had their ways, and no two marriages alike, that was what Ma always said. Most of any husband's ways made a woman's life a misery, in Figgins's opinion. If it wasn't blows and cuffs, then it was harsh words, and one almost as bad as the other to a young woman like Miss Alethea.

No, Miss Alethea was in the right of it, for all that running away from the home of your lawful, wedded husband would be considered a great wickedness. She had no choice but to flee, and if it was madness to reckon on dressing up as a man and setting sail to foreign parts, which only the freedom of the male would allow her to do, then let them both be mad.

They made a pretty enough pair of men, she thought, glancing at Alethea, who was sitting back on the squabs, her long legs stretched out before her in their pantaloons and boots, such female shape as she had left after all the weight she'd lost being married to that monster well disguised by the well-cut coat and folds of a neck cloth.

As for herself, she'd always been thin. Scrawny, like a chicken, her brothers used to say, and also that no man would want to marry her, and wake up to find themselves cuddling an armful of bones. Very well, but now, clad in the unobtrusive sober clothes of a manservant, no one would give her a second glance, or doubt for a moment that she was what she appeared to be.

The tale of what Miss Alethea had said to her sister, relayed to Figgins in breathless tones by a round-eyed Betty, had galvanised Figgins into action. She recklessly gave in her notice to Lady Fanny, first having filched some notepaper to write herself a character. Then she'd tipped her savings out of the cotton stocking tucked into her mattress and had made her way to Hertfordshire, getting a lift on a wagon as far as Butley and then walking towards the small hamlet of Tyrrwhit.

She had no definite plan in mind, all she wanted was to get near enough to Miss Alethea, by some means or other, and to be able to talk to her. Mind you, it wasn't going to be easy, not if Betty hadn't been exaggerating about the way Napier kept an eye on her.

She was in luck, however. Walking along the grassy path that led to Tyrrwhit, she had met a sobbing girl coming the other way. Common humanity, apart from insatiable nosiness as to what her fellow human beings were up to, made her stop and offer comfort and find out why the girl was in such a state.

Turned off by Napier, this Meg Jenkins had been; well, she knew all about that – without a character, and her only fifteen, and, she said between hiccups, she'd never agree to what Mr Napier wanted to do with her, she'd sooner rot in hell for ever and ever, and what was she to do? Her da would never take her back into his house now she'd been turned off.

That this was the reward for refusing to let your master have his way with her didn't surprise Figgins in the least.

'And that awful Mrs Gillingham, as is Mr Napier's fancy piece, she was that rude to me, saying I was a silly, prudish miss who didn't know which side my bread was buttered.'

Figgins's interest quickened. 'Fancy piece?'

'She's his mistress, has been for years, the others say, and they laugh at poor Mrs Napier for having to put up with having such a woman as a guest under her own roof.'

Laugh, did they? 'What are you going to do?'

The girl was intending to walk to London and seek employment as a maid in a respectable house. Figgins raised her eyes to heaven, gave the girl a hunk of bread and a piece of cheese – she'd been sent away without a morsel to eat – and gave her directions to Ma's house. 'You tell her what happened and that Martha sent you to her, do you hear me?'

Figgins watched the forlorn figure dwindle into the distance, shrugged her shoulders and went on toward Tyrrwhit. She reckoned the girl would never make it to Ma's; with those looks and that ignorance of how many beans made two, she'd be snapped up long before she got to that part of the town.

It had given her an idea, however. Where one maidservant had been turned off, another would be sought. Moreover, the hapless Meg Jenkins had mentioned that they were short-staffed up at the House, they always were. Figgins knew that when Napier turned her off on his wedding day, it was not for dislike of her; he'd no more noticed her than he would a cur in the gutter. No, it was because she was part of his bride's former life, and he wanted to cut her off from that as completely as he could. She felt she could count on his making no connection between his wife's former servant and a lowly new maid called Susan Peters.

Lucky for them both that her brother was apprentice to a tailor, to a man in a good way of business near the Corn

Exchange. He didn't cut and sew for the smart of smarts, but he did well enough by his prosperous and social-climbing customers, and Joseph Figgins had a flare for the work and had happily made several suitable outfits for Alethea, as well as more ordinary garments for his sister.

'I don't know what your game is, sis,' he'd said to her. 'But money's money, and I dare say you come by it honest, for if you didn't you'd be looking over your shoulder for Ma to strike you down. I reckon it's some prank to do with that Miss Alethea you was used to work for, and what tricks that sort of lady gets up to isn't anything to do with me. I don't ask, and I don't want to know.'

'Just as well, young Joe, for I wasn't about to tell you. And if Ma starts asking where I am, which she may, you tell her that I've gone back into service with my last lady, and we're away in – oh, I don't know, tell her, Yorkshire.'

'Are you? You don't look like you're in Yorkshire to me.'

'Don't be cheeky, Joe, and look lively about getting those shirts done for me. Then I'll hand over the ready for the coats and for you to pay the seamstresses for the other work, and you forget you ever had this little job to do. Seeing it's outside your regular work, and your master would hang you up by the fingers if he knew you'd been sewing on your own account, that's best for both of us.'

'It's not like making for strangers,' Joe said uneasily. 'It's my own flesh and blood, after all. There's no harm in that.'

'No, there isn't, and no harm in keeping your trap shut, neither.' She was busily tucking away coats, shirts and small clothes into a large bag she'd brought with her. Finished, she bent forward and gave her brother a peck on the cheek.

'Mind you visit Ma regular and don't let her get worrying about me.'

'And you did come by that money honest?' he asked again, as he opened the door for her.

'It belongs to the person as will be wearing those coats and trousers, and every penny of it rightfully' – a slight pause – 'rightfully his.'

And it was honest come by, too, Figgins reflected. Most of the roll of soft, as the gents called it, and a heap of clinking gold coins besides were now tucked away about Miss Alethea's person, with a reserve entrusted to her, more money than she'd ever seen in her life.

'Eggs in baskets and all that,' Miss Alethea had said. 'Go on, take it. We might be separated, and I don't want you alone and penniless in a strange country.'

Alone in a strange country? Perish the thought. And no danger of that, she was going to stick by Miss Alethea's side like she was her shadow. She felt in her pocket, where one of the notes was attached with a pin to the lining.

That had been a tricky moment, though, going into Trimble and Kedge's, jewellers to the nobility, with the diamond necklace and bracelet and hair piece tucked inside her cloak.

The jewellers were used to maids bringing in their mistresses' jewellery for cleaning or resetting, so the assistants took little notice of her, seeing to other more important clients first and leaving her standing until one of the more junior attendants found himself free.

She drew out the velvet box and laid it on the counter. Then she pressed the catch and lifted the lid. His eyebrows went up as he took in the quality of the diamonds lying there on their soft bed.

'For cleaning?'

'To be sold,' Figgins said boldly.

His expression changed. 'Sold? And how did you come by jewels such as this?'

'They belong to someone else, and she desires me to sell them on her behalf.'

An older, more experienced man, hearing her words, came over to his junior's side.

'She says she wants to sell these.'

'I'll call Mr Kedge,' the older man said smoothly. 'Leave it to me, you may go and attend that customer who is waiting.'

Mr Kedge was a lean, short individual with tufts of greying hair about a neat bald head. He glanced down at the diamonds, and then at Figgins.

'On your mistress's behalf, you say?'

'I do, and I have a letter to prove it.'

'Come this way.'

In the private room, he waved Figgins to an upright chair, and sat himself down on the other side of the table. 'I don't need to examine this set, I remember it well. Give me the letter, please.'

Figgins unfolded the sheet and passed it to him.

'These jewels were not included in the inventory of Miss Alethea Darcy's jewels at the time of her wedding. I believe they were left to her by a great aunt, and were lodged with us for cleaning. When I mentioned the oversight to her, she laughed and said it was of no importance, she would tell her father to make sure they were added to the list.'

Thank goodness Miss Alethea had never done so; by a lucky chance she forgot to mention them, and on her wedding day some instinct had led her to thrust them into Figgins's hands, bidding her in a hurried whisper to take care of them for her. Which she had, and what a blessing that was, for running away without a penny in your pockets was a sure way to disaster.

'They belong to Miss Alethea, personal, and she wants to sell them.'

Mr Kedge was quite used to ladies of the highest ton who needed to sell jewels for cash in hand, usually for gambling debts acquired without a husband's knowledge. In one or two cases he had known, the money had been needed to pay off a blackmailer. It was all the same to him. He recognised Figgins, who had accompanied Miss Alethea Darcy to the jewellers on more than one occasion. He knew all the Miss Darcys, as they had been, and was well acquainted with Miss

Alethea's father. Mr Darcy had dealt with his firm for many, many years.

If his daughter were in want of money, for whatever purpose, it was only right for him to help her out, in the interests both of business and of serving an old and valuable customer. As to Mr Napier probably being unaware of the existence of the jewels and almost certainly ignorant of the contemplated sale, that didn't bother him. He had taken Mr Napier in dislike the one time he had met him, and owed him no kind of loyalty.

'Normally, as jewellers, we advance only a proportion of the value of such a set,' he said to Figgins in an austere voice. 'For we have to make a profit when it comes to selling the items.'

Figgins was alarmed. A vision of the jewels displayed in the bay windows of the shop, to be recognised by a passing Darcy, or even Lady Fanny, came to her.

Mr Kedge read the alarm in her face. 'We are always extremely discreet in disposing of such jewellery. There is no question of the diamonds being set out on public display. And, in this case, it might be that at a later date, Mrs Napier may wish to re-purchase the set, given that they are family jewels and will have some sentimental value to her. So assure your mistress that I shall put them aside for a while, so that she can redeem them if she so wishes. Of course, we cannot keep them for ever, but shall endeavour to hold on to them for as long as seems reasonable.'

He opened the safe and drew out a money box. 'This is more than I would pay in normal circumstances, but I would not wish Mrs Napier to be the loser by any such transaction. Especially if she had immediate gambling debts, say.'

He handed her the notes and coins. 'Hide that away, if you please, and I will instruct one of my young men to summon a chair for you. You are not to be wandering about the streets of London with such a sum about your person.'

Gambling debts, Figgins reflected as she looked out of the

small window of the coach at a spring morning that promised a fine, warm day. Well, it was true in a way, for what Miss Alethea had planned was indeed a gamble.

Chapter Four

George Warren had no scruples about retrieving Manningtree's painting and passing it on, for a substantial fee, to His Majesty, George IV. By doing so, he would pay off several old scores against Manningtree, whom he held in dislike, he would earn the gratitude of his monarch, always useful to a man on the make, and he would pocket a tidy sum.

Scruples were for lesser men, he told himself, as he extended his neck for the slick flick of the razor. Trust, now, that was a funny thing. He trusted his barber not to slit his throat, for example, yet maybe it was only fear that kept the man from doing any such thing – and also the knowledge that to draw so much as a drop of blood was to lose his payment and also his customer.

Not that he cared one way or the other for this barber. Barbers, even skilful ones, were two a penny. This barber might cut his own throat, and it wouldn't bother him a jot, he wouldn't even have the inconvenience of finding another, equally skilled barber to shave him. His manservant would see to that.

Servants stayed with you and did their duty out of pure self-interest. You trusted them because it was easier that way, and because, with one's considerable knowledge of the world, one knew that a treacherous servant was easily spotted and removed. Provided one had an ally in the servants' hall, such as his own invaluable man Nyers.

He trusted Nyers, then. Yes, because the man relied on him for his wages, for a roof over his head and to keep up his reputation as a first-class gentleman's gentleman. If he,

Warren, let the man down by going to an inferior tailor or becoming careless about his neck cloths, then Nyers would up and leave him and find a better master. But while he remained in his service, he was trustworthy, simply because their interests coincided.

He tilted his neck so that the barber, whisking away a trace of soap from his chin, could attend to the hairline.

In the polite world, trust was a different matter. A man trusted a friend or a mistress at his peril. Either could turn on him without so much as a by your leave, and very likely would. Even so faithful, in her fashion, a lover as Mrs Beecham was worthy of no more trust than an afternoon's intimacy would warrant. And she had, he believed, a genuine interest in his well-being.

He trusted his stepmother. Probably no one else in the world did, for she was fickle and vengeful and spiteful. Her husband, his father, feared her, and her acquaintances were apt to be wary of her. But he trusted her with his money, his moods, his secrets.

He would go and call upon her this morning. She would be delighted to hear of his *coup* with regard to the Manningtree Titian, as he liked to call it, and sharing his scheme would add zest to the satisfaction of doing the man an ill turn.

She was delighted when he told her of it a mere hour later. He arrived without ceremony, her butler knowing better than to tell Mr Warren that Lady Warren was not at home. She was seated in her morning parlour, writing letters, a little heap of correspondence and invitations lying before her on her exquisite walnut writing table.

He regarded her with approval. Perfectly turned out himself, not the slightest crease in his coat or wrinkle in his pantaloons or the breath of a smudge on the mirrored surface of his boots, he liked to see a woman who took care how she looked, even when not, as it were, on duty.

Caroline Warren had never been a beauty, but she had taste and money at her disposal, and chose to present a stylish appearance both at home and abroad. The rich ginger of her dress suited her dark complexion, and the amber ornaments at throat and dangling from her ears complemented the silk admirably.

George had given her the amber pieces, and he was pleased to see them looking so well.

Lady Warren kissed her stepson, and told him that she had had the dress made up especially to go with the amber. This also pleased him, he liked his gifts to be taken seriously.

'Shall I be on the look-out for a fine cameo or two while I'm in Italy?'

She pursed her lips. 'Off again so soon? And to Italy, at this time of the year? Will it not be a tedious sort of a journey, with snow and avalanches in the Alps, and no doubt rivers in flood on the other side of the mountains?'

'How right you are, but it is a matter of business, urgent business that will not wait for more certain weather. Besides, spring is well advanced, I dare say it is all sunshine and daisies in the Alps.'

She gestured to a chair, and sat herself down on a chaise-longue. 'Business? What kind of business?'

'Royal business,' he replied with a wolfish smile. 'Money-making business, business that will put me in well with the king and may lead to more commissions of a similar nature.'

'Tell me.'

So he crossed one leg over the other with deliberate ease, leant back in his chair and told her about the missing Titian.

She laughed heartily at the thought of the rage that Titus Manningtree must feel when he had to accept that any plans he had of retrieving the painting had been thwarted by the cleverer plans of George Warren. 'Be careful,' she warned her stepson. 'He is an angry man when crossed, and a good shot.'

'Oh, a fig for that. He won't dare to do anything more than rant and fume, not once the painting's safely in the royal possession.'

'His father was quite a royal favourite, I seem to recall.

Mind you, he wasn't a man I ever cared for, and his son is just the same, hawk-nosed and far too sure of himself. I'm never impressed by these military reputations for courage and leadership, they are mostly made up after the event.'

'The son is no kind of a favourite with King George. Quite the contrary, in fact. There was some matter over a bill in the House, and it cost Manningtree his political career.'

'Everyone knows that.'

'Ah, but everyone doesn't know that his schemes so infuriated the king as to earn his most bitter enmity. That was why Manningtree had to give up any hope of political advancement. However much the country and Parliament alike hate the king, he still wields a lot of power, not to mention influence, and is well able to break a man if he chooses. Besides, Manningtree did himself no favours, he is too outspoken a man to do well in the House, and there were several others more than willing to see him brought down. No, he'll have to swallow his resentment over the Titian and retreat to Beaumont for another bout of brooding and temper.'

'He was hard struck by Emily Thruxton's rejecting him.'

George Warren's face lit up with the delight of a true gossip. 'Did he actually offer for her? Do you know that for sure?'

'I know that he wanted to marry her and that he's taken it very ill that she preferred an Italian nobody to him. What a blow to his pride! Not that it would be anything so very great, to get her for a wife, for she married beneath her, and that kind of thing carries a taint.'

'I knew of the nobody, of course, but I took it for granted that she'd married him because she couldn't bring Manningtree up to scratch. Well, well' – rubbing his hands together – 'so the Italian gets Thruxton's fortune, let's see how quickly he goes through that. Manningtree will be feeling sour indeed, and on top of it all he will have to watch his precious Titian flaunted before his eyes on the wall of the Pavilion or whatever other unsuitable place the king chooses to hang it.'

'When do you leave?'

'I'm posting down to Dover today, to catch the packet. I shall very likely pass through Paris either on my way out or on my return; are there any errands I may do for you?'

There were indeed. Silks smuggled in by George would save her a great deal of money, also scent. Her requests were precise, and George, who liked the ways of women, took a keen interest and made several suggestions of his own.

She kissed him on his cheek to send him on his way. 'Does your father know you are leaving the country?'

'I shall call on him, briefly, and tell him. I shall need some extra money, I suppose.'

His stepmother took the hint, and took several notes from the little drawer in her desk.

George ran lightly down the steps of the house, pleased with his visit. He had every intention of touching his father for some funds, as well; he would probably find him in his club at this time of day. One could never have too much of a good thing when travelling abroad. Who knew what expensive companions one might meet up with, or what objects of beauty or curiosity one might wish to acquire?

Chapter Five

The money stowed away inside her coat gave Alethea as much satisfaction as George Warren felt with his notes. As Mrs Napier, she had been allowed not a penny of her own. Upon her marriage, by law, everything she owned became her husband's. Her fortune, her jewels, her clothes, her books, her music, the very cream she used on her hands, it all belonged to her husband.

In practice in the modern world, women were no longer slaves to their husbands; indeed, Alethea doubted if most of them ever had been, even in mediaeval and historic times. Stern husbands, or would-be stern husbands, masters of their households, were usually no such thing. Look at her Cousin Fitzwilliam. Fanny let him think he was master in his house; while in fact, he was completely under his wife's sway.

She had had a friend, a young woman two or three years older than her, who had made a disastrous marriage. Seemingly pleasant, her husband turned out to be a tyrant within doors. A mere six months after they had left the church together, her friend was shaking the dust of her husband's house off her feet and driving back to her own family in a chaise and four.

Her father had not been best pleased, it was true, but he had felt a just indignation when he learned how his daughter had been treated, and in no way blamed her for fleeing the marital home.

As she was sure her own father would not blame her. She sighed inwardly. If only she had listened to Fanny's warning words about Napier when she had announced her intention of marrying him. Fanny had acknowledged the charm, but questioned the kindness of his nature. She had seen, as Alethea had been too distraught to do, the rigidity beneath the suave and pleasant surface.

'Take care, Alethea, that you do not throw away your life on a man for whom you have no strong feelings. You may not care much one way or the other just now, however, I beg of you to remember how binding are the marriage vows. Take your time, let us all get to know Mr Napier better, so that you and we may be sure he is the man you think he is.'

Fanny had been quite right. Her cousin might seem to be enclosed within serene and happy walls of domesticity, but she was a shrewd judge of a man for all that. And Alethea had a notion that she had a fair idea of what had passed between her and Penrose. A person of strict morals, Fanny could never approve of an illicit liaison of that kind. That was perhaps why Fanny had not been more forceful in her advice not to rush into marriage with Napier; she would think that what Alethea had done once, she might do again, and, in her view, the only safe place for such desire was the marriage bed.

Alethea blinked away the tears that started to her eyes at the memory of that night of stolen love. Wrong it might have been, misguided it certainly was, yes, and foolish too, but how very, very different it was from what passed for love-making between her and Norris Napier.

Well, all that was in the past. Her parents would be shocked to learn how her husband had treated her. How she wished that Papa and Mama were in England, that she could even now be heading for Pemberley.

They were not there; once her brother William was completely well again, running around the grounds at Pemberley and making his tutor's life a misery, Mr Darcy had responded to a request from the government for him to undertake a second diplomatic mission. His previous time in Constantinople had been highly successful; now he was to make a stay of some months in Vienna, accompanied, as before, by his wife. She no longer had any fears for William, she declared, and besides, Vienna was not Constantinople or China, they could very well keep in touch with their home from Vienna.

Alethea might have smuggled out a letter to them, once she had made contact with the resourceful Figgins, but she had hesitated. Letters could be delayed, opened, read, fall into the wrong hands. And what she had to say about her marriage was impossible to put down on paper. Then she had realised that she wasn't even sure she could say the words face to face; no one knew better than she how formidable Papa was when angry. Was there not a chance that he might feel she ought to return to the miseries of her marriage, try to make the best of it?

That was why she was on her way to Venice, not to Vienna.

Her sister Camilla and her husband were presently in Venice. Camilla, the second oldest of the Darcy daughters, was the one of her sisters that Alethea loved the best. She could trust Camilla with any secret and know that she would not be betrayed. Yes, and Alexander Wytton, too; he had more than once proved to be a man of his word, and was possessed of a keen sense of honour. Lucky Camilla, to have married such a man.

No, she wasn't going to waste time on such thoughts; that way lay self-pity, and self-pity was despicable. She must count her blessings; at least there was one person in the world she could speak to without reserve. She even felt that she might be able to reveal the worst aspects of her unfortunate marriage to so understanding a man as Wytton. Her sister and brother-in-law would take her in, they would advise how best she should approach her parents.

As the miles went by, she considered the journey ahead of her. One step at a time, that was what Griffy always said to her. When she plunged into a difficult sonata, or attempted a new dance or longed to be able to speak a language even before she had opened the grammar, Griffy would warn her to take it step by step. 'You can't jump down the stairs in one leap, however much you might wish to, and you even more surely can't jump up it, but one step and then the next and there you are, at the top or the bottom and not a bit out of breath or discomposed.'

Alethea knew herself to be, by nature, a leaper. She had leapt into love with Penrose and had leapt into marriage with Napier. If she couldn't have Penrose, she had recklessly persuaded herself that it didn't matter whom she married. Didn't many women make reasonably happy lives out of marriages to men they didn't feel any great love for? And she had acted precipitously for another reason, one that grieved her now: she had acted from pride, from the desperate desire not to appear distressed by Penrose's defection.

By becoming engaged so promptly to Napier, she had silenced the gossips; what folly to have allowed them to cause her a moment's concern. No, she wasn't going to let herself think either of Penrose or of Napier. She must not dwell on what was past. Soon, they would be in London. The transfer to the stage had been accomplished without a hitch, and any enquiries at the inn about carriages coming from the area of Tyrrwhit House would be met by the information that two young men had continued their journey northwards – if anyone at all remembered their being at a busy coaching inn on that particular day.

Napier would expect Alethea to be travelling alone; a woman without her maid and with no bandboxes would be conspicuous indeed; he would waste not a moment on accounts of any men travelling quite at their ease and headed in the wrong direction.

London, with busy hours spent in the acquisition of those necessaries that Figgins had been unable to obtain. Alethea had come, she reflected, out of her marriage as though reborn. We bring nothing into this world – the words from the burial service rattled round in her head as she hunted for suitable reading matter to sustain her on the long journey ahead.

The redoubtable Figgins had made all the arrangements. At the appointed hour they climbed aboard the Dover Mail – 'sixpence a mile, for each of us, why it's daylight robbery,' Figgins informed her – to find the other travellers already making themselves comfortable for the night with rugs, night-caps and even, in the case of one elegant young gentleman, a mask to cover his eyes.

'Though what for I can't imagine,' Figgins whispered to Alethea. 'It'll be pitch black as soon as we're beyond the town, on a night like this.'

For the weather had turned sour, with overcast skies and a thin drizzle to add to the discomfort of those who chose to travel on top of the Mail coach.

Alethea was convinced that she wouldn't sleep a wink. These coaches were designed for speed, not comfort, as she quickly discovered. None the less, the tiredness of one sleep-less night, the exhaustion of so much travelling, the turmoil of her mind and spirit which had worn itself into numb weariness all meant that her eyes were soon drooping, and within a very few minutes she was sound asleep, her head resting on Figgins's shoulder.

Catlike Figgins slept as well, although not deeply, on the alert for any movement from her mistress, any waking remark that might give them both away. But Alethea slept the miles away in utter silence, scarcely stirring for the various changes of horses, and did not wake until the coach rattled over the cobbles of the inn yard at Dover.

Dover, with the sea a heaving grey mass, matching the scudding clouds overhead. The packet rising and falling beside the quay, the seamen declaring that it was a capital wind, that they were destined for a swift passage. Then she and Figgins were down in the tiny cabin with its two berths, stowing the bags they had brought with them before going up on deck to say farewell to the white cliffs. Gulls swooped above the boat, their mournful, eerie cries echoing in their ears. The ropes were cast away, the sails filled, and the boat began to edge away from the shore.

As the vessel moved past the bar of the harbour, and hit the full force of the sea, Figgins announced that she would go below and get some sleep, if Mi . . . Mr Hawkins had no objection, and she – he, she meant – ought to do the same, while she could.

'Are you feeling unwell? Is it the seasickness?' Alethea enquired.

No, it was not the seasickness, it was merely the sight of all that nasty water. If God had meant them to travel on the waves he would have given them fins, and since he had not, the best way for a Christian soul to endure the voyage was to shut oneself away and pretend one was somewhere else.

Alethea remained on deck, revelling for a time in the rise and crash of the vessel, of the rattling of the halyards, the shriek of the rigging, the strong sounds of the sails. The white foam ran beneath her, the wind blew her cheeks into redness, the salt stung her eyes and she felt a wild exaltation.

She had done it. She had escaped from her cage, had left all that painful life behind her. She was off on an adventure into the unknown, and she was travelling, joy of joys, as a man, not a woman fettered by real or imagined frailty, long skirts and convention. She was a creature fully in charge of her own fate.

Then the motion of the boat became less agreeable, and her feelings took on a much more prosaic tone, as the first pangs of seasickness came over her.

*From Belinda Atcombe, in London, to her friend,
Lady Hermione Wytton, in Venice:*

This is not written in return for yours, for it is now three weeks since I had any word from you. The delights of Venice must tempt you out morning and night, for you were not used to be such a wretched correspondent. However, perhaps you are laid low with a cold or some such affliction, as I have been this past week. It is better when I am within doors and increases whenever I venture forth, but what is one to do, stay indoors yawning one's head off all day long? And this at the time of year when everyone who is anyone is in town and the list of gaieties is increasing every day.

Last night I was at the Quintocks'. Louisa is grown vastly fat this winter, I suppose in emulation of Henry Quintock's *enamorata*, and her posteriors are an astonishment to all. It will not do, though, for the *enamorata* is one of your ravishing sloe-eyed Latin beauties, whose amplitude of curves inspires universal admiration. Louisa merely resembles her overweight pug and her daughters are mighty cross with her for looking such a figure of fun.

You ask how the Youdall marriage has turned out. I have to say that the bride is a young lady not improved by marriage, as blushing shyness has given way to a pert boldness; not that her husband seems to notice. He is a fool to be so under his mother's iron control and now he has two of them to please so that his manhood must quite wilt and droop under their powerful rule. This perhaps accounts for the still slender figure of his bride who shows no signs of producing the heir that Mrs Youdall longs for.

People say he should have married the Darcy girl he was so hot for, your daughter-in-law Camilla's sister. She is something of a beauty, all those Darcy girls have good looks enough, but she made an ill choice when she took Norris Napier, handsome though he is. The *on dit* is that it is not a happy match. He has buried her away in the country, I hear no news of her being in the family way, and they say he makes her sing to him at all hours, even in the middle of the night.

The Napiers are not a family I would care to have any daughter of mine marry into, however fine and long their pedigree may be. There was that uncle who behaved so very oddly, do you remember him? They shut him away in the end. Lady Fanny Fitzwilliam, who is a dear friend, is very much concerned by the rumours, but as she says, what can anyone do? Married couples have to sort matters out between themselves as best they can.

How are Wytton and his bride? They are each as eccentric as the other, which may not make for an easy marriage. Pray remember me to Wytton, for whom I have a *tendre*, as you know. Were I twenty years younger, I should have cut him out with his rich Darcy daughter. Are they settled in Venice? He is such a gadabout, one hears of him now in Turkey, now in Egypt.

By the by, Alexander's old friend Titus Manningtree has left the country in his usual dramatic way, calling on his sister booted and spurred to announce that he was on the way to Falmouth to board his yacht and sail for France. He is still very cut up about Emily Thruxton's desertion, as he sees it, and doubtless feels that foreign fields will restore his equilibrium. If ever there was a man who needed to find a wife, it is Titus. Only who is there who could stand up to him and be the kind of companion he needs? One shudders to think of his sister-in-law ruling the roost at Beaumont, but that is how it will end; I fear he may have reached that age when marriage seems far too daunting an undertaking to be considered.

I am quite alone just now, with barely a cicisbeo or two left to bear me company. Freddie has gone away to Scotland and will not return this se'ennight, I wish him joy of the heather and the gamekeepers and am glad to be in London. An inclination for the wildness of the north is no bad thing in a husband; I could wish his brother shared it, the odious man came and sat a full hour yesterday, ungracious and surly, and not all my yawns served to get rid of him. Never was I more relieved than when his chair was finally called for and I could breathe again.

I was happy to hear that the weather in Venice has left off its fogs and when you next write I expect to have a good account of St Mark's gleaming in the sunlight and the waters of the Adriatic sparkling at your feet, not to mention the streets and canals thronged with handsome Venetians.

I remain, my dear, your most affectionate friend,

Belinda

PART TWO

Chapter Six

Paris.

A cold, grey day, with a wind ruffling the waters of the Seine and the trees still stark with the bareness of a late spring. Alethea and Figgins were heartily glad to have a respite from the interminable hours of travel they had endured since Alethea slid out of the window of Tyrrwhit House, but it was not an easy stay. Despite all that common sense told her about the unlikelihood of Napier knowing where she had gone, let alone setting off in pursuit, and the impossibility of his being now in Paris, Alethea couldn't help looking over her shoulder and jumping every time a carriage came into the Poisson d'Or where they were lodging.

Figgins was brusque. 'He can't be here, not without he's sprouted wings and flown across that dratted channel. It stands to reason; we came at such a pace, down to Dover and then straight on the road to Paris from Calais. If he should be on our trail, which I take leave to doubt, we'll be out of Paris and on our way to Italy before he sets foot on one of those dirty old bridges.'

Figgins didn't like Paris. In comparison with London, she said, it was grubby and mean-looking and she regarded the fine buildings with no enthusiasm. 'It's no good these Frenchies giving themselves airs for putting up one or two grand palaces, and they're most likely used as prisons or some such, look how they did away with the poor king and queen. And for every fine building there's a street full of hovels, and the streets aren't never cleaned, and they don't seem to have heard of gas lighting. Give me London any day. London is a city as is a city, and the people which live there are a respectable lot compared to these shifty types, cheat you as soon as look at you, you don't need to understand their language to know that, you can see it in their eyes.'

On the first occasion that Alethea had been in Paris, she had accompanied the Wyttons on a visit to her sister, Georgina, who was married to a rich Englishman. Sir Joshua had left England in a hurry after killing his man in a duel, and he had stayed in France ever since. Georgina had run off with him in the most outrageous manner, but that was an old scandal now, and one that had been well hushed up. As Lady Mordaunt, she was the mother of twin boys, and those who had forecast nothing but misery from the match had been quite confounded. Sir Joshua was dotingly fond of his beautiful young wife, and a proud father. Georgina had quickly found her feet in Parisian society, and had been at pains to show her little sister – who was quite half a head taller than her – how smart and infinitely superior this world was to London.

'Where the drawing rooms are full of bucolics, where eminent men are excluded from salons unless their fathers are lords. How much more civilised we are here in Paris! And so you will find when you have your come-out, I shall insist that Mama brings you to Paris so that you see for yourself how very superior the society here is.'

Alethea, who wasn't given to being impressed, and who had never had much respect for either of her twin sisters, had said that it seemed to suit Georgina, while privately thinking what a nonsense it all was.

And how different was her second visit to Paris in comparison with the prospects of delights that Georgina had planned for her. Alethea looked down at her drab coat and laughed.

Figgins was full of disapproval at Alethea's plan to call on her sister. 'Might as well announce to the whole world that you are here!'

'No, for I shall not call on her in her house, but send her a message to meet me somewhere quite private. A park, or some such place, where no one will take any notice of us.'

'And she'll bring that long-nosed husband of hers along with her, and he'll get on his high horse at the very idea of any young woman scurrying away from her husband like you have done, and say that you must stay under close supervision while word is sent to England of where you are.'

'Georgina will come alone, when she reads what I have to write.'

'And go dashing back to tell Sir Joshua the very instant she can.'

'Which will do her no good, for I shan't tell her where I'm putting up, and she wouldn't imagine for a moment that I'd stay in an inn such as the Poisson d'Or. Besides, she'll be looking for Mrs Napier, not for Aloysius Hawkins.'

Alethea donned her blue gown, which Figgins had thoughtfully put into her portmanteau, rolled up tight inside a pair of breeches, in case of a nosy chambermaid discovering it. Alethea hadn't thought it necessary to bring it, and said so, but Figgins knew better.

'Miss Camilla, Mrs Wytton, I should say, is very free and easy in her ways, but she didn't take to your hopping about London in breeches when you was younger, and you want her to help you when you get to Venice, not go exclaiming about you cavorting across Europe dressed like a man.'

It wasn't a smart gown, and it drew instant criticism from Georgina.

'You look such a dowd! And what an ugly bonnet, wherever did you buy such a dreadful thing?'

'It's the fashion in London,' Alethea said, untruthfully; she had sent Figgins out to buy the hat from a drapers in the next street to their inn.

Figgins had disapproved of it every bit as much as Georgina. 'For it is a nasty, unfashionable object, and one that no lady should be seen in.'

'I'm not a lady, I'm a man, and no one will give me a second look dressed like this,' Althea had replied.

'Does Mr Napier not give you money for your gowns?' Georgina said, unable to get over the shock.

'Never mind the gown.'

'Is Norris not with you?'

Alethea rushed her fence. 'Georgie, I have run away from him. He is . . . ' She couldn't finish her sentence.

'Run away! Do you mean you are here in Paris alone?'

'I have a servant with me.'

'A servant! Why have you done such a dreadful thing?'

'If you'll listen, I'll tell you.'

And she did, and Georgina did listen, but with no very sympathetic ear. 'You always were fond of dramatics, Alethea. It is wrong of you, very wrong, to run away from your husband. And I don't believe what you say about him. I heard from Letty, she says you were in Yorkshire complaining about Norris, and he was there with you, and she said she never saw such an attentive husband. You are making it all up, Alethea, you are in some scrape and think you can get out of it by running away. And coming to Paris! The very idea of it. The scandal, if it should become known.'

At first, Georgina had the moral advantage. Alethea felt shabby and ill at ease, and she hated having to say how things were between her and her husband. Just as she hated having to beg a favour from her older sister. They were attached to one another, but weren't close, and Georgina had always been a little afraid of her younger sister's sharp tongue and clever mind. Alethea's perception was as keen as her words, and she had the ability to make both the twins uncomfortable when she chose. Moreover, she laughed at them, and Georgina was one who took herself very seriously.

'Scandal! Any scandal there may be in my marriage is as nothing compared to the way you behaved when you ran off with Sir Joshua, yes, and lived with him before you were married and were his mistress before that.'

Georgina looked sulky. 'We were married almost at once.'

'Yes, and twins eight months later.'

'There is nothing to that, twins rarely go full term. There isn't a soul in Paris who does other than admire me for presenting Sir Joshua with an heir so promptly after we were married.'

'Well, I don't admire you for it.' She caught herself up. 'No, I didn't mean that, they are fine boys, and I am glad for your happiness. But can't you see, Georgie, that my marriage is not a happy one? Don't you wish for me to have the same pleasure in married life that you do?'

'Mr Napier is a proper man, he is handsome, rich, well-mannered, well-born, what more can you ask? He is a lover of music, that alone should make him acceptable to you.'

'That is the front he displays to the world. Let me tell you that once the door to the bedchamber is closed, he is a very different sort of person.'

'As to that, you are prudish, I dare say, and not quite used to what the marriage bed means. You will become accustomed by and by, and take pleasure in it.'

'I don't believe it is how Sir Joshua takes his pleasure of you.'

Georgina clapped his hands over her ears. 'I won't listen. You are making it up. Letty told me it would be so.'

'How heartless you are become, heartless and selfish.'

Georgina held out her hands. 'It is not so,' she said in cajolingly tones. 'Where are you staying? I will send a servant to collect your things; you may stay in Paris with us, you know, for as long as you want.'

'And Sir Joshua will send off an express this very day and before I have time to turn round, Mr Napier will be on the doorstep. I thank you, but no.'

'Alethea, you cannot walk away from your marriage like this, believe me, it is not possible. You have exchanged vows, you have been married so brief a time, just a few months. You have hardly had time to get to know one another.'

'It took one night for me to get to know what Napier is like.'

'Well, I do not want to hear another word about it. Is it to tell me all this that you have come to see me?'

It was a good question, and one that Alethea was asking herself. She knew why she was in Paris: it was a matter of convenience, a natural stopping place on her way to Italy.

As to why she had decided to call on Georgina, that was a more complex matter. It had to do with childhood alliances and sisterly solidarity, when they had tumbled in and out of trouble, she and Georgie and Belle. The twins were closest to her in age, and their heedless, careless approach to life had appealed to Alethea, with her innate appreciation of freedom.

Only now Belle was wrapped in feminine dreams of the happiness of approaching motherhood; she was a softened, more peaceful creature and Alethea would not have dreamed of approaching her for support or advice, not when she was so near her time.

Strait-laced Letty had behaved just as anyone could have predicted she would; there had been no point in expecting anything else from Letty. Wild, convention-flouting Georgie was another case – or so Alethea had thought.

Now, as she looked at her sister's beautiful, wary face, she knew she had made a mistake. There was no comfort or understanding or support to be had from her sister. She was happy in her marriage, secure in her position, not given to quick understanding of human relationships other than her own, reluctant certainly to take any steps of which her husband might disapprove.

As though she could read Alethea's mind, Georgina said, 'Sir Joshua does not consider you a good influence. Indeed, he says that the very idea of five sisters distresses him, he wishes to have my full confidence, he would be very angry if he discovered I was going behind his back in any dealings I might have with you or Belle or Letty or Camilla.'

In other words, Georgina would tell her husband that she

had seen her sister, even if Alethea begged her not to. She was a Mordaunt now, through and through, not a Darcy.

Alethea rose to go.

'Come back with me,' Georgina was urging. 'Take some refreshment, at least, and then we can talk further. You cannot stay alone in Paris.'

'I don't intend to.'

'Whatever do you mean? Oh, you are going back to England?'

'I am not,' Alethea said quickly, and added, 'I shall go to Austria.'

'You do not mean to go to Vienna! Only consider how angry Papa will be.'

It had been a mistake to have this meeting with her sister. She would run back to her husband with the shocking news; Sir Joshua would send word at once to Napier, and he would come after her, she was sure of it.

Let him, then, and let him go to Vienna. Once there, and finding no trace of her, she doubted if he would approach her father. He might be able to deceive Letty, who was a fool in such matters as these; he could hardly hope to hoodwink Mr Darcy.

Brushing aside Georgina's restraining hand, she walked quickly away from the park. Georgie might follow her, but she wouldn't get far, not in those shoes, and not alone. Alethea could vanish, in her dowdy gown, long before her sister could catch up with her.

'And I could have told you how it would be, and would you listen? No, and now it's hurry, hurry, pack up and go.' Figgins's voice was shrill and scolding. 'Without alerting the landlord that we're off at first light like a pair of scalded cats, if you please. An orderly journey, you said, that was what we were undertaking, an orderly journey. Well, so it could have been if you hadn't taken it into your head to visit Miss Georgina.'

Who had never knowingly helped another human being as far as Figgins was aware.

'For heaven's sake, keep your voice low. The landlord will grow suspicious if he hears your voice pitched so high.'

Figgins was silenced, but she muttered to herself as she deftly packed their bags. She'd known it would turn out ill. Miss Alethea didn't need to have another of her sisters turn her away, better not to ask for what you were sure not to get.

'It's lucky then you got the places on the coach booked. If you reckoned we'd need them, why did you go haring off after Lady M?'

'It was a precautionary measure,' Alethea said wearily. 'And a necessary one as things have turned out. Well, there is this to be said for it, the sooner we are on our way, the sooner will our travels be over. I can't wait to reach Venice.'

At least Miss Camilla wouldn't go giving her sister the cold shoulder. She was a lady as was up to snuff, as they said, and that Mr Wytton was no unworldly clergyman, he'd have no problems believing what Miss Alethea had to say about that husband of hers and his nasty ways.

Figgins pulled the straps tight with a satisfied grunt. 'There we are, all right and tight. I'll call the boy, and he can take this round to the posting office for us in his handcart. And do you cheer up, Miss Alethea. Every mile is a mile put between you and Mr Napier, and a mile nearer your family as is going to stand up for you. You longed to travel when you was in that schoolroom with Miss Griffin: how you used to listen to her stories of people going here, there and everywhere. All those wolves and bandits and spectres in the woods, I can see we're in for a lively time.'

'Yes, let us enjoy the journey as best we may, although I expect neither spectres nor bandits. A broken wheel is the most we have to fear, I believe.

Figgins saw with foreboding that a gleam had come into Miss Alethea's eye. 'Now, we have some hours to while away, let us not spend them cooped up in this inn. Young men such as we now are may go where we choose and enjoy all the delights that Paris may have to offer.'

Figgins cried out at that, but there was no stopping her mistress when she was in that kind of a reckless mood.

'The joy of going about with perfect freedom,' Alethea was saying. 'Only men have such freedom, so let us make the most of it.'

'And straight out into the Lord knows what dangers,' Figgins protested, as Alethea bundled her into her coat and out of the door.

Chapter Seven

In his youth, Titus had loved Paris. Dirty, positively mediaeval it might be, and half the size of London, but it was a lively city, where persons of every class rubbed shoulders and lived side by side. There were none of the rigid boundaries of London, no preoccupation with which addresses were socially acceptable and which beyond the pale. He liked the energy of the place, the outdoor cafés, the musicians and jugglers in the Palais Royale, the buzz of conversation in the streets, the courtesy of the Parisians, high and low.

Thirteen years after, he had found a different, darker city caught up in the aftermath of defeat. That had been in 1815; now, five years later, the city had come back to life. Building was under way, there was talk that something was to be done at last about the mephitic drains and the mucky, unpaved roads. Parisians were smart and full of chatter and vivacity once more, but to him it seemed an empty parade, and he wished he had not had to come. However, Bootle was sure that Paris was George Warren's destination, and wherever Warren went, he would follow, until he laid the wretch by the heels and seized his Titian from his clutches.

He had made his own enquiries, and was convinced that the painting must be in Italy. However, buying and selling could be done in Paris as well as anywhere; Paris was a city full of stolen and looted art of every description, anything was available if the price were right.

Bootle was being a damn nuisance. On his mettle in this city of fashion, he was being finicky over every speck of dust, demanding perfection of every fold of his master's neck cloth, insisting he wear the palest coloured pantaloons and then moaning when he came in with dirt upon them.

'Paris is a dirty city, Bootle. Three steps beyond the door, and all your perfection is undone.'

'In which case, sir, why is it that these Frenchies keep themselves so smart?'

Bootle had set out to find out what he could about George Warren's activities from the servants of English people currently residing in Paris. Titus visited art dealers, seeking out old acquaintances and finding who the new people were. Nobody had seen a Titian of the kind he described, no one had been offered any such painting, no one had heard any news of such a painting even existing.

'The late war,' said M. Dubenois, shaking his smooth grey head. 'So much of an upset to our business, such unsettled times. I fear that you must not place much faith in finding your father's painting.' His face brightened. 'However, the recent troubles have also brought their opportunities, I have some very fine items that I am sure would interest you.'

They didn't. Titus wasn't in Paris to inspect or barter or buy. Then he had news of George Warren: the wretched man was moving in his silky way through the ranks of society, relishing the gossip, picking up the threads of old friendships, exactly what so many of his compatriots were doing.

He seemed only to be passing through Paris. Titus was soon sure that his visit here was entirely for pleasure and would not be of long duration, and moreover that he was not undertaking any kind of negotiations that had to do with the world of art. He was frequenting the salon of a certain Madame de Faillaise, so Bootle informed him when he finally came to report that he, too, had drawn a blank with regard to the presence of a notable Titian here in Paris.

Titus remembered Madame de Faillaise. She had a pretty foot, yes, her charms were just such as would appeal to Warren. The fiend take him, why could he not stop his dalliance and continue his journey?

He resented the time spent there, was disinclined to enter into any social life and was annoyed when his cousin Eliza, a lively woman married to a diplomat, dragged him, reluctant and protesting, to soirées and balls.

'Titus, I declare you are behaving like a curmudgeonly old man, when I know for a fact you are not much above thirty. Here are beauties aplenty, French and English and every other nationality under the sun. If a man cannot find a delightful companion in this city, then there is no hope for him.'

'If by companion you mean . . .' he began.

She gave him a saucy look. 'I mean it is time you married and set up your nursery, all the family say so. Here is your chance, here are all these delightful creatures, spring is in the air, the very trees breathe *amour*. You must not sit and frown, but take your place in the dance and show that you can enjoy life.'

'Oh, as to that, I am a confirmed bachelor you know.'

'That's not what I heard. I heard that Emily turned you down, so you see you are a marrying man, and just as you get back on a horse when you have a fall, so you must enter the lists of love again, quickly, quickly, not fall into a melancholy because one woman rejected you. I have the highest regard for Emily, but she would not do for you, indeed she would not. She made you too comfortable, you need to find a young lady who leads you a dance and takes you out of yourself.'

Titus felt his anger rising. How dare she come trampling on his feelings like this? First his sister, and now his cousin. Why did women think they had the right to say whatever they liked on such matters? 'You do not know what you are talking of,' he said coldly.

'But indeed I do, and it is what everyone is talking of, and so you owe it to your family to hold your temper and show the world that you do not give a button for Emily, and that you have other amorous interests to amuse you.'

'Your levity and impertinence grow every time I see you,' he said crossly.

Eliza's withers were quite unwrung. 'How ungallant of you to make such a remark; why, you are a perfect bear. Come to my party tonight, I can promise you a bevy of pretty girls and beautiful women.'

He had gone, and had found she had spoken the truth. Pretty they were, indeed, and with some beauties among them, but they left him cold. He hadn't loved Emily for her beauty, although she had always been a well-looking and elegant woman, but for her humour and warmth and kindness.

The gaiety of the scene, the sparkling eyes and deliciously displayed bosoms, the inviting glances, the ripples of laughter, the perfumes lingering on the air – all this served only to enhance his mood of bleakness. The close presence of so many desirable women aroused his ardour, but the sensations brought him no sense of power or happiness. He could spend a night with any one of them and forget her the next morning. The emptiness in his life was for a different kind of woman, one who filled more than a hollow in the bed and an itch in the loins.

He made his excuses and left early. It was a warm evening, he would walk back to the Rue du Pelican, where Bootle would be waiting up to whisk away his evening clothes. He was in no hurry to get back to that nagging voice, and he wandered to and fro across the bridges of Paris, looking now into the murky depths of the swiftly flowing Seine, now across to the twinkling lights on each bank.

The city was alive and alert, and a more attractive place to his mind now that darkness had fallen, like an ugly whore who took on the lineaments of her youthful attractiveness in the soft light of dusk and candles.

He had just decided to return to the right bank across the Pont Royal when he heard a cry of alarm, a scuffle and the sound of running feet. The next minute a figure came pelting round the corner of an insalubrious street and ran straight into him.

The apologies were made first and instinctively in English,

then, as the slight figure regained his balance, he switched to French.

'English will do,' Titus said in that tongue. 'What's amiss? Were you set upon? You were a fool to go into such a street.' It was obvious that this was a very young man, no doubt visiting Paris with his father or a tutor; he was well spoken and seemed gently bred.

'I took a wrong turn and was lost in a maze of streets. Thank you, sir. My apologies for running into you, but the presence of another person has scared my pursuer off.'

'Why are you alone? Paris is a dangerous place after dark, or indeed, in those streets, at any time.'

They had moved into a pool of light flooding out from an eating place. Titus was struck by the youthful good looks, the soaring, well-defined eyebrows and the generous mouth. The face looked familiar, who was this handsome boy?

He caught himself up, shocked. That had never been his inclination, not even in his schooldays; not through lack of adventurousness or curiosity, but because his attention had early been drawn to the attractions of the fairer sex. Then it came to him. Christ, this was no well-bred young Englishman out a-whoring on his first trip abroad, as he had thought. It was a girl, dressed in men's clothes, doubtless out touting for those clients whose tastes lay that way.

To think that she had deceived him for even a moment, he must pull himself together. A good-looking girl, and young, it seemed a pity that she should have taken up such a life.

The boy-girl muttered a few words of thanks and then, before Titus could put out a restraining hand, had twisted away and was off.

The girl can run, Titus thought. I wonder where she learned to speak English like that. And then, I hope she comes to no further harm.

Which brought to his mind the shapely form of one Mathilde Rosarie, niece of the Comte de Montesquieu, whom he had met at Eliza's soirée. She had intimated that a late-evening caller might be made welcome. 'We play cards until dawn upon occasion,' she had informed him. He was not in a gaming mood, but he had a sudden craving for company, a wish to be away from these dark streets, and besides, who knew how a card game might end if the stakes were high? Mathilde had a head of glorious dark red hair, Titian red, the colour that went with a creamy skin and luminous hazel eyes. He imagined the hair spread in abandon across a satin pillow, and quickened his step.

Chapter Eight

Alethea judged it impossible to find Figgins out in the streets; she would return to the Poisson d'Or and await her there. She was worried; would Figgins, with barely a word of French, be able to find her way back to the inn?

Her fears were groundless. Figgins was ahead of her, waiting in her chamber, her thin face alive with concern. 'Well, there you are, Miss, I mean Mr Hawkins, sir, and here's me been sitting here this half hour on tenterhooks with no idea of where you might be or even if you was alive.'

'Why should I not be alive?'

'One minute you was standing there, beside me, in among all those jostling Frenchies, and I took my eyes off you for one moment, just to take note of a velvet gown cut in the new way, very smart, worn with a stomacher, and you disappeared like you were never there. What was I to think? So when I had done my best to find you, I thought there was nothing for it but to come back here and frighten myself into fits thinking what might have happened to you.'

She gave Alethea a shrewish look. Alethea, her colour as high as her spirits now that she had found Figgins safely back at the inn, lay back on the bed, her feet still on the floor and gave way to laughter.

'Why, I have had an adventure,' she said, when she had stopped laughing. 'And been rescued by a handsome English gentleman, who looked at me in such a way, and then with so much anger and puzzlement in his face that I had to run away!'

'Rescued!'

'It was when I was standing beside you, I was not wasting time on any velvet dress, but I was watching the fire swallower, I do long to know how he does the trick. Then I felt someone pressing against me, in a manner too familiar to be accidental. A lady of the night, I thought, but no such thing, when I turned round, it was a man. A kind of a man, that is to say, with so much rouge and such a soft mouth. He was tall and very elegantly dressed, not some thief with his hand reaching for my pocket as I for a moment imagined.'

'A gentleman, making up to you? I never heard of such a thing. How dared he?'

'Of course you heard of such a thing, for did we not find when we were out and about in our breeches in London that as many men as women gave us both the glad eye?'

'As to that, there are too many nasty men who like a lean boy instead of a woman, but here in Paris, on the street! Where anyone might see what he is about.'

'I didn't give him the chance to be about anything. I moved away from him, swiftly, as you may imagine, and that was when I lost sight of you. However, I had not shaken off this persistent gentleman, who was edging his way towards me again, so I dived into the crowd and took to my heels as soon as I could.'

'It's a wonder you didn't get lost.'

'Oh, but I did. I found myself in a maze of narrow, foul-smelling streets, I had no idea of where I might be.'

'Of course not, with dirty streets wherever you go in Paris. Whatever did you do?'

'Ran even harder, when I found my fine gentleman still coming after me. I tripped over a doorstep in my haste, and he caught up with me. So I shouted, in French and remembering to keep my voice as low as I could, while I kicked out at him. I think I hurt him, for he cried out and let go of me so that he could hold his leg. That was my chance, and I could see the river at the end of the street. The river, you know, is a great help in a city such as Paris. It was when I reached the corner that I ran into the other man, the one who wanted to come to my assistance.'

'And what was he doing, roaming about in such a district? Just such another, I warrant you, on the prowl for a molly or a slut.'

Alethea thought back. Her impression of the man had been swift, instinctive and favourable. She also felt that she had met him somewhere, and had not been at all surprised when he addressed her in English. Although there had been that glint in his eye; she did not care, these days, for a glint in any man's eye. Such glints had brought her nothing but trouble. At least Monsieur Rouge Cheeks only fancied her because he had mistaken her, reasonably enough, for a youth.

She yawned. 'Figgins, I neither know nor care. I shall see neither of them again, it was but a chance encounter in each case, and there's an end of it. Lord, how sleepy I am.'

Sleep didn't come swiftly or easily to her that night. She had tasted once again the delights of freedom, not merely freedom from the shackles of her disastrous marriage, but freedom from the constraints of the feminine world. However good a face she put on it, she had been frightened; she would not for the world have Figgins know just how frightened at the time, even though she could see the amusing side of her escapade once within the safe walls of the inn.

Both she and Figgins must needs be a great deal more careful. It was as well that their route would take them through no more cities such as Paris. Bern, for all she had ever heard, was a dull and sober city. They would find a respectable inn there, and in all the other towns on their way and not venture out. Her mind drifted away to thoughts of Venice, and of Vivaldi, whose music she had heard performed at the concerts of the Society of Ancient Music. To thoughts of canals and carnival and masks and, with a sense of relief, thoughts of her sister and Wytton.

Wytton would know what was best to be done, was her last

thought. Wytton and Camilla might be shocked, and angry, but they wouldn't turn away from her, as Georgina had done.

Chapter Nine

The mountains made Figgins stare. She twisted and turned to gaze up at the severe crags and peaks towering above them, peering out of the window of the lumbering coach as the steaming horses strained up the winding road towards the pass.

Next to her, Alethea looked out on the wintry scene with less astonishment. The majesty and stark white facets of the mountains filled her with awe, but she had known, in her imagination, how they would look. Living in Derbyshire, she was used enough to snow covering the high peaks for weeks on end, and she had read so many novels with accounts of Alpine journeys in them that she felt she had seen it all before.

'They aren't white,' Figgins said. 'Not like you'd expect. They're blue and purple and pink and more besides.' She heaved a sigh of vast content. 'To think that I should live to see this. Won't Ma's eyes be out on stalks when I tell her about it?'

'You'll have had enough of mountains by the time we reach Italy.'

They were alone in the coach. That was unusual, but there had been reports of late, heavy snow, of blocked passes and long waits. The coach driver scoffed at such talk, in guttural German that the innkeeper had to translate for Alethea. The other travellers, who had come most of the way with them from Paris, chose to remain at the last inn until more reassuring news should be brought down from the high mountain passes.

Alethea hadn't hesitated. They would continue their

journey. Familiarity bred carelessness; it would only be a matter of time before she or Figgins made a slip and gave their travelling companions cause to look more closely at these two young Englishmen. And apart from that, there was Napier, who might be close on their heels. She gave a little shudder, imagining him descending on Mordaunt's *hôtel* in Paris, the swift unfolding of details of her arrival, the false concern of her sister, the immense moral disapproval of her brother-in-law. No, Georgina's concern would not be entirely false; however such concern would not be for her sister, but rather for the family's good name, for her own now unassailable position as wife and mother, for the upholding of an orderly world where a young woman did not decamp from her husband's house.

And what if Georgina were somehow to discover just how she was travelling – dressed as a man? The rest would pale in comparison; for a female to step outside the circumscribed boundaries of her respectable life, not only in spirit but physically – that was more terrible than all the rest. To take on the liberty of a man's clothes and a man's identity was a threat to more than the seemly wearing of petticoats and the niminy-piminy steps of the elegant woman. It was a threat to the natural order of things; the merest idea of it would appal Sir Joshua and throw Georgina into the deepest alarm.

There was no way Georgina could know about her disguise, Alethea told herself. She had covered her tracks too carefully.

Did Georgina know about the previous escapades, when Alethea had crept out of the schoolroom to mingle with musicians in the breeches and coat of the professional player, blowing her flute at balls and assemblies, free as air to jaunt about the London streets?

Alethea thought not. She was confident that not a soul beyond Camilla and Wytton and Camilla's maid Sackree had ever heard about those times. She had no need to frighten herself. Napier in Paris, yes; Napier setting off for Vienna, yes, but Napier on her trail across Switzerland? No. She was safe from him, she must be safe from any pursuit.

The light was fading, sending final shafts of glowing red and orange light across the mountains as the weary horses drew up in front of the gasthof. Alethea looked with admiration at its huge sloping roof, snug under a deep covering of snow. From the numerous windows peeping out from beneath their own overhanging tiles, she surmised that this was the principal inn of the small town of Brig, and a hostelry where they might be sure of a comfortable room and good food.

Figgins wasn't fussy about a room, but she was anxious about supper. 'I'm hungry to my backbone,' she said, as they ascended the wide shallow steps that led into the inn.

Mine host was a small, sharp-eyed Swiss of some forty years or so, who mercifully spoke good English.

'It is needful, with so many English visitors coming this way now that the war is over. And those who speak German can do nothing with our Swiss dialects, for in my country, you know, every valley has its own tongue. They say the English have a hundred religions; well, we Swiss have that many versions of our language.' He laughed at his wit and rang a bell to summon a servant to take their bags. 'We have few visitors, the season has not yet begun, and late snow has caused many travellers to postpone all but the most essential journeys.'

His eyebrows rose in a question; Alethea was not disposed to answer him. She signed her name in the book, a flowing Aloysius Hawkins, with servant, of London, and passed it back to the landlord. She bespoke a room for only a single night, saying that they would continue their journey the next day.

Herr Geissler pursed his rather full lips and made a tutting noise. As to that, certainly the coach this morning had left at the usual time, but the one returning in the other direction was long past its regular hour and he doubted if it had set off at all, given that there had been such a heavy fall of snow. Still, if there were no more snow, and the wind continued in its present direction, then anything was possible.

'You will find a compatriot of yours in the coffee room,' he told her as he led the way himself up the ornately carved wooden stairs. 'One Signora Lessini; she is English although her husband is an Italian.'

Alethea had no interest in the company, English or Italian. She was so shaken and tired by the hard day's journey that she had no wish to make civil conversation with anyone. A meal, and then she was for her bed.

The landlord showed her into a pleasant chamber, its smallish windows tightly shuttered, its carved wooden bed spread with linen as white as the snow that lay thick outside on the mountain slopes. Figgins had a small adjoining room, and when the landlord had lit a lamp and taken himself off, she exclaimed aloud at the huge, soft quilts spread over each of their beds.

'Lor, do you sleep on that or under it?' She gave hers a suspicious shake. 'Foreign feathers. You don't know where those birds have been.'

'I believe you sleep under them,' said Alethea. 'Very comfortable, no doubt.'

'The linen is clean enough,' Figgins said in grudging tones. 'Now, you'd best bustle about if you're to dine below.'

Alethea pulled a face. 'I'd rather not, it will be some woman agog with curiosity as to who my father and all my ancestors are, and do I know Lady Such and Such and Lord This or That.'

'Why not an honest woman who has better things to talk about?'

'Because only women of a certain position in society have the leisure and the means to travel. One may meet many men upon the road, going about their business, but women are a different matter.'

Alethea pulled on her better coat, the one she hadn't

travelled in. It was a very dark blue cloth, and fitted her well; Figgins's brother Joe could be justly proud of his work. She peered at her face in the mirror. 'It will look odd, to seem to have shaved after a journey, before sitting down to a meal.'

'Many a fair-skinned young man uses his razor barely once a week. There is nothing wrong in not being an horrid hairy man that I ever heard of. Indeed, the ladies often favour a young man with a smooth cheek and no hair on his chest.'

'It is to be hoped that none such favour me,' said Alethea. She recalled her adventure in Paris. 'No, nor no men neither.' She laughed. 'It is a sad reflection on the morals of both men and women that I may be more exposed to insult as I am than were I travelling as a solitary female.'

Signora Lessini was a slender woman with an air of quiet elegance. Her gown was plain, as befitted a traveller, although well-cut; Figgins whispered in Alethea's ear that Mrs L was sure to have her clothes made in Paris. The cut and style vouched for that.

The Signore was not at all elegant, being plump and short with a wicked dark eye and a great sense of fun. He had, he informed Alethea as the soup was bringing in, lived in England for so many years that he thought of himself as perfectly English.

'Imagine my distress when my dearest Emily informs me, in the cruellest manner, that I could never for a moment pass as an Englishman. Now, sir, what do you think of that?'

'I think it is enough to be an Italian.'

'Oh, you are polite, you are so well-bred, you have such wonderful manners, you young Englishmen. Yet you despise all foreigners in your hearts, now admit that it is so!'

'Indeed, I do not. I have not met so very many foreigners; however I am acquainted with a compatriot of yours, one Signore Silvestrini, and I have the greatest admiration for him, I assure you.'

The words were no sooner out of her mouth than Alethea regretted them. What if he knew Signore Silvestrini, who had taught her singing since she first went to London? Might not her teacher, who knew something of her exploits when she dressed as a male musician, and most heartily disapproved of them, give her away at some later date?

She pushed the worry out of her mind. That was all in the future. Lessini was on his way to Italy, it might be many long months, years even, before he and his wife returned to England. He would not then recall a chance meeting with an unimportant young Englishman in an inn in Switzerland.

Unfortunately, the name of Silvestrini seemed to work a charm on Lessini. 'My dear friend, and his wife, ah, such a beauty!' He kissed his fingers in the air. 'So fair. You are doubtless acquainted with her.'

Alethea was eager to get away from the subject of the Silvestrini family, so she returned a non-committal grunt and attended to her soup. Her own, carefully instilled manners were a ladylike trap. Every mouthful she took had to be considered. She modelled her table manners now on those of her husband. How often had she not sat at the other end of the table from him, watching him eat, no appetite of her own, hating him with an intensity that made her feel quite sick.

Not that his manners were unrefined, but as Alethea had discovered in her former incarnation as a young man, men do things differently. There was a robustness to their style of eating, a vigour and enthusiasm that would have raised eyebrows in any polite company if adopted by a member of the female sex.

Alethea was sufficiently young and healthy to have something of a schoolgirl's appetite, and this was sharpened by the rigours of travel. So she drank her soup swiftly and without undue carefulness. Very differently, indeed, from the polite sips taken by Signora Lessini, who was sitting across the table from her.

Before the next course was brought in, there was a hubbub in the entrance, voices, English voices, exclaiming at the cold, the lateness of the hour, the tedious slowness of the journey, the need for immediate sustenance. 'I am sure,' came a high, well-bred woman's voice, 'that the other guests will forgive our sitting down to dine in our travellers' dust. For I confess I am famished, and want nothing more than a meal taken in front of a good fire.'

A man's voice, languid and affected, recommended that a meal be carried up to her chamber, where she might dine in peace and comfort, but his female companion would have none of it.

'What, after being shut up in a carriage for so many hours with only you for company, and so dull as you have been, complaining every league about how ill the carriage was sprung and how poor the roads? No, I thank you, Herr Geissler informs us that there are English people staying here. Let us join them and have the benefit of agreeable company while we dine.'

A glance at Signora Lessini's face told Alethea that her fellow guest had undoubtedly recognised the voice of at least one of the new arrivals, and that she did not care overly for the prospect of such company. However, as the new arrivals entered the dining room, she smiled and gave a courteous greeting. Her husband was more flamboyant, jumping from his place, ushering the newcomers to seats, calling to the waiter to bring more soup.

Alethea rose and bowed. She was aware of a penetrating gaze sweeping over her from head to toe, and to her annoyance, she felt a flush rising to her cheeks as she made her bow.

'This is my travelling companion, my cousin, Lord Lucius Moreby,' the woman announced. 'I am Mrs Vineham.' She nodded in Alethea's direction. 'I do not believe we are acquainted.'

'I have not had the honour of meeting you before,' Alethea said, resuming her seat as the others sat down. Which was a lie, for she had been introduced at Almacks. She heartily hoped that the encounter was not one that Mrs Vineham would remember. She had barely accorded the young debutante the civility of offered fingertips and a murmured, *Enchantée*; the dashing Mrs Vineham had no inclination to waste any time on an unmarried girl of no particular importance.

A lively girl, in her second season but in high spirits after the recent announcement of her engagement to an amiable and rich young man, had pulled Alethea away. 'She is a dashing widow,' she confided. 'She is prodigious fashionable, and they call her the Viper, for she has the keenest eyes and the sharpest tongue in the kingdom.'

Recalling these artless words now, Alethea found herself wishing that the new arrivals had been anyone but these two. For, on closer scrutiny, she realised that she recognised the nobleman who was escorting Mrs Vineham. If she were not much mistaken, this was the man who had edged up to her in the crowded street in Paris, and had pursued her through the streets. There was no look of recognition in his eyes, but there was a greedy spark there that boded no good to the lissom young man he took her for.

What a scrape to be in. She could hardly wait for dinner to be finished, good though it was, so that she might escape to her room. Upon the morrow, she and Figgins would be on their way once more, and with luck need not have another encounter with this pair.

In the event, Alethea couldn't escape so easily. The women withdrew to a small parlour, leaving the men to their wine, and she was reluctant to make herself conspicuous by not staying for at a least a little longer.

Figgins hovered, hoping that her mistress wouldn't make the mistake of matching the men glass for glass; might they find it strange if she didn't? She should have excused herself and retired, it was running into too much danger, sitting carousing with the gentlemen in there.

Her attention was caught by voices coming from the

parlour, polite female voices, but with an edge to them. One of the voices belonged to the woman with that Italian husband, such a pleasant-looking woman to go marrying a foreigner, only recently married, according to what her maid said, going to visit her new family. Fancy having a lot of Italians for your brothers and sisters, it didn't bear thinking of.

Not that Mr Lessini didn't look an agreeable man, if not English in his ways. His manservant said he was as good a master as ever lived and he wouldn't change his place for a position with any of your fine English gentlemen, who'd like as not damn your eyes as soon as look at you and throw a boot at your head.

Come to that, the Italian's manservant was a civil enough fellow himself, quite the gentleman's gentleman. Which was more than could be said for Lord Lucius's valet, a sneaky, sneery fellow if ever she saw one. He probably had to paint my lord's face for him every morning, a fine thing for a duke's son to have red lips and cheeks like he was on the stage.

The other woman, that Mrs Vineham, well she might hold her nose high, but if she was a respectable widow, what was she doing jauntering about Europe in the company of a loose screw like Lord Lucius? Anyone with eyes in their head could see he wouldn't be a-creeping into any woman's bed of a night, yet that fact still didn't make him the kind of company a lady should be keeping.

Her keen ears caught the name of Hawkins. She looked swiftly about her. No, not the door, some officious servant would be bound to come past and find her with her ear pressed to the keyhole. What about the adjoining door, where did that lead? She lifted the latch and opened the door a mere inch. It was a closet, with some linen and glasses. And every word from the parlour could be heard as clear as if you were in the very room.

Figgins slipped in and pushed the door to behind her.

Mrs Vineham was talking about her journey. How exhausting foreign travel was, how tiresome foreigners were, how even more tiresome it was to be constantly meeting with the very kind of English people that one had fled London to avoid.

'Do you find it so indeed?' Signora Lessini said. 'For my part, I enjoy travel, whether in my own country or abroad.'

An affected laugh from Mrs Vineham. 'Ah, but my dearest Emily, you have to decide which is your own country now that you are married to an Italian. I vow, I was never more shocked than when I heard of your marriage. To be marrying a Signore Nobody when you had Titus Manningtree at your feet. Or so the town said, although I know well enough that an attachment of one sort, be it never so tender, does not always lead to the altar. When that becomes a possibility, one's *enamorato* is suddenly elsewhere, do you not agree?'

'Lavinia, I shall not talk to you nor anyone else about my private life.'

'Private!' cried Mrs Vineham. 'Pray, how can it be private when all the world and his wife knew that your late husband wore the cuckold's horns on account of Titus Manningtree?'

A silence. It was wise of Mrs Lessini to keep her trap shut, Figgins felt. There'd be no getting the better of a woman with a tongue like that Mrs Vineham had on her.

'Of course,' Mrs Vineham was saying, 'we all understood your situation, married to a man you can never have cared for. It is always a mistake to marry outside one's circle, is it not?'

'Jonathan was beloved by me and by his numerous friends,' Mrs Lessini said with cold dignity. 'I count myself fortunate to have had such a happy marriage.'

That laugh again from Mrs Vineham. 'Oh, as to that, we all know what happy marriages are, they do not exist, they are a pretence we women weave about our lives. Is that not so? I appeared to the world a happy wife, but my late husband and I loathed one another most cordially, almost from the day we were wed, and counted it a fortunate day when we had cause neither to speak nor to see one another. And so it is with most women, nay, I would say with all women.'

'You speak as you find, I dare say,' said Signora Lessini. 'I count myself fortunate not to share your jaundiced view of married life.'

'Come, come now, we are women together. Confess if it is not better, infinitely better, to be a widow than to be a married woman.'

'You forget, I am a married woman.'

'Yes, and that amazes me. For your late husband must have left you a pretty fortune, and to enjoy it for so short a while before you place your life and happiness and wealth once more in a husband's hands seems folly indeed.'

'Does it so?'

'Perhaps Signore Lessini has virtues beyond the ordinary, although such as a man has to offer may surely be enjoyed outside the bonds of matrimony as well as within those shackles.'

'I don't think, Lavinia, that if you lived a hundred years you would understand what a man such as Lessini has to offer.'

And little chance of Mrs Vineham living that long, Figgins said to herself as she shifted her awkward pose for a moment. A glass slid along the shelf and tipped to the floor, breaking in a tinkle of glass.

'What is that?' cried Mrs Vineham.

'A clumsy servant has dropped something,' Signora Lessini said. 'Let me advise you to take a cordial for your nerves. I confess, to be travelling in the company of Lord Lucius would be enough to upset the nerves of a woman of even the least sensibility. You are on edge, I beg you to take care or who knows in what condition you may find yourself? Widowhood is not an easy state, you know; no one is ever very concerned as to the well-being of a widow. Her children merely count the days until they may inherit or be free of the burden of her support, and such gentlemen as she may be acquainted with fall off very quickly at the least sign of illness.'

Figgins approved thoroughly of this vigorous assault by Mrs Lessini. She had just decided that although it was entertaining to listen, she had best be about her business. But as she began to back out of the cupboard, she heard another reference to young Mr Hawkins, and all thoughts of duty upstairs fled.

'A pretty young man with manners to match,' Mrs Vineham said.

'I believe Lord Lucius finds him so.'

'I own, I find a fresh young man with a smooth cheek and blushing manners a delight. He is so very young, barely out of the university if he has yet gone. And a gentleman's son, one can see that at a glance. However, I don't know any Hawkins, it is not a noble name. I am not sure it is even a gentleman's name, although with families from the north and so on, it is so hard to say. Perhaps you are acquainted with him, since you move in a wider social sphere than most of us.'

'He has a look about him that reminds me of someone. I should not be surprised to find that I had met his father, even if I don't recall the name. Or his mother, he may favour his mother. It is of no consequence. He says that he continues with his journey into Italy tomorrow, and I believe we shall not be long after him. My dear husband is eager to be among his family again.'

'And where may that be?'

'He comes from Rome, we are heading for Rome, although we go first to Venice, where he has some commissions to execute.'

'Commissions?' There was a world of scorn in Mrs Vineham's rich voice.

'He is a musician, as I dare say you are aware. He is highly regarded as a scholar, his judgement is required as to the authenticity of a manuscript.'

Mrs Vineham laughed. 'A manuscript, well, men must

attend to their affairs. For some it is the running of an estate or the management of a large fortune, or the collecting of works of art. For others, it is a manuscript.'

Signora Lessini ignored the acidity of her companion's voice. 'We shall not linger in Venice. It is not a city my husband cares for. Romans do not, generally, I understand.'

'As for that, I am passionately attached to Venice. There is some excellent company to be had there just at present. We plan a stay of some weeks.'

Figgins was sorry to hear it. She felt that Alethea could do without the company of that pair, but then, it was unlikely that they would meet once in the city.

Mrs Vineham gave a prodigious yawn. 'Lord, how tired I am. I'm for my bed. Ring the bell, Emily, and I shall summon my maid. She will be down in the kitchens, no doubt, hob-nobbing with the Swiss peasantry.'

Figgins heard a door open, and Mrs Vineham told the inn servant to call her maid to her. It was too late for Figgins to slip out of the cupboard unnoticed, so she held the door to and waited, holding her breath until the click of the ladies' heels and the sound of Mrs Vineham's voice told her that they were on their way upstairs.

Time to see what was what with Miss Alethea. She hoped to goodness she wasn't still closeted with the gentlemen, that was no place for her, a foreigner and that mincing man who looked to be no more than a mollymop, just what Miss Alethea could do without.

The inn lay quiet beneath the shadow of the great mountains. A moon shone fitfully through a film of cloud. Shutters closed, lights extinguished, the villagers slept the sleep of those who work hard from daybreak to sundown, while the travellers enjoyed less solid slumbers.

Mrs Vineham's active mind brought her strange dreams and her eyes twitched under the dark shade she wore across them to keep out the least glint of too early morning light.

The Lessinis' bed was not a restful one, but its inhabitants enjoyed the other pleasures of the bedchamber with an ardour that did credit to a pair hardly in the first flush of youth; they might, so Lessini fondly told his wife in caressing Italian, be young lovers on their honeymoon, enraptured by the novel delights of wedded bliss. In the adjacent chamber, heedless of the sounds of love and laughter coming through the wooden walls, Lord Lucius tossed and turned, his mind fuddled still with the fumes of too much brandy.

Figgins slept the sound but wary sleep of the experienced servant, envied by Alethea, who could not sleep at all. She felt a heaviness in the air about her, an inexplicable sense of unease that kept her wide awake. She rose from her bed and went to the window. However cold the air, its freshness would clear her head. She opened the casement window and pushed back a shutter. The road lay gleaming in the dim moonlight and it seemed to Alethea that the way they had come was darker than the way that wound up the valley to the gap in the soaring mountains, the way they were to go.

Out of the darkness came the sound of hooves. A horse. No, two horses. She craned out of the window to see who was arriving at the inn at this ungodly hour. The first horseman was a tall man, cloaked and hatted and muffled so that his face was hidden. With him came a shorter man, a servant, judging by his actions as he jumped from his horse and ran to hold the other man's bridle.

A knocking at the door below. A long wait, then the sound of bolts being drawn back, the light from a candle spilling out over the threshold, voices, and then the door closing as the servant led the two horses round to the side of the inn where the stables were.

Intrigued by this late arrival, and now even more wide awake, Alethea was about to close the window when she heard the sound of more hooves, and of carriage wheels. Another late arrival? Was it like this every night at the inn?

No one but her stirred, how could everyone else be so soundly asleep?

It was another man, this time in a long drab coat, who descended from the chaise. He, too, was accompanied by a servant, and he too knocked on the door. His knock was loud and peremptory, the knock of a man who knows he has to arouse a sleeping house and does not care, thought Alethea.

Once again, the door opened. The voices were louder this time, and the language spoken was English. The man in the coat cursed the landlord for keeping him waiting, flung an order over his shoulder to his manservant, and entered the inn.

Alethea could not contain her curiosity. She pulled the shutter back across the window, flung her coat over her nightshirt and quietly opened the door of her bedchamber.

The rooms in this part of the inn were arranged around three sides of a gallery, and Alethea looked down into the hall. There was the landlord, still in his night-cap, and a sleepy chambermaid in a dress she had dragged on over her night shift.

The tall man, the first one, was talking now, in English, which was clearly his native tongue. He knew the second man, that was obvious.

'You're making the devil of a row, Warren. This is an inn, not a bear house.'

Warren ignored this remark. 'A large chamber, your best room, if you please,' he said to the landlord.

Alethea judged that the landlord was more than used to such requests; he spoke to the chambermaid in the dialect of the region, unintelligible to her and probably to the two men below. The tall man had the prior claim, but the landlord knew which of the two new guests was a troublemaker, and he was wise, Alethea reckoned to want to be rid of him as soon as possible, although she'd wager that the tall man got the better room.

She shifted her weight from one bare foot to another, and

then took a step back into the shadows as the slight noise she had made caused the tall man to grasp a candle from the table and hold it aloft. Keen eyes met hers for an instant, and she felt herself go hot to be discovered like this. And at the same moment, she fancied she knew the man, his voice seemed familiar. Good heavens, it was the man who had sent Lord Lucius packing in Paris. She wanted to laugh at the absurdity of it; was half of England bent on crossing the Alps by the same route, and had they all travelled here from Paris?

He was coming up the stairs now. She darted back into her room, pushed the door to, drew the bolt across, and stood, back to the door, breathing hard, as the masculine footsteps came along the gallery, paused for a moment on the other side of the door and then continued on their way.

Two more for breakfast, then, she thought as she gave a great yawn. Suddenly sleepy, she rolled into bed and drew the covers up around her.

Silence descended once more upon the inn. Alethea slept soundly, her slumber only broken for a moment by the crash and rumble of distant thunder. A storm, she told herself, turning over and paying it little heed. No rain lashed at the window, and no lightning flashes illuminated her chamber, there were no pyrotechnics in the night sky to disturb her further.

Chapter Ten

Figgins came into the room in a high state of excitement. 'And I didn't wake you earlier, Mr Hawkins, sir, because . . .'

In a second, Alethea was wide awake, and grasping for her repeater watch, bought from a shady jeweller by Figgins. She sprang out of bed.

'Whatever are you thinking of, Figgins? We were to be well on our way by this time, not lying abed.'

Figgins poured the hot water from the jug in a splashing stream. 'That's what I was about to tell you, if you'll give me half a chance. No one's going to be on their way today. There's been what they call an avalanche, which is, so that supercilious man of Mr Manningtree's who arrived like a heathen in the dead of night tells me, a kind of fall of snow where snow has no right to be. It's barred the road and all the paths, and neither man nor beast can get through until it melts or is shifted. There's ever such a hullabaloo downstairs; they're afeared lest people were caught in this avalanche and buried in the snow.'

'Or swept away down the mountainside,' said Alethea, patting her face dry with the towel. 'It is a kind of landslip, when a huge sheet of snow breaks loose and slides down the mountain, carrying all before it. I have heard of such a thing, only why, oh why, did it have to happen here? I dare say another year, we could stroll over the pass, with no snow underfoot at all. Well, we shall have to retrace our steps and travel to another of the passes.'

'They said in Bern that the others are closed, from having

heavy falls of snow. This way was supposed to be our best chance of getting across the mountains.'

'What a fix this leaves us in. Hurry up with those clothes, there, Figgins. I must consult with the landlord.'

There was a little crowd gathered around the landlord when she descended a few minutes later. 'What is this all about?' Alethea enquired of Signore Lessini. 'I trust no lives have been lost?'

'They do not yet know, but all those who live in these mountains go in the greatest dread of the avalanche, and all too often, such an event has no very happy outcome. However, we must hope for the best, and the fact that no carriages came through from the other side yesterday afternoon or evening gives us hope that they had some suspicion on the Italian side that this might occur. I believe they can judge by the temperature and wind and so forth as to the likelihood of a great shift of snow.'

'How long does he believe the pass will remain closed?'

Signore Lessini shrugged. 'It is too big a fall for any attempt to be made to clear the way. The only hope is for a thaw, and there is some expectation of that, he says. Indeed, that may be why the snow has shifted, it seems, the cause may be a rise in temperature.'

'I cannot wait. I shall have to retrace my steps.'

At those words, the tall gentleman who had been deep in conversation with the landlord turned and looked at Alethea. His cool eyes appraised her. 'As to that, sir . . .'

'My name is Hawkins,' Alethea said with a slight bow. 'Aloysius Hawkins.'

The eyes were thoughtful, but the man resumed. 'Titus Manningtree, at your service. Herr Geissler here informs us that we are cut off at both ends as it were. Ahead there is the snow, and behind there are floods. There has been a sudden rise in temperature, I dare say you may find that out for yourself should you step outdoors. The resultant thaw has filled the mountain streams and sent a positive torrent of water rushing down into the valley.'

Alethea stared at him. 'Then we are stranded, here in this inn?'

He bowed. 'There are worse places to be stranded, believe me. Here we have an excellent inn and food and fires.'

The other midnight arrival had been listening hard. 'True enough, Manningtree, though I don't doubt the ladies will be put out. Ladies always complain if things don't go just as they have planned. Landlord, where is the breakfast parlour?'

'That is Mr Warren,' Titus informed Alethea as she hesitated, wondering whether to go directly into breakfast, for she was hungry, or whether to wait in her chamber until the other English guests had finished.

Titus settled it by holding the door for her. She followed him in, with a word of thanks, and took her place beside Signore Lessini. He addressed himself to Titus with a frown on his face. 'Mr Manningtree?'

'Yes, I am Titus Manningtree.' He waited for the Italian to introduce himself.

George Warren, piling his plate with cold meats, raised his eyes, looked from one man's face to the other, gave a crack of laughter and took a roll. He sat back in his chair, fork poised to attack the meat. 'Allow me to introduce Signore Lessini,' he said. 'I believe you are well acquainted with his wife, Emily Thruxton as was.'

To Alethea's surprise, Titus Manningtree went pale and his mouth tightened. 'Indeed? I am happy to make your acquaintance.'

'Signora Lessini is with you?' George Warren went on. 'I was sure she would be, so recently married as you are. A honeymoon trip, one gathers.'

Titus rose, dashed his napkin down on the table and stalked out of the room. Alethea stared uncomprehendingly from Warren's mocking face to Lessini's red one. Before she could say a word, Lessini, too, rose and hurried from the room.

‘A pretty state of affairs,’ said Warren. ‘And you are, sir? Although I might put a name to you, surely you are a Darcy?’

Alethea was appalled. Her likeness to her father was unmistakable, but she had never dreamed she might find herself in company with anyone acquainted with her family. What a piece of ill luck! Warren was looking at her, curiously, a curl on his lip. ‘My name is Aloysius Hawkins,’ she said abruptly. ‘My uncle is Mr Fitzwilliam Darcy.’

Warren nodded, seemingly satisfied. ‘Knew I wasn’t mistaken. You’ll be his sister’s son, I dare say.’

He didn’t wait for an answer, but addressed himself to another helping of food. ‘Excellent ham, this. The reason for our friends’ abrupt departures, should you not, by reason of your youth, be *au fait* with what goes on in London, is that Lessini’s new wife was once very – how shall I put it? – close to Titus Manningtree. What a strange chance that brings the three of them together in this inn, especially now that we are likely to be here some little while. Tell me, are there any other English travellers?’

‘Two,’ Alethea said. She reached out for a roll and began to butter it, willing her fingers not to shake. ‘A Mrs Vineham and Lord Lucius Moreby.’

‘What,’ cried Warren, ‘Lavinia Vineham staying here? And Lord Lucius, a fool if ever there was one, but a damned fine card player. Ah, then it will not be so very boring, after all.’ He gave Alethea a hard look. ‘You will no doubt have charmed the noble lord, you are just such a morsel as he will fancy. My word, yes, I think we may pass the idle hours very pleasantly after all.’

Damn Warren’s eyes, Titus said to himself, for provoking him into revealing how he felt about Emily’s marriage to that Lessini fellow. How could Emily marry such a mountebank? One look at the man and you could tell he was nothing but a fortune-hunter. How could she have been so naïve, so downright stupid?

And now he was shut up here in this Godforsaken village, and with her new husband, and with Warren, not to mention that unpleasant pair, Mrs Vineham and Lord Lucius. There was that supposed boy, too, that woman masquerading as a member of the opposite sex. What was she doing here? He had taken her for a whore, but whores didn't end up at Alpine passes at this time of the year, quite at home in well-bred company. What was her game, for game there must be?

He frowned, puzzled as to where he had seen her before. Paris, yes, but even then he had felt a fleeting sense of recognition. No, he had met her before, in England. Not recently, he thought. No, it didn't come back to him. It would, he was certain his memory would duly deliver up the information he wanted from it. Meanwhile, he had to face up to the prospect of several days in this vile company. He was hungry, too; he had been quick to walk out before he was tempted to wipe that supercilious smile off Warren's face, and now he was breakfastless and therefore bad-tempered. 'Bootle!' he called out. 'Cut along to the kitchens and bring me up some breakfast. Quickly, now.'

Bootle was likely to prove a good source of information, as always. He'd have the gossip out of all the other English servants in a trice. Was that girl dressed as a boy travelling alone? He'd never heard of anything so scandalous. She could hardly travel with an abigail, however, and if she had a manservant, then that was even more shocking.

Bootle was swift to enlighten him. Young Mr Hawkins was accompanied by a manservant, he told Titus as he spread a white cloth on the table next to the window. 'A civil spoken, genteel kind of a servant, although on the small side for a gentleman's gentleman. One as had been in the service of Mr Hawkins's family for some considerable while, so he understood. Mr Hawkins was travelling to Italy to visit a member of this family, presently residing in Venice.' He straightened a knife, and whisked the cover off a plate of ham. 'All perfectly respectable, although I do not remember having heard of a Mr Hawkins, or of any Hawkins, being among those of the ton.'

Titus made a dismissive gesture. 'He's the sprig of some self-made man, I dare say. An iron master or someone in the City. That's where the money is these days, and such men send their sons off to Harrow or some other school for gentlemen's sons, and they come out indistinguishable from their fellow students as to manners and dress.'

'But not as to name, sir.'

'No, not as to name.' And this particular sprig had never set foot in Harrow School, unless to visit a brother there, of that Titus was certain. He'd make it his business to find out what the wench was up to, something smoky, he'd be bound; that at least might provide some entertainment until the snows melted.

It amused him that Warren hadn't noticed that the young gentleman Mr Hawkins was nothing of the kind. So much for his vaunted keen eye and keener wits. He wondered if Emily – no, he wasn't going to let his thoughts stray to Emily. He'd find himself in her company, sooner or later, that was unavoidable, but he wasn't going to let her intrude on his thoughts meanwhile. That whole affair was behind him, a closed book, a healed wound. 'Bootle,' he called out, 'hurry along with that coffee there.'

Refreshed, but hating the prospect of enforced idleness, Titus roamed restlessly about the inn. He wanted to be on the move, not cooped up at this wretched inn, his plans thwarted by the elements. He sent Bootle for his greatcoat, and took himself outside to walk off his ill humour. It was a raw day, with a wind whipping down from the mountains, and angry clouds scudding overhead. The sullen weather matched his savage mood and his sense of oppression.

Oblivious of the majestic scenery on every side, his mind turned yet again to Emily. What a misfortune to meet her here, and in Lessini's company. He reasoned with himself: whom else should she be with, but her new husband? Yet he would be, oh, so much happier not to have had this encounter. He had told himself that his feelings for her, his affection and his anger at her betrayal of him, were under control. Now he discovered that they were no such thing.

He quickened his pace. He would not think about her.

Warren. Let him think about Warren, damn the man. How much did the man know about the painting he was after? To him it surely meant no more than a fat commission and the favour of the king; he had carried out several such purchases for ardent collectors in the last year or so and had earned himself the reputation of a connoisseur. Titus was sceptical, he knew full well that in the London of 1820 a few fatuous words about light and shade and the placing of a composition were enough to set yourself up as an expert on art.

He climbed up the rock-strewn path, up and up, through the pine trees that still grew at this level. He disturbed a group of goats, extraordinary parti-coloured creatures with magnificent curved horns. The sound of rushing water was everywhere. What in the summer would be a mere trickle over the boulders was now a rushing torrent of mucky, icy water. This was a bad season to make such a journey.

Curse Warren for not waiting a few weeks, when this journey would have presented no such hazards or delays. Such haste spoke of unusual eagerness on Warren's part, perhaps the receipt of news about the painting, for he had chosen to leave London at the height of the season. He might have a doubtful reputation, but he knew everyone and was invited everywhere, relishing the social round, even though his flirtations caused most of the mothers to caution their debutante daughters against falling for his dashing corsair looks.

Poseur, Titus said crossly to himself. Fool, for finding anything to enjoy in the gatherings at Almacks, the balls, the routs, the receptions, the drums.

He had walked off most of his temper by the time he clambered down a precipitous path that came out to the rear of the inn. It was better, after all, if he had to be held up by the weather, that he had ended up in Warren's company. A couple of days sooner, and Warren might well have crossed to Italy with little trouble. Then he would have been days ahead of Titus, might have made contact with the rogue who had his picture before Titus had so much as set foot in Italy, let alone reached Venice.

Bootle was waiting in the yard of the inn, and ushered him in through the door, relieving him of his coat and advising him to put off his shoes. 'Lord Lucius was enquiring as to your whereabouts, sir. I believe he wants to make up a table for cards.'

'He can want away. I have letters to write, and besides, no one rises from a game with that man a winner. Let the others lose in his company, I will not play. You may tell him so.'

'Very good, sir.'

By the afternoon, Alethea was heartily bored. She had kept to her room for most of the day, aware that too much time spent in company as sharp-eyed and -witted as this collection of fellow guests might well lead to exposure. She had found a shelf of tattered books in the corner of what served as a writing room by virtue of two tables, one empty inkstand and a broken quill left in a drawer. She had no wish to write to anyone, but she was glad to find that there were books in French and English, and she carried away a lurid tale in marbled covers and a volume of Montaigne's essays.

Since the lurid tale was set in this part of the world, she opened that first. It was a fantastic account of abductions, incarcerations in wolf-bound forests, of wicked stepfathers and lost heiresses. Just the kind of story she liked, except that she found the hair-raising description of a crossing of the Alps at exactly this time of the year didn't appeal as it might have done in the comfort of an English sitting room or library.

She yawned and cast the book aside. Figgins appeared at the door, looking lean and mean.

'What a set of scoundrels; well, I'm used enough to the ways of servants being one of them, and familiar with indoors and outdoors staff, but I never met anything to equal this. They speak more free and easy with taking me for a man, and it fair makes your ears sting the way they go on, that Bootle and Mr Warren's man, Nyers. There isn't a scandal from one end of the town to the other, they don't have at their fingertips. Let them but fall to discussing your situation, your situation that is as they imagine it to be, and I shall put them right.'

'Oh, Lord,' said Alethea. 'A pack of gossiping servants, that's all we need, and if they talk about me, let them.'

'All servants gossip, just the same as their betters,' Figgins said with asperity. 'Bootle, though, he's Mr Manningtree's man, he's a more subtle one, not so free with his words but he's got his ears pricked up right enough. I shall have to guard my tongue.'

'Mind you do,' said Alethea.

'If ever they get hold of the merest glimmer of the truth about this escapade of yours, there won't be a soul in Europe that won't know about it, I tell you that straight.'

'Only they won't get even a glimmer if you keep your wits about you.' Alethea pulled her shoulders back and glared at her reflection in the rather green glass set on the table in her chamber. It sent back an eerie likeness, all too feminine she decided, trying to curl her lip in the way that Warren did.

'Have you got the toothache?' Figgins asked, staring at her.

'Maybe if I rub a little dirt into my cheek, just a touch of shadow, what do you think?'

'I think you'd best leave well alone and look like what you can well pretend to be: a callow youth who's hardly begun to use a razor.'

'Just the sort that Lord Lucius likes, I fancy.' Alethea let Figgins brush her short locks into a Brutus. A few snips of the scissors improved it, and Alethea turned her head from side to side to admire the effect.

'It's not as though you haven't been out in company all this time,' Figgins pointed out. 'In inns and in Paris and so on.'

'Yes, but never with people of this sort, who will quiz me as to who my father is and what his income and estate amounts to, and where I had my schooling and did I ever meet such and such.'

The best thing was, she decided, to stick as closely to the truth as she could manage. She could talk enough of Derbyshire and somewhat of London. Although her two Londons, that of the ballroom and polite society and that of the much more lowly, if more interesting, world of the musician she had passed as, were not the London that these men were familiar with. They frequented sporting taverns, no doubt, and gaming clubs, not to mention the gentlemen's clubs that any well-connected young sprig come to London belonged to. She'd never set foot in any such places; one inch into any of those male bastions in St James's and the whole sacred edifice would probably collapse about her ears. Sacrilege would be nothing in comparison.

Naïvety, then, and inexperience, and say as little as possible, and avoid the wine; she simply did not have the head for it. She closed her eyes and thought herself into the skin of the various boys and young men of her acquaintance. Ever the tomboy, she thanked God for the years of friendship with Giles, a neighbouring squire's son, who had been like a brother to her, included her in many of his youthful pranks and adventures about their two estates and confided endless tales of the brutality and inequity of schoolmasters and tutors. As to a boy's life on a country estate, she could hold her own. The awkwardness regarding any questions about her schooldays? She dismissed the problem. None of those present at the inn were interested in schoolboy doings.

No, it was London life where she could be found at fault. Very well, she would skate over it. Aloysius Hawkins had merely passed through on his way to stay with a cousin in Italy. She would pass as a milk-and-water youth, uninterested in the wildnesses of town that attracted every young man she'd ever been acquainted with. She could hint at religious principles, an interest in natural philosophy, perhaps, ancient music; dull concerns that stigmatised Mr Hawkins as a namby-pamby young gentleman, wet behind the ears, a bore to anyone who moved in lively London circles.

She smoothed out her shirtsleeves and cuffs, donned her coat, slid her feet into a pair of buckled shoes. Fanny had bewailed the size of her feet, just as she had fretted about her height; Alethea was thankful for them now. A ladylike frame and neat, delicate feet were exactly what she didn't need now. Her months with Norris had killed her appetite, so that she was far too thin for any feminine ideal of beauty. The leanness and the sharpness of cheek and jawbone were an advantage, making her look much more boyish than she could have done a year previously.

Figgins anxiously opened the door for her, bidding her to be mighty wary, she was fallen among wicked people and must not forget it. Alethea strode along the gallery, imagining herself to be the seventeen- or eighteen-year-old brother she didn't have.

Lord Lucius's door was ajar. A glimpse into the brightly lit interior, a blaze of candles burning within, showed his lordship seated in front of his glass. He had a kind of white sock drawn over his hair, to leave his face free of hair, and his valet was engaged in patting rouge on to his cheeks.

For a moment, her eyes met the knowing ones of the valet, and she drew hastily away from the door, annoyed to find herself flushing at the sight of a man prinking himself so and at the naked lasciviousness of the valet's glance. Lascivious on his own account, or on account of his master's predilections? It didn't matter, either possibility was disturbing and distasteful and made Alethea even more determined to keep well out of reach of the dandified, effeminate Lord Lucius.

The landlord had laid dinner for his English guests in a

private parlour which boasted a large round table. 'You will all be such good company for one another,' he said, rubbing his hands with satisfaction. 'All noblemen and gentlemen and ladies together, so fortunate that you are here together, to eat and make merry, it will be quite a party.'

It took some adroitness on Alethea's part to avoid having to sit next to Lord Lucius, which was what he had clearly intended. His red mouth pursed up in a moue of discontent as he seated himself beside Titus. At least his hand wouldn't stray on to Mr Manningtree's knee during the meal, Alethea told herself, suppressing a laugh. Titus Manningtree would have more congenial company on his other side, where Mrs Vineham, looking very elegant, was sitting. This left Alethea with Signore Lessini on one side and Mr Warren on the other. Informality was the order of the day, so she could devote herself to talking about music and Venice and Rome with the Signore, and leave Mr Warren to talk across the table to whom he chose.

It was an uneasy gathering, with too many cross-currents for comfort. To the landlord they might appear to be of one kind, with interests and connections in common, but among themselves there was too much history of one sort or another to ensure ease of conversation. Warren, urbane this evening, at once assessed the mood of the party and began to talk about painting. It seemed an innocuous enough subject, and showed him to be, in outward manners at least, a well-bred man. So why, Alethea wondered, was Titus Manningtree looking so vexed?

'I am a great admirer of the Italian masters,' Warren said. 'You have a fine collection, Manningtree, do you not agree with me? Perhaps that is why you travel to Italy, to snap up some canvases, so many possibilities now that the spoils of war are spread across Europe.'

'Unlike some men, I have no desire to profit by what others have lost. Those who have had paintings or any work of art stolen or looted are entitled to have them restored if ever they are found.'

'Ah, in a perfect world that would be the case. Unhappily, we live in a very imperfect world, and therefore it is a case of finders keepers, do you not agree?'

'I do not.'

The soup was cleared away and the table spread with a collection of covers, with delicious aromas wafting out from beneath each one. Alethea, who was extremely hungry, applied herself to her food. Let the others jostle and gibe. She would keep her head down, her mouth shut except for the food, and then it would soon be over and she could retire.

'Have you attended one of the universities?' It took her a moment to realise that the question was addressed to her. It was Lord Lucius who had spoken, and his eyes rested on her face with a look containing too much warmth for her liking.

'No. That is, I may go up next year. To Cambridge,' she added, improvising freely.

'Is that your father's university? Is it the custom for your family to go there?' said Mrs Vineham in silken tones. 'Or perhaps your father's education was of a different kind, is he more a product of the school of life?'

'My father was at Cambridge,' she said briefly and truthfully.

Mrs Vineham allowed a tiny frown to wrinkle her smooth brow. 'Indeed? You surprise me. And where did you have your schooling?'

Drat the woman. What did it matter to her what Mr Hawkins's background was? Alethea knew the answer to that. Since the end of the war, the people of good family, as they thought of themselves, had seen influence and status decline. The world was full of new men, mushrooms, with wealth far greater than old estates and land could possibly yield. A corn chandler's income might amount to fifty times that of a country landowner, with the money counting for far more than an ancient name and ancestors who had hobnobbed with the Conqueror. The part of society in which the likes of Mrs Vineham moved had drawn in on itself, excluding from its hallowed ranks anyone with the taint of commerce or new money.

If Alethea claimed to have been educated at Eton or Harrow or Westminster or another of the handful of schools to which the upper classes entrusted their sons, there would follow an interrogation: Mr Hawkins must be acquainted with such and such, he must know this fellow, have come across that friend's son. 'I was educated privately, at home,' she said. 'I was somewhat sickly as a boy.'

Mr Warren's face showed that he thought Mr Hawkins was still a weakling. Lord Lucius smiled across the table. 'I trust, however, that you now enjoy good health. Indeed, you must do so to be allowed by your doubtless loving parents to make a long and arduous journey. Tell me, why do you undertake it?'

'I am paying a visit to a cousin,' Alethea said. Couldn't someone else say something? Why should her concerns be of interest to the rest of the table?

'You travel to Venice, I believe?'

Alethea gave a slight bow of her head in agreement.

'Ah, how very delightful, we shall be quite a little crowd of English visitors. You must allow me to introduce you to society there, so many delightful people. Lord Byron is presently in Italy, and he draws quite a throng about him.'

Signora Lessini spoke for the first time. 'Such society can hardly be considered suitable for a young man, Lord Lucius.'

'Poetical society is surely the very thing for a young man to experience before embarking on a course of study at the University,' Warren said.

'Not that particular poet's society,' said Titus. 'Byron's a good friend of mine as it happens, but I wouldn't recommend his company to those of formative years.'

'May we ask what is the purpose of your journey, then, Mr Manningtree?' asked Mrs Vineham, with a flutter of her eyelashes. 'You are given to travelling, I know. Perhaps you seek to escape a romantic entanglement; they say that is a common reason to leave the country.'

Signora Lessini's eyes flashed with a quick anger, while Titus returned an adroit enough reply. 'Questions are such an unsatisfactory method of making conversation, do not you agree? Mr Hawkins, may I pass you this dish of goose, done in the Swiss style? Your plate is empty, I notice.'

Savouring the goose, which was cooked in a rich, sweet sauce, Alethea let the conversation flow about her. It was edgy, with undertones that she didn't entirely comprehend, and she preferred to remain, as it were, on the sidelines.

Her time abroad, brief as it was, had wrought a change in Alethea, a considerable change, and one that she was aware of as she contemplated those seated around the table. She was by a long way the youngest person present. The Lessinis were middle-aged, it seemed to her, in their late thirties or so. Lord Lucius must be even older, he looked to be of an age with her father, but might be younger and simply carrying his years less well. Mr Warren and Mr Manningtree were the closest to her in age, but they must be at least thirty, and very likely more.

Previously, she would have had no part in such a gathering. As a married woman, she might have expected to take her place in society and to mingle with a greater mix of company than was allowed to a young, unmarried girl. Given the peculiar circumstances of her marriage, however, she had gone from one form of protectiveness to another. Her sorties while still in the schoolroom had been brief and hadn't brought her face to face with the kind of sophistication and subtlety that she was now encountering.

The words these people spoke and what they meant by them were two different things. And they presented a very different aspect of the wedded state to any she was used to. Coming from a large and affectionate family, the youngest of five sisters, her experience of more complex arrangements was limited. The Fitzwilliams were another couple with a family and a regular way of life. So were the Gardiners, despite their great wealth.

But here was Signora Lessini, married for a second time at such an age, and to a man of quite a different rank in society. Having enjoyed a liaison, if Figgins's reports were true, of many years' standing with Mr Manningtree. He had, it seemed never married, his attachment to a married woman being a satisfactory enough arrangement, Alethea supposed. Mrs Vineham was a widow, had been a widow for two years, she had told Alethea. Now, according to what Figgins had gleaned from Mrs Vineham's discontented maid, she was on the look-out for a second husband. The first one had been drunk most of the time, and had defenestrated himself while on a drinking binge in a low part of town. Much to Mrs Vineham's relief, apparently.

So where did that leave the state of marriage and the chance of wedded bliss? Was her own matrimonial misery perhaps closer to the norm than the quiet happiness of her cousins, or the more lively but devoted relationship enjoyed by her parents?

Alethea had grown up supposing that in due course she would marry, as most girls of her rank and fortune might expect to. Married women had domestic duties and obligations, compensated for by the greater freedom allowed to a wealthy wife as to going about in company, attending the opera and musical performances and spending as much time on music as she wanted.

This, she now realised, was a naïve and ill-informed view of the world. No wonder the mamas and chaperons kept such a close eye on their ewe lambs, lest their charges become too aware of what made the world wag. Only those girls brought up in one of the great houses were likely to learn early on the reality of adult life; for the rest of her sex, innocence was indeed bliss, if a bliss destined to be shattered with marriage and entry into the polite world.

One thing she was now sure of: she would never go back to her husband. With some men it might be possible to work out a *modus vivendi*, but not with Norris Napier. With her travels had come competence, independence and a quickening of maturity. With every league covered, every change of coach, every new arrangement made, Alethea felt more confident. She liked paying her way, she liked coping with strange people and strange situations. She liked using her schoolroom languages and she envied other travellers their greater fluency. She was eagerly looking forward to Italy, something she would not have believed possible only a little while before. Then she had only imagined a difficult, unsettling journey that would end in the relief and security of joining her sister and Wytton.

Titus had been observing Alethea as she ate her way steadily through the meal. Why was she abstracted? What was she thinking about? She certainly had the appetite of a young man rather than of a young woman. Could he be mistaken? No. Had any of the others noticed what was so obvious to him? Apparently not. It was such a preposterous notion that a young woman should be travelling disguised as a man that the idea wouldn't enter their heads. The too-smooth cheek would be taken as evidence of his youthfulness, while her voice, unusually deep for a girl, gave nothing away, and the slim, athletic frame and her height were well suited to her pretence.

His attention was caught by a new subject; Lessini had turned the conversation, showing himself to be possessed of better manners than Warren or that scrub Lucius Moreby, who were supporting Mrs Vineham in her focus on the impertinent and personal.

'While you are in Venice,' Lessini was saying to Warren, 'you should visit Delancourt. He is an art dealer of some renown, and I have heard that he has some very fine paintings in his hands just now.'

Warren's face gave nothing away, he had a card player's

ability to remain expressionless. Only for a second, by the flicker of an eye, did he betray himself to Titus.

Delancourt. It was not a name he knew, and Warren had recovered and was now holding forth to Lessini about coins from the ancient world. Coins, forsooth – George Warren hadn't the least interest in coins.

What could Emily have seen in Lessini? He supposed the man to be a pleasant enough fellow, not one to set the world alight, yet there must be some hidden virtue in him for Emily to turn him, Titus, down in the Italian's favour. Titus winced as the thought crossed his mind that perhaps Lessini embodied the traditional view of the Latin lover. Only he and Emily had been well-suited between the sheets, he could not be mistaken in a matter such as that, setting aside normal masculine pride and disinclination to consider oneself in any way lacking in the amorous arts.

It was not as though the late Mr Thruxton had been a tyrannical or overbearing husband. He had been an amiable, good-tempered man, with no particular interest in the female part of humanity; a scholar and a man concerned about his estates and his horses. He had known of his wife's particular friendship with Titus, had never played the cuckold, had been grateful to Emily for preferring to spend most of the year apart from him. She favoured town over the country life, and this suited Thruxton, who had been perfectly happy to pass a twelvemonth without visiting London. He had found solace, so Emily said, in the arms of a local woman; there was nothing in that marriage to make Emily fall into the arms of a man on account of his being kinder or more easy-going.

Whatever it was, Titus wished from the bottom of his heart that he was not fixed in this inn with the pair of them. It still wrenched his heart to be in Emily's company, and she was avoiding him, deliberately avoiding him. Not that he would force his attentions on her, but surely he deserved an explanation?

Well, it was clear he wasn't going to get one. The sooner

he was out of here and out of her company, and on his way to Italy, the better. Women, he told himself, were simply too much trouble. He had learned his lesson. He had loved Emily, and look at the suffering that had brought him. Better to set up an expensive mistress who would go on her way without a backward glance when the novelty wore off. No ties, no strings, no eyes eating into one's heart and making life a misery.

They were talking about music now, and this appeared to be a subject that made the disguised girl come to life. So she was a musician, was she? That wasn't surprising if she had had the kind of upbringing he was coming to believe she had. Only, the question remained: if she were a gentleman's daughter, what on earth was she doing togged out in a pair of pantaloons and boots, travelling virtually alone across the continent of Europe?

The landlord was pleased to inform his guests that the instrument in the parlour was in good condition, and that they were more than welcome to use it if they chose. He had few other people staying at the inn at this season of the year, and there could be no objection to the English party, as he thought of them, amusing themselves with some music.

'There is a good fire in that room, and you may drink your coffee in there and the waiter shall bring wine or brandy for the gentlemen, as you wish.'

They made their way to the parlour, led by the rustling skirts of Mrs Vineham. Lord Lucius was muttering about cards, but she quelled him, saying there was time enough for that later, with an entire wearisome evening to be got through before it was time to retire. She paused for a moment at the threshold of the room, said that it would do well enough, and asked the landlord whether there were any news on the state of the passes.

He shrugged. 'There is more rain to come, and that will melt the snow. However, if the rain is too fierce and the thaw too sudden there is the problem of floods, of streams overflowing, of mud – all hazardous to the traveller. I believe you will be at my inn for some little while longer.'

'Lord, what a bore,' said Mrs Vineham, glancing around the room before appropriating what she considered the best place to sit. 'We shall be forced to all kinds of stratagems to entertain ourselves; it will come to charades and recitations, Lucius.'

'Not if I have anything to do with it, it won't,' he said, sitting down discontentedly before the fire and stretching out a hand to the blaze. He wore a huge solitaire ruby and tilted his head to admire the deep colour of it in the firelight.

Signore Lessini, with no more than a brief look which showed what he thought of Lord Lucius's underbred ways, ushered his wife to a comfortable seat. She touched his sleeve, giving him a look of such affection that Titus felt as though he'd been kicked in the chest.

'You had best play for us, my dear,' she said. 'Perhaps Mrs Vineham will honour us with a song?'

'Not I,' said that lady. 'I gave up all pretence at accomplishments years ago, I have better things to occupy my time. Mr Hawkins, you are a young man recently out of school, did they teach you to sing there?'

Her voice had a touch of contempt in it, but the so-called Mr Hawkins appeared not to notice.

'I can sing a little, ma'am.'

'If you studied with Silvestrini, then it must be more than a little,' said Lessini as he turned over the music that lay on the pianoforte. 'I never knew him take on an indifferent pupil.'

Alethea bowed, said that she would be happy to oblige, begged Signore Lessini to favour them with a performance on his own to begin with. Then she settled herself down – in the darkest part of the room, Titus noticed.

Signore Lessini played a sonata by Clementi, a delight to those present who took any pleasure in good music. That did not include Lord Lucius, who yawned and fidgeted his way through the piece and only came to life when Lessini was joined by Alethea.

His lordship's rather protuberant eyes swivelled to focus on the slim figure standing very upright, one hand on the pianoforte.

'A high tenor voice,' Mrs Vineham whispered to Warren. 'Almost an alto.'

'What did you expect, from a eunuch?' was Warren's reply. Mrs Vineham laughed, curled her lip at Signora Lessini's sshing sound and sent Titus a provocative look over her shoulder.

He ignored her. He was held by the song, by the voice, by the singer. So that was who she was. That was why he had all along had a sense of recognition. She was Wytton's sister-in-law, Fitzwilliam Darcy's daughter, no less. He couldn't believe the evidence of his ears at first, but no, he couldn't doubt it. His memory carried him back to Shillingford Abbey, to those days when the happy company gathering there for its owner's nuptials had taken him out of himself and dispersed some of the bitterness left by his stalled political career.

He had admired the music and the musician then. It had crossed his mind that when she came out, in a year or so, she would stand out among the usual insipid crowd of young ladies being paraded on the marriage mart.

She had married, of course, very soon into her first season; he had heard of it from Wytton, when he ran across him in Constantinople; his friend and neighbour had mentioned that Napier was a musical connoisseur, which would, he hoped, create a bond between the couple.

Not such a bond that she hadn't swiftly got up to mischief. An intrigue, an adulterous intrigue, must be the reason for this escapade. But, good God, what a risk she was running. Was Napier aware of where she was? Could he possibly have any inkling what she was up to? His own position was damnable, too. A total stranger cutting up such a lark might merely be amusing, but when it turned out to be someone very much from his own world, it was different.

He frowned. He was no kind of a hypocrite, he could not pretend to be a keen protector of the married state, but were he in Napier's shoes, he would feel great indignation if a fellow countryman didn't step in to send the errant wife scurrying back to England before anyone else found out who she was and what she was up to.

'Bravo,' Lord Lucius cried, as the song wound to its end. 'Give us the pleasure of another tune, Mr Hawkins, you have a fine voice, indeed.'

Signore Lessini was nodding in agreement. Warren and Mrs Vineham had their heads together; Titus heard the word 'castrato', and another peal of laughter broke from Mrs Vineham. She waved a hand in a languid gesture. 'Let us have no more music, enough is enough. The card table calls to us, does it not, Lucius?' Then, in a lower voice, 'For heaven's sake, stop gazing at the young prodigy as though you would gobble him up. That is not the way to coax him to your will, I assure you, you will merely embarrass him.' Louder, 'Mr Manningtree, do you make up a four?'

Titus declined, quite brusquely. Signore Lessini stepped forward, with the proviso that he would not play for high stakes, but otherwise was happy to oblige so that the others might have a game.

Warren raised an eyebrow, Lord Lucius looked huffy, Emily Lessini appeared relieved, and Mrs Vineham lifted an elegant shoulder in acquiescence. 'It will be but dull sport; however, anything is better than more music. I protest, I find such an unsexed voice quite devoid of charm. I dare say,' she added, noticing that Mr Hawkins had heard her words, 'that your voice will deepen as you grow older and can boast some hairs on your chin. You need not despair of such an outcome, I believe it does happen, even to young men in their twenties.'

Lord Lucius was calling for cards. Titus hesitated. He longed to go and sit beside Emily, perhaps to snatch a few private words with her, but she had brought out a piece of embroidery and stretched herself out on the little sofa where she sat so there was no room for another person. A dull evening indeed. He could retire with a book, or go out for a damp walk in the dim moonlight, only he fancied neither course of action. Very well, he would sit beside Alethea Darcy, Alethea Napier as she now was, and see if he could glean something of the truth from her, ascertain if there were any reason why he should not send word to Napier of where his wife was.

He caught himself up at this thought. Not a hypocrite, indeed. He had never cared for Napier, considered that the surface man and the essential Napier were two very different creatures. What the devil business was it of his whether Napier and his wife fell out or not, and why should he play the moralising parson by putting an end to whatever game this Darcy girl was playing?

He owed it to Fitzwilliam Darcy and Mrs Darcy? He did not. He knew them, but did not move in the same circle, could in no way describe himself as intimate with the family. With Wytton's family, yes, he was on very close terms with them, and therefore with Camilla Wytton, who was, of course, this hermaphrodite's elder sister. Even so, to betray her whereabouts to her husband or her father might be to cause the very scandal he preferred to spare his old friend and neighbour. Besides, he couldn't be so very sure that Wytton would regard this jaunt of Mrs Napier's in the same disapproving light as the rest of the world assuredly would. You could never tell with Wytton.

There had been a look of intelligence in Titus Manningtree's eye that made Alethea's heart give a lurch of alarm. Had he smoked her out? Had he recognised her? Their acquaintance had been brief, and in the two years since then, she had changed. She had grown, she had become thinner, she had had a love affair and become a married woman. In so many ways, she was a different person, and with short hair and these clothes and the admitted relationship to the Darcy family to account for the likeness to her father, why should he doubt her? It was her experience that people generally took you at face value and accepted that you were what you claimed to be.

Like Napier. No, she wasn't going to think about Napier. She was going to lounge in this chair, stretch her long limbs out, be at her ease and think herself into her part. I am Aloysius Hawkins, she told herself. A young man of promise, on his first adventure out in the world.

Titus offered wine, she was about to refuse, then thanked him as he called to the servant hovering at the door to the room.

'You may bring us a bottle of wine, and don't leave that door so wide open, it makes the fire smoke.'

The man scurried off, and Titus, too, stretched out his still longer legs, crossing them at the ankle and looking from under his eyelids at Alethea.

'You are not previously acquainted with any of this group of stranded travellers?' Titus enquired.

'No, sir. I have led a somewhat secluded life.'

'Your father's estate is where?'

'In the north.'

'Derbyshire?'

'I have spent much time in that county, with my cousins.'

'Ah, yes, of course.'

They fell silent. Alethea wondered whether to venture a remark of her own, but thought that a callow youth would let the older man determine the subject of any conversation.

'You have made a study of music,' Titus went on. 'Your performance is beyond that of the amateur.'

'I was fortunate in my teachers.'

He was finding this hard work, Alethea could see. She was boring him. Very well, let him be bored. She hadn't asked him to come and sit near her and ask awkward questions. The weather – that excellent conversational standby of anyone with a drop of English veins in his or her blood – let them discuss the weather.

'The landlord is vague as to how long our stay here is likely to be.'

'The landlord,' said Titus, 'is very happy to have a party of travellers holed up in his wretched inn, running up long bills and filling his rooms at a time of year when he must have little trade.'

'Wretched inn? I find it very comfortable.'

'Do you? I spoke figuratively. The beds and the public rooms are well enough, but I count any place wretched where I am forced to stay against my will. However, do not believe all the landlord said. Snow, at this season, is destined to thaw and floods subside. The way he speaks, we are likely to be here for at least a se'ennight; I do not think so. Another day or so, and the pass will be open, provided one has a good guide and takes care how one goes.'

'Have you often crossed the Alps?'

'Several times, although not usually so early in the year.'

'The business that takes you to Italy is urgent, then.'

'I wish to be away from here, because I find it tedious. I am quite sure, though, that the business I am upon will wait until we are released from imprisonment by snow and water. I have a rival in what I have come to acquire, but he is not yet in Italy.'

There was a grim note to his voice, an uncompromising look to his jaw; Alethea felt rather sorry for the rival, whoever he was.

'And you are going to stay with my good friend Wytton and his wife, who is, of course, your cousin.'

There it was once more, that edge to his voice. Sharpness? Mockery? She glanced at him again and found his expression to be one of bland politeness.

Scenery, then. 'The mountains have a grandeur beyond anything I expected,' she ventured. 'From the descriptions of them that I have read, and people's accounts of them, and engravings – and so forth. I was still not prepared for such majesty.'

'They are very big, are they not?'

There was unquestionably a mocking tone there. 'You are used to them, sir, they inspire no awe in you as they must in one who has never seen them before.'

'You are mistaken. Mountains inspire awe in any human person who has a soul. They remind us of our frailty, our unimportance, of the briefness of our span upon this earth. They touch the heavens, and sail serenely at an altitude beyond even the imaginings of a mere mortal. I assure you, even those like Herr Geissler, who has seen the mountains every day of his life, never lose their respect for the mountains. They are cruel, dangerous and possessed of a beauty one can never weary of.'

Titus had raised his voice slightly as he spoke, and Mrs Vineham's keen ears had caught his words. 'Of whom are you speaking, Mr Manningtree?' she cried across the room. 'Who is the cruel and dangerous beauty? I am sure I must know her.'

'We are speaking of the mountains, ma'am,' said Titus.

'The mountains! The world would be a better place without mountains. They are much admired but the picturesque is not as fashionable as it was used to be, and for my part I can do without mountains.'

Lord Lucius impatiently called her attention back to the cards and Alethea gave way to the laughter that was welling up inside her.

Titus watched her trying to control herself. 'A sip of wine?' he suggested.

Gasping in her efforts not to laugh out loud, Alethea took a large gulp of her wine, and nearly choked on it. She coughed and spluttered, aware that Titus was watching her with a sardonic expression on his face.

'Are you quite recovered?' he asked.

'Yes. It was so absurd, you see, about the mountains—'

'Do not think of it, or you will succumb to your laughter, and bring Mrs Vineham's contempt down upon you.'

The thought of Mrs Vineham's tongue quite took away any desire Alethea had to laugh, and she composed her face.

'We have spoken of the mountains, and of the weather,' said Titus. 'Have you any very striking observations to make upon the subject of your travels? Did you enjoy Paris?'

Alethea started. Did he connect her with the boy who had bumped into him that night in Paris? Had she mentioned the city? She thought not. 'I did travel by way of Paris, but that is a city I have visited before.'

'You have another cousin there, no doubt.'

She stared at him, nonplussed for a moment. Cousin? Of course, Georgina.

'Lady Mordaunt is a cousin of mine.'

'Did you see her while you were there?'

What business was it of his if she had? 'I did myself the honour of calling upon her,' she said stiffly.

'You sampled the many delights Paris has to offer a young man, I dare say.'

Now he was teasing her, she was sure of it. 'If you mean the more salacious pleasures the city is famous for, my inclinations do not run in that direction.'

'No? *Un homme serieux*, I perceive. Very well. Did you visit the site where so many unfortunates lost their heads, and trace the last footsteps of the late King Louis the Sixteenth?'

'I am not a ghoul, and history does not interest me,' Alethea said. She was growing hot under her starched collar. He was playing with her as he might a puppy. That was the kind of man he was, one to use his superior years and experience to make a green young man feel ill at ease and inadequate. She had thought him a man of uncertain temper, with the habit of command, one used to having his own way, a man well able to deal with the unexpected, whether in the form of an attack from bandits or a Mrs Vineham. He was all that, but he stood convicted, in her mind, of a cold callousness that she didn't care for.

Then he smiled, and his face was transformed. 'You rebuke me, Mr Hawkins, and with reason. I am out of sorts this evening, fretful for the delay to my journey. I am not a patient man.'

A better man would feel contrite, Titus told himself, for goading her like that. He didn't. He had to admire her coolness under fire, however. A keen observer could notice nothing malapropos about her behaviour or responses; they were just those that might be expected of a callow young man such as she was pretending to be.

Had he ever been such an one? He judged her to be eighteen or so. Yes, for Camilla Wytton had said that she was sixteen when they were at Shillingford Abbey for the wedding. 'So, Mr Hawkins, you will proceed to the University. Do you have plans beyond that? The law, perhaps, or the Church. Perhaps you are fortunate enough to be an elder son, and will inherit an estate and have no need of a profession.'

'It is still some while in the future.' She made a visible effort to continue the conversation; one that clearly made her uneasy. 'I might enlist in the Army.'

His eyes flickered over to her, his eyebrows lifted. His mouth twitched. 'I am not sure that such a life would suit you.'

'No, sir? Are you familiar with army life?'

'I was a soldier for several years.'

'Did you fight at Waterloo?'

'I did, much to my sorrow.'

While she had doubtless been taking her first unsteady steps around the nursery, he had joined his father's old regiment and gone to war.

That had been the kind of young man he was. Brave, hot-headed, impetuous, longing to fling himself into battle against the foe. At that age, any foe would have done. How he had loved the life, then, with all its privations and hardships and dangers. For five years he had soldiered in the Peninsula; five years that saw him grow from eager youth to competent manhood. He had made friends and endured the bitterness of watching them fall in battle or die by the roadside of dysentery. He had served under good men and indifferent men and downright dangerous officers. He had laughed and fought and wenched his way across Spain and Portugal and back again. He had been sickened by the terrible sights at the siege of Ciudad Rodrigo, exulted by the victory at Salamanca, bored by retreats, driven on by his thirst for danger.

'That was a great battle,' Alethea said politely. Apart from the reported death of their neighbour, Tom Busby, which turned out to be no such thing, merely a case of amnesia, she had been untouched by the war, and by the end of it that came with Waterloo.

'War is a terrible thing, Mr Hawkins,' said Titus sombrely.

His hot blood had deserted him when he was what, five-and-twenty? Until then he had been immortal, and utterly sure that he had been born to be a soldier.

Two things had happened, apart, he reflected, gazing with unseeing eyes into the flames, from the inevitable fact of his growing up. He had received a savage wound, which had nearly cost him his life, and he had seen his oldest friend, a companion from his childhood and schooldays, die in agony from a bullet that lodged in his guts.

He fought on, serving his country to the best of his ability, but the guiding light had gone out of his life. The burning desire to fight and kill the French had become a cold matter of duty, and he despised himself for the life he was living. He had acquired a reputation as a hard man. New recruits, as fresh-faced and smooth-cheeked as this girl sitting here by the fire, arrived and had him pointed out to them. 'Don't cross the Major,' his men warned. 'He has the very devil of a temper, and never, ever, be seen to neglect your duty while he is about.'

It occurred to him that Alethea had the rare gift of being contained within herself, unbothered by silence. She had made attempts at conversation, as manners dictated, but now that he was lost in his thoughts, she left well alone. No doubt she had thoughts of her own to occupy her mind, although he sincerely hoped ones less grim than his.

Waterloo. He sighed, closing his eyes for a second only to see the muddy ground churned up by tens of thousands of hooves and boots. Mud, itself besmeared with blood. Death everywhere, the stink and horror of death. Wellington, with tears coursing down his drawn face as he read the list of men lost in battle.

'Waterloo was terrible,' he said aloud, though speaking really to himself. 'Don't ever believe it when men tell you of the glory of victory. There was no glory that day.'

Titus had sold out of the Army at the end of the Peninsular campaign. His elder brother had died of an ague, and his father wanted him to learn to manage the estates that would one day be his. He had given up the life of a soldier with considerable relief.

Only to return to it with a heavy heart, driven by his keen sense of duty, when Bonaparte escaped from Elba and it became obvious that, once again, war-weary England must fight yet another battle. What choice was there? This was not a war of expansion, a war waged at the whim of political masters or the kings of olden days. This was a war to keep the England he loved safe. Where would he be now, or those others keenly watching the fall of cards, or Emily, setting her stitches with such precision under the light on the round table over there?

What of Alethea Napier, so improbably sitting there in her man's clothes? She would have grown up in an England whose ancient liberties and independence were cast aside by a Napoleon. If that man had achieved his goals of France's hegemony over the whole of Europe, what a different world they would all be living in. Not a better one, neither, whatever one's sympathies for the Revolutionary cause might be.

For a moment, he wished he were eighteen again, on the threshold of his adult life, with no war to be fought and won, with no savage memories to etch themselves on his unwilling brain. He envied Alethea, with a spurt of feeling that astonished him by its intensity, for her youth, her ignorance of such horrors, for being at that age when an adventure was just that, an adventure, and a good night's sleep cured all ills.

Looking up, he met her eyes. He was even more startled by what he saw there. Not innocence, nor ignorance. This chit was carrying horrors of her own, he was sure of it. He began to wonder what kind of man Napier might be under that pleasant exterior, and exactly what he had done to his young and beautiful wife, not merely to cause her to run away, but to carry that look of absolute bleakness in her eyes.

'Drink your wine,' he said abruptly, wanting to jerk her out of whatever personal hell her mind had taken her to. 'It will do you good.'

'Your hands are like ice,' Figgins scolded, chafing them with her own. 'I thought as how there was a fire in there.' Lordie, she hated to see Miss Alethea look like that. Whatever had turned her spirits, when she had been so light hearted and sure that she was doing the right thing all the way here?

'It's this waiting about and not knowing if we're going to be swept away by snow or floods.'

'Mrs Lessini's maid speaks some Italian, she's half Italian herself, as you can tell from that dark skin and those eyes like they have. I dare say it's handy for her mistress, having a servant that can understand what's been said around her.'

Figgins sounded aggrieved, and she was. Used to relying on her keen ear and quick wits, she found it hard not to know exactly what was going on.

'However, she looks a frail creature,' Alethea said. 'Mrs Lessini may yet wish she'd brought a stout English abigail with her. After all, once she is in Italy, she may engage any number of Italian servants, all speaking the language fluently.'

'I don't have anything against Maria,' Figgins said. 'And it's useful, what she picks up from some of the people here at the inn. Half of them seem to speak Italian as well, for all that country's over the other side of these dratted mountains. She has told me that the snow is melting away in the warmer air, and that we may expect to see the first arrivals from the other side at any moment.'

Alethea looked more cheerful. 'I most sincerely hope so,' she said, with a yawn. 'I long to be away from here, and apart from this company. The Lessinis are the best of them, but there is such tension in the air – I suppose on account of Mr Manningtree and his previous connection with Mrs Lessini – that even they are not such agreeable companions as they might be in different circumstances.'

Figgins gathered up Alethea's cast-off shirt. 'I'll be off and wash this out, you haven't so many that you can leave any behind, and who knows, we may be off tomorrow.'

Chapter Eleven

A thunder of knocks at the chamber door. Footsteps echoing on the wooden floor above. An Englishman's voice shouting for his boots.

What was going on? Alethea, still half-asleep, sat up in bed, tousled and bewildered, to find Figgins stuffing clothes into her portmanteau.

'Get up,' she was crying out. 'For if we are not ready inside a quarter of an hour, we shall miss our chance.'

'Our chance for what?' said Alethea, tumbling out of bed and taking the shirt Figgins held out to her.

'Our chance to be away over these dratted mountains and down into a place where, please God, May is May, with no snow nor floods of icy water.'

'What time is it? Do we leave at dawn, is that the plan?'

'Dawn! No, indeed, it lacks some few minutes to three o'clock, there is to be no idling about until dawn. You must be quick, for they will not wait for us.'

Alethea hopped about on one foot, trying to pull on a boot that seemed to have shrunk since she last wore it. 'Do we travel alone?'

'We do not. They will not have it, we travel as a party or not at all, there are not the drivers nor the guides to take us separately.'

A strange cry rent the air, making Alethea jump.

'There's Mrs Vineham screeching at Sarah, I wouldn't be an abigail to that woman for a hundred pounds a year.' Figgins gave a tug at a buckle and tucked the leather strap in place. 'There, now, and what's forgotten will have to wait.

I've a bag full of wet shirts and I don't know what else; it's to be hoped we find a decent inn on the other side.'

'It may be a night on the bare mountain,' Alethea said, reaching for her greatcoat. 'Where is my hat?'

Figgins passed it to her, and Alethea jammed the beaver over her short, springy hair.

They were downstairs with barely a moment to gulp down a bowl of strong black coffee before Herr Geissler threw open the doors to let in a gust of icy wind from the darkness outside.

Mrs Vineham gave another screech and wrapped her voluminous travelling cloak more securely about her person. 'Give me that,' she said, snatching a huge muff from her maid's hands. 'And mind you stay within earshot, you stupid girl, in case I have need of you.'

'The servants will travel in a separate vehicle,' the innkeeper told her. 'The carriages must stay close together, to be of assistance in case of an accident.'

'Accident,' cried Mrs Vineham, drawing back into the shelter of the inn. 'What is this about accidents?'

Oho, thought Alethea, she is going to make a scene and delay us all. Look at the inn servants eyeing her as though she were a creature in a zoo. If I were in my petticoats, I too could flutter my eyelashes and cry out in alarm. Signora Lessini, in complete contrast, stood cool and collected as she waited for her husband to escort her to the chaise.

'My dear Mrs Vineham,' Signora Lessini was saying, 'calm yourself. Remember that every journey involves danger, and any crossing of the Alps is bound to be a more arduous journey than most. Place your trust in God and I am sure we shall arrive safely on the other side.'

Mrs Vineham's maid took her arm. 'Come, madam, the driver is waiting, if we do not go now, we shall be left behind.'

Alethea heard Bootle muttering under his breath that if God had any sense, He'd strike Mrs Vineham a swift one with a thunderbolt and spare them all a deal of playacting, and she grinned inwardly.

'Mr Manningtree,' Mrs Vineham called out as Titus's tall figure appeared at the door. He was booted, cloaked and crackling with energy as he swept Alethea and Figgins before him, telling Mrs Vineham that the party was leaving, and it was up to her to stay or go as she chose. 'We have a long journey ahead of us, and cannot delay a moment.'

Outside, Alethea felt heady as she breathed in the clean, fresh mountain air. It was a perfect night, the velvety sky thick with stars, stars that were more than usually dazzling in the pure atmosphere.

A touch at her elbow brought her back to earth, and she went to board the waiting chaise that Titus was indicating to her.

Mrs Vineham, she was thankful to see, was travelling in the other chaise. Complaining still about her rude awakening, the unreasonableness of the hour, the darkness, the cold, she climbed in beside Lord Lucius, and could be heard demanding to borrow his smelling salts.

'Never tell me that man carries a vinaigrette,' Alethea said, as the carriage jolted into motion and she was flung back against the seat of the chaise.

Her travelling companions were Titus and Mr Warren; the Lessinis were with Mrs Vineham and Lord Lucius. Titus found the vinaigrette amusing, too, but George Warren looked at her in a bored way and said that many men of fashion carried smelling salts.

Alethea took no notice of his early-morning sourness. For herself, she was in high spirits, glad to be away from the confines of the inn and relishing the prospect of an exciting journey through the mountains.

'Why such an early start, sir?' she asked Titus, who was leaning in a corner of the carriage, his long legs stretched out crossways.

'The journey will not be an easy one, and can take many

hours; we are unlikely to reach Domodossola before the late afternoon.'

'Mrs Vineham will not be pleased to hear that.'

'Which is why we all took pains not to inform her of it.'

Warren snorted and pulled his hat down over his eyes. 'I intend to sleep, since it is the middle of the night,' he said. 'Therefore, I would be obliged if you could refrain from conversation.'

Titus shrugged, raised an eyebrow at Alethea and withdrew into himself. For her part, she was happy to travel in silence; she wanted to savour every moment of her journey. The carriage was cold, and she was glad of the hot bricks put in by the inn servant as she looked out at the wintry scene, the snow high above them gleaming under the starlight in contrast to the patches of deepest shadow cast by pine trees and the mountain itself.

At first, there was no snow on the road, and the coaches kept up a steady, slow pace, climbing all the while. The sky lightened, turned to a pale grey streaked with pink, and, as the sun rose, Alethea saw the drifts of snow on either side of their wheels. The May sun was blazing with a summer's heat, but now they were high enough for it to seem more like a cold, bright January day.

The mountains seemed to be closing in on them, vast snow-covered peaks above and walls of snow on either side. For the first time, Alethea felt a stirring of fear. Seen from down in the valleys, the mountains were immense, but distant, like the sky or the stars, indifferent to humanity. Now, as they climbed towards the distant peaks, winding their way up into the heart of the mountains, they became threatening and hostile.

In his corner, Titus stirred out of his reverie. 'This is where it becomes interesting,' he observed.

George Warren slept on. 'Should we wake him?' said Alethea. 'He must be sorry to miss such sights.'

'I dare say he's seen it before, and he's a surly fellow in the morning; let him sleep off his temper until we have to leave the chaise, then we can rouse him.'

'Leave the chaise? Do we continue on foot?'

Titus gestured to the window. 'See for yourself. Those great swathes of snow are from avalanches, and the streams have turned into torrents; they bring boulders and rocks down with them. I don't doubt they have blocked our path in places, and we shall have to descend from the chaise and walk part of the way.'

Titus was right. Within a half hour, the drivers were calling out to one another in their unintelligible Schwyzerdütsch and the chaises came to a standstill. Titus thrust his head out of the window. 'It is as I thought,' he said, drawing it back inside before unfastening the door. 'There is heavy snow ahead, and a stream beyond it. They will take the horses and carriages through, but we shall have to go on foot.'

Warren woke up, stretched, yawned and swore in disapprobation when informed that they had to descend from the chaise. 'What a cursed bore,' he said. 'And in May, it's too bad, we might as well be here in February or March for all this trouble.'

'I hope you find your journey worthwhile,' Titus said.

'I shall, Manningtree, I shall,' Warren said with a curl of his lip that might have been a smile, but could just as well have been a sneer. It certainly didn't reach anywhere near his eyes. What a disagreeable man he could be, especially when there were no ladies about to put on a pleasant face for.

What was the cause of the hostility between the two men? Alethea asked herself as she jumped down to the ground. It was icy and slippery underfoot, and she would have fallen if Titus hadn't put out a strong hand to steady her. An old rivalry? The contempt of a soldier for the man who prefers not to fight? Some ancient family feud? Although they didn't, apparently, hate one another to an equal degree; it seemed to be Titus Manningtree who was full of anger against Warren, while Warren seemed merely to dislike the other man.

Her attention was drawn away from such theorising and to the immediate, physical certainties of the icy water swirling above her ankles. Stream, indeed. This stretch of water, that tumbled and sucked against the stones and boulders carried down by the volume of water, was a positive torrent, and one that she would much rather not cross.

Mrs Vineham's rising notes of complaint stirred up her courage, and there was a resolute Figgins ahead of her, sliding and stumbling, but making steady progress and, she noticed, never more than knee-deep in the water. As women, they might be able to exclaim and help one another; as men, they would be expected to take it in their stride.

How much of women's weakness was genuine, how much a matter of expectation? Triumphantly arrived at the other side, Alethea removed a boot to shake out the freezing water, leaning on Figgins's shoulder as she did so. She did the same with the other boot, watching from the corner of her eye the uncertain crossing of Mrs Vineham, held aloft by two sturdy Swiss, who stoically ignored her shrieks and cries to heaven. They set her down on her feet, none too gently, and plunged back into the water to tender assistance to Lord Lucius, who had lost his eye-glass.

Signora Lessini had waved away offers of help, relying instead on the support of her husband, and they came across in a resolute fashion, her skirts raised well above the surface of the water. This drew another scream from Mrs Vineham, a genteel scream against such immodesty as a lady revealing her legs in the presence of so many men. 'Not all of whom have seen them before,' she added.

Titus gave her a look of contempt. Lord Lucius, his glass restored, tittered, and George Warren laughed aloud, the laughter resonating back off the sheer cliffs to either side.

Signora Lessini took no notice of the vicious remark, nor the laughter, but pulled a large handkerchief from her husband's pocket and calmly set about drying her feet and legs as best she could.

'I admire her for that,' Alethea said, *sotto voce*.

Titus, standing within earshot, and obviously possessed of keen hearing, nodded his agreement. 'An admirable woman,' he said quietly.

They made their way back into the coaches, somewhat chilled, and glad to learn from their driver that the first rest house was only a little way ahead.

Alethea had never in her life enjoyed coffee more than the steaming bowl offered at the guest house. She sniffed the aroma, blew on the surface to cool it enough to drink, and sipped it sitting on a bench in the hot sunshine looking out across snow so bright it hurt her eyes.

The drivers chivvied them back to their places. Still damp, but warmed by the coffee and the sun, Alethea sank back, leaning her head against the seat, feeling suddenly very tired. She pulled her greatcoat closely around her and felt her eyelids droop.

The scrunching of the wheels through the snow, the clink of the horses' bits and the incomprehensible sounds of the Swiss coach drivers merged in her head to form an uneasy lullaby. She didn't sleep, but fell into a drowsy state, the chill from outside seeming to creep within her. Images came unbidden into her mind; images she had no power to resist, unwelcome as they were.

Instead of Mr Manningtree and Mr Warren, she had a fancy that she was in a coach with Penrose, and for a moment she felt a rush of joy. Then Penrose's face distorted and grew dim, and, clear as though she were physically there, in London, she was back at the dance, that fateful dance, at the Danbys' house.

She was wearing her aquamarine ball dress. Looking down at her skirts, she could see the tiny bouquets of flowers on the festoons of flounces in perfect detail. The dress was a favourite one, net over a satin slip, falling in full folds that allowed her much more freedom of movement than many of her ball dresses.

He was standing before her, with a smile on his lips and admiration in his eyes. Charles Danby, a cousin on Penrose's mother's side, made the introduction. 'May I have the honour to present . . . ?' Penrose made a leg, begged the favour of a dance. He had on a blue coat. She wore a diamond necklace, he had a chaste but fine diamond pin in his gleaming white stock. He was young and handsome and tall enough not to make her feel uncomfortable as he took her hand and led her into the dance.

Alethea struggled to escape from these vivid, unwelcome memories. But the snow blinded her eyes when she opened them, and she sank back into her restless, dreamlike state.

Another night, another ball. She was in white. Her dress had spangles, which glittered slightly as she moved. Thinking only of the moment when she might see him again, she was oblivious to the attention she attracted upon her entry into the ballroom; the glow of happiness and expectation enhancing her looks and turning more than a few heads in her direction.

It was a much grander occasion than the Danbys' dance. That had been little more than a family affair, not a formal ball. There were above five hundred people crammed into the ballroom at the back of the huge house in Berkeley Square, all the great and the gay, the rich and the fashionable, were there, packed tight, waving fans, exclaiming at the crush and the heat, tripping over one another on the dance floor.

Words drifted past her ears as she waltzed with Penrose.

'Oho,' said Snipe Woodhead. 'Is that another of the Darcy girls? It must be, it's her father to the life. Young Youdall seems to take a deal of pleasure in her company.'

'It's their second dance, and I saw them sitting out together in one of those little alcoves,' said Lady Naburn, who was passing. 'Shocking behaviour for such a young girl, barely out of the schoolroom. A very forward miss, indeed.'

'They say she sings.'

'So do cuckoos.'

Oblivious to the clack of vitriolic tongues about her,

Alethea danced with a spring in her step and a lively beat to her heart. She found Penrose utterly delightful. He was funny and quick-witted, and shared her passion for music. With him she felt no shyness, no reserve, no wish that she could be somewhere else. All the creeping boredom of her first few parties had vanished. Where he was, there was gaiety and amusement and an ease of companionship that was extraordinary after so short an acquaintance.

Other scenes sprang before her eyes. Riding in the park, falling behind the rest of the party, returning to Aubrey Square in a glow of happiness that made Fanny smile and Fitzwilliam shake his head.

Their engagement began to be spoken of as a likely event, indeed possibly even as a matter agreed between the families but not announced, not with the Darcys fixed at Pemberley, anxious for the health of their youngest boy, who had been suffering from a low fever that caused family and physicians some alarm. That was why Alethea was in Fanny's charge, and how glad she was of it, because she knew, deep down, that Mama and Papa might not approve of the time she spent with Penrose.

Only those close to the Youdalls begged to differ, saying there was no question of an engagement, that Penrose was too young to be thinking of setting up his own household, that Miss Alethea Darcy, although a very good kind of young woman, was something of a flirt, and there was nothing serious in the young people's friendship.

Frozen in time, she saw Mrs Youdall in another house, at another ball, gazing at her in a most disagreeable way. Only a fool could not have noticed it. 'Why does your Mama so dislike me?' she asked Penrose as they circled the floor together.

He flicked a quick glance to the side of the room where the dowagers sat in a clutter of turbans and feathers, and smiled down at Alethea.

'How can you say such a thing? She admires you greatly,

she told me so herself. She remarked how pretty you are looking, and how much your liveliness adds to your looks.'

Alethea did not think that Mrs Youdall looked like a woman who valued liveliness, but she kept her counsel, and said that doubtless Penrose knew his mother better than she did.

They ventured into the garden, where the air was warm with the lingering heat of a May day. The scents of the flowers wafted over her as they walked along the lamplit paths that wound into the shrubbery. An inviting bench placed discreetly behind a tree, his arm around her waist, tightening its grip, and they lost themselves in a passionate embrace.

In the coach, Alethea turned her head, and murmured his name.

'Did you say something?' Titus Manningtree's voice rang in her ears, and she dragged herself out of the May garden, back into the chilly heights of the Alps. He was staring at her, an inscrutable look on his face. She flushed, and struggled to a more upright position.

'I fell asleep,' she said lamely. 'I was dreaming.'

'So I gathered,' he said drily.

Alethea sat up, yawned and looked about the carriage. For some reason, her senses retained a strange, lingering clarity: the set of Titus Manningtree's masterful nose, the way his coat fell across his muscular thighs, the dense black curls of George Warren's hair beneath the curved brim of his hat, the intense masculinity of both men.

She shook away the last of her sleepiness. She felt uneasy; she was out of place, had no business being here.

'We're going dashed slowly,' Warren complained. 'Manningtree, put your head out and ask that lazy clown of a driver whether he or the horses have fallen asleep.'

'If you care to look out, you will observe for yourself that the snow is deeper. I am not sure that the chaises will be able to go much further.'

'What, are we to be stranded?' Alethea asked, forgetting

her intention of maintaining a suitable indifference to discomfort and danger.

'They may have to hoist the carriages on to runners,' Titus said.

'God, what a bore,' said Warren. 'One always forgets how tedious foreign travel becomes as one leaves civilisation behind. One must, I suppose, render thanks to the Emperor for building this road, I shudder to think what such a journey was like in the last century.'

Alethea didn't like to display her ignorance, but Titus caught her blank look and enlightened her.

'Warren is referring to Napoleon Bonaparte,' he said. 'He had this road constructed some ten or twelve years ago, when he wanted to bring troops across into Italy and Austria. It is a remarkable feat of engineering, and I dare say the Swiss may grow to be grateful for its building, but I do not think they thought well of it at the time. It cost a great many lives, I believe, to blast such a road through the very rock itself.'

Titus had a tolerably good idea of what was going through Alethea's mind. For one of her generation, the years of war with France were no more than a memory, a backdrop to childhood. In 1815, as the war ended with the guns of Waterloo, she would have been under the care of her governess, learning French verbs, stitching a sampler and putting in her dutiful daily hour on the pianoforte or harp.

Although not the last activity, he suspected, not in Alethea Darcy's case. For her, music was a passion, and he guessed that any stitches she was obliged to set were probably ragged and resentfully done. He pictured her as a tomboy, rolling down grass banks, climbing trees and running wild with no care as to the dirtying of dress or shoes.

Such girls usually grew out of their wildness, and became well-dressed, poised young women. Clearly something had gone amiss with this Darcy daughter; he was amazed that her parents had not had more control of her. To run away from a husband, to roam Europe disguised as a man indicated a distinct wildness of nature.

He utterly disapproved of such behaviour. Hoydens had never appealed to him. Yet, against his better judgement, he felt a reluctant admiration for her as the journey became slower and more and more difficult. Three times more, they had to descend from the carriage and wade through torrential streams. Emily was sensible and stoical; this reckless girl, though obviously tired and anxious, made little of the trials of their journey.

Look at her now, reeling as she was nearly knocked off her feet by a stronger than expected current of water. 'The water is so cold, and the air so fresh and clean, I have never known such air, it quite goes to my head,' she said breathlessly.

'That is the altitude,' Titus said, as he hauled her, none too gently, aside from a wavering boulder.

'And the snow, so dazzling and with such perfection about it, I never saw such smoothness and brilliance. And yet, the sun is blazing down. It is all so different from anything I have ever experienced.' She gave him a quick, sidelong glance. 'I dare say none of it is new to you, you will have made many such journeys.'

'On the contrary, I find this journey a revelation in many ways, and it is quite unlike any of my previous crossings of the Alps, I can assure you.'

She wasn't listening to him, but was looking intently at the men who were busying themselves about the wheels of the chaise. 'What are they doing, sir?'

'They are attaching the runners I spoke of to the chaise,' said Titus. 'Where the snow is deep and the passage impossible with wheels, they are accustomed to make the chaise into a kind of sleigh.'

'A sleigh!' Her laughter chased the care from her face, and the clear sound made the labouring men look up and stare at her with the tight eyes of those who spend time in the sun in the high mountains. They returned to their task; Titus moved over to speak to Emily.

'Our young friend here is amused by the novelty of our situation,' he remarked. 'I wish I could share his enthusiasm for this very inconvenient mode of travel.'

She gave him one of her direct looks. 'I am sure that when you were a young man, you would have found it an adventure. It is a sadness of growing older that we lose our ardent appreciation of what is new and different and difficult.'

'I stand rebuked.'

Signore Lessini had been regarding them with a smile on his face; he came across to join them. 'Well, this is something, Mr Manningtree, we are to turn into Russians and travel across the snow as on a sleigh. We should have bells and make a merriness of it.'

'As you say.' Titus's voice was cold. Try as he might, he couldn't dislike the amiable Italian, although every fibre of his being resented the man for usurping his place in Emily's life, in her heart as well as her bed, to go by the look on her face. Damn her, he said inwardly, damn all women, so deceiving, so inclined to do the unexpected.

'You look to be in a temper, Mr Manningtree,' Emily said in a kindly way. 'Perhaps you are a trifle liverish, in which case the jolting I fear we are about to receive in our progress across the snow and ice will stir that organ up for you, and restore you to your customary good humour.'

He eyed her uncertainly: was that a note of irony in her voice? He was not a man known for his good humour, although when he was younger, he had had a happy, open disposition and was not given to displays of irritation or anger. 'That is another change the years have wrought,' he said to Emily. 'We have to have regard for our livers.'

'Nonsense, nonsense,' cried Signore Lessini. 'I have the greatest respect for my liver, and it causes me no discomfort whatever, and as for dear Emily, she is never in any kind of internal disorder, all is in harmony with her.'

The next part of the journey was enough to tax the strongest stomach and nerves. The rock faces towered above them on one side, with waterfalls roaring and foaming down them; on the other side yawned a chasm.

'I trust there are railings,' Warren said. His jaw was tight and, unlike Titus, who was regarding their dangerous progress with detached calm, he was ill at ease, peering first up at the crags and peaks above, then sliding along the seat to look down into the steep gorge stretching away to a snaking river far below.

'Wishing you hadn't come?' Titus asked.

'It is not a matter of wishing or not wishing; my mission will not wait,' Warren said testily.

'What are those men perched so perilously alongside the way?' Alethea asked. 'They are waving at us.'

'They are not waving; they are indicating to the coachmen where the edge of the road is,' Titus said, after a brief look. 'The railings are covered with snow, and without those workmen posted here, we would no doubt plunge over the edge.'

Warren's face turned even paler, and he shut his eyes. 'Almost I wish we might plunge,' he murmured. 'That would at least be an end to this interminable misery.'

'Are we near the top of the pass?' Alethea asked, sinking back into her seat. While not as disturbed as Mr Warren appeared to be, she found she didn't care for the sheer drop to the depths below, so few inches away from the wheels of their carriage.

'By no means,' Titus replied. 'We have several hours of ascent ahead of us.'

'Look there, at that rock fall, quite half one of those great cliffs appears to have come down,' she said.

'Then let us pray the other half does not tumble down upon us,' Warren said, without opening his eyes ... heerful

His ill humour persisted, but Aleth... enjoy the

when the way became wider

sunshine, the mountains and the novel sensation of being drawn over the snow on a sled. Hadn't Mama told them that in winter one made much of the journey from Vienna to Turkey in horse-drawn sleighs? With armed guards to keep away bandits and wolves; how she would love to go upon such a journey. She remembered her sister Camilla exclaiming how much she envied her parents their journey to Constantinople and their stay there among the mosques and the musselmen.

Now she could appreciate Camilla's feelings; how well suited she and Wytton were in that respect. Her brother-in-law was an energetic soul with a curious, scholar's mind, eager always to be off exploring ancient sites in remote parts of the globe. How different from Napier, and at the mere thought of her husband, she shivered.

'Cold?' enquired Titus.

'No, merely an unpleasant thought that came into my mind,' said Alethea. She closed her eyes again, disinclined to enter into conversation with Mr Manningtree, who had too much perception in his eyes for her liking.

Unpleasant thought? If only he were merely a thought, and not a man, flesh and blood and money and power. And her husband. She forced herself not to give in to the fear that flooded over her. She was out of his reach now, and would never return to that terrible house again.

The same dreamlike state overcame her, but this time she slipped back into the nightmare world that she had escaped from; escaped physically, that was, but with the months of her time with Napier scored deep into her soul.

And there she was, back in the drawing room at Dundon House, after dinner, waiting for the gentlemen to reappear. A young woman with soft brown hair and big, rather protuberant brown eyes came and sat beside her. She was a good deal [illegible] than Alethea, with a neat figure and a voluptuous [illegible] which reposed a very fine pearl necklace. She [illegible] as Diana Gray, and complimented Alethea on her performance at the pianoforte. 'I myself play the harp, but I cannot lay claim to half your accomplishment.'

'I do not regard music as an accomplishment,' Althea said.

'Do you not? How strange. What is it then?'

'An art.'

'Oh, that is all above my head. I have nothing to do with art, I think it an unsuitable subject for young women to contemplate. I don't mean I don't dearly like to look at a picture, I much enjoy going to the London exhibitions of paintings. However, it is for the men to take that kind of thing seriously, do not you agree?'

'No,' said Alethea, disliking the way this girl was looking her up and down with such a complacent stare, and wishing that the men would come in and she could enjoy Penrose's company.

It hadn't turned out that way, with the odious Mrs Youdall drawing that Miss Gray away to talk to her son.

'Miss Alethea, here is a gentleman who wishes to have the honour of an introduction. May I present Mr Napier, Mr Norris Napier?'

She smiled and nodded and said what was civil, and spoke a few words to him, hardly aware of his presence, how could she be, when Penrose was in the room?

Several of the gentlemen begged Alethea for a song, and Mr Napier paid her the compliment of giving her performance his undivided attention, and afterwards his praise was genuine and full of real enthusiasm and understanding. He talked sensibly about Mozart and Rossini, about French songs and about singers in London and Paris. He said he envied Penrose his ability to play the violin, 'Alas, I never achieved more than a modicum of success upon any instrument, although it was not for want of trying.'

'I merely scrape,' Penrose said with a laugh, 'alth
confess I have great pleasure in pl
in Miss Alethea's leag
to music.'

'You have acquired another beau,' Diana Gray remarked as they waited for the carriages. 'We other young ladies are quite cast in the shade.'

'Another beau? What can you mean?'

'There is Mr Youdall in constant attendance upon you, as all the world knows, and now Mr Napier evidently takes great pleasure in your company.'

'Mr Napier and I were talking of music.'

'Oh, is that what you have in common? And what do you discuss with Mr Youdall?' This was said with a sly, knowing look that made Alethea flush with anger.

The memory faded. A tear slid unnoticed from beneath her closed lids as she stretched and turned, trying to blot out these painfully intrusive recollections.

Why, she asked herself, had Napier appeared so normal, so pleasant? Such a man should have had some mark of Cain about him to warn her that he was not to be trusted; some indication of his unnatural ways and the cruel spirit that lay hidden beneath the charm.

She shook herself awake, felt the dampness on her cheek, remarked that the sun was making her eyes water and determined to doze no more. What was it about this unreal place of snow and ice, so far above the normal world, that brought these miserable thoughts into her head? She longed for the journey to be at an end, but was assured by Titus that they were no more than halfway.

They travelled on the runners over the snow for nearly two hours, before the cavalcade once more came to a halt and the wheels were restored to the chaises. More hours passed, as they climbed higher and higher towards the summit. The sun was too dazzling to look out at, and Alethea was forced to close her eyes. She was determined to keep alert and in the [illegible]ent moment, but weariness overcame her and once again [illegible] back into her uncomfortable half-doze.

[illegible] dream of all, a familiar one that often

came stealing into the troubled hours of her sleep at Tyrrwhit House, increasing her wretchedness.

She was in the country this time, at Holtmere, the seat of Lord and Lady Milton. She was with Fanny, come to join a considerable house party, and among her fellow guests was Penrose. Nothing and no one else mattered, as far as she was concerned; and she looked forward to spending so many happy hours in his company.

He was in love with her, as she was with him. He hadn't proposed, but never for a moment did she imagine that he would not, and very soon, too. Attraction had deepened into love, and with that love went passion, physical passion. The sensations she felt in his presence and the heat of her blood when they snatched moments alone together made her dizzy. Her ardour matched his; no wonder she had heard one crotchety old dowager remark with the frankness of her generation that the sooner she and Penrose were man and wife and bedded together, the better.

'Youth will to it,' the dowager said to Fanny. 'Push the business forward, before their passions turn out to be stronger than their morals.'

Fanny, of a more mealy-mouthed generation, protested at any such idea. 'Alethea has been strictly raised, she knows just how she must behave, she would let neither Mr Youdall nor any other man go beyond the line of what is acceptable.'

'Strictly raised, indeed, but all of that can fly out of the window in the case of a young woman with strong feelings. You heed my words, Lady Fanny, and see to it that the nuptial knot is tied before mischief is done.'

Alethea, whose hearing was acute, had overheard this conversation as she sat in the window embrasure of the gallery where the ladies were gathered for the hour before the men returned from shooting. Her cheeks blazed, from temper as much as embarrassment, and she had to suppress an urge to tell the dowager to keep her unwanted opinions to herself.

There was a wildness in Penrose that evening, a recklessness that made her catch her breath and feel a glow. When he stole a kiss by lingering in the shadows as the company gathered to say their goodbyes, he surprised her by the hard urgency of his lips. His voice was rough as he whispered in her ear, 'Alethea, my love, my only love.'

That night, he stole into her room. Only Figgins, her maid, saw him come and go, and she, although uneasy, knowing as she did what men were, and what trouble they could cause, also knew how to keep her mouth shut.

For Alethea, there was no unease, no uncertainty. Nor any maidenly hesitation or modesty. Her feelings for Penrose were too strong and it was with rapture mingled with curiosity that she sank into his embrace, secure in his love and with only a moment's concern about anticipating their wedding night. What could it matter? They would be married very soon, and this passionate coming together was the seal of their love. There might have been some awkwardness of coming to what the country folk called the right true end of love, but not with Penrose, not with the passion he aroused in her.

'Like music,' she said drowsily to Penrose as he slipped out of her bed when the light of dawn began to trickle round the shutters at the window of her chamber.

The dowager gave her a very sharp look when the ladies met for luncheon and pursed her lips in an irritatingly knowing way. Alethea raised her chin and refused to look at her. What did all these dull women know about love? Had any of them ever found the perfect delight and rapture that she had experienced in the intimacy of her night with Penrose? She was very sure they had not.

Another night, another day with no proposal. Indeed, she saw much less of Penrose than she had expected. A loud woman, one Mrs Gray, the mother of the little brown girl with the bosom, claimed his attention. Instead, she spent time with Norris Napier, who found her out in the music room and charmed away the afternoon by playing for her to sing and joining her in some *duetti* that they found lying on the pianoforte. There was an old harpsichord in there as well, and he tuned it so that they might amuse themselves with some of the airs of an earlier age.

The mere thought of Penrose was enough to keep Alethea happy, and so she was well able to enjoy the complex music and take pleasure, of a different kind, in another man's company.

Which earned her a smilingly spiteful remark from Diana Gray, who fixed her large brown eyes on Alethea and Napier as they played to the company after dinner.

'You've certainly made a conquest,' she said afterwards, as she and Alethea stood together at the tea table. 'He is rich, Mr Napier, and on the look-out for a wife they say.'

'I am not on the look-out for a husband, however,' Alethea flashed back.

Miss Gray raised her eyebrows. She had a smug look about her this evening, a cat-that-had-licked-up-the-cream expression on her rather uninspiring countenance.

'Perhaps that is as well,' she said enigmatically, and went off to join her mother, who still had Penrose pinned to her side.

The next day was to bring the break-up of the party. Alethea rose late, after a night alone. She felt some slight sense of disappointment, but Penrose had no doubt stayed up late playing cards and had not liked to disturb her in the early hours. She came yawning into the morning parlour where the dowager sat in solitary state amid a majestic collection of silver pots and jugs, drinking her coffee.

'You are late up, Miss Alethea,' she said. 'Several of the guests have departed and you have missed the excitement of the news of an engagement.'

Alethea stretched out her hand for an apple. She was not especially interested in the gossipy goings on of her world. 'An engagement?'

'Yes, for Mr Penrose Youdall is to marry Miss Gray.'

The dowager watched as the colour fled from Alethea's cheeks and she dropped the apple with a little thud on to the table.

It couldn't be true. This malicious woman was playing a joke on her. Penrose and Diana Gray?

'Their mothers have arranged the match, of course. There is land to be considered, the two estates border one another, and she is her father's only child. It will be a substantial inheritance apart from her fortune, which is eighty thousand pounds.'

The dowager's vulture eyes were on her face, but try as she might, Alethea couldn't keep a calm countenance. It was impossible. Penrose was in love with her not with Miss Gray.

'I don't believe it. You are mistaken, ma'am.'

'No, child, I'm not mistaken. It is you who has been mistaken, and so I warned Lady Fanny. She should have taken better care of you. I'm doing you a kindness to tell you this in private, to allow yourself to comport yourself in a proper way and to take your leave without anyone suspecting your heart is broken, as I dare say it is. Hearts mend, let me tell you. The poets say women only fall in love once, and after that it is mere repetition and habit. I wouldn't know how it is with you young creatures, so full of romantic notions and sensibility as you are. I can assure you that you will recover, and marry some excellent man, and also that Penrose Youdall, whom I have known from his cradle, is no proper match for you; he is not up to your weight.

A cry of protest broke from Alethea's lips before she could prevent it.

'Keep such histrionics to yourself is my advice. You aren't the first young lady to find yourself in such a predicament, and you most assuredly won't be the last. If you don't wish to be an object of pity and conjecture, as well as gossip, for that can't be avoided, then you must show a serene and indifferent face to the world. I don't say Penrose isn't in love with you,' she added, with a touch of what might even have been kindness in her voice. 'However, he is not a strong character, and his mama has long been plotting for him to marry Miss Gray. You may have won his heart, but she has his hand and will have the wedding ring on her finger; there is nothing to be done or said about that.'

The dowager departed in a rustle of silk skirts. Alethea sat alone in the parlour, unable to think or feel or do anything. The shock was so great that she could hardly breathe; she was winded by this news.

Thoughts began to dart through her mind. It was false. The dreadful old woman had made it up, to make her betray herself. Then recollections crowded in, Penrose's odd behaviour these last few days, the smug cattiness of Diana Gray, the hostility Mrs Youdall had always shown towards her.

She sat motionless, unaware of the door opening. Fanny was beside her, her voice soft with compassion, urging her to rise and come away upstairs. 'For you must make an effort, you know you must. Only let us be away from here, I have ordered the carriage, you must control yourself and say all that is proper to Lady Milton, you cannot leave without that.'

'I know,' Alethea said, moistening her lips with her tongue; they felt dry and swollen. Her eyes were dry, too, she hadn't shed a single tear. She would not break down here, she would not let anyone see how keenly she felt Penrose's betrayal. The mere sound of his name inside her head brought a pang to her heart and she cried, 'Fanny, let us go at once.'

The words echoed in her ears, at once, at once, and she was overwhelmed by unhappiness. The memory, the dreadful memory of her wedding night, in such stark contrast to her night of passion with Penrose, flooded into her mind, the contrast more than she could bear. Then her tired spirit at last relented, and she slid into a deep, restorative sleep, where no demons could pursue her.

Titus watched her curiously. He knew enough of troubled youth to sense the demons, and he felt strangely disturbed by the misery that seeped out with the involuntary tears. Just what had she been through? Was it possible that the daughter of Mr Darcy should have endured such suffering as was indicated by the turmoil of her dreams? He told himself that she was no doubt inclined to give in to her emotions, that she had learned to let her sensibilities rule her reason, but he didn't believe it.

This young woman was, he concluded, haunted by some grim event in her past. And she was too young to realise that there was no escaping by means of any journey, however adventurous, or to however different a place, since, as her dreams looked to be telling her, one took one's problems and sorrows with one. A harsh or unkind husband, probably; well, there was no cure for that. It all went to show what a minefield marriage was, a trap, indeed.

It took them eight hours altogether to reach the top of the pass, and Alethea blinked as the chaise rolled to a standstill and Titus roused her from her slumbers.

Blinking away the traces of sleep from her eyes, Alethea looked out over the vastness of the prospect before her. The view took her breath away, and the brilliance of sun and snow, and the majesty of the scene made her head reel. For a moment, time seemed to still, and an extraordinary sense of peace and of oneness with nature and these awe-inspiring mountains came over her. The past faded from her mind, as though a cleansing wind swept through her, and for the first time in many, many months, she felt at one with herself and the world.

'We are lords of the earth here, are we not?' Titus remarked, as he came to stand beside her.

She noticed, with the clarity that had suddenly come to her, that his eyes were elsewhere, dwelling on Emily's radiant face as she leant close to her husband, exclaiming with delight at the majesty of the sight laid out before them.

'How the ugliness of the world vanishes from such a height,' she said.

Mrs Vineham had swathed her face in a green veil, to ward off the sun. 'You will become so very brown if you stand in the sun like that, Emily. There is nothing worse for the complexion.'

Lord Lucius had adopted a wide-brimmed hat to shade his painted face. 'Let us return to the chaise, out of this blinding light.'

'Those workmen have red eyes,' Alethea said to Titus as they climbed back into the coach.

'It is the glare of the sun that makes their eyes so sore,' Titus said. 'The ugliness of the world doesn't entirely vanish, you see. The Swiss pay a heavy price for guarding the ways over the high mountains.'

'For God's sake, Manningtree, you grow sentimental,' Warren said. 'They are only peasants, after all, and I dare say they are glad of work, even if it be up on the peaks in the dazzle of the sun. And if I were you, sir,' he added, speaking to Alethea, 'I would not look down at the path we are to take on the downward journey.'

Alethea , filled with a new energy and courage, looked out of the window without apprehension. 'It is very steep and looks extremely perilous.'

Warren eyed her with disfavour. 'There is something tiresome about the buoyancy of youth, do you not agree, Manningtree?'

'We all had it once, and are sorry to lose it.'

'You may be sorry, but I prefer a rational mind, that marks danger where it exists. I have no doubt but that we shall break an axle on our descent, or have to stop to replace a pole. That is, if the horses don't bolt with us.'

'You should be travelling with Mrs Vineham,' Titus said. 'You could comfort one another with the horrid prospects ahead. You haven't mentioned bandits, I'm sure a troop of them will await our arrival on the lower slopes.'

'I need have no fear of bandits with a warrior such as you for a companion,' Warren said coldly. 'I am sure you have not forgotten your skill with the sabre or the pistol, or are your fire-eating days quite behind you?'

'Bandits?' said Alethea, startled. 'Do you really think so?'

'No, I do not,' said Titus, laughing despite his irritation with Warren and his needling remarks.

Chapter Twelve

In the chaise carrying the servants, the subject of bandits had also been raised. Why, Figgins wondered, was Bootle so determined to frighten Nyers, Warren's man, out of his wits? The unfortunate man was suffering terribly from the motion of the coach; he was, he had informed them all, prone to travel sickness. They had made him sit by the window, telling him to hang his head out if he felt inclined to vomit. Only Signora Lessini's abigail showed him any sympathy or kindness as he moaned and groaned his way over the pass, and even her goodwill began to run out as he set up a wailing at the sight of the downward path.

'Come, brother, bear up,' Bootle said, with an evil grin. 'Don't ever you worry yourself about the dangers ahead. Aren't there bears in these parts, as well as wolves?' he added inconsequentially.

Mrs Vineham's maid Sarah gave a squeak at that. 'He's trying it on,' Figgins reassured her. Hemp, Lord Lucius's man, gave a sycophantic laugh, and Figgins glared at him. To think that, disguised as a man, she should still have to put up with leers and lascivious suggestions and seeking hands on her knee. She had found herself sitting next to him, by his contrivance, and very uncomfortable it made the first part of the journey.

Not that she hadn't been deflecting the unwanted attentions of men since she was no more than a slip of a girl, and this weedy specimen presented no great problem. However, he was a nuisance, and she was disgusted by his open attentions, as though the danger and the journey in the carriage excused him from any normal caution or restraint. She had, in the inn, had her suspicions that he was cast in the same mould as his master, but there he had behaved in a more orderly way, doing no more than murmur a suggestion or two in her ear as she passed, or allow his nasty little eyes to dwell on her as she went about her duties.

And inside, she wanted to laugh; what a shock he would get if he knew who or what he was making up to! Like Miss Alethea couldn't help giggling at Lord Lucius trying to make up to her; at least this sodomite didn't paint his face and ogle at her through an eye-glass, which was what Miss Alethea had to put up with. She had been afraid more than once that her mistress was going to laugh out loud at the absurdity of the situation.

She had managed to keep herself very much to herself at the inn, what with having the little chamber beside Miss Alethea's one instead of sharing with two or three of the others in the servants' quarters. She ate her meals quickly, keeping mum but watching and listening with her usual inquisitiveness. You could never know too much about those whose company you were forced to keep, that was her maxim.

Now, however, in the closeness of the chaise, she felt she might venture some questions. She had changed places with Sarah after the first halt, and so was out of reach of Hemp's pawings and hot breath in her ear.

Bootle's tone had changed, which was odd. Having done his best to make Warren's man feel thoroughly out of sorts in mind and body, he was now oozing consolation and concern. 'Let us talk of other subjects, to take our minds off the present danger and discomfort,' he said. 'Mr Figgins, you are very quiet, and we have seen little of you at the inn, so attentive as you are to your young master. Yet he does not seem so very demanding. Where are you bound for?'

'Venice.'

'To see the sights? Young gentlemen are always eager to see the sights.'

Hemp gave a cynical laugh. 'Bare bosoms and gleaming thighs aplenty, if your tastes lie in that direction.'

'Which yours and your master's don't,' Figgins flashed out. 'And nor do my master's, though not for the same reason. He comes to visit his family, who are respectable people.'

'Not if they live in Venice, they aren't,' said Sarah firmly. 'Respectable English folk don't go a-journeying to Italy and staying in Venice.'

'That's what your mistress is doing,' Bootle pointed out.

'She isn't what I'd call respectable,' Sarah said calmly. 'Like I told you before, she's husband hunting, and, having had no luck in England, is trying her hand abroad.'

'She's a widow,' said Maria.

'Yes, but not a rich one, or not rich enough. She's got her eye on your master, Mr Bootle, for he's as rich as anything, so she tells me.'

Figgins could see that for all his eagerness to start a conversation, Bootle wasn't about to discuss his master. It had been the same in the inn, he was perfectly willing to gossip about the other people in the inn, but not about Titus Manningtree.

'You know why his lordship is going to Italy,' Hemp put in. 'So there's no need to go asking questions about it.'

'What his lordship says is the purpose of his journey and what it actually might be are two different things,' said Bootle.

Figgins saw that Nyers was looking more alert. He was an inveterate gossip, and this seemed to be a titbit that Bootle hadn't thought fit to dish up at the inn.

'It's no secret,' Hemp said, uneasy now. 'He's a-visiting of Lord Byron, the poet, who is part of the time in Venice and part of the time in a palazzo in the country near by.'

'Where he keeps company with a married woman,' said Bootle.

'Shocking,' said Sarah, her eyes huge and round.

'But that isn't the only reason for his lordship's journey, one hears,' Bootle went on. 'There was some unpleasantness, was there not, with regard to Lord Sevington's middle boy? All hushed up, of course, not a word to be spoken of it.'

'So how came you to hear of it?' said Hemp.

'I come to hear a lot of things. Lord Sevington felt that it would be best for Lord Lucius's health if he was to spend a time – a long time – abroad. And him being related to Lord Lucius and having a lot of powerful friends to recommend the same removal to foreign parts as being best for Lord Lucius's health, why, his lordship heeded the advice. Which is why you are here now,' he added in silky tones.

'All lies,' said Hemp.

Nyers was looking much brighter. 'I heard something about that. My master said there was some reason why Lord L was on the move. I never heard the details.'

'Mr Warren not being the kind to confide in his gentleman's gentleman? He plays his cards close to his chest.' Bootle was sympathetic now. 'It's the same with Mr Manningtree. If I was to ask him, where are we going and for how long or why or anything of that kind, he'd give me an old-fashioned look and tell me to mind my duties and not go thinking I had any right to know anything. Mumchance, that's what our masters are, am I not right, Mr Nyers?'

Nyers straightened in his seat. 'It may be so with you, Mr Bootle, but Mr Warren is not such a close gentleman, and since I make all the arrangements for his travel, for our travel, I should say, it's only natural that I should know more than you seem to.'

Figgins had to give Bootle credit where credit was due. For some reason he wanted to know where Warren was going, and why, and he was going to wangle the information out of Nyers as sweet as taking the juice from an orange.

'As you say, Mr Nyers.' Bootle didn't sound in the least convinced.

'It is as I say, Mr Bootle. I know it all, down to the last detail. My master has business in Italy. Important business for a very important personage.'

Figgins had the impression that none of what Nyers had said so far came as news to Bootle. There must be something more that he wanted to know. Why? she wondered. Nosiness? Or did his master want the information? Miss Alethea had told her that the two men didn't seem to get on, although she herself wasn't sure who Mr Manningtree would get on with, he seemed always about to lose his rag, and the way he looked at Mr Lessini, well, it was just as well that looks never harmed anyone. Lord Lucius he seemed contemptuous of, as though his presence didn't matter to him one way or the other, which there was no reason why it should.

A spirit of mischief prompted her to join in alongside Bootle. 'An important personage, Mr Nyers? Is your master one who moves in such high circles?'

'The very highest,' Nyers said impressively. 'None higher, in fact, not in the whole kingdom.'

Sarah made a pooh-poohing noise. 'You're having us on, Mr Nyers, for the highest in the land is the king, and what should Mr Warren do for the king?'

'It is a matter of the greatest delicacy,' said Nyers with satisfaction. 'It is to do with a work of art.'

'Lord, is Mr Warren an artist, then?' said Figgins.

Nyers flushed. 'He is no such thing, he is a thorough-going gentleman and you shouldn't go speaking disrespectfully of him. Artist, indeed! No, it is that the king is a great patron of the arts, which is something you would hardly know. He wishes to acquire a certain masterpiece of Italian painting, which my master happens to have heard of, and so he sends my master to obtain this painting for him.'

'And is this a great secret?' asked Bootle.

'There are others who might be interested in getting their hands on the painting, and there is some slight doubt as to the ownership of the work, so it needs a man like my master to carry out the task in a discreet way.'

'And so you go to Venice, just to bring back a painting?'

Nyers grew suddenly wary. 'I never said we was bound for Venice.'

'Oh, are you not?' said Figgins. 'I thought I heard Mr Warren speak of Venice as though he was going there.'

Nyers's face relaxed. 'Anyone may go to Venice. Or Milan or a dozen other Italian cities.'

'After you've been to Venice. If your master finds the picture is not there, perhaps,' said Figgins, all innocence.

'My master is not in the habit of traipsing about foreign countries in search of this or that. He knows where what he seeks is, and that is where we shall go.'

The chaise jolted, stopped, swayed and tilted to one side as it took a very tight corner. Nyers went pale.

'It seems to me that the sooner you get to your destination, the better for your health, Mr Nyers,' said Bootle.

'And it cannot be a moment too soon,' cried Nyers with sudden animosity. 'This cursed chaise, I never travelled in anything so ill sprung. And there are four more days of such misery!'

From the flash of triumph that passed over Bootle's controlled countenance, Figgins guessed that he had gleaned the information he wanted. Four days' travel to wherever Mr Warren was going. She'd ask Miss Alethea where that might be, but she thought it was likely to be Venice; hadn't she spoken of three or four days and nights on the road once they were across the Alps?

Bootle was a subtle one, she thought with some respect.

Titus was growing bored with the journey. He felt restless, eager to be cracking along at a better pace. Had Bootle managed to worm anything out of Warren's man? He would rather not have to follow Warren like some sneak thief after his prey; how much better if he could discover his destination. The Titian could be anywhere in Italy, in Rome, in Verona, in Venice, in any one of a dozen cities.

He glanced over to where Alethea was now sound asleep,

and frowned. Her face was flushed from exposure to the sun. Relaxed in slumber, it was also, he realised, quite remarkably beautiful. He had thought, when he had first met her at Wytton's wedding, that her charms lay in her vitality and humour; now he could see that it was also a matter of bone and inborn beauty. He felt a surge of vexation. She should not be out alone. She had a servant, true, but unless his wits were astray, Figgins was no more a man than Alethea was. Two innocents abroad, and in Italy, never the safest place, even for one experienced in foreign travel and used to being on guard against mishaps and dangers.

There was nothing he could do about it. It was none of his business, to be keeping an eye on stray rollicking females. If she got into trouble, it would be her own fault. Even as he said this to himself, he knew that it was false. She was the sister-in-law of one of his oldest friends, and the daughter of an acquaintance. She was of his world, could he simply abandon her to her fate?

He would have felt less annoyance if she had been less carefree, less openly relishing the novelty and perils of the journey. Women were not intended to take such risks as she was exposing herself to.

Had he ever drawn back from risk and danger? No, but it was different for a man. A life without risk or danger became tedious, and even if he no longer felt a passionate desire to set about an enemy in war, he still wanted challenge and drama in his life. Women faced their own, domestic risks: that of childbirth and of illness and perhaps of domestic disharmony.

How tedious. For the first time in his life, he wondered if women found it tedious. Women could be intrepid. Emily was being intrepid, damn her eyes, marrying a foreigner, out of her class, out of her kin, and setting off with him to live in Rome. Yet she seemed not to worry a whit about what unforeseen hazards might lie ahead, and this perilous trip across the mountains hadn't caused her the least alarm, from what he had seen. She took it in a cooler spirit than the Darcy girl, who had embraced it with such wild delight, but she was no shrinking violet. Mrs Vineham, now, her reaction had been more what he would have expected, a purely feminine expression of dismay and fear.

Which irritated him. Besides, he had a suspicion that very little actually daunted Mrs Vineham, whatever her shrieks and pretence at helplessness. You couldn't have been married to Vineham these ten years and survived without you were as tough as old boots.

Wytton's mother, Lady Hermione Wytton, had often chafed him on his misapprehension of women. 'It is why you have never married, Titus,' she had said more than once. 'You do not make any push to understand what you consider the weaker sex, and your life is the less interesting because of the lack of any such rapport.'

'I have all the rapport with the female sex that I desire,' had been his cross reply; was she questioning his manhood?

'Oh, you have commerce with women of the usual kind, and there is Emily to cosset and comfort you, but you may believe me when I tell you that you have not the slightest notion what is going on inside Emily's head – or her heart, for that matter.'

His private opinion, that what might or might not go on inside a woman's head was of little importance, he kept to himself – wisely, for Lady Hermione Wytton had a sharp tongue when she chose to use it.

Had she been right about Emily? Of course not. This marriage to Lessini only proved that you couldn't trust a woman's heart or reason. She had clearly taken up with the man on a whim, seduced by his amiable manners and charming smile. How like a woman to be seduced by what had no substance.

Opposite him, Alethea stirred, yawned, stretched. Lithe as a cat, and with about as much sense, he thought disagreeably. He need not rack his brains over what to do about her immediately, however. She was heading for Venice, and it might very well be that he was doing the same. In which case he could ensure that she was safely handed over to Wytton, and then he could wash his hands of any responsibility for her. God knew what Wytton would make of this excursion of hers. If he had any sense, he'd at once send word to Darcy – wasn't the man in Vienna just now? – and leave it to him to sort the whole sordid business out. He doubted if Napier would take his wife back after such a jaunt; she would have to live quietly, abroad, under the care of some duenna.

'Why do you look so severe?' Alethea asked him. 'Is it to do with our journey? Is there some further delay?'

'I? Look severe? I'm sorry you should think so. No, we are very near Domodossola, I am sure. There is a spittal there, where you may rest.'

'Spittal?'

'It is a hostel, a place where travellers stay, with beds and food.'

'But I understand it is possible to leave for Milan immediately. It is late afternoon now.' She pulled out her half-hunter. 'Our journey has taken some fifteen hours. Fifteen hours!'

'Fifteen of the longest hours I ever wish to spend,' said Warren from his corner.

It was with great relief that Titus got down from the chaise, and turned to hand Alethea down. She had forestalled him, jumping down to the ground beside him, and looking around with alert, interested eyes, every fibre of her being alive with anticipation.

'I long for food,' she said. 'Then I must find when I can continue my journey to Milan.'

Titus strode over to a fat man in a long apron, who was talking to one of the outriders. He spoke in rapid Italian, and then came back to Alethea.

'The coach for Milan leaves in less than an hour and travels through the night. You will be too tired, I think, to undertake another journey immediately.'

She stiffened, caught sight of Figgins and called out to her. 'Figgins, see to the luggage, for we go directly on to Milan.' Then, to Titus, 'I am not at all tired, you know, for I have slept on the way down. I wish to be in Venice as soon as I can. Do you make a halt here? It seems a very gloomy kind of a place, this spittal.'

Warren had drawn apart, and was dressing down his valet, who looked very much the worse for wear.

'We go on tonight,' Warren was saying. 'It is a flatter journey, you will not mind it.'

'Is it not unkind to bring such a poor traveller with you on such a journey?' Signora Lessini asked.

'He looks after my clothes and my person too well to be left behind, ma'am,' said Warren shortly.

'If you go on tonight, you will be in Milan in good time tomorrow,' Titus said to Alethea. 'The roads are supposed to be perfectly safe.'

'I was quite disappointed that we met with no mountain bandits or bears,' Alethea said blithely. 'Do you make a stay here?'

'I think not.'

Titus strode into the spittal, shrugging off his greatcoat as he went and calling out to a servant to bring him food and wine, immediately, he had no time to lose. A nimble waiter followed him, saying '*Si, si, signore*,' in cheerful tones, and dived ahead to open a heavy wooden door.

'A private room,' the waiter announced with satisfaction, then added, 'Except for the English signora,' and whisked himself away.

Emily was sitting on a chair beside a window. Outside, sun slanted down across the mountains, sending brilliant rays to light up an otherwise dingy parlour.

Titus glowered at her and then began to prowl about the room, picking up ornaments, looking at a book, casting it aside, glancing at a newspaper, sending frowning sideways looks at Emily as he went to and fro.

'Sit down, Titus, for heaven's sake; you make me feel quite queasy, pacing up and down like that.'

'Thank you, I have been sitting for so many hours, I need to stretch my legs. Where's that husband of yours?'

'Mr Lessini has gone for a walk in the town, to stretch his legs and to buy one or two items we need. May I recommend you take a mountain walk, to work off your fidgets?'

'I have no time, I go straight on to Milan.'

The waiter flew in with another cup. 'The signore can take coffee while his food is being prepared.'

'I said wine, I don't want coffee.'

Emily gestured to the chair on the other side of the low table where the coffee pot stood. 'If you don't sit down, then I shall go and find somewhere else to sit, where I may be more comfortable.'

'Oh, very well.' Titus lowered himself into the chair. Damn Emily, always so calm, and, now he came to think of it, always telling him what to do. 'You're managing me, Emily. I find I don't care for that.'

'I don't suppose you do, not now.'

'What do you mean by that? Not now? Not ever.'

'Nonsense, my dear. I've been managing you for years, and you have never complained. It was one of the reasons you sought my company.'

Titus felt a surge of anger rising in his gullet. He took a hasty gulp of coffee, swallowed it the wrong way, and succumbed to a fit of coughing. 'Now look what you've made me do,' he said, when he had recovered.

'Did it burn your throat? I'm sorry for it, but it is not wise to drink hot liquid when you are breathing so heavily.'

'I was not breathing heavily.'

'You were. It is something you always do when you are working yourself into a rage.'

Titus felt it wiser not to argue this point. 'I resent that

remark about your managing me, I resent it very much indeed. When one is in love with a woman, one seeks her company for reasons very different than a wish to be ordered about.'

'Managing is not precisely ordering about, and you were not precisely in love with me.'

He stared at her. Had she taken leave of her senses? 'Dear God, Emily, we have been as close as two human beings can be these five years and more. How can you say I was not in love with you? I suppose what you are saying is that you were not in love with me, and that's obvious enough, now that you have chosen to marry another man.'

'We dealt very well together, and I took great pleasure in your company, in bed and out of it, if that is what irks you.'

'Dealt, took, all in the past tense, all finished now that Thruxton is dead,' he said bitterly. 'The minute you were a free woman, you deserted me.'

Emily was a most patient woman, but her mouth tightened at this. Titus was too preoccupied with his own resentment and hurt to notice. 'I dare say that you felt I had deserted you, merely because I happened to be out of the country at that time. But, Emily, you must have known it was no such thing. A word from you, and I would have been at your side. By the time I heard that you were a widow, you were already planning a trip down the aisle with a damned Italian music master—'

He stopped, realising from the flash of fury on Emily's face that he had gone too far.

'Carlo is a fine and distinguished musician, and it is a profession that I happen to honour,' she said coldly. 'I know I am considered to have disgraced myself; I was born an Uppinger, daughter of a baron, and here I am married to a foreigner who writes music. Do not forget, however, that my impoverished, if noble, father sold me to Thruxton, who was not a member of an ancient and noble family but a brewer, albeit a very wealthy man who had inherited the business together with considerable estates. His money made him respectable and kept me, just, within the circle of society in which I had been born.'

'And now you have excluded yourself from it, for ever.'

'With very few regrets. London society has its ways and manners, but I have lived in that world for long enough. I crave a new life, new places, new people, and it so happens that I fell in love with Carlo almost as soon as we met.'

'And when was that? Exactly when did you meet this paragon that you've chosen to marry?' Good God, had she been in love with the fellow even when she was still his mistress? Look at the blush on her face, she knew she was in wrong.

'Where and how I met him is entirely my own business, Titus. Had you been in England when I was widowed, it would have made no difference. I would under no circumstances have agreed to become your wife, Lessini or no Lessini.'

He couldn't believe his ears. 'What?'

'No, Titus. I loved you dearly, and always will, in a way, but you need a different kind of wife from me. We should not suit as man and wife, we would have a very disagreeable life together. We came together when you were lonely and unhappy, and I gave you comfort and consolation, and yes, a great deal of love. We had merry times together, with no ties, and we met one another's needs.'

'And what is so very different about a marriage?'

'We should never be equals.'

Titus frowned. Equality, between a man and a woman? What nonsense was this? 'A man is master in his own home.'

'Or so he likes to think, but that is precisely my point. I manage you, as you put it. I have cosseted you, and made allowances for your temper and nightmares, and given you some peace of mind.'

'You make yourself sound like my nurse when I was a boy.'

'Exactly, Titus. And how very cosy it has been for you, but

I find I do not care to have a husband who needs so very much looking after, and indeed I believe your needs now are not the same. You should look for a wife that you have to take some care over, and yet one whom you may respect. As she will respect you, for indeed, Titus, you are a rare man and are destined to make some woman extremely happy. Find someone you can laugh with, and admire, and who loves you wholeheartedly – as a man and as an equal.'

Titus heard her words, but felt that he could not grasp their meaning. 'Is it because you are two or three years older than me? Is that it? Does such a trifling difference in age matter?'

'I am four years older than Carlo.'

'Lessini, Lessini, that is all you can talk about. Curse him, I wish I could run him through with my sword and put an end to his husbandly capers.'

'Titus!'

'Oh, you know very well I would do no such thing. However, ma'am, I consider that you have made a bad choice, and one you will live to regret. I bid you good day, and wish you a comfortable and safe journey, and, of course, my best wishes for your future health and happiness. Waiter! I will eat in the dining room, and send my man to me.'

He flung himself out of the parlour, almost sure that he could hear laughter from within as he slammed the door behind him.

Alethea had also been shown into a room with one of her fellow travellers, but she was even less happy about it than Titus.

'Lord Lucius,' she said, stopping in the doorway and making as though to retreat.

Moving with remarkable swiftness, he had shut the door and drawn her into the room before she could protest. Angrily, she shook his hand from his arm.

'My dear Mr Hawkins,' he said, standing much closer to her than she cared for. 'Pray call me Lucius as my friends do, for we are quite well-acquainted enough for such familiarity, do you not think so? And I am sure we are going to be friends, very close friends. I shall call you Aloysius.'

'I would much prefer that you did not, sir,' said Alethea, trying unsuccessfully to edge away. Whatever perfume did the man use? He smelt like a civet cat. She wrinkled her nose in disgust.

'Ah, you are admiring my scent,' he cried. 'It comes from Paris, I have it made up especially for me, it is extremely expensive. I shall give you a bottle, as a token of my esteem.'

'Believe me, I want neither your perfume nor your esteem, my lord,' said Alethea, eyeing him warily. Was he going to lunge at her? He was, but she was quicker on her feet than him, and she sidestepped him neatly. Not such a good move, however, for now she found herself hemmed into a corner. What could she do? What would make him keep his wretched hands to himself? For if they wandered where they undoubtedly would, he might discover that she was not at all what he thought her, and then the fat would be in the fire.

'Excuse me, sir,' she said, raising her voice. 'You are blocking my way to the door. I wish to leave.'

'Not so fast, my pretty young man.'

He was leering at her in what he presumably thought was an alluring way. 'Do not be so hasty, do not scorn my company. I know what you are, I have lived a little longer in the world than you, and know what's what about men.'

A little longer! He must be at least forty, thought Alethea indignantly.

'I am a man of wealth and influence, and my friendship can be very rewarding.'

'I am sure that is so, my lord, for those who share your tastes, but I assure you, I am not one of them.'

'You are very young and inexperienced, you do not yet know what pleasure is.'

Alethea struggled to compose her face into an expression of gravity. The situation was so absurd. A swift kick in his breeches might put a stop to his capers, or would that create the very scene she was anxious to avoid? One thing she knew about travelling in disguise: never draw attention to yourself. Leaving Lord Lucius rolling on the ground in agony might be satisfying, but it would not be prudent.

He lunged, she let out a furious yell, and punched him hard, in his stomach. He was momentarily winded, but hardly deterred, and the simpering look had quite gone from his face. He was, Alethea realised, bigger and stronger than her, however effete his manners. She had to escape from this room. 'Waiter,' she shouted in her most powerful voice. 'Here, immediately.'

'He will not come,' Lord Lucius said. 'I have paid him to leave us alone.'

He was right, and the waiter didn't come, but Titus Manningtree did. He flung open the door, made an exasperated sound, and in two quick steps was shouldering Lord Lucius aside.

'Leave the boy alone, Lucius.'

Lord Lucius went pale with anger. 'Manningtree, mind your own damned business. Barging in here, into a private parlour, without so much as a by your leave. You will answer for this.'

'Stow it, Lucius. Your reputation is bad enough without your foisting your attentions on young men like Mr Hawkins, who is no meat for your plate.'

'Much you know about it.'

'Much I do know about it, indeed. And I know the boy's family; you'd best not try your tricks here, or it will be very much the worse for you. Good God, man, when you've had to leave England in such a hurry, do you want another scandal rocketing about your ears?'

Alethea was growing angry. 'I can speak for myself, Mr Manningtree. I have told Lord Lucius I do not want his friendship, as he calls it, and I am sure he knows I mean it.'

Lord Lucius rounded on her, as though to strike, but she held her ground and his gaze without flinching.

'Come along,' Titus said to Alethea. 'I came to offer you a place in my coach. I can take you as far as Milan, should you care to accompany me.'

He could see the hesitation in her face, then she gave a quick nod of agreement. 'As long as you have room for Figgins.'

'Your man? He may travel outside with Bootle. Only you must be quick. Where is your luggage?'

'Lord, I'm glad to be out of his company,' said Alethea, as they crossed the yard outside to the waiting chaise.

'Whatever possessed you to be alone with him? Do not you realise what kind of a man he is?'

Yes, and I know what kind of a man I'm not, Alethea said inwardly. She laughed aloud. 'I do, indeed.'

'And you find the situation you were in humorous?'

'I think it is very funny, much funnier than you know. Whose carriage is that leaving now?'

Titus looked across to the arched gateway. 'Warren's, the fiend take him. Bootle! Bootle, where's Mr Hawkins's man? Find him this instant, we leave at once, there's not a moment to lose.'

'Why the hurry?' said Alethea breathlessly, as he pushed her unceremoniously into the chaise.

'Oh, I wish to reach Milan as soon as may be.'

Liar, thought Alethea. You want to keep an eye on Warren, and I do long to know why.

My dearest Hermione

How I envy you, being away from London just now. Rain sweeps over us all, the streets are thronged with bumpkins and cutpurses, and there is no news worth the hearing.

Except that Norris Napier, the husband of the youngest Darcy girl, appeared in town in a terrible temper, and left post-haste for Paris. I have heard that his wife was not left behind in the country, as is his usual practice – he pretends she has no liking for London – but has broken out of the matrimonial fetters and gone to France to stay for a while with one of her sisters – the beautiful Lady Mordaunt, who has made such a stir in Paris. It was Sir Joshua who informed Napier that Alethea was there; one wonders where Napier thought her to be. Perhaps he is quite in the habit of mislaying his wife.

Well, that is not all, for it is rumoured that Mrs Napier was not to be found at her sister's house, but has travelled on across the Alps to Austria, to pay a visit to her parents. I do not believe it; young married women are not much in the habit of setting off across Europe simply for that. Either she has eloped with another man, or she has returned to Tyrrwhit House to await her lord and master. Where he is, is uncertain, although people say that it is he who has gone to Vienna to see the Darcys – it is all to do with money and settlements.

Sadly, I think this prosaic explanation is the correct one, although I would much prefer an elopement – for the sake of a little excitement, you understand, in this dull world. However, I dare say Camilla would be horrified to think of her sister running away from her new husband, so pray don't mention it to her. For my part, I should not blame Alethea for escaping from Tyrrwhit House and what I fear is not a happy marriage. How can it be, with such a husband? You never saw a man eat up with rage the way Napier was when I saw him – mercifully briefly – when he passed through London.

Next week I join Freddie to ruralise in Sussex, where I shall have to be civil to his mother, who grows crosser and more disagreeable with every passing year.

Do write to me soon, to tell me how you do and what news there is from Venice of Byron – I dare say you are often in his company. Is his latest mistress as lovely as they say? Is it true his valet puts curl papers in his hair at night to preserve the romantic Byronic look?

I suppose you can hardly ask him, but I long to know.

Your most affectionate friend,

Belinda

PART THREE

Chapter Thirteen

Water rippling with reflections of the buildings on either side of the canal. A sense of lightness, despite the murkiness of the water through which the gondola moved with swift, silent ease. Voices ringing out across the water and snatches of song, gulls, the sound of pulleys as blocks of stone were winched off a barge rang out across the grand canal.

Venice, Alethea said to herself. They were actually in Venice.

Figgins was staring open-mouthed at the palaces lining the canal, the bridges, the people walking to and fro alongside the canals and up and over the arched bridges.

'You said they had water for roads, but I never would have believed it, not without seeing it with my own eyes. How come they to build a city in such a damp place? The mould there must be, why, you can see it for yourself, all that green slime. How they must suffer from the rheumatism! Whoever would choose to live in such a place? Mrs Wytton must have taken leave of her senses.'

'It is so very beautiful, Figgins. The light, and the reflection of the buildings in the water, and the movement of so many boats up and down the canals. It is all built on islands within a lagoon, you know, I remember learning all about it with Griffy.'

'Then it must be the only thing you remember of your lessons apart from all that music,' said Figgins.

'It captures the imagination, a city built on water, and indeed, it is far more beautiful than one could believe possible.'

'It is also a city of smells: faugh, what a whiff of dead things. If you fell in this water, I doubt they'd bring you out alive.'

'It isn't so very clean, but what does that signify? Do you realise that Vivaldi lived here, and wrote much of his music in this city? It was performed by girls who came from an orphanage.'

'Dressed as boys and men, were they?'

'They were not, for it was not considered at all wrong for women to perform music in public. They were excellently trained and the music they played was greatly admired.'

'It is a pity you weren't born here in that case. Is this Mr Vivaldi still living in the city?'

'No, he died many years ago.'

'Of some disagreeable disease caught from the water, I dare say.'

'Of old age, Figgins. He was a composer of the last century, he lived here a hundred years ago.'

Alethea was about to trail her hand over the side of the gondola, but she thought better of it. Another gondola drew level with them; two gorgeously dressed ladies sat in it, being serenaded by their gondolier; they made eyes at the young Englishmen as they glided past.

'Hussies!' said Figgins.

'That gondolier has a good voice,' Alethea said. 'The Italians are born to sing. Signore Silvestrini claims it is in their blood, and certainly it is a country full of music. While we are here, I shall hear as much music as I can.'

Figgins didn't appear overjoyed.

'I shall be sorry to become a woman again,' Alethea went on. 'Dresses are so uncomfortable and impractical when compared with trousers.'

'Yes, but not respectable, and I've travelled all these miles with my heart in my mouth lest someone should recognise you, or that Lord Lucius try a trick too far and discover you are not at all what he thought.'

Alethea thought back to the spittal, and Lord Lucius's overt attempts on her person. Serve him right that Mr Manningtree had come in just then, although his lordship didn't seem so much embarrassed as annoyed by the interruption. She supposed a man of those tastes was used to brazening it out. Titus Manningtree hadn't seemed shocked, either, he'd been more angry than shocked.

Mr Manningtree puzzled her. His definite ways and air of authority reminded her of her father, but he had less of reserve and more inclination to black moods than Papa; he'd been in a most dreadful temper all the way to Milan. Then, although she had been more than grateful for the place in his carriage, she wasn't sure she altogether cared for the forceful way he had arranged for the rest of her journey in his company, once he had arrived in Milan and decided he was going to continue to Venice.

Odd, to come all the way to Italy and not be sure where you were going. However, from one or two things he had said, she understood there was a woman in the case. Perhaps it explained his bad temper, although she'd thought at first that had more to do with Emily Lessini. She wondered at Mrs Lessini, for although the Signore was a delightful man, Mr Manningtree was—

She pulled herself up short. He was no more than another arrogant member of the opposite sex. Wise, sensible Emily Lessini , to opt for the warmth and lively humour of her new husband instead of taking on the moodiness and difficult nature of a Titus Manningtree; there was another man who would make life wretched for a wife.

She wondered why he had never married. Easier for him to carry on with another man's wife – yet Mrs Lessini must have entertained a warm affection for him to have so lasting a liaison. She sighed; perhaps no relations between men and women were what they seemed, and she was sure that they were never easy, however serene a front a couple might present to the world.

And Titus Manningtree was clever, that was unquestionable. She liked a clever man. Had Penrose been . . . No, she wasn't going to think about Penrose.

At least, she reflected, they had managed to give Mr Manningtree the slip when they reached Venice. She had told Figgins that she didn't want him to know where they were going and they had seized their opportunity when there was some argument between Bootle and a waterman about luggage to slip away unnoticed into the little crowd of visitors arriving and departing.

Alethea's Italian was stretched to the utmost; the Venetians seemed to speak an entirely different kind of language to the one she had learned and sung. However, the gondolier had nodded when she gave him the address, and set off with skilled enthusiasm to thread his way through the knot of boats and gondolas and out to open water.

Not that the canal itself was easy going. 'It's as crowded as Piccadilly,' Figgins complained. 'Only in London you are at risk of falling under coach wheels or being trampled by a horse, which is a Christian end, not like drowning in this canal.'

The gondolier left the wide canal and turned with an elegant swoop into a much smaller one. Houses were so close overhead that people on one balcony might almost reach out and clasp hands with a neighbour opposite. Washing fluttered from lines strung from the windows, and there was a hubbub of noise: voices talking and singing and calling out.

They slid past another gondola coming the other way, Alethea holding her breath; it seemed impossible for the two boats not to crash together, or for the single oars to become entangled.

Then a wider canal, and the gondola drew into the side, beside some steps leading up to a narrow alleyway. Alethea stood up carefully, and gave Figgins a shove on to the side. She dug her hand into her pocket to find the coins to pay the gondolier, accepted his exaggerated bow of thanks – she must have tipped him too heavily – and sprang on to dry land.

It was mid afternoon, and the sun was still beating down on them as they walked along the way the gondolier had directed them with graceful gestures and a torrent of Italian.

'I think this is the one,' Alethea said, pausing outside a narrow house of some four storeys. A woman who looked like a servant was passing by, and Alethea stopped her to ask if this house was the one she wanted. The woman nodded, bursting into a flood of unintelligible Italian. Alethea thanked her, shrugged at Figgins, and went up to the front door. The house had a shuttered look, but that might be normal in a country where the sun was an enemy to be kept out of the house at all costs. She lifted the knocker.

There was no response, no sound of footsteps within, no voice calling out. She tried it again, and stepped back to peer at the upstairs windows, her hand sheltering her eyes against the brightness of the sun. The shutters were closed on the upper floors as well. Could the whole household be asleep?

It could not. There was the servant whom she had stopped, talking too fast to be understood, but waving her hand in a distinctly negative gesture. What was she trying to say? She appeared to have given up on her attempt to communicate, and instead, tugging Alethea by the hand, begged the signore to come with her to another house.

The other house was the one next door, where the woman worked. Her mistress was at home, a plump beauty with sleepy dark eyes, who spoke much more the kind of Italian Alethea could understand.

What a pity. Had they come a long way? For the English couple, the Wyttons – she pronounced it in a charmingly un-English way – were not at home, were not expected to be back for some weeks. They had, she informed them, left only the day before, for Rome. So the young English gentleman must return next month, if his stay in Venice were to be that long.

Chapter Fourteen

The wretch, Titus said to himself when Bootle informed him that the young gentleman and his valet were nowhere to be seen.

'Shall I make enquiries as to which way they went, sir?' Bootle asked. 'Although I fear that in this city, with its warren of streets and waterways, it may be impossible to trace their path.'

'No, leave it,' said Titus. Bootle was looking alert and curious; he didn't want to seem over-interested in Hawkins, or Bootle would make it his business to find out why. 'His man, Figgins, what do you think of him?'

'He kept himself to himself, for the most part, but has quite a good hand with a shirt and a boot.' Nowhere near my standards, his tone implied, but quite good enough for a young man of no particular importance. 'I would say a shrewd head on his shoulders; a lad like him has to rely on his wits to keep himself out of trouble, for there's no brawn there to protect him.'

'Very true,' said Titus. 'Call a gondolier.'

'Where are we going, sir?' Bootle's voice held the slightest note of aggrievement; he liked to know what was what, and his master had been vague about where they were to stay in Venice.

There was a reason for this, for Titus had been exercised in his own mind as to whether to make his visit in the serene city anonymous or if it were better to mingle with such of his friends and acquaintances who might be resident there at present. On balance, he thought it wisest to be open about his presence. He would be recognised sooner or later, if he were to make other than a short stay, and it might be easier to keep tabs on Warren that way. Warren wasn't going to hide himself away, however secretive his mission, Titus was sure of it. Warren enjoyed society too much not to be out and about in it.

'The gondolier can carry us to the Palazzo Borosini.'

'Mr Hellifield is presently in Venice, I take it,' said Bootle, with some satisfaction.

'Yes, and you may wipe that smirk off your face. I know you hanker after high living; well, you shall have your fill of it over the next few days, unless Hellifield has lost all his fortune at the gaming tables.'

Sitting in the bobbing discomfort of the gondola, Titus's thoughts returned to Alethea. He was sure she must be at Wytton's by now, in the safe hands of her sister and brother-in-law, able to put off her ridiculous imposture and resume her place in the world as a young woman of good family. He wondered how she was going to explain her presence in Venice to an irate husband, but that was no concern of his. The Darcys were well able to look after their own, as indeed was Wytton. Wytton had confided that he never liked the marriage, so perhaps the girl had shown some sense in flying to his protection.

How would she look, dressed again in feminine clothes? Her beauty was more marked than when he had first seen her at Shillingford, with the traces of girlish plumpness about the face planed into a structure of bone and flesh that—

That nothing. He swore at a rowing boat that came perilously close, sending drops of water flinging across his face, told the gondolier to mind his steering in a few pithy Italian phrases, instructed Bootle to move his legs over to make more room, and sank down into the velvet cushions.

'Titus, by all that's wonderful! What a fellow you are, not to send word of your coming so that I might roll out the red carpet and slay the proverbial calf and so forth.'

'Harry, how glad I am to see you.'

The two men matched each other for height, but Harry Hellifield looked to be the taller, as he was of slimmer build, and had a lightness and quickness about him that was in stark contrast to the energy and vigour of his friend.

Titus was always astonished afresh at the sight of Harry's opulent surroundings. Harry had inherited a fortune and huge estates from his English father, and this palazzo and another great fortune from his maternal grandfather. He had been raised and educated in England, but the strain of Venetian blood inherited from his mother ran strong in his veins, and as soon as he could, he left the English estates in the capable hands of his steward and made his home in Venice.

'Another month, and I'd be gone, and then you'd have to find some humbler lodging, Titus.'

'Gone?'

'To England, for my annual visit; as you know, if you bend your mind to it, I spend July in the country at Milverley, dealing with my affairs; so tedious, I can't tell you. Then in August I go to the mountains, for the air and to restore my system, so that I may return refreshed to my life in Venice.'

As he spoke, liveried servants were swooping to take Titus's coat, remove his bags, usher Bootle to what the valet knew would be excellent quarters; no dingy, stifling attics for visiting servants in Mr Hellifield's houses.

'That coat, Titus,' Harry was saying as he led him up the sweeping marble staircase to the first floor. 'Where had you that? So dull, so sombre.'

'It does for travelling, and we can't all prink ourselves out in brilliant colours, Harry. I'd look like something out of the circus if I wore a coat such as you have on.'

Harry clapped him on the shoulder, and called for hot towels to clean the hands, wine, refreshments. 'Then you may go and take a bath and shift out of those clothes, my dear, you do look as though you had slept in them.'

'And so I have, I have travelled day and night since crossing the Alps. Yes, I shall like to bathe.'

Harry's habits of cleanliness always amused Titus. Even when they were on campaign together, Harry contrived to keep himself and his clothes far cleaner than anyone else in the regiment. He had travelled in Turkey, and loved the traditional steam baths of that country, and was a collector of basins and fountains, evidence of which passion was to be seen on all sides.

'Damn it, Harry, I believe you were a fish in a previous existence,' Titus exclaimed, as he traced the sound of rippling water to a deep marble shell set into the far wall of the great room in which they sat. 'What do the Venetians think of this fascination that water has for you?'

'Why, they live in a watery world themselves, so what's to say? Some purist fellow took exception to my fountains within doors, saying it was not in the Italian style, but it is my house, and I shall put fountains wherever I choose.'

Titus was not one to be wearied overmuch by a lengthy journey, but he felt an unusual comfort steal into his muscles as he bathed in a room set aside for that purpose, tiled in Venetian glass in sea greens and blues, with servants gliding to and fro with hot water, scented soaps and, finally, enormous towels. He was shaved and barbered, then recommended to take a brief rest after the exertions of the bath. He had no intention of doing any such thing, but consented to put his feet up for a few minutes while Bootle finished choosing such garments from his wardrobe as he felt might do his master most credit.

Titus awoke with a start some two hours later, thoroughly refreshed, to find Harry laughing at him. 'You are getting old, Titus. I never knew you to sleep during the day.'

'No, and I would not have done so, were it not for your infernal pampering bath, hot water, scented towels and the rest of it. However, I feel the better for it, so you may make all the remarks you wish.'

'I must say, you look in fighting trim,' Harry observed, as Titus pulled on a clean shirt. 'You always were a restless person, I dare say you keep yourself in good form with striding about in that tiring way you have. Do you still go regularly to Angelo's?'

'I do.' Titus was not a remarkable swordsman, but he found that a few bouts with a tough opponent gave him great satisfaction as well as an opportunity to vent the built-up anger and aggression that had once served to send him flying into battle against a real enemy.

'Then I shall challenge you to a few sessions with the foils while you are here. By the way, do you care to tell me why you are here? I never knew you to travel anywhere without there being some purpose to your journey.'

Titus smiled. 'I have come in search of a woman, Harry, and that is as much as I propose to tell you at present.'

'A woman!' Harry's eyebrows rose. 'Never tell me so, you gave up pursuit of the fairer sex long ago, to my certain knowledge. What with Emily Thruxton and the inclination of certain women to seek your company, what need have you to go on the chase? Do not tell me you have fallen in love at last.'

'Certainly not.' Titus felt unreasonably annoyed at the suggestion. He had grown more cynical about women over the years, and now, with Emily's betrayal, he was in no danger of falling in love with any woman, however desirable or bewitching. Pleasure, yes; love, no. 'Any nonsense of that kind lies back in my youth, I thank God for it. However, this beauty I must have, and when you see her, you will agree with me that she is worth the trouble.'

'I look forward to it with the liveliest expectation; she must be unusual indeed, to arouse such enthusiasm in such a hard-heart as you are become. Now, for this evening's entertainment, we shall dine at home, and then venture out into company. Let us see if some Venetian lady cannot tempt you with a flashing oriental eye.'

'Do you know that scrub Warren?' Titus asked a little while later, when he had dined extremely well and was feeling more mellow than usual.

'George Warren? I should hardly call him a scrub, he spends a lot of time in Italy and has many friends in this country.'

'Including you?'

Harry considered. 'No. An acquaintance, merely. I don't find him so very amusing, and we do not move in precisely the same circles. There are doors that are closed to him, but some of our circles overlap. I do not think he is in Venice. If you call him a scrub, I suppose he has done you some disservice, and you have no wish to seek him out.' He sat up, suddenly alert. 'Unless you seek him for another purpose, do you intend to run him through at dawn? Is he a rival for your fair beauty?'

Not for the first time, Titus was taken aback by the extraordinary way his friend had of coming in a flash, and without any obvious thought or reasoning, close to the truth of a matter.

'In a way I suppose you may say he is, but I assure you, I don't intend to call him out, I have no time for that kind of nonsense.'

'A pity,' said Harry with a sigh. 'I dearly love a duel, and it is some while since I was called upon to play the part of a second. Once, you were more of a fire-eater, when I consider how often I was there to hold your pistols or mop up after one of your bloodthirsty affrays.'

'Those days are long gone,' said Titus.

'Like love.'

'Oh, the devil with you, Harry. What we did back then, when we were soldiers together, that belongs to a different world, and one I am very glad to turn my back on. Grown men have better things to do than take shots at one another or cross swords in earnest.'

'Not here in Venice, they don't.'

'I am no Venetian.'

Chapter Fifteen

An enquiry of the Wyttons' obliging neighbour had led Alethea and Figgins to modest lodgings in the nearby Pensione Donata, where a heavy-browed landlady with suspicious eyes agreed that they might rent two rooms on the second floor for a night or so.

'It seems clean enough,' Figgins said, after an inspection of dark corners and a quick peer behind the huge cupboard that stood between the two deep windows of the room they had been shown up to. 'Only what are you going to do until Mrs Wytton returns? Do we stay here in Venice?'

Alethea sighed. In truth, she felt as downhearted as she ever had. Arriving in Venice, at her journey's end, she had felt a flush of pride and achievement and a great deal of relief. Now, instead of finding herself in the safety of her family, able to shift out of her men's clothes and become herself again, she was faced with no very certain date for Camilla's return and decisions to be made.

'I do not want to stay here for some weeks, idling our time, perhaps running the danger of my husband coming to look for me. I think we had best set off tomorrow for Rome, or even think of going on to Vienna, to my parents.'

Figgins pursed her lips. 'It seems to me, Miss Alethea, that Vienna is more than likely where Mr Napier will go hunting for you, if he suspects you are gone abroad. It is what you have said, all along.'

Alethea did not really want to go to Vienna. To appear on her parents' doorstep there was going to be much more difficult than explaining to Camilla and Wytton what she had been driven to do. Although, once they reached Vienna, she might change back into women's clothes and pretend, perhaps, that she and Figgins had travelled in the company of some respectable woman friend.

Mrs Vineham, for example, and she laughed out loud at the thought. She had a very good idea that Mrs V would certainly not count as respectable company, and as for Lord Lucius – well, it was a good joke, and one that might be shared with Camilla, but not, she thought, with Papa and Mama.

'I am quite starving,' she said. 'Let's go and find somewhere to eat, and then we can find out how best to travel to Rome.'

'You'll never set off this evening!' cried Figgins. 'Haven't we been jolted to bits for long enough? Can't we take a night's sleep like Christians in our beds?'

'I don't think we can make arrangements so quickly. Tomorrow will be soon enough. Besides, it is so interesting here that I should like to spend a day or two exploring the city. Who knows when we may get another chance?'

'Never, I hope and pray,' Figgins said. 'Damp and dirty is what I call it, and say what you may, God never intended us to live in a lagoon, or He would have made us water rats, not human beings.'

'Where's your spirit of adventure?' said Alethea, her own spirits rising at the prospect of dinner and a night's sleep for which, although she didn't care to admit it, she was quite as eager as Figgins.

The food was delicious, in Alethea's opinion, and she made a hearty meal, while Figgins picked at this and that with her nose wrinkled in distaste.

Ironically, it was she, not Alethea, who awoke in the morning with vile stomach cramps and not the least inclination to venture out.

That settled it; they would not be on their way to Rome today. Alethea knew that Figgins was sometimes prone to bilious attacks, and hoped that this would prove to be no more than one of those. If she were taken really ill, then she must find a physician, but she wasn't going to think about that for the moment. Figgins assured her that although she felt mortal poorly, she would soon be on her feet again.

The landlady perked up when she heard that Figgins was unwell, she was obviously the kind of woman who liked illness and misfortune. She promised to take her up some herbal decoction of her own, a certain remedy for any disturbance of the stomach, she assured Alethea. Relieved that Figgins would be taken good care of, Alethea set off with a light heart and a great sense of freedom, to explore this strange and fascinating city.

It was a city, she rapidly discovered, that was full of music. Voices came from churches, the sound of a flute or a fiddle wafted over the water from open upstairs windows, there was a quartetto rehearsing in a room beside yet another church and, as she crossed the square, she heard the sound of a soprano about her scales. All this was a great joy to her, and she spent a happy day, ending up standing under the dome of San Marco to listen to the sung mass. She was entranced by the music, dazzled by the gleaming, glittering mosaics above her head, fascinated by the popish ritual and horrified by the overt religious enthusiasm demonstrated by the congregation, which seemed to consist largely of elderly women in black, who crossed themselves at frequent intervals and broke into a kind of wailing chant during the prayers.

Much refreshed in mind, body and spirit, Alethea found her way back to their lodgings, to find Figgins looking pale and thin, but assuring Alethea that she felt much, much better, and would travel instantly to Rome, to China, to anywhere that was out of reach of the landlady's kind ministrations.

'I do not think there is a question of instantly,' Alethea said. 'I am glad to see you recovered, but you are still quite weak and tired, and after all, there is no great hurry. How say you to a visit to the opera? I have found a theatre where there is a performance this very evening, and I long to hear an

Italian opera here in the very country of its composition, with Italian singers and musicians.'

Figgins didn't share Alethea's love of music, but she liked a spectacle well enough, and Alethea could see that she would rather not be left in the care of the landlady for the whole evening. 'Only if you feel well enough,' she said. 'We need not stay for the whole performance.'

Her head abuzz with tunes from the opera, Alethea paid little heed to Figgins or to her surroundings, and they had walked for a little while in the hot, water-scented air before Figgins enquired if this was the right way, for although all those bridges and canals looked the same, she didn't remember that they had come through these very narrow streets, hardly more than passages, on their way to the theatre.

Alethea blinked, and came out of her musical reverie. 'I believe you are right. We shall have to retrace our steps.'

An hour later, they were thoroughly lost. This part of the city was darker and quieter than where they had been, with only the sound of a rat slipping into the canal close to where they stood and the distant sound of a voice carrying over the water to be heard.

'If we can come to where there are gondolas,' Alethea said, 'then we can ask to be taken back to our lodgings.'

Figgins, her London-bred senses all alert to city dangers, nodded. 'I think we'd best be away from here as soon as may be.'

They came out of the narrow maze of streets and on a wider canal, where light spilled out from behind open shutters and there were one or two people walking along the canals and over the bridges.

'Surely—' Alethea began, and then she felt a savage pain on the back of her head, and her eyes were dazzled with stars before her world went dark.

Chapter Sixteen

Titus woke with a sense of immense well-being, only marred by a slight, nagging feeling that he couldn't at once identify.

Something to do with Warren, no doubt, a worry that he had let an evening slip away in pleasure and dancing when he could have been out on the hunt for Warren.

If that was the case, then the nag should have taken itself off with the arrival of Bootle, accompanied by servants, in morning livery now, bearing the inevitable water and towels, a barber, and the major-domo who came to assure himself that Signore Manningtree had passed his hours of sleep in supreme comfort, with nothing to mar his slumbers.

He managed to get rid of them all, noticed that Bootle had a great air of self-satisfaction, and asked him what he was looking so pleased about.

'It happens that one of Mr Hellifield's servants is fluent in English as well as in the Italian, a knowing and likely man, so I persuaded him to make some enquiries on your behalf as to the whereabouts of Mr Warren.'

'You've found Warren? Good. Where does he lodge?'

Bootle consulted a slip of paper that he held in his hand. 'In the Via Orsini, which I understand is not far from here.'

'I'll ask Mr Hellifield if one or other of his subtle servants will keep an eye on the fellow for me. He may think it odd, but I'm sure he'll oblige me in this matter if he can.'

It was swiftly arranged, Harry being more than happy to send one – 'or several, if you wish it' – of his servants on this mission. 'It'll give them something to do, I have so many that most of them are kept very idle. Being Italian, they love an intrigue, so I'm sure you'll get all the information about Warren's movements that you can wish. Quite like old times, when I used to send out intelligencers into enemy territory, do you remember?'

'And a set of ruffians they mostly were. I hope your servants here are a more respectable lot of men.'

'One does not reside in Venice to be respectable, Titus. We can leave that to the Shires and the dowds in Bath. By the by, are you still at all interested in paintings? I remember that at one time you seemed likely to follow in your father's footsteps as a patron of the arts and a collector of pictures.'

There it was again, that home thrust. Not done with any vicious intent, but disconcerting the way he seemed almost to be aware of what was uppermost in his friend's mind.

'Why do you ask?'

'My dear, this is Venice, the very birthplace of so many great paintings, and since the war finished, Italy has been a sea of flotsam and jetsam of paintings, sculptures, fine old books, masterpieces of all kinds. Napoleon and his banditti were great removers of whatever took their fancy, as you well know. Officially, to take it back to Paris, centre of the new regime. Unofficially, to benefit by whatever could be stolen or hoaxed out of someone else's possession. Even, I'm told, some fair dealing with a price offered and paid. There is lately come to Venice a fat rogue by the name of Delancourt. He has found himself a Venetian wife and set up shop in a crumbling palazzo where the most dazzling works of art as well as the most obscure may be seen and purchased.'

Delancourt! That was the name that Lessini had mentioned. 'You interest me, Harry. Go on.'

'They say that what is on show is but a fraction of the goods he has to sell, and that he has remarkable sources of supply, can obtain for you a classical urn or a Tintoretto at the drop of a hat, should you so wish it, and should your pockets be deep enough. He is an engaging fellow, not to be trusted an inch, but I hardly need to tell you that.'

'Do you buy from him?'

'I am no collector, and I was fortunate – this house and its contents were never ransacked, neither by the French nor by the Austrians. My uncle, my mother's brother, has many useful connections, and so, although I was unable to live here at that time, for obvious reasons, he saw to it that my property emerged intact.'

'You always were lucky.'

They were sitting in yet another exquisite room, and Titus watched the play of light and shade, as rippling flashes from the water outside were reflected back into the high room by artfully placed mirrors. 'Your palazzo is itself a work of art. Quite perfect. The coolness of the marble, the red silk on the walls, the light and air from the balcony, it is all charming.'

'Soon the smell from the canal will become unendurable, and then the windows will be closed, and the room not used again until the autumn. For the moment, we can enjoy it. So do you wish to call upon Delancourt? I shall send round to make an appointment, he allows only one client at a time. He will be delighted to see me, I can promise you, he resents the fact that I do not buy, and is always hoping to persuade me to acquire a nymph, or a drawing by da Vinci.'

'I should very much like to see the man.'

'It will be a day or so before he can fit us in, he likes to keep his clients waiting. Meanwhile, there are all the delights of Venice to savour – it is some years since you have been here. My gondola is at your disposal, go on a tour, remind yourself of its beauties.'

Titus looked across at Harry. 'What are you doing today, if you want to be rid of me?'

'No such thing. I have my lawyer calling round this morning, and I must attend to some matters of that sort. After that, I'm entirely at your disposal.'

'Are you? What became of the fair Cecilia? You can't have grown bored with such a glorious creature.'

'No, indeed. She prefers to spend much of her time out at Moli, where I have a house. We shall visit her there, I know she will be pleased to see you again.'

'You'll have to marry one of these days, Harry. Otherwise, what will become of your inheritance?'

Harry sighed. 'I know, I know. My uncles, of whom I have far too many, are always harping on that theme. I swear that I shall come to London next year for the season and find myself a bride.'

'Next year? Why not this year?'

'What with one thing and another, I have left it too late.'

'Why not an Italian bride? Will an English miss take to living in Venice?'

'The English miss, who will rapidly become an English matron, will produce a son or two, and then she may live in England, at Milverley, and I shall return to my life in Venice.'

Titus frowned. 'That's mighty cold-blooded of you.'

'Marriage is a matter of business. And you're in no position to cast stones, I don't see you filling the nursery at Beaumont.'

'I have a brother who has four sons.'

'Yes, and that sister-in-law of yours, what's her name? Christabel, that's it. An appalling woman, who longs to lord it at Beaumont.'

'I know it.'

'Don't you mind?'

'The only way she can lord it there is if I'm no longer on this earth, in which case I do not suppose I will mind very much who is there. The boys are well enough, and I find the idea of marrying merely to produce an heir very distasteful. I would not choose to marry without affection, and as I told you, the time for that is past. If one does not marry young, I'm of the opinion that it becomes harder and harder to take the plunge, and when you reach my age, it is almost an impossibility.'

Harry was amused. 'You speak as though you are in your dotage. Since we are almost exactly of an age, I take exception to that. My case is different. I adore Cecilia, and have no room in my heart for another woman.'

'Marry Cecilia.'

'Cecilia is already married.'

Titus sat up at that. 'I had no idea. Where is the complaisant husband, or do you live in daily danger of being run through by an exasperated cuckold?'

'I do not. Her husband is not quite right in his wits, and is cared for by his loving family. He had a fall from a horse or some such thing, and never fully recovered. Cecilia is a Catholic, and bourgeois to her soul. Even if her husband were to die, she would not marry me. She considers my world far too wicked and immoral for her to wish to become part of it.'

How strangely people's lives turned out, Titus thought, as Harry went out, leaving him to enjoy another pot of coffee and read the English newspapers which Harry had brought from England every week. When one was young and romantic, things were so clear. One consorted with women of the town or had a mistress or kept an opera dancer. Then came marriage, setting-up house, becoming a family man. With adventures on the side if so inclined, although for many men, a new sense of morality crept up on them, and they settled down to enjoy a more domestic kind of existence.

Only if you kept your eyes open, you soon noticed how many exceptions there were. Those such as Lord Lucius went one way, a widowed Mrs Vineham another. Somehow there he was, back to thinking about Emily. Harry had no idea how fortunate he was to have his voluptuous Cecilia, no chance of her upping and marrying some stranger and proceeding to set up a new life, jollying about abroad, never a backward glance to her years with her lover.

The coffee tasted bitter, and some grains caught in his teeth. He put his cup down with a sharp bang; at once a servant leapt forward to replenish the cup or remove it, whatever the signore wanted.

He didn't know how Harry could bear having this soft-footed tribe of immaculate servants hovering about the place. And no, he didn't want the gondolier to be summoned, he'd go about on his own two feet, thank you very much.

Chapter Seventeen

Alethea was in the nursery at Pemberley. There was a storm outside, which would account for the thud of thunder in her head and the flashing light wavering across her consciousness. She was ill, that was why she was lying down. Here was her nurse, bending over her, coaxing her to swallow the bitter mixture she was holding to her lips. What was her nurse saying? Why did she speak in so odd a way?

That must be her governess, Griffy, lurking there in the shadows, now speaking to her in a firm voice, telling her to take the medicine. It wasn't Griffy's voice, though. It was Figgins who was speaking to her.

And she wasn't in Pemberley, no, she was a thousand miles away, in Venice, and not lying in bed in any nursery, but propped against the stone corner of a bridge. The nurse wasn't a nurse, but a short man with a face like a walnut. Only the foul taste of the medicine was the same, Alethea thought, as she swallowed some with an involuntary gulp, and felt her stomach heave. Smelling salts were waved under nose; she loathed the smell of smelling salts. The ammonia caught in her nose, made her eyes water, but it served to clear her head.

'Figgins?' she said, struggling to sit in a more upright position. She put a hand up to her aching skull and looked with dismay at the red patch on her fingers. 'Did I fall?'

'You did not,' said Figgins, cutting across the torrent of Italian from walnut-face. 'You was attacked and robbed, and so was I. At least I escaped with my head unbroken, but they slit and took my coat, the same as they did with you.'

That was why she was in her shirtsleeves and waistcoat.

'Oh, Lord,' she said, putting up a grubby hand to shade her eyes. 'All our money?'

'All of it. This kind gentleman happened to come round the corner, otherwise I think you'd have been tipped into the canal and never lived to tell the tale.'

Alethea managed the shadow of a smile as she thanked the little man. He waved her thanks away. He was an apothecary, he said, which is why he had the restorative draught and the salts about him. Where were their lodgings?

Through the haze of pain in her head, Alethea grappled with the fact that they were now penniless, in a foreign country, with no acquaintance to call upon for help, even had they not been passing themselves off as men. Imagine arriving at the door of some acquaintance of Papa, and saying, I am Alethea, Mr Darcy's daughter.

One thing was clear, she and Figgins couldn't return to their lodgings. They owed for a day's stay already, and the landlady was not the sort of woman to take kindly to excuses for non-payment. The mere sight of them in their shirts would tell her what had befallen them, and Good Samaritan was unlikely to be her middle name. She'd seize their luggage, demand payment, make a scene, call a constable; no, it was not to be thought of.

It was now quite dark. She and Figgins had to find somewhere to stay. 'I can't remember,' she said to the man, gingerly feeling the back of her head.' And to Figgins, a quick *sotto voce* instruction to look dumb and say nothing.

'Your servant, he must know the address,' the apothecary said with a frown that made his eyebrows meet.

'He is not very quick-witted, speaks not a word of Italian, stays with me but has no notion of his way about Venice.'

The little man shrugged. 'Then you had best come with me. I can only offer you a poor room, but it is a roof over your head, and a clean bed. With a night's sleep, your head will clear, and in the morning you will remember where you are staying. Do you know your name?'

Alethea thought it wise to shake her head, immediately regretted the impulse, and so made a negative gesture with her hand.

'Ask your servant.'

'He wants to know my name,' Alethea said to Figgins.

Figgins pursed her lips. Miss Alethea wasn't as gone in her wits as all that.

'Say it,' Alethea hissed at her.

'Mr Aloysius Hawkins.'

'Very well, Mr Orkins, if you will lean on me, it is but a step to my shop. We live above it, myself and my wife.'

Figgins wondered what was in the evil-smelling liquid the apothecary had brought up for Alethea to drink. This being Italy, where poisonings were as common as sneezes, she hadn't wanted Alethea to touch a drop of it.

Nor had Miss Alethea seemed very keen, only she said that her head hurt abominably, and the apothecary was certain that it would ease the pain and help her sleep.

'It is nonsense, Figgins, that all Italians carry vials of poison about with them. We are not living in the Middle Ages.'

Yes, Figgins said inwardly, you and I know that, but do they?

However, it seemed to have worked. There Miss Alethea was, sleeping peacefully enough, and that was the best thing for her. If she had stayed awake, she'd be fretting over her predicament, and what was the use of that?

It was a practical matter, Figgins decided, and one that she would have to resolve. She knew what it was like to have no money, while Miss Alethea had not the least notion of it. And the lack of so much as a penny in their pockets would like as not make her mistress fret and worry, and that wasn't going to help her head mend.

Could she safely leave her for an hour or so? She looked around the small attic. It had a narrow bed, on which Alethea lay, a chest, a small table and a single chair. A pallet had been brought up and laid down by Mrs Apothecary; Figgins had slept on worse. The only window was a tiny one, that barely opened. If the apothecary knew that Figgins had gone out, would he come creeping up the stairs to his victim?

She spied a key attached to a short piece of string, lying on the narrow shelf beneath the window. She tried it in the door, and it worked. What if Miss Alethea woke up, called out, and no one could get in to her? She glanced again at the sleeping form on the bed. Didn't look like she was going to wake up, not for hours. She'd have to risk it. She went out of the room and locked the door behind her. Then down the steep stairs and down a second flight, slightly less steep. The apothecary and his wife slept in a chamber behind the shop; she paused, listened, not a sound to be heard. She eased open the door that led into the shop, and tiptoed to the entrance.

The door was locked, but not barred, and there were few locks that could defeat Figgins. Not all her brothers were as upright as Joe, and her next brother, Will, had had a successful career of crime in his youth before he had come to see the error of his ways and settled down to serve his apprenticeship as a locksmith. He had taught her the tricks of the trade, and in such a shop as this, there was bound to be what she needed to pick the lock.

Two minutes later, she was out in the deserted street. English she might be, but she was city born and bred, and to her mind, one city was very like another when the lights were out and the rats were abroad. Tonight, she was going to play rat.

Alethea woke coughing. The room was hot and airless; Figgins had carefully closed the window before settling down on her pallet. With all that water about, there would be a terrible miasma wafting in, if allowed.

Alethea blinked, and looked at the sleeping hump that was Figgins. Sliding out of the bed, she stood up carefully. No dizziness, and only a dull ache where there had been that shattering pain. Good. She stepped over Figgins and pushed at the window until it creaked reluctantly open. She stood there, breathing in the morning air. How long had she slept? She could hear the sounds of the household stirring, and outside voices rose in cheerful greeting; a man was calling out that he had most excellent fish, fresh fish for sale. A dog barked, a brief quarrel broke out on the water.

Normally, all this would have raised her spirits, but after a moment of pure pleasure, the events of the evening before flooded back to her. They were in a real scrape this time.

Her eyes fell on the table, where Figgins had laid her trousers. There, beside them, was a leather purse. Alethea snatched it up and opened it. It wasn't bulging with coins, but there were enough to draw a clear line above destitution. What had Figgins been up to?

She was about to shake her maid awake, but stopped. Figgins was usually an early riser; if she was sleeping soundly at this hour of the morning, she must have come to bed late. Alethea could remember little of the night before, only that she had taken some drug given to her by the apothecary. Then she had fallen asleep, she supposed. Had Figgins gone out? Alone, in this strange city? And how had she acquired the purse? Or did it belong to the apothecary, left on the table while he attended to her head.

She dressed, wrinkling her nose at putting on such a dirty shirt, and sat down in the chair to wait for Figgins to wake.

'Oh, that,' said Figgins, looking sideways at her mistress. 'We have to have money, we cannot survive without we have coins in our pockets.'

'I'm not one to preach morality,' said Alethea. 'Whose money? Not the apothecary's, I trust. He has been very kind to us, as has his wife.'

The apothecary's wife was a plump woman, as smooth skinned as her husband was wrinkled, but otherwise rather like him. She had fed Figgins, food that Figgins didn't much care for, but food was food, and had tucked Alethea up with the greatest care.

Figgins was shocked. 'I'd never steal from anyone I knew. Not that I make a habit of stealing anyhow,' she added quickly. 'I got in the way of knowing how it's done, though, when I was a nipper. My ma didn't half wallop me when she found out what I was up to, it's not what she holds with. My brother Will used to do it for larks, and I went along with him sometimes.'

'So you stole the purse?'

'Forked it, smooth as butter,' said Figgins.

'And fled?'

'Not I. Went on my way innocent as can be. No need to draw attention to yourself, that's what Will used to say. Mind you, he could slip away like an eel if he had to. It wasn't necessary last night, the gentleman as I came up against being rather the worse for wear.'

'I hope he could afford to lose the coins.'

'He had the price of several purses on his back.'

'Well, as long as you didn't steal from widows and orphans, then I must say I'm glad for the use of the money.'

'I don't do widows and orphans,' Figgins said virtuously.

Alethea wasn't to know, and Figgins had no intention of enlightening her, that the reason for this restraint was that stealing from widows and orphans had its point, in that such people were easy victims, but with the downside that the pickings were generally meagre.

Alethea stood up. 'This will keep us for several days, if we're careful.'

'It won't take us to Rome, then?'

Alethea shook her head. 'It would cost more than we have, even travelling in the cheapest way possible. Rome is not just around the corner.'

'I can try again.'

Alethea felt alarmed. 'No, by no means. I hope that in a

day or so I may have come up with some other means of our getting by, but no more pick-pocketing for you. Why, if you were caught, the Lord knows what would happen to you.'

She was very grateful to Figgins for what she had done, but realisation of how big a risk her servant had taken was beginning to steal over her. It was wrong, she had dragged Figgins out of England, and it was up to her to make sure that Figgins came out of all this safe and sound.

'Shall we go back to our lodgings now?'

Alethea considered this. 'No, for the rooms are expensive, and to pay for last night and another night would take much of what we have. No, we'll have to leave that woman to cry for her money for the time being. Wytton can settle with her in due course.'

'What of your things?'

'We can manage without them meanwhile. It is so warm, you can wash our shirts at night and they will be dry by the morning. Mrs Apothecary will bring us water, I feel sure.'

'Shall we stay here, then?'

'I mean to ask if we may. They can hardly charge much for the room, and I shall say it is only until my memory returns.'

The apothecary was agreeable and his wife was happy to provide an evening meal for a modest sum.

Figgins and Alethea went out into the sunlight. Another dose from the apothecary had soothed Alethea's head still further, and this one would not make her sleepy, the apothecary had assured her. 'Although I advise you not to attempt to walk far, especially in the heat of the day. One should rest after such a blow.'

Their first need, Alethea decided, was for coats. 'We are conspicuous without them, only we need to buy them as cheaply as possible.'

'Dead clothes are cheapest,' Figgins said helpfully.

'Dead clothes?'

'Taken from the dead, and sold off at very low prices, specially if they died of some disease.'

Alethea knew that her revulsion showed in her face. Figgins took it in good part. 'It's how most people get by, Miss Alethea.'

'Mr Hawkins, for heaven's sake; God knows who may be passing by who understands English.'

The task of acquiring a coat to wear taxed Alethea's energy to its limits. Figgins had come up with the idea of visiting a tailor's shop. 'Not one that the nobs use, but a respectable establishment,' she said.

'A new coat? From a tailor's? Are you mad? We can't afford any such thing.'

'Listen, will you? There are always coats made, and waistcoats and trousers and breeches too, if it comes to that, that are never collected. The customer finds he has no money or is ill or finds a tailor who makes a coat that suits him better. So the tailor is left with his work done and no one to pay for it. If it's a common size, then he can unpick it, with luck, and remake it for a new order. If not, he hangs it up and hopes that someone may come in to buy it off the peg.'

'Am I not a common size?'

'Course not. You're tall and thin, how many tall, thin types have you seen around? These Italians are no higher than I am.'

Alethea was doubtful, but anything was better than having to resort to more theft. Her shirtsleeves were attracting some attention, too, she noticed.

'What about you?'

'I can't go buying a gentleman's coat, that'd be daft. I can pick one up, cheap, later. No one's stopping to wonder why I'm in my waistcoat. It isn't seemly for a gentleman's gentleman, I'll admit, but who's to know that's what I am?'

By the time they went down two dark steps into a third tailor's workshop, Alethea's head was beginning to thud again in a most alarming fashion. But Figgins's instinct proved correct. The tailor positively fell over himself in his hurry to whisk a coat from a dark corner. It had been ordered by a

Frenchman who had never returned, never paid him for it, he would be delighted to sell it to an Englishman instead, and he was sure it would be a perfect fit.

Perfect it wasn't, but it was good enough. Not good enough for Figgins, though, who made the tailor sit down then and there and turn up the sleeves and take in the seams at the back, before insisting that Alethea haggle over the price.

The coat was dark green and fortunately plain, sporting no outlandish collar or trimmings on sleeve or vents. Alethea was relieved to be able to put on her disguise again. She was uncomfortable going about in her shirt and waistcoat; she felt sure she looked less masculine than when wearing a coat.

They emerged into the sunlight, and she faltered slightly as the glare struck her eyes. It was no good trying to hide this fact from Figgins, who took one look at her and declared that they were to go back to the apothecary's. 'You'll not go out again today,' she said roundly.

Alethea resented her physical weakness, and her sense of uselessness. Figgins deserved better of her than this. If only her head was clearer, she could no doubt think up a way out of their present fix, but for the moment the thoughts just chased one another round and round inside her head.

'It's so hot and stuffy there.'

'That's as may be, but you can lie down out of the sun and rest. I'm not taking no for an answer, for you're no use to yourself nor me without you get back on your feet again. I don't want to have to go round knocking on doors to find some English people to save us, now do I?'

'Perish the thought!'

'There you are, then. It's what I'll have to do, if you don't watch it.'

Alethea lay down on the narrow bed, hot and uncomfortable, but grateful to be in the shadows and to be able to close her eyes. The apothecary came tripping up the stairs with a new dose, although he declared that he took a sanguine view of her case. His patient was so young and strong, he had done too much too soon, that was all. Sleep was the answer. Another twenty-four hours, and it would be a different story.

Alethea didn't sleep, but lay brooding, an unusual condition with her. Figgins sat perched by the little window, which afforded her a narrow view of the canal and the streets beyond. She was perfectly happy to sit and watch barges and gondolas and rowing boats come and go, gulls fighting over scraps from the morning market, children playing and skipping in the street, two elderly women going past, their tongues moving a great deal faster than their legs – an endless procession of humanity to amuse and interest a mind at rest.

Alethea was not perfectly happy, nor was her mind at rest. She had brought Figgins into danger and discomfort – for what? So that she could escape from her husband. Women escaped from their husbands all the time, no doubt, but they didn't go haring off to Venice dressed up as men, not that she'd ever heard of. They escaped into adultery or their family's care. Why had she had to end up here, with no money and a cracked head and a nervous inclination to start every time she heard footsteps approaching from behind?

Because she had no one to turn to in England. So, whom had she to turn to here in Venice? She had chosen what seemed the easiest path – the only path – from her state of virtual imprisonment in England. It made sense to seek out Camilla, the sister who best understood her, and rely on her and her capable and understanding husband to sort out the situation with Papa, and rely on Papa to deal with Napier. Even if Camilla happened to be residing in Italy.

What if Papa wouldn't, or couldn't, deal with Napier? What if Napier threatened legal action? Could a wife be dragged back to her husband's care? It seemed gothic, but then the law was gothic, everyone said so. And Napier was certainly gothic, if not deranged. Was the fact that your husband was mad sufficient to justify a separation? Would Napier appear mad to anyone who hadn't been in his power when the doors were shut and he had drunk too much wine and brandy? Maybe most men were like that.

Not Papa, though. Nor Wytton. Mr Barcombe? Surely not, Letty was far too smug for that to be the case.

The hot, pungent air from outside floated in, making her wrinkle her nose in distaste. She yawned, and moved her head carefully on the pillow. The heat was oppressive, and she was overcome with longing for the cool green lawns of Pemberley, where the oaks would be rustling with their fresh May foliage, the rose garden alive with new leaves and buds.

Sights and memories from earlier, happier times came chasing into her head. The long shadows of a summer evening, the sound of voices, her sisters' laughter, one of her little brothers racing over the gravel on sturdy legs, shouting and calling to his mother.

Herself in a girl's muslin dress, playing the pianoforte in the music room, its long windows open on to the terrace, a warm breeze stirring the summer curtains. The sound of bat and ball as the twins played their own private version of cricket. Horses grazing in the paddocks, flicking tails and shaking their manes to ward off flies, a dog asleep in the shade cast by the stable clock, the clock itself, ticking away the peaceful hours.

Tears trickled out beneath her closed eyelids. That was childhood. That was gone for ever. Pemberley – did Pemberley actually exist? – was no longer her home. Did she have a home at all? She turned again, pulling at the bolster tucked beneath her head.

Figgins was beside her. 'Does your head hurt?'

Alethea quickly brushed away the traces of tears with the back of a hand. 'No, not at all.'

'Has the medicine not worked? Has it not taken away the pain?'

'I told you, my head doesn't hurt.' Alethea knew her voice sounded fretful. She made an effort. 'This bolster is very firm, that is all. Go back to the window, I shall be asleep in a moment.'

Figgins went back to her stool, watching Alethea with sidelong glances.

'Stop looking at me as though I were about to expire,' Alethea said crossly, and closed her eyes again.

Money. They needed money. She must owe the apothecary for his draughts. The coat had cost several of their precious coins. They had to eat, to keep a roof over their heads. How could she get some money? Suddenly, Figgins's threat of knocking on doors to enquire if anyone English lived there didn't seem so far-fetched. She winced at the prospect, the discovery, the scandal, the disgrace. She could hear Letty's appalled tones in her ears: 'You should have thought of that before you did such a wicked thing, that was always your way, heedless and careless and never a thought for other people, or your family.'

Damn Letty, she muttered. Damn her self-righteousness. Damn Georgina for being under her husband's thumb; perhaps he was a brutal husband, for all his apparent dotingness. Damn Belle for being so blissfully happy in her marriage and getting pregnant just when she might have been of use for once in her life. She almost damned Camilla for going off to Rome, but stopped herself in time. Camilla was the only person in the world who might help to get her out of this mess, she wasn't going to damn Camilla's eyes, however inconvenient her trip out of Venice was.

'I could find work as a musician,' she said, speaking aloud without being aware of it. 'Like I did in London.'

'I doubt it,' said Figgins, without turning her head from the window. 'It seems to me as how this city's crawling with musicians. I expect it's the same as London, where you have to know people to get your toe in the door, no matter what your lay is. You don't know a soul here, musicians or anyone else. Not that your playing isn't a deal better than some of the dreadful sounds I've heard here.'

Figgins was right, of course. You needed an introduction to be on the circuit. She could have arranged it in London, with the friends she had made during her visits to Silvestrini for lessons. His house in Bloomsbury was always full of musicians, who took her as they found her.

That was another door that had closed with a slam on the day she had ascended the altar steps with Norris Napier.

She thrust the memories of music and camaraderie out of reach, down into the deepest layers of her mind to join the green swards of Pemberley and the evenings of ecstatic happiness with Penrose. It did one no good to dwell on the past, the only place to live was the present, with the expectation that, against all odds, there would be a future where things were not so very bad.

Courage, her better self urged. These weeks of pretending to be a man might have been folly, but they had brought her a degree of freedom and independence she had never dreamt of. There was the feeling of competence earned by difficulties surmounted; they had achieved a great deal, she and Figgins. Were they to falter now, lose heart, when with a little determination and luck, they would accomplish what they had set out to do?

No, they were not.

Chapter Eighteen

The palazzo must once have been a most magnificent building, but it had been sadly neglected.

'French and then Austrian troops were quartered here,' said Harry. The gondolier made the boat fast and Titus sprang on to the steps of the palazzo.

'Savages,' he said, looking up at the façade.

'Venice was crumbling from within, before ever Napoleon arrived.' Harry gave instructions to his gondolier and then joined Titus on the steps. 'We do not enter here, we need to walk round into the piazza.'

As they turned the corner, Titus stiffened. He stopped, and drew back into the doorway of a building.

'What is it?' said Harry.

'Just someone I know and whom I don't wish to be seen by.'

'That man in the blue coat. Why, damn me if it isn't George Warren. He's been in to see Delancourt. Wait, here comes one of my men.'

A suave servant, out of livery, came up to Harry and bowed before making his report. This was the English gentleman's first visit to the art dealer. Yesterday he had taken coffee at Florian's, visited a house in the Grand Canal where an Englishman and his wife presently lived, friends of the poet, Lord Byron. He had spent the evening at the gaming tables.

'Let's see if we can worm out of this Delancourt what interests Warren.'

'Fat chance,' said Harry, as they knocked at the dilapidated wooden door. 'You couldn't worm the time of day out of Delancourt.'

The dinginess and decrepitude of the palazzo from outside gave no hint of the glories within. Titus caught his breath as he spun round on his heels to scan the wide, marbled room they were being led into.

Women's faces gazed out on him from every side. There, the beautiful, serene face of a Madonna: here, the lascivious eyes of a peachy beauty painted by Giorgione. He noticed the knowing look of a crone, peering from the corner of a vast canvas by a Venetian painter he couldn't at once identify; the languid gaze of a Canova – surely that was a very modern work to be among these other pieces? A Roman matron drooping over an urn had, he thought, a pleased look to her grief. Happiness is widowhood, as a friend of his had once remarked.

An altar piece was propped up in glowing splendour on a worm-eaten chest, with two Marys kneeling before the cross, one in blue, one in red, one looking stricken, the other with an air of anger about her. Which was mere fancy, Titus knew. Paintings of that time did not depict emotion of that sort.

Worse than all these varied aspects of the feminine, he had an uneasy feeling that Emily's eyes were looking out at him from canvas after canvas, through the sightless stare of a classical bust, from the blue orbs of Diana clad in no more than a wisp of clothing and her virtue among a pack of hounds, from the satisfied expression of a middle-aged noblewoman in a green gown.

Titus shut his eyes for a moment. How dare Emily wind through his mind like this? Everything between them was over, and after her appraisal of his character, he had few happy memories left behind to soothe the sense of pain her defection had caused him. Think of the scores of women, he urged himself inwardly, all more agreeable, more honest, more worthy of his attentions than Emily, that were to be found within a stone's throw of this place. Even before he began to think of Paris, of London—

He pulled himself together, and began to wish he hadn't come. It was improbable that this man would have any knowledge of the whereabouts of the painting. If so dazzling a work had appeared on the market, it would have been snapped up at once. The woman in the Titian was neither Emily nor a harlot nor a saint. Any man would long to possess her. She would never belong on the walls of this damp, decaying place.

His attention was caught by a painting he had missed at first. It was small, fifteenth century, he supposed. Men before a castle, about to set out on a hunting expedition. They wore the particoloured hose of the time, and some women looking down from the tower had the pointed headdresses that belonged to the world of fairy tales. One young man stood slightly apart. He had a falcon perched on his wrist, and they were looking at each other, man and bird, with the same hawkish expression.

It was Alethea Darcy to the life; her dark brows and challenging look were caught to perfection, and the sight of the figure, standing there with such grace and courage, made his heart stop.

'Seen a ghost?' Harry said in his ear.

Titus stood back, took a deep breath. 'A remarkable painting,' he said.

'If your taste runs in that direction,' Harry said indifferently.

Delancourt came mincing out to meet them. Difficult, thought Titus, to mince when you had a dozen chins and a preposterous belly, but mince he did. Sharp eyes looked out from a roll of fat about his eyes; a hand, as neat as his small feet and covered in rings, was extended to the visitors. A thoroughly untrustworthy individual, and obviously so, how could he survive in a business that depended so much upon trust and an assumption of expertise?

'Welcome, Mr Hellifield,' Delancourt said in strongly accented English. 'And you have brought a companion.'

Titus would rather have remained anonymous, but Harry said, 'Allow me to name Mr Manningtree, a good friend of mine, lately arrived from England.'

Delancourt bowed, or at least tilted slightly forward. Perfectly judged, thought Titus; an inch more, and he would surely have toppled over.

'The son of the late Mr Severus Manningtree?' the dealer asked.

His words took Titus by surprise.

'I knew your father, in Rome, oh, many, many years ago. I was desolated to learn of his demise, so fine a scholar, so keen a connoisseur of art. I recall that he bought a Titian, what a *coup*! I feel sure you have inherited his eye for a fine piece.'

'Perhaps.' Titus found he didn't care to discuss his father. 'That is a Giorgione you have over there, heavily restored, I believe.'

'Ah, yes. Clumsy work, done by one of my fellow countrymen, I regret to say. However, the true glory of the original is still there in places, would you not agree? The hand of a master is always apparent to those who have the eyes to see.'

'The Canova is not quite in keeping with the rest of what you have on show.'

'You are right,' Delancourt cried, clapping his hands together in a grotesque display of boyish enthusiasm. 'A part payment. I reverence the work of Canova, he is an artist one cannot admire too highly. Also, on a more practical note, I foresee his reputation remaining high and outlasting the vagaries of fashion. There is always a market for marble depicting the human form in such a manner.'

'I dare say. It is not what I would choose to buy.'

'But do you wish to buy something? That is charming. How often have I trailed tempting morsels before the feet of Monsieur Hellifield, and always in vain. Now he makes recompense, by bringing his English friend, and no less a man than Monsieur Manningtree's son. What a delight!'

Not so at all, Titus said to himself. If he was not much mistaken, there had been a sudden flash of alarm on the Frenchman's face when Harry had said his name. Moreover, that immediate association of his father with Titian was suspicious. His father had only ever bought that single Titian in his life – well, how many men could say even that? – but he had not gone out of his way to search out and acquire a painting by that master. His father's famed collector's taste lay in a different direction; the Titian had been an aberration. Which was why, perhaps, Severus Manningtree had made no great effort to trace the painting during the troubled years of the war. He had left it in safe-keeping, he had told Titus shortly before his final illness. If it were still there, then it would be restored to him in due course. If not – he had shrugged. War had brought greater tragedies than that to so many families.

Unfortunately, his father had taken the name of the guardian of the painting with him to the grave. Which was a pity, for to have that piece of information might have saved him the devil of a lot of trouble, Titus reflected. Yet here was this Frenchman, raising the subject of Titian, associating his father's name at once with the painter. His father might have come across Delancourt in Rome; Titus doubted if he had ever had any dealings with him, he was far too canny a man for that.

What would he say, if he could see his son standing here now, a man grown into maturity, no boy full of wild ideas and schemes, yet so obsessed with denying his king possession of the painting that he was talking to Delancourt like a keen customer, prepared to do business with him, if there were the least chance that the man knew where the Titian was?

'I saw another old acquaintance of mine just now,' Harry was saying. 'One Mr Warren, another compatriot. I did not know he was an *aficionado* of art.'

A blank look spread over the jowly face. 'Mr Warren? I don't think I—'

'Come, come, man, we saw him leave. Dark as to complexion, wearing a cherry-coloured coat.'

'Ah, Mr Warren,' Delancourt said, strangling the name so that it sounded like Mr Venom. 'He called on behalf of another client, that is all. I know nothing about him.'

The man was a good liar, but not good enough. Why deny that Warren had been there, and then make up a feeble tale about his representing someone else? Of course, that was exactly what Warren was doing, but Titus doubted if he would have revealed to Delancourt that he was acting on behalf of King George. Warren was not the man to show the cards in his hand; although the mention of such an eminent patron might tempt Delancourt to bring forth the jewels in his collection.

Titus felt it was time for him to play a bolder hand. 'You spoke of Titian,' he said. 'I see no works here of his.'

Delancourt's mouth shaped an unpleasantly moist moue of sorrow. 'Alas, alas, a humble man such as myself would consider himself the most favoured of beings were he to come into possession of anything by that master.' He kissed his plump fingers in an extravagant gesture. 'So few pictures, all of them so prized, so many collectors panting, yes, panting, I say, to obtain even the least of his canvases. I cannot help you there, greatly to my sorrow.'

'Oh, I don't want a Titian,' Titus said. 'I have my father's one, after all, which should be sufficient for the heart of any man, don't you agree?'

'You have his Titian?' cried Delancourt. 'How can this be?' He recollected himself, and Titus noticed with interest that beads of sweat were forming on his forehead. 'I had understood that in the confusion of the times the painting had been lost.'

'Not at all. It hangs at Beaumont, which is my country house. In the library,' he added untruthfully. That was where he had a place earmarked for the painting; at the moment a lugubrious ancestor looked down from the wall from there.

'I am amazed. Overcome. I had understood—' Delancourt produced a large red silk square and mopped his brow, leaving unpleasant streaks behind on the flamboyant handkerchief. He stuffed it back into his pocket. 'I take a great personal interest in the works of this artist, and I had thought I knew where all his paintings are. But I stand corrected.'

'You do, indeed. Few people have ever seen it, I live in a remote part of the country and entertain little there. Perhaps that is why it has never come to your notice. Although my late father's purchase of the work in question is a matter of record.'

'Records! If we were to rely on records—'

'Quite.'

'What was all that about?' Harry asked as they watched his gondola approach the steps and come to a standstill with an elegant twist of the gondolier's oar. 'You had the old rascal looking quite pasty. Makes a change, I think it's usually his customers who end up poorer and paler.'

Titus was following his own train of thought. 'He is up to something with Warren.'

'Oh, that's clear enough. What's it to do with you? Do you really own a Titian, by the way? I don't recall it, but then I only ever paid you one visit at Beaumont; time spent at my own house is time ill spent enough, without going visiting anyone else's draughty residence.'

'I do own a Titian, yes.'

Harry was a dear friend, but he was a gossip. Able to keep his mouth shut when it came to matters military, or even political, he would regard Titus's quest for the Titian as of no great moment, and therefore a good story to pass around. He was big with curiosity as to exactly why Titus had chosen to visit Venice now; he knew Titus well enough to be aware that he did nothing without a reason or a purpose. Idling his time away amid the fleshpots of Venice was not Titus's style, yet it would have to suffice as an explanation for the present. Once the Titian was recovered, Harry could regale the whole of Venice with the tale if he wished.

Once it was recovered. What was Warren up to? Why had he gone straight to Delancourt? Why was Delancourt so twitchy on the subject of Titians, and of the Manningtree Titian in particular? Ha, he'd given him something to think about, saying it hung at Beaumont. It was the last thing Delancourt would want, to sell a painting to a man like Warren, especially if he had, after all, named his illustrious patron, and for the ultimate purchaser to find the painting had a twin.

He felt cheered. What he had most feared was that the trail would go cold here in Venice. 'Can your men continue to keep watch on Warren?' he asked Harry.

'If you wish it. Only, hear me, Titus, I shall want an account of this as soon as you are able to loosen that padlocked tongue of yours.'

'Yes,' said Titus, stepping down into the gondola. He wondered how much Delancourt might want for the fifteenth-century painting.

Chapter Nineteen

'My head is quite healed,' Alethea told Figgins in the morning. 'So we must be up and about, finding a way to make some money. You may take that mulish look off your face; I'm not saying we won't steal sooner than starve, but it must be the last resort.'

'For young women stranded in a big city, there isn't a heap of choice,' said Figgins. 'There's stealing, of all sorts, there's being a whore, which my ma is dead against, and there's being taken into keeping by a man, which isn't a lot different, just that you only go with the one.'

'We aren't stranded young women. We're stranded young men, and that's much better. Look, the sun is shining – in England I dare say it's pouring with rain – we have the day ahead of us, and enough money in our pockets for a meal or two. Perhaps I can find some lost English people who are looking for a guide and interpreter.'

'Go on. What kind of a guide would you be, a stranger here yourself?'

'I can invent plenty of stories about the houses and palaces as we go along. Griffy taught me to make up tales about anything.'

In Figgins's opinion, Miss Alethea had lived in a land of make believe for too long. Now she was landed right in one of those fanciful tales Miss Griffin made so much money out of, quite famous she was now, only where was the masked admirer who was going to appear from nowhere to whisk them to safety? It would come to pick-pocketing, there was no doubt about it. For her part, she'd rather do it sooner than later, and have the coins sitting snug in her pocket.

'Where are we going?'

'First, to have breakfast, I'm famished.'

That was another thing. Figgins was used to going without food, and she could last well enough on a meagre diet. It looked like Miss Alethea, now that she was away from that wretch of a husband, had her appetite back with a vengeance. It might have been subdued while she had the headache, but Figgins's experienced eye told her that her mistress would be back to her old ways. Ate like a wolf, she did, when given the chance. And it looked like she'd grown again, where was it going to end?

'A crust of bread and a glass of thin ale?' she suggested.

'A pot of coffee and a plate of pastries,' said Alethea. 'We'll go in a new direction this morning, to see what's afoot. Chance, you know, plays a chief role in all our lives. Who knows what we may find around the next corner?'

'Trouble, like as not,' said Figgins, but not in her wildest imaginings could she have hit upon what they did find around the first corner.

'Look at the fat cove all perspiring and done up like a preacher, in those old-fashioned clothes,' she said.

'A clergyman!' Alethea said. 'An English clergyman, as I live. He may be lost, this could be my chance to act as guide. My word, I do believe it is a bishop, I saw a flash of purple. How absurd to wear such clothes when you are abroad. I have a cousin who is a bishop, mind you, who is just such an idiot.'

The man in black, who was consulting a small book, seemed to hear the English words hovering on the air, for he lifted his eyes from the book and stepped backwards, colliding with Alethea, who had begun to prowl forwards.

To Figgins's astonishment, Alethea gave a kind of eldritch screech, cried out, 'Fiend take the man,' and took to her heels.

Figgins was quite taken aback, but only for a moment. Seeing that the portly clergyman was about to address her, she ducked sideways and followed Alethea who had vanished into an unsavoury underpassage.

The sound of their running feet echoed about her ears, easy enough to keep track of Miss Alethea, but what if the man came after them?

'No danger of that,' Miss Alethea said, panting as they emerged into a small square. 'He is much too dignified to give us chase, and why should he?'

'Why, then, did you run from him?'

Alethea was struggling to restrain her mirth. 'Because I know him! You'll never guess who he is .'

'Oh, I can guess, with our luck he'll be that cousin of yours, as you said was a bishop. And if you know him, he'll know you, and now the fat's truly in the fire.'

'Not a bit of it,' said Alethea blithely. 'It is some years since he saw me, I was a girl then, with my hair in a plait and wearing my best muslin dress. Why should he associate that with a young man in Venice?'

'It'd be different if you weren't the spitting image of your pa.'

'I am like him, it's true, but then people do often look like other people in the most surprising way. He is a cousin on Mama's side, not on Papa's, so he will merely assume I am a Darcy, he cannot know all Darcy's relatives.'

'He looks to me like the kind of nosy gent as would make sure he did know all his noble relatives, that's how he comes to be a bishop, I expect.'

'Well, he may wonder about the likeness, but there is nothing more he can do about it. We shall have to make sure we don't run into him again, that's all. Dressed up like that, he is instantly recognisable.'

Figgins ate her roll with a heavy heart. If it wasn't one thing, it was another. They'd survived bludgeoning and destitution – at least for the moment – only to meet up with a bishop.

'I told you,' Alethea said, her voice light-hearted and

happy, 'you never know what the next hour is going to bring.' She paused, a pastry suspended in the air as she listened. 'Hark, I hear a singer, beginning the day with scales. Not quite true on that note, but it is a good voice.'

She got up, pastry still in her hand and walked to the centre of the square, her head on one side. She was joined by the barman from the establishment where they had bought breakfast.

'Mollini,' he said, jerking his finger towards a third-floor window. A babble of unintelligible Italian followed, with Alethea looking bright and alert, and stopping the man when she didn't understand. Then she nodded her head and thanked him gracefully.

'She is a soprano at the opera. We are in the theatrical district here, it seems, where several opera companies put on performances. If we wander about, I dare say we shall hear some more music.'

'It's early in the morning for musicians to be up and about,' said Figgins. She finished her coffee and wiped her mouth with the back of her shirtsleeve.

'The day is still cool, it's a good time to practise,' said Alethea. 'Let's wander about the nearby streets and see what we find. Look, there's a flybill on that wall, an announcement of an opera by Rossini. He no longer lives in Venice, but I dare say they still perform his music. Yes, at the Teatro San Benedetto, *L'italiana in Algeri*. Don't I wish we might go.'

There was something to be thankful for, Figgins thought: with no money in their pockets there was no way she could be dragged off to endure hours of caterwauling.

'Do you suppose we might be able to sneak into the theatre?' Alethea was saying. 'It happens in London.'

Figgins sighed.

The name at the foot of the flybill seemed familiar to Alethea, but she couldn't place it. She didn't know any Italian of that name; where had she heard it mentioned, and recently?

It would come back to her, as long as she didn't dwell on it. Meanwhile, this was a delightful area, despite Figgins's wrinkled nose. It might be close and fetid at street level, but above their heads, brilliant flowers tumbled over balconies and voices and laughter – and music – came out of open windows, still unshuttered in the comparative cool of the morning.

A tall, thin priest in a shabby soutane went past, gave them a curious glance, and disappeared into the side door of one of those unexpected churches that looked out over a small square. A lean, keen-eyed cat sat on a doorstep, washing itself while keeping a wary watch on the world.

Another singer trying out his voice, a tenor this time, a rich and vibrant voice, singing an unfamiliar aria, a showy, flowery piece; Alethea stopped to listen, regardless of the steady stream of people who had to pause and walk round her. Friendly and not so friendly admonitions were called out as people went past, but she stood quite still until the singer stopped, coughed, gargled and began again.

A flute was being played further along the street, and Alethea paused again, her ears on the trills, her eyes riveted by a shop selling music. 'How I wish we had money to spend,' she said.

She gave a quick, laughing glance at Figgins, she knew what her maid was thinking. 'I have quite enough music, you believe, but that's no longer the case. What was mine was taken by my husband' – she spat the word out – 'detestable man, he burnt much of it, and only kept the music he liked. So you see, I have to begin my collection all over again.'

Alethea saw the tightening of Figgins's lips. 'No, never look like that. I don't want sympathy, you know. I have broken away from him, and I shall never go back; they will never force me to.'

'I reckon as how your father will go straight to England with a horsewhip in his hands, once he hears how you've been treated,' Figgins burst out. 'Why, even my pa, who's only a groom, wouldn't stand for a husband carrying on like that Mr

Napier did. And your father's a rich man, with an earl for a cousin and powerful friends, he may do as he chooses.'

'I hope so. Not as to the horsewhip, never that, but as to agreeing with me that my marriage is over and that the conditions imposed upon me by Napier were intolerable.' She shrugged. 'I don't want to think of the man. He poisons the air by mere mention of his name.'

In that strange way the mind had, the surge of hostility she felt at the thought of her husband jostled the memory of that name on the flysheet into the foreground. Salvatore Massetti was an impresario Lessini had mentioned, when they were at the inn, as being a great friend and former colleague of Signore Silvestrini, her singing master in London.

Better, perhaps, not to have brought Figgins in with her, but Figgins was there beside her, clearly not intending to be shut out, or worse, left loitering in the street.

Salvatore Massetti had a face like a skull and a voice like a corncrake. Which was interesting, Alethea decided. Maybe his work in opera was a compensation for possessing such a dreadfully harsh and untuneful voice. Were his ears of the same kind, then it was a mistake to be here.

As Massetti swept an inscrutable gaze from her head to her toes, his eyes lingering where Alethea least wished him to take notice of her anatomy, she felt herself grow uncomfortable. Never mind the voice, this might be a mistake by anyone's reckoning.

'So,' he said at last. 'A pupil of my good friend Arturo Silvestrini, who abandons his homeland for the cloudy streets of London, where musicians hardly grow on every tree. He takes many unpromising pupils, to make ends meet; this is the way it is in London.'

That, to Alethea's certain knowledge, was untrue. The man was goading her. Had she not had an exceptional voice, Silvestrini would not have agreed to teach her, rich man's daughter or no. His reputation was so high that he could afford to pick and choose those whom he wanted to teach, and he only taught the best. So she said nothing, and waited for Signore Massetti to continue.

'I run an opera company, my business is music, and by music I mean what entertains and amuses the public and brings them to buy their seats and boxes. You say you are a singer. Very well then, sing.'

Taken aback, Alethea stared at him. Sing? Sing what? Where was an accompanist?

Massetti flicked his hands in the air. 'No voice, suddenly. What has Silvestrini taught you to sing? English ballads? These are of no interest to me.'

'I shall sing Mozart,' Alethea announced with some defiance. 'From *Le Nozze di Figaro: "Non so piu cosa son, cosa faccio".'*

His eyebrows rose. 'How interesting, that you choose to sing a woman's part.'

'I worked on the role with Maestro Silvestrini. My voice is an unusual one.'

'It must be.'

He walked to the instrument that stood in the corner of the room, a pianoforte with a shabby case and, she realised as he began to play, a tinkly sound. No matter, it would do.

She sang, finding that to sing for your supper was very different from singing to a roomful of friends or musicians who knew you and what you were. She had chosen the Mozart aria in a moment of desperation; it was a part she had studied in depth with Silvestrini, and she could remember it all, here and now. But this man wasn't interested in Mozart. Mozart belonged to the last century, Mozart was old fashioned. Novelty held sway in the operatic world in Italy. Silvestrini had often said so, and she could see for herself, by the posters around the walls, that Massetti's business was with the new.

He continued to play after she had finished singing, toying

with the theme, embellishing it, picking out a variation. He was a musician, Alethea had to admit, corncrake or not.

'That is an unusual voice, as you say,' he pronounced finally, swinging round on the stool to face her. 'A remarkable voice. Were I to hear it without seeing the singer, I might be in doubt as to whether it was a man or a woman singing. The power is that of a man, the range that of a man who has no balls. Have you lost your balls, Mr Hawkins?'

Alethea had expected that. She lowered her eyes to the ground. 'An accident in childhood,' she said.

He came over to her, raised her chin in his hand and looked critically at her, turning her face from side to side. Alethea had to control herself, beating down the urge to pull away; Napier had often held her so, in a tight and painful grip, while he demanded that she sing to him. She held her breath and looked back at the skull with unwavering eyes.

Then, before she knew what he was doing, he had moved his hand down to run it across her breasts and, with the other hand, grasped her between her legs. Now she did move, even as Figgins sprang up from her chair in the corner, and she gave Massetti a violent cuff to the cheek with her fist.

Figgins had turned into a ferocious nag. 'No, Miss, I mean Mr Hawkins, I won't be quiet. You can't do it, indeed you can't. It's bad enough to go jauntering about foreign parts dressed like a man, but to go on the stage! An opera dancer, there's no way anyone in your family will forgive you that.'

'I'm not going on stage as an opera dancer, but as an opera singer.'

'There's no difference, everyone knows what those women are. They show their legs and worse, and all the men are after them.'

'The men won't be after me, for I shan't show my legs, and they won't know I'm a woman.'

'Then you'll have the likes of Lord Lucius backstage, and if that isn't just as bad. Oh, dear, what are we do?'

'Go down on our knees and give a prayer of thanks,' Alethea said. 'I've no patience with you. Here is a way out of our present difficulties that is neither criminal nor immoral, and all you can do is protest about it.'

'Not immoral! How can you say that? Of course the stage is immoral.'

'I'm earning a living doing what I'm trained to do, which is to sing. God gave me a gift, and now, when we're in such trouble, it's going to save our skins. I want to hear no more about it. We must hurry, for Massetti wants me back to rehearse within the hour, and we must settle up with the apothecary.'

Figgins stopped dead. They were on a bridge, and Alethea took advantage of the pause to watch a boat carrying brilliantly coloured flowers, a floating flower garden, gliding silently beneath them. 'Now what's the matter?'

'Settle up with the apothecary? Where are we to sleep tonight?'

'In a house owned by Mr Massetti.'

'A house owned by . . . To be sure, I know what his game is, even if you don't. I shan't let you stay in his house, and that's my last word.'

'He doesn't live there. It is where he has rooms for his singers, the ones who come from other parts of Italy and have no home in Venice.'

'What, a lodging house full of opera dancers? Bringing back their fine bucks for a quick one-two? How you can think of it!'

'Singers, not dancers. There's a housekeeper, I'm sure it is all quite respectable. We are to share a room, you and I; naturally I can't share with either the men or the women, lest my secret should be discovered.'

'It didn't take him long to discover it, with his nasty hands roaming where they had no business to be.'

Alethea's first reaction, after the blow to ward the man's probing hands off, had been fury that her sex had been discovered, and that her plan to seek employment in the chorus at the opera house had come to nothing.

Salvatore Massetti had other plans, a scheme of his own. Had she studied the whole of Cherubino's part? Mozart of course was no particular draw these days, although there always was some audience for *Figaro*, for a good *Figaro*. It was a shame she was not a professional, when she could have sung Rossini or Spontini or Figlioni, all infinitely more popular composers than Mozart.

Nevertheless – and he stalked round her, examining her from every angle. 'It is indeed remarkable,' he said, 'that any young woman should look so like a boy. This is no doubt why English women are so cold, they are not truly women.'

Alethea, who hadn't found a woman's lot to be an agreeable one, didn't want to argue this point with the Italian. And there was some truth in what the man said, take herself, certainly as cold as ice where men were concerned. Napier had cured her of men for good.

Mozart it must be, and so the rate would be lower, and lower also because she was a woman. Had she been a true castrato – he cast his eyes heavenwards at this point and kissed his fingertips at the thought – then no sum would be too great. For one performance only, and there was the expense of coaching her for the role, not only the voice, but the acting, the moving on stage, there would naturally be a reduction.

Could she be ready in time? *La Cenerentola* had been announced for Friday, but his Don Ramiro had a bad cold, the substitute had a voice like a gondolier, and now he too was beginning to sniff. *Figaro* could be put on in its place, a spate of posters and word spread about the fashionable world, that word being castrato, should do the trick. He hoped she were up to it; even if she could only stand and sing, with that voice and a handkerchief stuffed in her breeches, then the audience would be pleased. Audiences today adored a novelty, and a freak was better still.

She must take great care that none of the company learned her secret, since they would spread the truth abroad if they knew it. Then the audience would fail to flock, the performance would be a disaster.

He turned clinical eyes on Figgins. 'Is he your lover, that he accompanies you everywhere?'

'She is my maid.'

A skull grimace, and a shake of the head, and then they had both been dismissed to find their new lodgings.

'Here we are,' said Alethea.

'Looks dirty to me,' said Figgins.

'It's a roof over our heads, and a bed each, and it's costing us nothing.'

'When's he going to pay you? You'll like as not go out and ruin your reputation for ever, should anyone ever find out, and when you've finished, he'll say he won't pay you. You won't be able to argue with him.'

'He's paying me some money at once. I told him I wouldn't do it otherwise, and that I'd have expenses.'

'Like what?'

'Like my costume. I have to find a costume for myself.'

'Costume?' said Figgins, grumbling up the cracked marble staircase behind the immense bottom of the housekeeper. 'What costume?'

'Man's dress of the last century, and a woman's dress also.'

Figgins looked around the tiny room, with a single bed, a sagging bed, a rickety washstand and a skylight of a window. 'Makes the apothecary's look like a palace, this does.'

'It's only for a few nights. Then we'll have money in our pockets, we can go back to the pensione and collect our bags, and find somewhere clean and cheap to await Camilla's return, or go on to Rome, just as we choose.'

'Clean and cheap! Fat chance of that, in this city. Now, what's this about a costume?'

Alethea perched herself on the other side of the bed, and

launched into a description of the plot of *The Marriage of Figaro*.

Figgins's eyes were like saucers. 'I never heard the like, what a wicked man that count was, to behave in such a way. I know many men of his kind, disgraceful coves. And this part you play, a page dressing up as a woman, and in love with the countess. Such goings on! How can you say it's more respectable than being an opera dancer?'

'I don't show my legs, you see. Or, at least I do, but clad in breeches. Perfectly proper.'

'There's nothing proper about you, Miss Alethea, and your dressing up as a man, and I've known it from the start.'

'Admit, Figgins, you've taken to being a man as though you were one of your brothers. Think of the freedom it gives you. And how pleasant not to be accosted by men.'

'How you can say such a thing, when we travelled in the company of Lord Lucius and that creepy valet of his, is what I don't understand. And it's been a shock, let me tell you. I'm used to men, what with the stables and brothers and all that, but what those men talk about among themselves, well, it'd make your toes curl.'

'I'm sure London will seem most dreadfully boring when you return there.'

'I return? I won't be returning without you go back as well, miss – sir – and that's flat. I've been turned away the once, but I'm not being got rid of again. Where you go, I go, and if you aren't returning to London just yet, then nor am I.'

'Oh, Figgins, don't say that. I may never be able to return to England. Women in my position often have to live out their lives in some spa town in France or Germany.' A foreign Bath, dowdy, respectable and dull.

'I don't see you settling down in no spa town, that's where all the gouty folk go for the cure. It wouldn't suit you one bit, and your family wouldn't stand for it.

'I do hope not,' said Alethea.

Chapter Twenty

Bootle stood before him, sleek, obsequious and triumphant.

'Are you sure about this?' said Titus. 'You tell me that Warren's man, Nyers, was in his cups, was not quite aware of what he was saying. You were companions in some tavern, were you drinking, too? Perhaps you were not quite aware of what you were hearing.'

This was unjust, and Titus knew it. Bootle was an abstemious man, especially when on what he perceived to be his duty, out and about on behalf of his master.

Bootle grew taller and thinner and more dignified. 'I would not so demean myself as to drink the brandy that Nyers was imbibing. I value a clear head in such circumstances and a little wine was quite sufficient to ensure that Nyers felt I was matching him glass for glass.'

'What had he to say in this drunken state that's of any concern to me? Servants' gossip, as you know, is not to my taste.'

'I am aware of that fact, sir. Nyers was bragging about how his master, Mr Warren, had acquired what he came to Italy to obtain, viz. a certain painting by an old master.'

'Both you and I know that is why Warren came to Italy, and you also know that we are here for the same purpose. Come to the point, Bootle. Which painting does Mr Warren have? Where is it? From whom did he acquire it?'

'It is at present in the possession of Mr Delancourt, the foreign person you honoured with a visit yesterday.'

Bootle's mouth twitched, and this faintest of movements revealed to Titus just how his valet's mind was working. He,

Titus, had spent an hour with Delancourt, and all the while the picture he so longed to find had, no doubt, been concealed on the premises. His Titian beauty, tucked away in a damp ground-floor room or behind a bundle of engravings in an attic.

Delancourt had, it seemed, taken Warren to wherever his place of concealment was, and had there concluded a bargain that the dealer must have known was a dubious one. If Delancourt's claim to the painting, as owner or go-between, had any vestige of validity, the painting would surely have been on show, inviting offers from the highest bidder.

Why had the Frenchman not tempted Titus with the picture, thus raising the eventual price he might be able to get for the painting? It was a question scarcely worth the asking. The oleaginous rascal knew perfectly well that Titus owned the picture, and would be unlikely to pay a further large sum of money for what his father had already bought.

Warren, with the king's name and wealth to support a collector's greed, was the kind of customer that men such as Delancourt dreamt of. The more secrecy, the better, no awkward questions to be asked or answered.

'Mr Warren is to arrange the transfer of funds immediately, so that the painting may be packed up. He plans to take it with him, back to England. Nyers has to make all the arrangements for the journey today. And I don't I wish him joy of it with the head he must have on his shoulders this morning,' added Bootle with righteous savagery.

Titus didn't hear these last words. He was lost in thought and temper. Curse Warren to hell and back again, for achieving the purpose of his visit so easily. He was no doubt full of self-satisfaction. He stood to gain a large sum of money and the goodwill of the king, all for the most trivial expenditure of effort. Well, he wasn't going to find it as easy as he imagined, not while Titus was in Venice.

'Of course, there is no knowing whether the painting Mr Warren buys is the one I'm looking for.'

Bootle's face took on a closed look. ' The goddess Venus, I believe, is the subject of the painting, clad in nothing very much as to garments. A harlot, Nyers called her. He said it was a depiction of a harlot displaying her wares.'

'Nyers's opinion is not of the least interest to me,' said Titus. He snapped his fingers for Bootle to bring him his coat. His valet eased it on to his wide shoulders, smoothing it down the back and setting a sleeve exactly to rights. Titus gave an angry shrug, the effect was ruined. Bootle sighed. That was what came of working for a master who had served in the army. Neat, yes, but nothing of the dandy about him.

'I know what you're thinking, Bootle,' said Titus. 'You're thinking how exquisite in his dress is Mr Warren. So would I be, if I didn't have better things to think about than a wrinkle in my pantaloons or a neck cloth a fraction of an inch out of true. Ask the major-domo if I may have use of Mr Hellifield's gondola, it will be quicker than walking.'

Up the steps of Palazzo Tullio again, and across to the entrance in the square, where a suave doorman bowed, refused him admittance, denied that Delancourt was within, relented on receipt of a coin, retired, returned with the same information, accompanied by a knowing smile. Which vanished swiftly from his face as Titus thrust him aside, flung open the door and stalked inside.

Delancourt was there, of course, as Titus knew he would be. He was not expecting a client, that was clear from the vast loose robe he wore and the cigarillo that he held between his fingers.

'My dear sir,' he said, waving Titus to a chair opposite the table upon which reposed a coffee pot and a small spirit stove. 'What an unexpected pleasure. However, I cannot be of much assistance to you this morning. I only see clients by appointment, as I am sure M. Hellifield explained to you. I need my hours of solitude to restore myself. Working with art takes a great deal out of oneself, as you will appreciate.'

There was a whiff of something in the air which Titus

couldn't quite identify. Then it was lost, as Delancourt attended to the spirit stove, which lit with a little whoosh and a splutter of noxious fumes. Delancourt flapped a pudgy hand. 'These are wonderful devices, I am such an admirer of all the benefits that science brings, but unfortunately, progress often means smells. It will pass, I assure you. Do you care for some coffee? Perhaps you like it made in the Turkish way.'

Titus didn't. He preferred his coffee strong and black, and considered the syrupy brew offered up in the coffee houses of Venice to be undrinkable. In any case, he didn't want to drink coffee with Delancourt, he wanted an explanation.

'You have sold a picture to Mr Warren. A Titian, I believe. A reclining Venus, with Cupid in the background.'

'Yes, indeed. One of several depictions of the goddess of love painted by Titian in his erotic period. The exquisite beauty of the flesh tints! I am sure you are familiar with the Diana and Actaeon, another of his masterpieces from those years.'

'I'm not concerned with other depictions of classical subjects. This particular painting does concern me, however, since I have reason to believe that it belongs to me. I have the paperwork for the original purchase, which was made by my father in Rome, eighteen years ago. There is a detailed description of the painting.'

'Ah, such troublesome years we have all lived through since then,' said Delancourt, with a profound sigh. 'The Emperor's triumphs and defeats, and all Europe in turmoil. So many possessions changed hands. Countries, land, houses, furniture, paintings, jewellery. All spoils of war, so disgraceful to men of culture such as we are, Monsieur Manningtree.' He made an eloquent waving gesture, which allowed the frills of an over-ruffled shirt to spill out of his robe. His voice grew a shade more silky. 'Besides, I understood that the Manningtree Titian hangs in your library, you told me so yourself. Did your late father then buy two Titians?'

'If you will permit me to see the painting, then I can assure myself that it is not my Titian. If it is, then I am sure the provenance I can provide will convince a reputable dealer such as yourself that the picture is not yours to sell.'

Delancourt shook his head, the picture of regret. 'Why do so many Englishmen lie to me? You have lied to me, Monsieur Manningtree. I was so happy to hear that your Titian was safe and sound in England. It is a pity that your father was unable to take the painting back to England at that time; of course, the circumstances were such that travel was an uneasy business.'

He sat back in his wide-armed chair, which made a loud creaking sound, and took a few slurping sips of his coffee. 'As to the painting which is the subject of our conversation, I bought it in good faith. I am afraid that it is impossible for you to inspect the canvas, I am desolated to say that it has already been packed up. And since I am well aware that the ultimate purchaser of this masterpiece is no less than a king, it would almost amount to treason for you to question the painting's ownership.'

'A fig for treason!' Titus was outraged. He had fought for king and country, and respected the institution of the monarchy, but he had not the least respect for the gross Hanoverian who presently sat on the throne in London. 'If the King buys, he buys as a private individual, such a painting is destined for his personal collection. It is a matter between gentlemen, not kings and subjects.'

'Such niceties are beyond me. I have a painting, I have sold it, I await the final payment, and then the whole business is out of my hands. Perhaps you might care to discuss it with Mr Warren. But for now ' – he leant forward and picked up a gleaming gold bell, which he tinkled vigorously – 'for now, I very much regret that I have to dress and must deprive myself of your amiable company. Guido will show you out. Good day to you, Monsieur Manningtree.'

'Well, if he don't care to let you get a peep at it, and he insists it's his to sell, I don't see what you can do about it,' said Harry, when Titus finally told him about the Titian.

Titus was lunching with his friend in another exquisite room, this one a blaze of cream and crimson and gold. 'It sounds to me,' Harry went on, 'as though Delancourt rolled you up, horse, foot and guns.'

'He wants the picture off his premises and into Warren's care as quickly as may be so that he can wash his hands of it,' Titus said. 'Mind you, he's as nervous as a cat about it, sweat breaking out all over him, quite revolting.'

'You can be a frightening fellow in a temper,' Harry observed. 'Or out of one if it comes to that. You've got such a devilish frown, and the sort of countenance that warns the most hardened villain to be on his guard.'

'Nonsense,' said Titus, annoyed. 'I do lose my temper from time to time, I admit, but other than that there is nothing threatening about me at all. I am the kindest of men.'

'No need to flare up at me. There's no one I'd sooner have beside me in a scrap, no, nor a friend I'd rather turn to if I were in difficulties, but then I've known you since we were boys, and Delancourt hasn't.'

'I'll have to have it out with Warren, that's all,' Titus said. 'I'd hoped to keep one step ahead of him, and prevent him ever getting near my Titian. Too bad that it hasn't worked out that way.'

'My people say he's not been back to his lodgings for a while. A servant there tells them he's gone to stay with friends elsewhere in the city.'

'You mean your men have lost him.'

'It does seem that he's given them the slip, yes,' Harry admitted. 'Which means that he probably noticed them watching him. Warren has a guilty conscience, not surprisingly. He is the kind of man who must always be up to mischief of one sort or another. He may not connect the watchers with his purchase of the painting at all, he may consider it prudent to be elsewhere for any number of reasons. He is bound to show up sooner or later.'

'His man says he's preparing to leave as soon as he has the painting in his hands.'

'The painting is still with Delancourt?'

'So Bootle said, after his conversation with Warren's servant.'

'Then my singularly useless people may redeem themselves by keeping a close watch on the Palazzo Tullio. Not a water rat to leave the premises without it is noticed. Is it a large canvas, your painting? One trusts it has not been removed and rolled up, in which case it will be a less bulky object.'

'Even rolled up, it would be hard to hide.' Titus, too, hoped Delancourt had no such intention; it would do an old painting like that no good at all to be removed from its stretcher and carried about in a roll. No, Warren wouldn't risk the chance of damaging anything so valuable, and why should he? Speed was what he counted on, speed and the advantages of having the painting in his possession, doubtless with a sheaf of genuine-seeming papers from Delancourt to satisfy any nosy customs official who chose to make an enquiry about it.

'Possess your soul in patience, my dear,' Harry said, watching his friend with laconic amusement. 'Like padding around after Wellington, skirting round the enemy, wondering if we'd ever come up to an actual battle.'

'Warren is hardly Marmot.'

'No, nor Soult. So take it all in your stride, Titus, take it in your stride. You are eager to have your Titian back, an understandable desire, but do not lose your sense of proportion. There is something middle-aged about lusting after a picture.'

'Harry, how dare you say such a thing?'

'A very beautiful woman, I dare say, but Venus herself on the wall isn't half so satisfying as a stirring beauty in the flesh. Talking of which,' he said, rising, 'I'm off for a pleasant hour or so with Cecilia. Come with me this evening to a masked ball; the company will be amusing, and you are certain to run into some old acquaintances.'

'A ball? I think not, my dancing days are behind me. And why a masked ball at this time of year? I thought the Venetians worked that out of their system at carnival time. Is that not in February or March?'

'How stuffy you are become. It is a masked ball because the Venetians love to dress up.'

'Well, I don't.'

'I tell you what it is, Titus: you're bored. You've got no outlet for that damned energy of yours. It's a pity you ever sold out, or that there isn't another war where you could fight yourself out of your fidgets.'

'Never pray for another war. We've had enough of war and bloodshed these last years, more than enough.'

'Even so, you need some purpose in life, even if it's merely slaying your fellow men.' Harry lifted a slender hand. 'No, no, do not frown at me, I know your distaste for the battlefield, and after Waterloo, who can blame you? Go back into politics, bloody a few noses in the House, for God's sake. Or take up a cause, anything to direct your attention in a more active way. This sniffing about after an old picture is not the way to spend your life. A passion for collecting, such as your Governor had, why, that's a different matter.'

'Leave me alone, Harry. I've done with war, I've done with politics, and all I want is to thwart the king's lust to possess my Titian.'

'There's no reasoning with a man who has a maggot in his head.'

'Besides, I have no mask.'

Lights, colour, smells from the canal mingling with candle wax and the scents of humanity, perfumed and powdered humanity. Titus, resplendent in a dark green coat and silk breeches, and taller by a head than most of the men present, stared out over the restless throng of guests. He took a glass of wine from a passing servant and lingered by a deep window overlooking the canal. It was still busy, even at this time in the evening, when shadows had fallen over the city and torches flared by the steps of the palaces and houses lining the sides of the canal.

He felt a light touch on his arm, and turned to find a woman, not young, by the look of her neck, but with amused, ageless eyes glinting through a velvet mask. 'Mr Manningtree, alone, in Venice? How is this possible?'

Titus made his bow. 'Your servant, ma'am.' He'd have known that voice anywhere. How well Lady Hermione Wytton was looking. She must be well past fifty, no, nearer sixty, but her eyes still held the sparkle that had made her, so his father had told him, the toast of the town when she was a young married woman in London. The Wyttons were Titus's closest neighbours in Herefordshire. He had known Lady Hermione all his life, and been somewhat afraid of her ever since he was in short clothes.

'Harry Hellifield told me you were here. Tell me why you are in Venice. Have you run away from London on account of Emily's marriage? I was astounded when I heard about it, and of course the polite world is, or pretends to be, shocked, yet I think it will answer very well. Emily is not the kind of woman to dwindle into comfortable widowhood. I dare say you might have married her, but that would be too much excitement in her life, she will be better with a more even-tempered husband.'

There it was again, first Harry, now Lady Hermione passing remarks on his temper. He took it amiss, he really did.

'No, never look so darkly at me, for if I can't say these things to you, who can? Now, let us find you an enchanting companion to ease the ache in your heart.'

'I assure you, there is no ache.'

'So much the better, then you can flirt desperately with all the prettiest women. How did you leave your brother?'

'He was well when last I saw him, which I admit was a while ago.'

'It is such a pity that he married such a poor creature as Christabel, and it's a miracle that the boys are turning out so well.'

'She is a good mother, I believe.'

'She is a guileful woman.' While she spoke, Lady Hermione's eyes were darting about the room. 'There is Lady Mesurier, you must know her, in the cat's face mask, what a good choice. Or can I introduce you to Valentina Heybrook, she of the feathers and beak? She is a charmer, only her husband is inclined to be jealous, and you are looking so handsome this evening, it might not be wise.'

'As to charm . . .' Titus said, his face breaking into the smile that wiped all trace of severity from it and caused several ladies in the vicinity to flutter their fans and widen their eyes at him. Lady Hermione had more charm than any woman of his acquaintance, that rare gift of the gods that outlasted beauty and rank and defied any ravages that age might bring.

Despite himself, despite his wrath at Warren's underhandedness and Delancourt's two-facedness, Titus found he was enjoying the occasion. There was a vitality here that he hadn't expected, for his view of Venice was a jaundiced one. He saw it as a gorgeous but dying city, whose attractions had faded with her power; he could see no future for Venice, once the greatest maritime power of her day, in a world torn asunder by revolution. The Palace where centuries of Doges had ruled was left bare-walled and empty ceilinged by the rapacious greed of the invaders; the great chambers where powerful men had held court and sat in judgement and schemed and planned and plotted were deserted now, nothing there but the ghosts of red-robed figures who had once held an empire in their hands.

Yet here was life and movement and laughter, music and

graceful figures, a moment captured out of time, perhaps, a reflection of a happier and more glorious age.

'So pensive, Titus?' said a soft Italian voice at his elbow.

'Paolo, by all that's wonderful,' Titus said, shaking a mask of comedy warmly by the hand. 'What are you doing here? I thought you were settled in Vienna for the duration. How is diplomacy?'

The man swung his mask, which he carried on a stick, aside from his face. 'As tedious as ever, and your handshake is the same formidable one I remember. Pray do me a favour, and greet me with a bow when next we meet. It is not enough that you tower over me, but you have to crush the life from my bones as well.'

Titus looked down at the slight man, who had a face like a wicked faun, with great benevolence. 'I was reflecting on Venice.'

'Alas, she is somewhat bedraggled, a woman past her prime, still clinging to vestiges of beauty. I am not a Venetian, so I can regard this without emotion. For me, there is altogether too much water around Venice. I do not care for the sea, and these canals are depressing to the spirits. And the Venetians! They are a subtle race, intrigue is in their blood; one can never get a straight answer from a Venetian.'

'Diplomats do not generally deal in straight answers, I believe.'

'Ah, we live behind masks much more effective in their disguises than these we see tonight. What brings you to Venice, Titus?'

'A woman.'

The faun's eyebrows rose. 'A woman? This is not like you. Last time we met – it was in London, at a rout, such a crush, such bad food, I left early – you were in company with Emily Thruxton.'

'She was widowed and has remarried. An Italian.'

'So now you come to Italy in search of an Italian of your

own? Or is it a fellow countrywoman who is the object of your pursuit?'

'She is a Venetian.'

'Present now?' said Paolo, interested.

'I'm afraid not.'

A thought had struck Titus. 'Paolo, have you encountered a Mr Darcy in Vienna? Mr Fitzwilliam Darcy?'

'Oh, that one, what a man, how formidable, the kind of controlled and clever Englishman that frightens us on this side of the Channel. So reserved, so keen-witted. With a delightful wife. Yes, he is attached to the legation for some months. We shall all be happier when he departs for his native shores, and is replaced by a more stupid man.'

Paolo was about to add something, when his attention was caught by a slim, elegant creature in a golden half-mask, who put a hand through the Italian's arm and whispered into his ear. He vanished into the crowd, and Titus was drawn into the dance that was just starting by the ruthless tactics of his hostess, a woman he had exchanged bows with on his arrival, who showed herself to be as bossy as any of the patronesses at Almacks as she presented a young woman with flaming hair and a beribboned mask to him as his partner.

He took it in good part, not least because while his partner's face might be covered, her white bosom was mostly exposed, and he dwelt on her plump form with satisfaction and appreciation.

'Look, but don't touch,' Harry murmured into his ear as they passed one another in the dance. 'She's a Pisani, and the families in the Golden Book guard their womenfolk jealously.'

Titus's private opinion was that the Signorina Pisani was more than a match for any fathers or brothers who might try to control her. Immuration in a convent might restrain her, but not any masculine moral disapproval, he felt sure. She was lively, conversable in delightful broken English as well as in Italian, flirtatious and more than capable of arousing Titus's ardour, menfolk or no menfolk.

Disappointment, as she was swept away at the end of the dance by an Italian nobleman with flashing eyes and a rakish smile, whose company she clearly intended to enjoy.

'Cut out by another Italian,' Titus said to Harry.

Harry laughed. 'The night is young, and also hot. If you have had enough of dancing, I propose a stroll, to calm the fevered brow and spirits.'

Titus looked around at the jostling, murmuring, brilliantly coloured throng of dancers and onlookers. 'A moment, while I find Lady Hermione.'

'There you are out of luck, I observed her leaving some thirty minutes since.'

'I can call on her tomorrow, I suppose.'

'Today,' Harry said, taking his friend's arm and guiding him from the ballroom, nodding and bowing to his numerous acquaintances as he went. 'It is past three.'

'Is it really?' said Titus as they came out of the stuffy rooms into air that was hardly less hot. 'There is no coolness in the air.'

'We are in for a thunderstorm, so the fishermen say, but not yet.'

Moonlight gleamed and danced in the water, the moon riding so high and clear in the sky that its beams reached even the darkest and most shadowy of the canals they crossed in a meandering walk across the quiet city.

'Only whores and malefactors abroad at this hour,' said Harry. 'And revellers such as ourselves. The citizens of Venice dine and retire early.'

Whores there certainly were, standing in doorways and advancing to accost the two of them. Coaxing suggestions of unrivalled pleasures to be had, offers of reduced rates for the pair of them and curses when they walked on, unmoved, rent the air. The Rialto bridge was astir with gaudily attired women, flashing bosoms and legs at passers-by, and equally so with slim, beautiful youths in tight breeches, showing rippling muscles beneath smooth skin.

'All tastes catered for,' Harry said. 'I would not advise you to keep company with any of these, however. Should your ardour be high, let me recommend one of the better *casini*, where the women are prettier and cleverer in conversation as well as the arts of love.'

Titus scowled. 'I don't want to lie with a whore.'

'No, you want to lie with Emily, but you cannot, and I do not suppose you intend to embark on a lifetime's celibacy on account of that.'

'Androgyny is a strange thing,' Titus remarked, as a slender figure stepped out in front of them. 'Put that youth in a fine dress and mask, and you would take him for a woman. Or it may be that he is in fact a she, a woman pretending to be a man to attract a man who likes men but who is only satisfied with a woman. How close the sexes sometimes come to one another. It is as much a matter of behaviour and the sphere in which they move that separates the masculine part of humanity from the feminine.'

'What nonsense,' said Harry. 'Are you saying that you cannot distinguish a man from a woman?'

'I'm saying that besides women who are always unmistakably women, there are others just as female in their nature and desires, who may pass for a man while they are young. Just as that effeminate youth we passed a few paces back could, as I said, pass as a woman in any light.'

Harry shook his head. 'You have drunk too much wine, your judgement is warped.'

'I have known such a case,' Titus said. 'Of a young woman passing herself off as a man, with complete success.'

'She deceived you?'

'Not I, for I knew her as a girl.'

'You haven't taken up cradle-snatching, have you, Titus?'

'No, I have not; my tastes do not in the least run in that direction, I'm thankful to say. The person of whom I speak is none of those, she is as well-born as you or I.'

'Never say so! Who is this freak? She is surely not an

Englishwoman. Why does she wish to pass herself off as a man? How do her family permit it?'

Titus could hear the zest for scandal in his friend's voice, and he laughed. 'I shan't say any more about her.'

'There's sluttishness in the soul of any woman who would stoop to such a trick,' Harry said, annoyed.

Titus whirled round on him. 'You know nothing about it. There is courage and bravery and foolhardiness, yes, but there is nothing of the slut about her at all. That isn't the game she plays; in fact she plays no game at all.'

'You intrigue me,' said Harry after a moment's silence. 'I see that she has intrigued you, this minx of yours.'

'She has done no such thing. I merely spoke of her in the context of my musing on androgyny.'

'Where is this marvel of nature?'

'I have no idea, I have no interest in her beyond remarking upon the success with which she carries her disguise. I doubt if we shall ever meet again; our encounter was the result of chance, no more.'

The minute the words were out of his mouth, he hated himself for uttering them. It felt as though he were forswearing Alethea, and it hurt him to the quick to do so. Damn it, what did it matter? It was the truth. Alethea Darcy – or Napier as she was, of course – was up to some scheme of her own, a desperate affair, he must assume. It was nothing to do with him.

For a horrid moment, the figure of Mr Darcy appeared in his mind's eye: tall, cold and accusing.

To hell with Mr Darcy; if he had brought up his daughters to behave so imprudently, so hoydenishly, or had permitted one of them to marry a man like Napier, then he must bear the blame for the consequences.

'Observe the exotic carving.' Harry waved his quizzing glass to a relief of a man who at first glance appeared to have a third leg between his other two.

'Good lord,' said Titus, his laughter echoing across the water.

'Note his companion, she has a flame between her legs. I told you we were come into the lewdest part of town.'

'It would never be permitted in London, not in such a public place.'

'England is, as ever, a puritan country. Venice has often felt the need to encourage what it considers the right end of lust; too many Venetian men have in times past preferred the company of their own sex. But we are back to the forbidden subject of androgyny once more. If we walk through here, we shall soon be home.'

He ducked through a dark arch, shouldering aside a man who slouched towards them, and led the way at considerable speed through a maze of narrow streets that opened unexpectedly into silent squares, the flagstones and walls washed into an eerie paleness by the moonshine.

As they crossed one such square, Harry paused by the marble well in the centre and waved up to a set of lighted square windows. Titus could see a crystal chandelier ablaze with candles, a painted ceiling, and hear voices, music, laughter.

'A *casino*,' said Harry. 'One of the most elegant, only the most ravishing girls work there. Are you not tempted?'

'No,' said Titus.

'The trouble with you is that you're heartsick, not loinsick. It's a dangerous state to be in.'

'Because I don't fancy a night with a whore? You draw your conclusions too swiftly, you know nothing about my heart. Nor do I, for it's not anything I ever think about. I'm not some sentimental youth languishing for love.'

'Here's a fellow is much the worse for love,' said Harry.

A man emerged from the ground floor of the *casino*, escorted by a liveried servant. He balanced himself for a moment against the pillar beside the door and then launched himself on a wavering path across the square.

'By God, it's George Warren, as I live,' exclaimed Harry. 'What's he cradling there, is it a bottle?'

'No, a shoe,' said Titus, as Warren drew nearer. 'Hey, Warren, a word with you!'

Harry caught his arm. 'Leave him alone, Titus. He's drunk.'

'*In vino veritas*.'

Warren stopped and stood swaying, his hand, clutching a lady's shoe, dropped down by his side. His face was flushed and his eyes bright. 'Titus Manningtree, or am I so foxed that I'm seeing visions?'

'You aren't. I'm glad to meet up with you, Warren.'

'Can't return the compliment. Don't want to meet up with you. Not now, not ever, not anywhere. I bid you goodnight, gentlemen.'

Before he could reel on his way, Titus had hold of him. 'Not so fast. You're in no state to make your way home alone. Pray tell us your direction, and we will accompany you to your door.'

Harry uttered a protest, but Titus ignored him. Warren looked at him, and his lip curled. 'My direction? I think not.' He tried to shake Titus off, but Titus's grasp held firm, and forced the drunken man round to face him.

'I want my picture, Warren.'

'Picture?'

'My Titian. The painting you have acquired from Mr Delancourt was not his to sell. It is mine, and I want it.'

'Go to hell, Manningtree. Or back to cloud cuckoo land where you must have come from.'

'Amazing,' put in Harry, 'being able to get that out when he's intoxicated.'

'He's not half as disguised as he makes out,' said Titus. 'Just worked up over that damned shoe.'

Warren waved the shoe in the air. 'This belongs to Flavia, who has the prettiest foot in all Venice. In all Italy! Do you malign her fair name? I'll meet you for that, Manningtree.'

'Don't be absurd. Is my painting still with Delancourt?'

Warren sobered up again, and gave a titter of laughter. 'Wouldn't you like to know, and don't I wish you may go there and ask for it again. Delancourt will be waiting for you this time, and he don't like troublemakers, I tell you that for nothing.'

'There's no point in you taking that painting back to England, Warren, for I will dispute its ownership every inch of the way.'

'What, with the king? I doubt it. Anyhow, he knows it belongs to you, or rather, belonged to your father, because I told him so, and he don't give a damn. Nor do I. All's fair in love and war, Manningtree, and that painting's a spoil of war.'

'That for your damned impertinence,' said Titus. His rage rose in him, and he gave Warren a back-handed slap across his cheek, making such a resounding noise that the girls at the windows above, who had crowded to watch the altercation in the square, exclaimed and cried shame on him.

Warren wrenched himself free, flung aside the shoe and made to pull his sword. Titus's hand was already on the hilt of his own weapon, when Harry pounced on him and dragged him back. Servants were spilling out of the *casino*, and two of them caught hold of Warren. One pinned his arms behind his back, the other took possession of his sword.

'You can't fight here,' Harry was saying to Titus. 'You'll land yourself in jail. They don't like sword fights in public places, and the magistrates will have no mercy on a pair of Englishmen. Put up your sword, no, put it up, I say, and listen to reason.'

'Reason!' spat a struggling, breathless Warren. 'I'll have reason of him. Name your seconds, sir, and then we'll see who has reason on their side.'

'Harry?'

Harry groaned. 'For God's sake, Titus, let it go.'

'Oh, no, Hellifield. You shan't get him out of this. He struck me across the face, you saw it. On no provocation. I want satisfaction, and by God I shall have it. Swords or pistols, Manningtree, I can make an end of you equally well with either.'

'That is for the seconds to agree,' Harry said quickly. Titus understood why: Harry knew Warren for a famous swordsman, while he supposed Titus would have a better chance with pistols.

'I can cool his blood with a bullet as well as with a sword,' said Warren. 'My supporters will call upon you later today, Hellifield, and then we'll have an end to this.'

'I do believe he means to kill you,' Harry complained at breakfast much, much later that morning. 'A surly fellow, barely worthy of being called a gentleman came by while you were still sleeping, demanded to see me, said he hoped Mr Manningtree wasn't shy, as an apology wouldn't be accepted.'

'I've no intention of apologising,' said Titus. 'Any apology due must come from him. Moreover, apologies are beside the point. The matter may be resolved by his returning my painting.'

'I do not believe he sees it in quite those terms. And I believe you are longing to let blood, and his will do as well as anyone else's. So much for the savagery of war being behind you. To fight over a painting, I never heard of anything more absurd.'

Titus rose from the table. 'Where and when do we meet?'

Harry sighed. 'What a bore all this is. We have arranged, this unsavoury friend of Warren's and myself, that you are to meet at a spot near the Arsenale, a deserted spot since Bonaparte's men sacked the place. You may escape the notice of the authorities there, and I hope you do, for the Austrians rule here, remember, and they frown on duels in the city.'

'Austrians are always duelling.'

'That is different. You aren't Austrian, nor is Warren. It is to be pistols. I've a pair you may borrow, since I don't suppose you thought to bring duelling pistols with you.'

'When should I be ready?'

'The gondola will be here at half past five in the evening.'

'There will be shadows at that time.'

'Better than under a noonday sun.'

'Who's the little man like a monkey?' Titus asked, as he tucked his stock more firmly inside his coat. Buttoned tightly into it, he was shelteringly hot and he found to his dismay that sweat was trickling down into the palms of his hands.

'The surgeon,' said Harry.

He was carrying a flat case beneath his arm, and he now approached the man standing on Warren's right. They drew apart, and Harry laid the case on a plinth that had once held a statue. Titus watched him flip open the lid of the gun case and draw out a pair of long-barrelled pistols.

The world about him seemed to have slowed to an unreal pace. A gull flapped from the balustrade of the stairs over the canal; with such leisurely wings, how could it keep aloft? A clock in the distance struck the quarter, but the sound of the bell stretched out across minutes. A sandalo came past, an oarsman at each end, working their oars as though in a dream where time counted for nothing. They looked curiously at the figures in the table on the patch of waste ground, heads moving round in slow motion, soundless words coming from their lips as they commented on the scene to each other.

Then time played her next trick, speeding up so that he could hardly draw breath. Harry was beside him, handing him a pistol, the other second was pacing out the distance, gulls were mewing, a gondola flashed past, a streak of black, the gondolier ducking his head as the boat shot under the bridge before vanishing. Harry spoke staccato words of encouragement and warning, the pistol was in his hand, hot and heavy, a purple cloud billowed up from behind the walls of the Arsenale and blotted out the sun.

Titus shook his head, trying to restore a sense of order to the minutes. He glanced down at his gun, and saw that his hand was holding it so tightly that it shook. He prised his fingers away, and shook them, then wrapped them around the pistol butt again, weighing the balance of the weapon. His feet carried him to the spot indicated by Harry, he turned mechanically sideways, the gun at his side. The surly man swept a grubby handkerchief into the air, where it fluttered like a dying bird before he dropped it and the gun went off in Titus's hand.

A bullet screamed past his ear, and then time stopped again. Paces away, Warren sank to the ground, his hand holding his arm, blood seeping through the fingers. Titus could see the blood fall to the ground, drip, drip, drip.

He could smell blood all around him, the blood of men and of horses. His eyes were raw from the smoke, his throat dry and choked, his hands raw and blistered. Around him men cried out and horses screamed and the guns sounded, over and over, the guns that had begun firing on the day God made the world and would never stop.

'Titus.' Harry's voice was urgent in his ear. 'Titus, you're shaking like a leaf. Here, have some brandy.'

Titus tried to shake his head, but the flask was at his lips and the spirit searing down his gullet, startling him back into the present.

'Have I killed him?'

'No, unless he dies from loss of blood; he's bleeding like a pig, but the surgeon will attend to that. You caught him on the arm, did you mean to hit him?'

Had he? Duellers were more likely to harm an opponent by not aiming at them than by taking careful aim, duelling pistols were temperamental weapons, and hardly accurate, even in the hands of a master shot. Yet he had had murder in his heart when he struck Warren across the face, and murder in his mind when he raised the pistol.

For what? For a painting! For a tawdry few square feet of canvas, a two-dimensional image of a pagan goddess, Titian's whore, people said. A thing of beauty, but to take a man's life in cold blood on account of a picture was irrational, pointless, chillingly futile.

Warren was sitting up, now, supported by the surgeon. He was pale, and his eyes were closed.

'He'll live,' Harry said.

'Thank God,' said Titus. 'I've killed enough men in my life. Christ knows why I should take it upon myself to hustle another out of this world.'

'He wronged you.'

'He annoyed me. Is that a reason to take a life? Let him have the picture, let the king hang it in some private chamber and lick his lips as he goes past his goddess. I want none of it. This whole affair has been a wild-goose chase of the most extreme kind. What a fool I have made of myself!'

Titus kissed Lady Hermione's hand.

'I'm happy to see you, Titus,' she said. 'Come and sit by the window, where there is more air, such a sultry day. My dear man, how tired you look. The hot weather doesn't suit many Englishmen, I know, although with your service in Spain, I would have thought—'

'It isn't the heat, ma'am,' said Titus. 'I slept ill last night, that is all.'

He had, in truth, passed a wretched night. Waves of regret over losing his temper with Warren and wounding him mingled with nightmares of his fighting days, and through all his bad dreams, he was searching, desperately and in vain for someone. At first, in his half-dazed state he had thought it was his Titian beauty, but in the early hours, sitting on the side of the bed, spangled with moonlight and with his tousled head in his hands, he realised that the elusive figure was Alethea.

How could he simply let her walk away and make no effort to ensure that she reached her destination safely? There was no reason to suppose she wouldn't, but then the image of Mr Darcy rose in his mind again, severe and condemnatory. He had been so obsessed with his Venus that he had failed as a human being. Alethea was in trouble, or she would not be running across Europe in trousers. Had he made any real effort to find out what kind of trouble? No, he had assumed an unhappy marriage, an adulterous affair; he had made no attempt to get at the truth of her situation.

She would have resented his trying to ascertain what had happened to goad her into this wild scheme; she was, he suspected, a private person, disinclined to pour out her woes to others. None the less, he could have tried, and he hadn't. He made up his mind. As soon as it was *convenable*, he would call upon Lady Hermione and learn whereabouts in the city her son resided. Then he would pay a visit and if it embarrassed Alethea to encounter a witness of her unconventional disguise, that was unfortunate, but would not deter him.

He might well find they were all gone to Vienna; Camilla Wytton could have decided that her father was the best person to deal with Alethea's problems. Only he was of another generation, and Alethea's behaviour was so very shocking; might not an affectionate sister want to keep this information from their father?

'I want to call upon Alexander while I'm in Venice,' he said to Lady Hermione. She had ordered glasses of the light white Veneto wine that everyone drank in Venice, a chilled and refreshing beverage on such a day, and he was drinking his gratefully.

Lady Hermione put down her glass. 'I am sorry to tell you that you have missed him. He is gone to Rome, with Camilla, for a visit of some weeks.'

He was relieved, if a little disappointed. 'I should have made my visit sooner, when I arrived in Venice.'

'When was that?'

'Ten days ago.'

She shook her head. 'Then you were too late in any case, he and Camilla left a fortnight ago.'

Chapter Twenty-one

Entering the theatre, Alethea crossed into another world, of music and gossip, glitter and sweat, harmony and backbiting. An artificial world, the stage a little place of its own within the larger arena of the auditorium, and quite disconnected from the sun-soaked streets outside the theatre.

It was a ridiculous, gruelling enterprise. She was not in vocal practice, not after her time on the road. The San Benedetto was a huge theatre, and not all her work with Silvestrini had prepared her for such demands on her voice. She had the voice, that was admitted grudgingly by even the least enthusiastic of her fellow thespians, but did she have the stamina?

For a castrato, they whispered, the voice was undeveloped. In her few snatched hours of rest, Alethea explained this to Figgins, who was severe and disapproving at men singing women's roles, women dressing up in men's breeches to entertain the crowd, and of the foreign idea of men being emasculated to preserve their boyish voices.

'It isn't done at all these days, the few remaining castrati are older men.'

'If men you can call them . . .' Figgins said with a sniff.

'The quality of the castrato voice lies in the combination of a boy's high, pure voice with the physique, the lungs and chest of a grown man.'

'How came these men to be eunuchs? Were they captured by pirates and cut?'

'It is an operation, on a boy of nine or so, a simple incision is enough.'

More sniffs. 'Then it's a pity it's going out of fashion, for it would be doing women a favour for many men to lose their balls.'

Alethea wasn't sure of the anatomical details of castrati. 'I believe, that although they are unable to get children, some of them—'

Figgins lifted her hands. 'No, tell me nothing more about them. But if they can have the pleasure without the consequences, we'll need to lock this door, I know what kind of women those opera singers and dancers are.'

Which was more than Alethea did, for she was, and felt, a complete outsider. The only bond she shared with the other singers was music. Otherwise, she was an intruder, a foreigner, an inexperienced non-professional interloper, a sexual freak, a favourite of Massetti's, and, however friendly she was, of quite another rank. Not all her goodwill or acting ability could wipe away the years of upbringing in an English great house, as the daughter of a rich man.

Her knowledge of the Venetian dialect of Italian increased greatly, although most of her new vocabulary was of a kind that could never be used in polite society. Half the singers and dancers and musicians regarded her with obvious distaste, if with a morbid curiosity as to what there was within her slightly baggy trousers, while the other half took a prurient interest in her genderless state, and considered her fair game.

She owed much to Massetti's uncanny ability to appear whenever situations promised to get out of hand. And for his swift decisions when it came to her garbing herself in women's clothes in her role as the page. He provided a screen, and was invariably there to keep curious onlookers at bay.

Alethea had never worked so hard in her life, had never finished a day so utterly exhausted. Thank God for the theatricals she and her sisters had revelled in during those distant Pemberley days, when most holidays saw productions of scenes from Shakespeare or whole plays from contemporary authors when time allowed. She had always enjoyed being before an audience, and although too young to take on key roles, had learned much from watching and copying the one or two really talented actors that their neighbourhood afforded.

Her head buzzed with Mozart's music, her own part and everyone else's. She moved and sang and ate and slept as though in a dream, while the intrigues and strains of life in the count's house became more real than her own life. For the first time she began to realise what the opera was about, that the ravishing music was more than just that, that the whole work was a profound and searing commentary on the nature of men and women and marriage. Which only made the hours more unreal and more tiring, for her own experience of marriage had been so entirely out of the sun that she had never stopped to think what marriage might really be about.

It took a while for Massetti to coax her out of her English reserve. 'You sing like a virgin, like an English spinster,' he complained to her privately. 'Yet you are no virgin.'

How did he know?

'How old are you, seventeen, eighteen? Then you can enter into Cherubino's passion, his for women, as yours is for a man, or men. You look scared, put out of your mind the memory of the men who have mistreated you and given you a distaste for their sex, and remember the time when you loved without fear or unhappiness.'

Alethea shifted unhappily, what gave him this perception into her amorous experience?

'Ardour is what we must see in Cherubino, he is a wicked boy, desperate for every woman he encounters, he is shameless in his wooing and his desires. Prim and reserved will not do; you are in Italy now, a country of warmth and passion.'

'I'm not prim.'

'You are cold, and the voice is too pure and therefore unreal and unconvincing. You are on stage now, you have to perform, there can be no holding back. The role demands heart, passion; the notes, however beautiful, are not enough.'

So she unwillingly dragged up the passion she had felt for Penrose, the ardent yearning, the whole-heartedness of young love. She found it curiously cathartic, how odd that one should be able to make emotions come and go at one's bidding, that the bitter feelings engendered by her marriage to Napier could be put aside when she summoned the remembrance of her attachment to Penrose, and poured it into the music.

'Now you sing,' Salvatore Massetti said with approval. 'Like this, you move the audience's heart, and that is what they are paying for.'

No, it isn't, Alethea said inwardly. The audience was paying to stare at a prodigy.

Titus strode along the narrow streets, bounded up and down the steps of the steeply arched bridges, a man in a hurry, citizens remarked as he swept past them. The heat came back at him from the walls as though he were walking through a furnace; he was quite unaware of the temperature, so intent was he on reaching his destination.

He wasn't entirely sure what purpose going to Wytton's house would serve, but it was a starting place. Ten days ago, Alethea must have been there. Perhaps a servant had stayed behind in the house, a housekeeper who had taken Alethea in to await the return of her sister and brother-in-law. In any event, it was the last place he knew Alethea to have been, it was there that he must enquire for her.

No housekeeper responded to his violent tugs on the bell pull, nor to his thunderous knocks on the door. After a few minutes, he desisted and stood back, shading his eyes to look up at the shuttered windows.

From a balcony next door came a voice, asking him whom he sought, saying that the only residents of that house were

Signore and Signora Wytton, who were at present away from Venice.

Titus thanked her for the information. He was seeking an acquaintance of the Wyttons, a young man who would have called some ten days ago.

'An Englishman, like yourself?' Yes, she remembered him quite clearly, a very young man, accompanied by a servant. He had been much cast down at the Wytton's absence, he was a relative, she understood. She had suggested that he try for lodgings near by, but as to whether he had taken the advice, she could not say. Titus might enquire there, if he wished, it wasn't far, the Pensione Donata, two streets away, over the bridge and to his left by the mask-maker's shop.

Titus followed the directions and found the pensione, a building with a faded and crumbling façade, but a clean entrance way and a respectable-looking if glum-faced landlady. His heart rose; if Alethea were here, she might be safe enough.

Two sentences were sufficient to disabuse him of any such hopes. He was English, too, was he? Like that rogue of a young man who'd flitted owing two nights' rent, and his baggage worthless, no more than a thief, she was sure, else why would he have a woman's dress rolled up in his portmanteau, yes, and another one in the servant's bag. No, she had no idea where he might be, if she had she'd have sent her son after them to get her money.

Nonplussed by this flood of ill-will, Titus stepped back into the street, trying to gather his wits together. Alethea had been here, but not for more than a week. By the sound of it, all her possessions were here. What had happened to her? What ill fortune had taken her from the shelter and safety of the Pensione Donata? She had seemed to be in funds, was it merely that her money had run out, that she only had enough to reach Venice and no more?

His blood ran cold at the thought of the perils a young woman without money or friends would be exposed to in a city like Venice. How could she contrive? She must have other acquaintances in the city, have blown discretion to the winds and asked for assistance.

In which case, why had she not returned to pay her bill and collect her possessions, or sent her servant? Unpaid bills never loomed large in the minds of young gentlemen, he knew, but she wasn't a gentleman, and she would surely want her portmanteau returned to her.

Or maybe not, if it contained men's clothes. He knocked once more on the door of the pensione. The landlady frowned out at him, what extraordinary eyebrows she had, to be sure, and made as though to slam the door in his face. An intention that changed rapidly at the sight of money in his hand. No, she hadn't yet disposed of the young scoundrel's baggage, although she was going to do so as soon as she had a moment to spare. The money owing? She named a modest sum, adding an amount for her inconvenience, Titus was sure, and he counted it out into her outstretched hand.

The door shut in his face, and then, a few moments later, an upstairs window opened and a leather portmanteau that he recognised as being Alethea's sailed out, only just missing him as it landed with a thump. It was followed by a canvas bag and the triumphant clash of shutters closing.

Hot, alarmed, and cursing himself for letting Alethea's welfare concern him so much, Titus arrived back at Harry's palazzo, and handed over the portmanteau and bag to a surprised servant, with orders to convey both items to his room.

The Signore was at home, he had company.

The last thing Titus wanted was to be in company. He began to mount the stairs.

The Signore had requested that Signore Manningtree should join him when he returned.

Cursing, Titus followed another servant into the wide, high-ceilinged room on the second floor.

'Here you are, Titus,' Harry said, raising his hand in

greeting. 'Champagne for Mr Manningtree, he is hot and exhausted. What have you been up to, dear fellow? Here is Lady Hermione come to call.'

And there she was, cool and composed and looking rather amused.

'Such a fire-eater as you are, Titus,' she said. 'You never told me that you'd been out at dawn to meet your man.'

'It was in the evening,' said Titus, flushing with vexation that word of the affair had so quickly got around.

'In Venice, we all know each other's business,' she said. 'And it was a public affair, not a sneaking off to the mainland to kill a man and flee the repercussions.'

'I am profoundly grateful that I merely winged Warren,' said Titus, taking the proffered glass of champagne, an exquisite, slender glass ornamented with gold that set off the foaming, chilled wine. 'Your health, ma'am. It was a stupid business, and one that I feel ashamed of. My hope is that it will be soon forgotten.'

'Oh, yes, certainly, as soon as the next scandal comes along,' said Lady Hermione tranquilly. 'You left in such haste this morning, that's why you omitted to tell me of the duel, I dare say.'

'Hardly a fit subject for a lady's ears.'

'How pompous you are become,' she said. 'I'm not a squeamish modern miss, I thank you. My husband was forever fighting duels when I first knew him; I was heartily glad when they began to go out of fashion. So dangerous, for one may be killed, or kill the other man, and then there is so much distress and trouble. What had Warren done to rouse your ire? It was over a woman, rumour says, but that is what rumour always says.'

'We fell out over a painting,' said Titus. 'However, I wish that you will keep that information to yourself; it does neither of us much credit.'

'A painting! You cannot be serious.'

'He is, he is,' said Harry. He waved to the servant to fill

Titus's glass again. 'I admit, I never heard of men meeting over a painting, but there is a first time for everything. The fact is, Titus's father owned a painting which was unfortunately in Italy and not in England, and Warren came to Venice to buy it illicitly, knowing full well that it belonged to the Manningtree family.'

'A special painting, one assumes.'

'A Titian.'

'A Titian! Indeed, and in whose possession in Venice was this painting?'

'One Mr Delancourt, a dealer in such works,' said Titus.

'What does Warren want with such a picture? I never heard of him as a collector of paintings?'

'He was buying on behalf of the king.'

'I see, which makes it all so awkward. This painting, was it one of Titian's voluptuous nudes? I can't imagine Prinny, the King as we must now call him, longing to possess one of Titian's religious masterpieces.'

'It is a Venus, a reclining Venus.'

'With no clothes on, and a very come-hither expression on her eyes and that Titian coloured hair? With a blue riband around her neck, and behind her Cupid at a window and a bird in a cage beside a mirror?'

Titus stared at her. 'You know the painting?'

'I caught a glimpse of such a painting in Delancourt's establishment when I was there some three or four weeks ago. It was propped on an easel, with a young man painting away.'

It took a moment or two for her words to sink in. Painting away? Realisation dawned. 'A young man, painting? Restoring the canvas do you mean?'

'I do not. I mean he was working on a fresh canvas and painting from life, his model was a very beautiful girl with the true Titian hair and not a stitch on. I caught the merest glimpse, as I said, through a gap in the curtain, I was not meant to see any of it, I'm sure. I pretended I had noticed nothing, but I thought it odd at the time, and wondered if Monsieur Delancourt was up to some trickery.'

'He could never hope to pass off a copy,' exclaimed Titus.

'Don't see why not,' Harry said. 'I dare say Delancourt had seen your painting at some time or other, and could instruct his artist, his faker, as to the composition of the subject. Copiers in Venice are very skilled artists, one would have no trouble turning out a Titian – it happens all the time, I'm told. With the secrecy of this purchase, it's unlikely that the buyer will place it where the few people in a position to identify it as a fake would ever see it.'

Titus was aghast. He had felt fool enough calling Warren out, and now to discover that the supposed Titian, his Titian, was no such thing, but a fake. He had nearly taken a man's life over a mere copy, the shadow, not the substance.

'You are sure, ma'am?' he asked.

' I am very sure that Delancourt paints, or causes to have painted, as many canvases as he acquires in the normal way of trade. Did you not smell the linseed oil when you were there? Some might be used for restoration, but the place has the distinctive odour of the artist's studio; it is unmistakable if you are used to it. I have had my portrait painted several times, so I am quite familiar with the smell.'

Titus began to laugh. 'Good God, so Warren has a bullet wound and a picture which he will hardly dare to offer to the king when I have told him it is not by the hand of Titian.'

'My advice to you,' said Harry, 'is to say precisely nothing on that to Warren. If you did so, I doubt if he would believe you, and how much more delightful for the rest of us to know that the king has parted with a large sum of money for a worthless painting.'

'I've wronged Warren enough by attempting to kill him; he would be in serious trouble if he passes this picture off a genuine Titian.'

Harry shrugged. 'That is his affair. He entered into what he knew to be shady dealing, let him suffer the consequences. Like as not there will be none.'

'The king's advisers will tell him they doubt the authenticity of the painting.'

'Why should they?' said Lady Hermione. 'I am of the opinion that Monsieur Delancourt is a very clever man. I dare say his copies are very good indeed, and the king won't be the first Englishman, no, nor Italian or Frenchman, to hang a fake upon his walls in the conviction that it is by a master. I agree with Harry, let the matter rest.'

Titus looked from one to the other. 'Your morals are shocking.'

'We are pragmatists, that's all,' said Harry. 'And now you have got this bee out of your bonnet, you may settle down to enjoy what Venice has to offer. For I sincerely hope that you are not still determined to find your missing painting, the true, the genuine Titian.'

'No.'

'What's the matter, Titus?' Lady Hermione asked. 'You have the exact same look on your face you used to have as a boy, when a favourite dog went missing or you lost that special ball your mother gave you.'

'Have I?' Titus didn't care for her perception, and he certainly wasn't going to discuss Alethea's predicament with her or Harry. He remembered the lost dog, which had been recovered after some hours from an irate neighbour's barn, and the missing ball had bounced down from the branches of a tree several days later, causing an under housemaid who was passing by just then to have a fit of hysterics.

He hoped that Alethea would turn up in as happy a condition, but a young woman alone and, he feared, penniless in a foreign city was not the same thing at all.

Lady Hermione glanced at him, and turned the subject. Were Harry or Titus acquainted at all with the Bishop of Wroxeter?'

'An Anglican bishop, one assumes,' said Harry. 'I'm glad to

y that I'm not acquainted with a single English bishop. I number a few Jesuits and a cardinal among my acquaintance, but that's as far as it goes. Perhaps Titus knows the man.'

'Never heard of him.'

'Why do you ask?' said Harry.

'It is odd, that's all. This bishop is a self-important man, not at all clever, and a connection of the Darcys'; he is cousin to Fitzwilliam Darcy's wife, as he informed me, at tedious length. You must know the Darcys, Titus, and of course Alexander's wife, Camilla is a Darcy, so I felt I had to be civil. He told me the strangest tale, that there is an impostor abroad, a young man claiming to be a close relative of Darcy's, a nephew, in fact. Mrs Vineham, who is such a tittle-tattle, told him that they were travelling companions across the Alps. A pleasant enough young man, she told Mr Collins, by the name of Mr Hawkins. She supposed him to be the son of Darcy's sister, Georgina. However, the bishop asserts that Darcy has but the one sister, and she is not married to anyone called Hawkins, she is married to Sir Gilbert Gosport and her son is presently at Magdalen College, Oxford. His name is Christopher Gosport, so you see there is no possibility of confusion there.'

'I expect he is a connection of Mrs Darcy's,' said Harry, whose nose for scandal was not yet twitching, and pray God it wouldn't start, Titus said inwardly. Damn this inquisitive bishop, what business had a bishop to be in Venice? He would set Mrs Vineham's tongue clacking, and she was a shrewd woman who might well put two and two together.

'No, no, Mr Collins is certain it is not so. That isn't all, for the bishop tells me that only two days ago, he had an encounter with a young man who was the very image of Darcy. He bumped into him, and was about to apologise when he took the likeness. Before he could say anything, or ask who he was, the youth let out a very rude exclamation – so the bishop says, but I dare say his sensibilities are extreme – and was off like a startled hare.'

'The mystery is no mystery,' declared Harry. 'This elusive Mr Hawkins is a by-blow of Darcy's.'

'Camilla has never mentioned any such person to me.'

'She has too much delicacy of mind, or maybe is not aware of her half brother from the wrong side of the sheets.'

Lady Hermione laughed. 'Delicacy of mind! How gothic you sound, Harry. I'm glad to say that Camilla is not a prude, and it is not a secret she would keep from Alexander. So you are doubtless right, and she doesn't know of the boy's existence. Mrs Vineham says he is a mere stripling, cannot be more than seventeen or eighteen, which does make it more shocking, since the eldest Darcy daughter is all of three and twenty. I think it is all a hum, Mr Darcy is not that kind of a man. And I have experience in these matters, for my husband was a complete rake. It is a matter of temperament as much as of upbringing, you know.'

Titus could see from Harry's expression that he had no belief in anyone not being that kind of a man. 'Two days ago, you say? Did the young man look to be in any particular distress?'

'Why should he be? Oh, because he ran away. There is nothing in that, I'm sure; I would have run away from the bishop if I could. No, Mr Collins said nothing about that. He hopes he may meet him again, I feel sure; you know how these clergymen love to sniff out wrongdoing, even though if he should be a Darcy by birth if not by name, it would be a dreadful shame to bring the secret out into the open.'

'Where did he have this strange encounter?' asked Titus.

'He did tell me, but I wasn't paying attention: he is so very tiresome when he proses on about this and that in his pedantic way. Does it matter?'

Titus's mind was in turmoil. Mrs Vineham might mention that he, too, had been in the group of travellers that included the putative Mr Hawkins. In which case, Lady Hermione would find it extraordinary if he didn't mention it.

'I was with Mrs Vineham and Lord Lucius, and indeed,

George Warren was one of our number, as were Emily and her new husband. I took no particular notice of Mr Hawkins; he was a well-bred young man, travelling abroad to join a cousin, I believe. He did admit he was related to the Darcy family, the likeness was there, but not so marked as your bishop seems to think. I have no recollection of his claiming to be a nephew. I think Lavinia Vineham is out to make mischief.'

'Now, that I can believe,' cried Lady Hermione.

How startled and alarmed Alethea must have been to encounter a clerical cousin, in Venice of all places, a man very likely to recognise her at once. He felt unaccountably more cheerful to think that she was on her feet and had her wits about her so recently as two days ago. She was not dead or destitute, by the sound of it. Wretched girl, she had probably fled from the bishop and collapsed in laughter as soon as she was clear away.

Lady Hermione had risen, and was preparing to go, but not before she had reminded Harry that, before Titus had come into the room, she had invited both men to accompany her to the opera. 'It is a performance of Mozart,' she told Titus now. 'With a remarkable Cherubino, they say.'

Titus, who loved music and never missed a *Figaro* if he could help it, accepted the invitation with real pleasure, and Harry, claiming that he much preferred more modern Italian operas, said that he would none the less join their party.

'For Lady Hermione always gathers a crowd of interesting people about her,' he said when she was gone. 'One is sure to be amused in her company.'

Figgins was dressing Alethea, the task could hardly be entrusted to anyone else. To Alethea, enraptured by the life of the theatre, despite the evident hostility of her fellow musicians, Figgins's continuing disapproval and dislike of the opera house was extraordinary.

'I'm ashamed to be here, among these actresses and

dancers,' said Figgins. 'They may play the part of countesses and who knows what, but it still isn't a place where you should be singing, and nothing you say will make me think differently. Every time I think of what Lady Fanny would say, if she knew, or Mr Fitzwilliam . . .' She closed her eyes in horror.

Alethea had a very good idea what her cousin Fitzwilliam would say. A pillar of domestic rectitude, with firm views on the need for women to be counselled and protected and guided, he would probably suffer a seizure if he had the slightest notion of what she was up to. The mere donning of masculine apparel would appal him; to run away from a husband, to travel abroad alone would be acts almost beyond his comprehension, and as for singing in public in Venice, in a breeches role – no, she couldn't imagine his reaction.

Lady Fanny would be shocked, Letty both shocked and full of outraged virtue, and as for her parents, she didn't want to think about what their feelings and opinion might be. In her heart of hearts, Althea knew that even Camilla and Wytton would consider her appearance in public, in an opera, to be quite dreadful.

Only what choice had she? Would it be better to starve? Or come upon the town? This way, she could earn the money she needed for her and Figgins to survive, and survive in a respectable way, until her sister came back to Venice.

Besides, she wouldn't have missed this opportunity for anything. It fascinated her to be among women who earned a living, a living that Figgins might consider far from respectable, but indeed, many of the singers were married women with children, living quite ordinary lives away from the paint and the footlights. Men had their independence; even if they had a satisfactory income, they could practise the law or go into politics or the Navy or, lower down the social scale, any number of trades or jobs. Women of her class could write – if, like Miss Griffin, they had the knack of it – or become governesses, that was all. Where was the justice in that?

Figgins, her mouth pursed, fitted Alethea into her breeches, and closed her eyes as her mistress set about creating a realistic swelling with a crumpled handkerchief. 'I have to, with these skin-tight breeches, or they will catch on that I'm a woman masquerading as a castrato. In which case, they will probably throw eggs and rotten tomatoes at me, and I don't care for that idea.'

'They never would!'

'Italian audiences are extremely volatile, and quick to show their appreciation or contempt, that is what Massetti says.'

Figgins didn't trust Salvatore Massetti, no, not an inch. He was a scheming, devious foreigner, who wished Alethea no good, only she was too entranced by all this theatrical nonsense to realise it. True, he had handed over quite a reasonable sum of money, but Figgins doubted if they'd ever see another penny. Once the performance was over, and he didn't need Alethea any more, that would be the end of it.

She helped Alethea into the coat, a yellow coat that went over a natty waistcoat. She had to admit, as she stood back to admire her handiwork, that Alethea made a striking and convincing young man. Her straight, masterful eyebrows helped, as did her slim form and long legs, hardly a curve in sight, that was what came of half-starving herself in her unhappiness.

At least she wasn't unhappy now. No, far from it: she was keyed up and elated. Well, Figgins had seen that glinting look in the past, there'd be tears before bedtime, as Ma used to say.

'I think I'm going to be sick,' Alethea announced.

'Not in that coat, you aren't,' said Figgins, removing the coat with one hand and passing a basin with the other. 'Nerves, that's what it is. You haven't got the temperament for all this, not like these girls who were showing their all on stage when you were stitching your sampler, they're bred to it, you aren't.'

'Don't be so tiresome,' Alethea said, pale now after a violent fit of retching. 'I'll be all right once I start singing, that's what Massetti says.'

Figgins removed the basin and set about putting Alethea's foaming neck cloth to rights. 'You watch out for that chit as is singing Susanna, there's a saucy number for you. She's got hands where they shouldn't be, she'll be having a grope to see what's what if you take your eyes off her for a moment, and that'll be the cat out the bag along with that handkerchief you've got down your breeches.'

'I'll be on my guard,' Alethea promised. 'Listen, there's the overture, I must go up. Won't you wish me luck? You'll watch from the wings, you'll have to, to be ready with my dress.'

Figgins was dreading every moment of the performance. Fear flooded through her: fear of exposure, fear of Miss Alethea singing so badly that she was booed and jeered off stage, fear of her forgetting what came next; how could anyone remember all that music without getting it wrong? She didn't know how she was going to be able to breathe until the curtain came down on those dratted peasants prancing about the stage, when it would, thank God, all be over.

Massetti was pleased with the audience, a full house, he murmured to the baritone who went past. All his publicity had paid off, a young fresh castrato was a novelty these days, this had been a highly profitable venture.

He was pleased with Alethea, too, Figgins could tell that from the smile wavering about his thin lips. He snapped his fingers with delight at the storm of applause that came after Cherubino had sung that first solo; it was quite a catchy tune, it was true, but one that Figgins never wanted to hear again.

The last act began, the setting shot through with the darkness of night, a darkness echoed in the words and music, a brilliant contrast to the essential comedy of the piece.

Figgins noticed none of it, she was simply counting the minutes until it was all over.

'Ah,' said a cold, familiar voice in her ear. 'Mr Figgins, isn't it? I wish to speak to your mistress. Will she come off this way?'

'Yes. That is – I don't know who you mean.'

'Oh, but you do,' said Titus in a voice that made Figgins wish she'd never been born.

My dearest Hermione

I write no more than a note, in haste, to tell you of some news I have just heard that may be of interest to Camilla, for it is to do with her father and sister.

Mr Darcy's secretary in Vienna is Charles Ingham, who is Freddie's nephew; a younger son, you know, and destined for a career in the diplomatic service. He had occasion recently to write to Freddie about some family matter, and mentioned an odd thing that had occurred. Mr Napier had been in Vienna, not calling directly upon Mr Darcy, as might be expected, but asking about as to whether anyone had seen his wife!

This came to Charles's ears, and, intrigued, he arranged to meet Napier, who interrogated him at length, almost accusing him of lying, and only the fact of Mr and Mrs Darcy's not being presently in Vienna, they having gone to Turkey again, convinced him that Charles was telling the truth.

It seems that Napier expressed his intention of going on to Venice, to call upon the Wyttons, who were no doubt hiding his wife. Naturally Charles was fascinated to know why Napier's wife should be hiding from him, but at this point Napier realised that he was saying too much and went away in what Charles described as the devil of a taking.

So where is Alethea? Supposedly, she came back to England after visiting Georgina Mordaunt in Paris, but if so, she did not return to Tyrrwhit House. Napier has managed to cover up her continued absence and is clearly intent on tracking her down.

I know you would have told me if she had been in Venice. I do wonder where she has got to. Is it possible that she has run away with a man? One shudders at what Mr Darcy would have to say about that, if it were true.

However, now you are forewarned, for Napier sounds to be in a very disagreeable way, and I dare say he may turn up on your doorstep in due course. I expect to hear from you the moment he does, my life is very dull just at present and I long to hear of any excitement elsewhere in the world.

Believe me, as always, your most affectionate friend,

Belinda

PART FOUR

Chapter Twenty-two

'Must you yawn so?'

His voice betrayed how angry he was with her, although he could see that Alethea was drained to her bones. Perhaps all singers felt like this, night after night; no wonder they were a temperamental lot. Or was it the novelty and her inexperience, having to perform on her nerves, that left her so weak, mentally, physically and emotionally? 'I cannot understand how you came to think up such a hare-brained scheme.'

'Mr Manningtree' – another prodigious yawn – 'you have hauled me here by main force, abducted me, in fact, and when Figgins and I try to leave, you will not let us go.'

'No, by God, I won't. I've been chasing all over Venice looking for you, my concern mounting day by day. I had such a dread of – but never mind that. You may wait here until Lady Hermione returns, which will be very soon now, she cannot have been far behind us.'

'Lady Hermione?'

'Lady Hermione Wytton, Alexander Wytton's mother. You don't know her?' Voices, swift steps outside. 'I expect this is her now.'

'Good gracious,' said Lady Hermione, as she came bustling into the room. 'Cherubino, no less. Such pleasure as you gave us all this evening, such a voice.'

'Ma'am, may I present Mrs Napier?' said Titus.

Alethea looked as though the breath had been knocked out of her, and the colour fled from her face. Distraught, she rose and faced him. 'How did you know? Never tell me you are a friend of my husband? To track me down, and to betray me, there was no reason for you to do such a thing.' Too dismayed to be polite, she ignored Lady Hermione. 'Do not call me by that name, or I am quite undone.'

'Mrs Napier – why, good heavens, you aren't a boy at all. You are Alethea, Alethea Darcy as was. Now I come to look at you, of course you are. With the make-up you are quite different, what a look of your father you have about you. We have never met, which is a cause of regret to me, for I know how attached Camilla is to you. My dear, please don't cry.'

'I'm not crying,' said Alethea, dashing her hand against her eyes. 'It is just that I have tried so hard to keep my disguise, and now it's all in vain. When did you discover my identity, sir?'

'I've known that you were not a man from our first encounter in Paris. With your likeness to your father, it did not take the mind of a Newton or an Aristotle to deduce who you were.'

'Sir, you do not properly understand my situation. I must not be known to be here, not as Mrs Napier, not on any account. Oh, why did you have to interfere? What business is it of yours who I am or what I do? Why have you hunted me down?'

'As soon as I learned that the Wyttons weren't in Venice, I set out to find you. A young, gently bred woman alone in Venice; it is not to be thought of. I am acquainted with your father, Wytton is one of my oldest friends, no man of honour could do less.'

'And now it will all come out, and I shall be ruined, completely ruined.'

'What the devil do you expect to be when you run away from your husband and travel, as a man, across Europe?'

'Is that what you have done?' cried Lady Hermione. 'I am amazed, my dear, amazed; what intrepidity! How did you manage it? You must tell me all about it, but first, I shall order some refreshments. You look in need of food and wine.'

'First, Mrs Napier should change out of those pantomime

garments and put on clothes more suitable for her sex and rank,' said Titus. The sight of her in the velvet coat and tight-fitting breeches offended his sensibilities – had the girl no shame?

Up went her chin, and she gave him a level look. 'I have no gown, and if I had, I should not wear it. Good God, how awkward you make things for me, my coat and trousers and shirt are all at the theatre.'

'Your portmanteau is being brought round, should be here by now.'

'My portmanteau?'

'You left it at the Pensione Donata. I assume you ran out of money; how like a woman to plan such a journey with insufficient funds for your needs.'

'That is not true,' said Figgins, who had been silently watching her mistress. 'More than enough, she had, and you've no call to go saying such things. Miss Alethea was robbed, beaten to the ground and robbed.'

'No!' said Lady Hermione, horrified. 'Is that why you were singing at the opera tonight? For money?'

'Of course.' Alethea's voice was calm, but the look she shot at Titus defied him to comment or find fault.

'It didn't occur to you to ask for help from one of the many English families settled in Venice, who would know your father and mother and—'

'And spread the tale all about the city and back to England in the twinkling of an eye,' said Lady Hermione. 'That's enough, Titus. Alethea has coped magnificently, she is a brave young woman indeed. Here comes a servant – a glass of wine will restore you, and then you must eat.'

'I was sick before I sang,' Alethea said, eyeing the plates of cold meats and fruit. 'Nerves. So I am very, very hungry.'

It was all of a piece, Titus thought indignantly. To behave in a way so outrageous as to place herself quite beyond the pale of her upbringing and social world, and then calmly to announce that she was hungry. Was she not ashamed of what she had done?

Clearly not. Was Lady Hermione to be trusted with her secret? Without a doubt. Lady Hermione was one of those rare women to whom a man might turn for assistance in a crisis such as this. Emily was another, but Emily was not here, Emily was no longer part of his life. Yet, why did he need assistance? How had he become caught up in this imbroglio, which had the makings of exactly the kind of scandal he most disliked?

'It is impossible for Mrs Napier—'

'I wish you will not call me that,' Alethea said through a thick mouthful of ham. 'Miss Darcy, if you please, or Alethea, I have no objection to your using my name.'

'May she stay here with you, for the present? There is no woman in Harry's household – how did you get rid of him, by the way?'

'He met a friend, they were going to go backstage, to ogle the opera dancers I suppose, and catch a glimpse of the castrato.'

Titus sighed. 'You see, ma'am' – to Alethea – 'what company you have been keeping, what dangers you laid yourself open to.'

She gave him a very direct look. 'One may lay oneself open to far worse without setting foot in a theatre, indeed, without stepping out of doors.'

'Titus, stop it,' said Lady Hermione. 'Alethea has been through enough without you preaching at her. Since when did you grow so remarkably righteous and moral?'

Titus was silenced. He didn't care to admit to himself, let alone to Lady Hermione, that he hated the idea of people peering at Alethea, had hated seeing her the focus of all eyes when she was on stage and hated himself for the admiration that he had felt, despite himself, for the way she had sung. To undertake such a mad scheme was beyond what any young woman should be capable of, but then to pull it off, to sing in a way that moved his heart – that was unforgivable.

'You aren't attending to what I say.' Lady Hermione's words broke through his reverie, he started and apologised.

'It is impossible, in the circumstances,' she began.

Voices, footsteps on the marble outside, heavy footsteps, with a slightly creaking shoe.

'Lord, we are quite undone,' cried Lady Hermione.

Titus looked at her, astonished. Had she a lover? Visiting her at this hour? It was not inconceivable, although she was by no means young, but somehow he had never imagined – someone disreputable, perhaps, he knew of women who took their pleasures with a handsome young gondolier, or – no, the voice was speaking in English, loudly and deliberately, so as to make himself understood by the Italian servant, saying that Lady Hermione's instructions to deny herself to visitors did not mean him, he was a guest, not a visitor.

The same horror seem to have transfixed Alethea. Ha, so her insouciance was not invariable. Only, why did she look quite so panic-stricken? She had been happy enough to pass herself off with English people formerly. Sartorial considerations? The coat and breeches she was wearing looked decidedly *outré*, but this was, after all, the city of masks and costumes.

Lady Hermione and Figgins were dragging a large screen away from its place against the wall. It was painted in the classical style, a pastoral landscape with nymphs, that matched the elegant trompe d'oeil figures on the walls. Althea darted behind the screen, just as the door opened and a ponderous clergyman, purple chested and pink faced, entered the room.

Alethea emerged from behind the screen equally pink faced some fifteen minutes later, when Lady Hermione had finally got rid of the man. Her pinkness was due to suppressed mirth, to which she succumbed as she slid into a chair.

Titus, indignant at having to spend even five minutes in the company of such a man, was demanding of Lady Hermione what on earth had possessed her to give house room to that prosy bore. Then he rounded on Alethea. 'This bishop is your cousin, I dare say.'

'He is,' said Alethea when she could stop laughing. 'And he is the most dreadful man, is he not? So pompous, and always moralising; how we used to dread his visits.'

'I'm surprised your father let him in the house.'

'There's no keeping him away. Cousin Collins is a very persistent kind of person. His wife, Charlotte, is a great friend of Mama's, so she bore with him for the sake of seeing her. Papa was rarely there when he came, he always seemed to have urgent business in town on those occasions. My cousin goes and stays with my grandfather, too, in Hertfordshire, for he will inherit the estate there, it is an entail or some such thing. He cannot believe that Grandpapa is so hale and hearty, I'm sure he expected to step into his shoes years ago.'

'He is the kind of man whom there is no resisting,' Lady Hermione agreed. 'He announced his arrival in Venice by telling me of his intention of staying with me on account of there now being a connection between our families, and there was no refusing him, he is an immovable force. I dare say that is how he became a bishop.'

'I've never had a high regard for the bench of bishops,' said Titus, 'but how a man such as that has reached such eminence, I cannot think.'

'He is not a proper bishop,' said Alethea. 'He has no seat in the Lords, which is what he would love, and I don't suppose he would be much noticed there, as they are all so boring.'

'Not a proper bishop? You mean he merely dresses like one? Masqueraders seem to run in your family.'

Alethea found her mind wasn't working as clearly as she should like, and it was beyond her powers just at present to explain what she meant.

'He is the Bishop of Wroxeter,' said Lady Hermione, 'not of Gloucester or Durham or any such seat as that. Can we leave Bishop Collins to his own devices for the moment? As you heard, he was retiring for the night, and he will sleep soundly, with the most prodigious snores for the next many hours. However, you understand why Alethea may not stay here with me.'

'I can't pass myself off as Mr Hawkins for more than a minute with him,' said Alethea. 'Even though he is a stupid man, he is not so stupid as that. I bumped into him a few mornings ago, and I had to be off like a flash before he recognised me.'

'He is the kind of guest who wanders about, poking his nose in everywhere he is not wanted,' said Lady Hermione. 'Alethea may sleep here tonight, and indeed I think she is about to fall asleep in front of our eyes, but it is too risky for her to stay any longer. Don't look so cross, Titus, I shall contrive something. Now, take yourself off, and you may call in the morning. The bishop sets off for several hours of sightseeing every morning at ten o'clock, he loves to visit churches and be appalled by the Catholicism all around him. I thought I would have to apply smelling salts when he came back from San Marco.'

Alethea, once again yawning her head off, bid Titus a cold if sleepy goodnight, and followed her hostess out of the room.

How pleasant it was, how very pleasant, to wake up to find oneself in a wide comfortable bed, lying between clean sheets, with a smiling maidservant fastening the shutters open and offering a dish of chocolate.

The chocolate was followed by a tray with rolls, preserves, fruit and a pot of coffee. Alethea polished off every crumb, and leant back on the soft pillows to consider her situation.

'You will have to wear this dowdy gown that was in your portmanteau,' said Lady Hermione, coming in with Figgins. 'For you are too tall by far to fit into any of my clothes.'

'Must I dress as a woman?'

'Yes, for I think both Mr Hawkins and Cherubino will have to vanish.'

Alethea sighed, and eyed the gown Figgins had laid on the bed. 'It is so very comfortable to wear trousers and breeches, ma'am.'

'A gown will be cooler in the heat, you will find. And you cannot be a man for ever, you cannot become a man.'

Alethea wished, as she had many times before, that she had been born a boy. How different her life would have been. How different it was for her younger brothers, how their independence was encouraged, what liberty they would grow up to in comparison to her narrow world. For the first time since she bowled away from Tyrrwhit House in that carriage, she felt completely at a loss.

'I don't know what to do,' she said, twisting the fine linen of her bed sheet between her fingers. 'How long will it be before Camilla returns? Could you lend me sufficient money to travel to Vienna, perhaps?'

Lady Hermione settled herself on the velvet stool that was placed between the windows. 'As to that, I have some news for you about Vienna.' She glanced at Figgins.

'I have no secrets from Figgins,' Alethea said at once. 'Indeed, she is my dear friend, and I should not have survived without her.'

'Well, then I shall tell you what I have heard from London, where a great friend keeps me abreast of all the news in town. It seems likely that your husband, that Mr Napier, is on his way to Venice.

Alethea went pale and clasped her hand to her mouth. Napier here in Venice? 'With my luck, I shall run smack into him the minute I set foot out of doors. What am I do? Where am I to go?'

'That is what we have to discuss. Wait, though, there is more from London, and it is best that you should hear it. There are strong rumours of an estrangement between yourself and Mr Napier, and people are saying that you have run away with another man. London loves a scandal, especially an adulterous one, and people in society have such commonplace minds that they always hit upon a story of this kind.'

Alethea was silent for a moment. It had been bound to happen. Sooner or later her absence even from Napier's country fastness would be noticed and commented upon. She felt it was the least of her worries.

'There is no possibility of a reconciliation between you and Mr Napier? You could perhaps meet him here, with others present, if need be, myself, or your cousin even.'

'Cousin Collins! I think not. No, ma'am, I shall never, ever go back to Mr Napier. I don't care if I have to live in disgraced seclusion for the rest of my days. Nothing could be worse than to be back in his company, in his power. I truly think it would end in his killing me.'

Alethea regretted blurting the words out. They sounded melodramatic, and she had no wish to go into the horrors of her marriage with a woman who, however kind and well-meaning, was a stranger.

Lady Hermione had no such inhibitions. She was determined to get to the bottom of this. Titus might put it down to a careless upbringing and a wild and reckless disposition; she knew despair and deep unhappiness when she saw it – and neither state seemed at all natural in one of Alethea's temperament and character.

'You will tell me about it,' she said firmly.

What a difference a dress made, Figgins thought, as she fastened Alethea into the plain gown.

'Oh, how stuffy it is after trousers to wear petticoats again.'

Figgins was thoroughly glad to be back in her own clothes. 'It's time all that pretence was over, always looking over one's shoulder and waiting to be found out. I'm not saying it didn't work – and we must be grateful for that, for here we are, with people to help you – but my heart was in my mouth every minute for fear we would be discovered.'

People to help her, yes, that was true. Which was more than her own sisters were prepared to do; at least Miss Camilla would have helped, had she been able, but as for Miss Letty and Miss Georgina – for she still thought of them by the names they had had when she had waited upon the family in Aubrey Square – they hardly deserved the name of sisters.

Easy enough to dismiss others' problems when you had none of your own. If they'd heard half of what Miss Alethea had related to Lady Hermione they must have cried out in sympathy for their sister, but they hadn't wanted to hear any of it.

Miss Alethea was unusually silent while she finished dressing her and did her hair. Thinking, no doubt, working out some new scheme to plunge them into more trouble. That Lady Hermione had a head on her shoulders, and for all she was a great lady, she had a practical outlook on it all. She'd wasted no time on pitying Miss Alethea, which was as well, for you could see that she was buttoning up and wishing she hadn't spoken out like that. It had to be told, however, for now her ladyship would not dream of suggesting that husband and wife try to make up their differences.

'I think we should go to Rome,' Alethea said. 'I can stay there safely with Camilla and Wytton, and I do not suppose that Napier will follow me there. Then, when Papa and Mama are back in Vienna, I am sure they will escort me there, one or other of them.'

Rome! Figgins didn't in the least want to go to Rome. Still, if that was where Miss Alethea had made up her mind to go, then to Rome she had no doubt they would go.

'Lady Hermione is sending me out this morning, with a maid of her own who speaks English and Italian, so that I may buy more clothes for you, and for me, too, she says.' She would enjoy that, how different to be out and about in your own skin, not on guard for every moment of the day, nor having to worry over what your mistress might take it into her head to do next.

The mere thought of the night before, the opera house, the performance, made Figgins feel queasy. Thank God that Mr Manningtree had chanced to attend the opera, and had behaved with such presence of mind. How different it might have been if Miss Alethea hadn't given him the slip when they first arrived in Venice.

Still, no good ever came regretting what was past, you couldn't undo it, so you might as well put it out of your mind.

A knock on the door, a curtseying maid, and Miss was to attend on Lady Hermione if she were ready.

Miss Alethea surveyed herself in the long glass without enthusiasm. 'I make a much prettier man than a woman,' she said under her breath as she walked from the room.

Titus did not agree. He saw before him a young woman who had fulfilled all the beauty that her sixteen-year-old self had promised. He took her hand and raised it to his lips. Her regard was cold and reserved, the look of one who neither liked nor trusted him.

However, she remembered her manners and thanked him, a little stiffly, for bringing her and Figgins to safety in Lady Hermione 's house. Then she turned to Lady Hermione, who was sitting on a sofa looking at them both with a keen, interested expression on her face.

Lady Hermione was not a woman to betray a confidence, but she was shrewd enough to know that she was going to need Titus's help in sorting out Alethea's affairs, and that it would be best if he knew, starkly and without embroidery, what Alethea had had to endure during her months with Napier.

It had not come as a great surprise to him, neither the nature of the man's behaviour, nor that Alethea had been driven to escape from him at any cost. 'My father sat as a magistrate on several such cases,' he had told Lady Hermione.

'It is unpardonable, a man who treats a woman, any woman – or indeed any creature in their power – in such a way puts himself beyond the protection of society.'

'Is Napier deranged?'

'Any reasonable person would call such behaviour the acts of a man outside his wits, but no, I do not think one can say he is insane. There is the sexual pleasure, that goes without saying, but in this case, there is also an exaggerated sense of power, an assertion of patriarchal authority coupled with the demands and ties of domesticity that an immature man may feel reluctant to assume, which is sometimes combined with a fear of effeminacy. There is no excusing such a man, of course, whatever his perverse reasons are for such cruelty.'

'Alethea seems to think the law will support him; he led her to believe that he had total ownership of her body as well as her property, that she owned nothing that he did not choose to grant her.'

'The law would not support him. A separation would be the normal course, and perhaps, in time, divorce. In most such cases, the woman returns to her family.'

'As to that,' said Lady Hermione, 'Alethea tried, in the absence of her parents, to enlist her sister Mrs Barcombe's support, but Napier, weasel that he is, charmed her and persuaded her that Alethea was suffering from no more than an excess of maidenly modesty.'

'Maidenly modesty! I doubt if Miss Darcy – for I refuse to call her Mrs Napier – has ever had an ounce of maidenly modesty.'

'Do stop pacing up and down and sit beside me, here, and take a cup of coffee, or there is wine if you prefer. Alethea will be down directly, and then we must put our heads together and see what is to be done.'

And here was Alethea, a little wan, dark circles beneath her eyes that it pained him to see, but with no inclination to show a single sign of weakness. Had he not met her, had he not seen what she had done – and understood, now, why she had done it – he would not have believed that any woman alive was capable of taking her life into her own hands in the way this young woman, hardly more than a girl, had done.

Announcing, in the calmest way, that she intended to go to Rome.

She shot him a glance from pale, resolute eyes. 'Don't look like that, Mr Manningtree. It is for me, and me alone, to decide what I shall do and where I shall go.'

'Not so high, Alethea,' said Lady Hermione. 'Wherever you go, you will need an escort and I have no wish to go to jauntering about Europe in all this heat. Titus, however—'

'I need no escort.'

'In Italy, you do, believe me, you do.'

'I have no intention of leaving Venice at present, as it happens,' Titus began, then bit off the words as Lady Hermione gave him an exasperated look. 'Perhaps it will be best if Miss Darcy stays here in Venice until arrangements of some kind can be made for her to go wherever she decides.'

'Titus, do not be tiresome. Alethea cannot stay here, not with her cousin on the premises.'

Titus had forgotten the bishop. 'The devil with the man, you'll have to send him packing. Surely you can get rid of him somehow.'

'We never could,' said Alethea. 'Whatever we did, he always stayed his time out. I remember once we dressed up in sheets and—'

'I can well imagine it, if your sisters are anything like you,' said Titus. 'How long a visit does he propose to make, ma'am?'

'Another fortnight at least. I shall go to my house in the mountains, I always do for the heat of the summer months, you know, so I shall bring my departure forward. He may stay on alone, if he wants to.'

'Mountains! Why should not Alethea go with you?'

'My dear Titus, I thought men were supposed to have rational minds. Should Napier come to Venice, he will seek me out as soon as he finds Camilla isn't here. It will hardly be a problem for him to discover my address in the hills, it is barely a half day's journey from here and there he will be, on my doorstep and looking over my shoulder at Alethea.'

'The same argument surely applies to Rome. Once he finds Camilla and Wytton are there, he may try his hand in Rome.'

'Rome is a big place, why should he find them?' Alethea said.

'Wytton has a wide circle of acquaintance,' his mother said. 'When Wytton can tear himself away from his inscriptions and old monuments, he and Camilla will go out in society. The English community isn't so large, it would take a man like Napier no time at all to track them down.'

'Is there nowhere I am safe from him?' Alethea said.

'I think,' said Lady Hermione, 'that the safest place for you at present is England.'

'England! I cannot possibly go back to England. Where should I go?'

'Lady Fanny would welcome you with open arms, I am sure. I am surprised you didn't seek refuge there in the first place.'

'Lady Fanny might welcome me, but Mr Fitzwilliam wouldn't,' said Alethea roundly. 'He cordially dislikes me, and always has done, and he would make me go back to Tyrrwhit House. He is stupid and stuffy and has no idea—'

'When he learns how vilely Napier has treated you,' Lady Hermione said, 'I think his attitude will change. You are one of his family, he will support you.'

'No, he won't, no more than my sister Letty did.' She took a deep breath in an effort to control herself. 'I do not assert that he would approve of . . . of how things were between my husband and me, just that he would refuse to listen if I tried to tell him. He never does listen to anything I say.'

There was a rising note of panic in her voice, and Titus, who knew Fitzwilliam only slightly, had a strong suspicion that she was right, he looked like the kind of man who would turn ostrich to avoid anything disagreeable on the domestic front. A brave soldier in his time, but storming a wall at Badajos would come much easier to him than admitting to such a degree of marital disharmony and wickedness within his circle.

'In that case, you must go to the Abbey,' said Lady Hermione.

'Abbey?'

'Yes, to Shillingford Abbey, Alexander and Camilla's house in Herefordshire.'

'But is there anyone there?'

'The housekeeper. I shall give you a letter for her, and she will make you quite at home.'

'A good solution,' Titus said. 'Perhaps the polite world may be led to believe that she has been there all this while.'

'She is known to have been in Paris.'

'Paying a visit to her sister, what could be more normal or less worthy of gossip?'

Alethea was beginning to look more hopeful. 'Georgina is just as likely to tell everyone that I fled to Paris to escape from Napier.'

'A letter from your father will quell any desire she may have to say such a thing; all she has to do is to keep her mouth shut.'

Alethea had moved over to stand beside one of the long windows that overlooked the quay beneath and the canal, wide and sparkling in the sun. She turned the handle to open the door and stepped, blinking, into the sunlight.

Titus heard a commotion below, and stepped forward to pull Alethea away from the window. He fairly pushed her back into the room and then looked over the edge of the balcony.

Straight into the enraged, upturned face of Norris Napier.

Chapter Twenty-three

Lady Hermione, appraised of what had happened, swept into action. 'Napier is doubtless come to visit me, to find out if I know where you are, Alethea. I shall receive him in the salon, and he may say what he chooses – I shall deny everything.'

Alethea was numb with apprehension. Titus's sighting of Napier had unnerved her completely, bringing back as it did so many memories of unhappy times. And now, she told herself, just when she was in most danger, her courage had deserted her.

Figgins was having none of that. 'Miss Alethea, rouse yourself, this is no time to fall into a melancholy.'

'No, indeed,' said Lady Hermione. 'This is time for action. You are to change at once back into your breeches and boots.'

'He will know me, whatever I wear.'

'He will not, for he shan't see you,' said Titus.

Lady Hermione took no notice of Alethea's dismal words. 'Titus, you are to escort them to England; no, no buts or ifs. You will travel on your yacht.'

'My yacht?'

'Yes, she lies at Livorno, you told me so. Take a chaise to Livorno, and sail at once for England.'

'Is that wise?' asked Titus. 'Scandal piled on scandal, if ever—'

'Don't you come the prig now, Titus. Let them behave with circumspection, which they are well able to do, and no one need ever know. Alethea has taken risks enough, what is one more? She must return to England as swiftly as ever she can, so that Napier is left looking the fool with his belief that he saw her in Venice.'

'He will be on my heels, wherever I go,' said Alethea.

Titus was impatient. 'You have given him the slip before, you shall do so again. Go with Figgins, and while Lady Hermione makes him welcome, we shall be away.'

He addressed some words in rapid Italian to one of Lady Hermione's servants, and stretched out a hand to Alethea. 'Up, and go quickly to your chamber to change back into your breeches,' he said.

His energy was infectious, and Alethea found herself coming out of the hopelessness that had overwhelmed her. Still, she hesitated. 'I think, if he encounters me while I am in men's clothes, it will make matters worse even than they are.'

Figgins propelled her out of the room. 'That isn't possible, Miss Alethea, so don't you go fretting about it.'

Voices in the hall below. Napier's like a knife, cutting through the servant's words of enquiry, demanding to be taken at once to wherever in the house Lady Hermione was to be found. Indeed, he could work out for himself which room to go to, for he had seen people just this minute, on the balcony.

Alethea darted back inside the door. Then, as Napier, despite his protests, was ushered into the salon below, she and Figgins fled upstairs.

The salon door was closed. Lady Hermione was speaking in a quiet way; Napier's replies sounded barely civil as they crept past on the stairs and descended into the hall.

The gondola was waiting, bobbing up and down in the wash from a barge that was passing by with a large bronze statue of a man on a horse lashed down on deck.

Titus handed Alethea in, then Figgins. 'Sit on that side, if you please. Keep your heads well down and your face shaded by that hat, Alethea.'

'Must we go past him? Cannot we go the other way?'

'No, this way is better. He will not be expecting to see you, and I need to go this way, I shall have to stop to collect my man and to arrange for a chaise.'

'He will follow us, all the way to the Alps and beyond,' said Alethea desolately, as she sat on one of the black stools the gondolier provided for his passengers.

'Not a bit of it,' said Titus. 'Now, take care to appear quite at your ease.'

'Can you see him?' whispered Alethea, not daring to look up.

'He is standing on the balcony, addressing himself to Lady Hermione with some vehemence. How fortunate, his being there at that exact moment when I stepped out on to the balcony, so that we knew he was on your trail. Now, you may be easy, we are past him, he looks after us, he notices nothing, he has gone back to haranguing Lady Hermione.'

'He was bound to turn up, he will be like a bloodhound, following every trail. It is enough that Lady Hermione is Alexander's mother. I dare say he called at Camilla's house as well, and he will pursue any acquaintances I might be supposed to have in Venice.'

'Think no more about him,' said Titus. 'We have got clean away. Now all we have to do is get out of the country. And don't I just hope that Lady Hermione introduces him to the bishop.'

Titus Manningtree's yacht lay at Livorno, or Leghorn as the English less euphoniously called it. He had sent it on to Italy when he had disembarked after crossing the channel, and it had lain there after a leisurely passage, with the crew awaiting further orders.

The captain of the vessel, a young ex Royal Navy officer who had been sent ashore on half-pay after Waterloo, like so many of his colleagues, and had taken up private service, was enjoying himself. He liked the climate, he had the pleasure of the company of any number of ravishingly pretty females, both respectable and not so respectable, and he found the Italian wine and food quite delicious.

He was in his cabin, taking a nap after a night of merrymaking, when a sudden energy coursing through the yacht roused him. A knock sounded on his door. 'Mr Thorogood's duty and compliments, sir, and Mr Manningtree has just driven alongside in a coach and four. A prime team, and sweating like Lucifer himself had been driving them. Mr Manningtree looks in a black mood and he's got a young gent with him and that Bootle with a face like a wet weekend, and they're all coming aboard.'

By the time he had delivered his breathless message, Coletree was pulling on his coat and diving on deck. There was an end to his idyll, here was trouble on the way if ever he saw it, and no chance to so much as say goodbye to any of his new friends.

'Are you ready to leave, Coletree? Are all the crew aboard?'

'In half an hour, sir,' he said, thanking God internally that he took his master's standing instructions always to be ready to sail quite literally.

'We are going back to England,' Mr Manningtree said. 'Have a cabin made ready for my guest, Mr Hawkins. His servant will share his cabin.'

Which was unusual, but it wasn't Coletree's place to question his orders. England! Well, that wasn't so bad. The cricketing season would be in full swing, and his mother and sister would be pleased to see him, as they always were.

'As fast as you can,' Mr Manningtree added. 'There's not a moment to lose.'

The winds were favourable, so much so that the yacht was set to make a record passage across the Mediterranean. Heeling right over, a fine show of sails white against the brilliant blue sky, the water creamed along her side as the vessel surged through the warm sea. And day after day, Alethea lay in her small, stuffy cabin, wishing she were dead. After the first few days, she staggered, at Titus's insistence, into the fresh air on deck, and managed to swallow a morsel or two of food, an infallible cure for the seasickness, the officers assured her.

With disastrous results.

Figgins plied her with watered wine, wiped her brow and fanned her burning face. Her own momentary queasiness had soon passed, and she couldn't understand why her mistress was taken so mortal bad. She dosed her with laudanum, which soothed Alethea's retching, but brought her troubled dreams.

Titus came down to sit with her, sending Figgins on deck for air and a rest, although it wrung his heart to see Alethea so pale and in such distress, tossing and turning from the effects of the opiate and muttering incoherent sentences. It seemed to him that she was afraid all the time of Napier, feared that he would come through the door at any moment and haul her back to the caged misery of her marriage.

Marriage, he thought to himself as he took his own paces round the deck. What a pitfall it was, what a torment when it went wrong, as it so often did. He paused to stand beside Figgins, who was leaning over the highly polished rail and gazing at the brilliantly clear water.

'It's like there's another world down there,' she said, pointing at a group of brightly coloured fish darting about in their deep and salty domain. Figgins was now deeply tanned from the Italian sun. Skinny, wiry as a cat, Titus thought, and she'd taken, barefoot and momentarily carefree while Alethea slept, to joining the younger members of the crew skylarking about the rigging.

He'd been alarmed at first, fearing she might fall, but Coletree had watched her with an expert eye, and said reassuringly that the young man was like a monkey, just the sort he'd liked having on a ship when he was still in the Navy.

'Salt of the earth, sir, or maybe we should say salt of the sea, those are the men that saved our skins, and protected our country's freedom, over and over again.'

Not quite, Mr Coletree, Titus said to himself, but again he returned to the vexing question of how both Figgins and Alethea coped so extraordinarily well in a world entirely restricted to the masculine half of nature.

Titus had noticed before that normal notions of rank were suspended at sea, and a division was drawn instead between the seamen and officers, in charge and in their element, and the passengers, mere landlubbers. Here he could have a conversation with Figgins that would have been impossible on land.

She, too, was willing for once to let her guard down. Titus wasn't aware that she had decided quite some time ago that he was one of that rare breed, a man who might be trusted.

She had told Alethea as much, sitting beside her for long hours, talking to her about anything that came into her head, not sure whether Alethea heard a word of what she was saying. 'For all his hot temper and anger, he's not got a trace of that Napier nastiness in him. He sits with the ship's cat curled up on his lap, reading a book written all close, tickling puss under the chin, gentle as you please. And he's civil to the men on the ship, never a harsh word. He doesn't like to be crossed, and he hasn't got enough to keep him occupied, well, that goes for most of the gents in this world, but he's a man you can rely on.'

She pushed back a strand of Alethea's dark hair from her troubled brow.

'Just as well, circumstanced as we are. You can see why Lady Hermione entrusted you to his care, she's a wily one as is alive to every suit, she wouldn't stand for no nonsense from anyone.'

'Is Mr Hawkins feeling any better?' Titus asked Figgins.

She shook her head. 'No, and won't be until she's safe ashore, and even then, I think her spirits are so wore down it's no surprise if she doesn't stay low. For she's in a rare tangle, and no way out of it that she can see, or no way that isn't going to mean a way of life she's no fancy for.'

'Why did she marry Napier?' Titus's voice was bitter. 'How came she to make so great a mistake? Why did her family permit it?'

'He was charming and handsome and all over her, and oh-so-keen on her music, that's always been the way to win her favour, and all her parents could think about was her little brother, and no blame for that, for his life was despaired of at one point. And tongues were wagging, about her and Penrose Youdall, that everyone thought she was going to make a match of it with, only he upped and married a little dab of a creature which his mother had picked out for him.'

'Penrose Youdall?' A wave of jealousy swept through Titus, so intense and so unexpected that it took his breath away. He controlled himself, although his knuckles, grasping the rail, were white and taut. 'She cared for him?'

Figgins shot him a quick, knowing glance.

'Deep in love with him, she was, like girls are when they first meet a young man they can fancy.'

'You are a cynic, Figgins.'

'I don't know about that, since I don't rightly know what it means. But I do know how it was between Penrose and her, and I knew from the start it wouldn't do.'

He grasped at the straw. 'Not do? Why not?'

'He wasn't right for her, that's why. He was four and twenty, and still under his mother's thumb. Oh, he was dazzled by her, he fell in love with her just like that. You see her now, worn out and thin, but she's a beauty, Mr Manningtree, too tall and too unusual for some men, but the kind of girl to break hearts. Only it was the other way about, he broke her heart.'

'Curse the fellow, I hope his wife makes his life a misery.'

'No, he'll do well enough with her, they deserve each other those two. Ordinary, that's what he was, when you peeled away the good humour and high spirits and lively talk, and that'll be gone before he's thirty.'

'He sounds a dead bore.'

'He wasn't to my mistress, for she'd never have given him the time of day if he had been, but it's what he'll become.'

'So she married Napier on the rebound.'

'She married Napier to silence the gossip, the backbiting of her enemies and the pity of her friends, she can't be doing with pity. It's the Darcy pride got the better of her. She wouldn't let the world see how much she cared, and marrying a man of fashion and fortune silenced the sour talk. It's best to be off with the old love before you are on with the new is what they say, and it's true enough, if she'd given herself time to get over Mr Youdall, she'd have taken a different view of Napier. As it was, I think she thought that if she couldn't marry Penrose, it didn't matter much who she did marry.'

Figgins became confused for a moment, as though she had said too much. 'You'll forgive me speaking so freely, sir, but it's hard to bottle it all up, and I'm that worried about what's to become of her. Now, if you'll excuse me, I must get back to her.'

Alone at the rail, Titus reflected on Alethea's future. He deliberately refused to dwell on his own feelings for her; he hadn't needed that reaction to Penrose Youdall's name to be made aware of how strongly he was attracted to Alethea, an attraction that had grown into an attachment that alarmed him by its intensity.

He knew, better than Figgins, what awaited her: the condemnation of society, for rustling the curtains pulled around the marriage beds of the upper classes. Napier was rich and well-connected, and Alethea, some people would say, had behaved badly in exposing him for what he was.

Separation was the likely outcome, followed by the tortuous unravelling of all the legal and financial ties that were bound into a marriage between rich families, Napier no doubt fighting every inch of the way the efforts of Alethea's family lawyers to wrest some part of what had been a considerable fortune back for her support. A Bill of Divorce in Parliament, the sordid details of a failed marriage printed up into broadsheets and hawked about in the streets for any Tom, Dick or Harry to read and salivate over.

For Alethea, withdrawal from all the pleasures of London life. She could, if a different kind of person, attempt to brazen it out. Titus thought she would want none of it, it was a world that had served her ill and not one into which she could ever easily have fitted. Knowing her as he did now, he couldn't imagine her as a dutiful debutante, and yet that was what she had been so short a time before. She had experienced more in the few months since her come-out than most women of her position and background did in a lifetime.

After a period of discretion and withdrawal, she might be able to marry again. Divorced women, the few of them that there were, divorce being so exceedingly difficult and degrading, often did remarry, with great happiness in some cases. If your husband had deserted you, committed adultery openly and spitefully, had foisted illegitimate children on you, then you might well, after a decent interval, hope to find a man of better character and make a success of a second marriage. If you had suffered at the hands of a husband in the way that Alethea had, what chance was there that you would allow yourself to feel for any man again?

How much courage and heart and optimism for the future would Alethea have left when she had endured what undoubtedly still lay in store for her, in addition to all she had been through?

The sickness and dizziness subsided, and Alethea, weak as a kitten, felt her head clear for the first time since she came on board. She insisted on getting dressed and making her way on deck, this time gratefully taking great gulps of the fresh, salt-tanged air, and rejoicing in the sparkle of sun on the water, and the surge of speed as the boat sang through the waves.

Figgins brought her broth, which she wolfed down, and there was even a touch of colour in her cheeks when Titus joined her, expressing his pleasure at her recovery in careful, formal tones.

She smiled past him, her eyes on the narrowing landmasses on either side.

'The Straits,' he said. 'Over there is Spain, and closer at hand is Gibraltar.'

'The scene of some very stirring actions during the last war,' Coletree said from behind them. 'Take my glass, sir, and you may see the Barbary apes on the peak there.'

'Were you involved in any of the actions?' Titus asked.

'As a very young mid, I was present at a lively action, here in the straits, with the Spaniards and Frenchies lined up against us,' Coletree said, his face brightening at the recollection.

'A crucial engagement, as I remember it. You naval men had it all your own way in those days.'

'Ah, but then it was up to you in the Army, sir, how we cheered when we heard of Wellington's victories in Spain. We drank to our colleagues on land in three times three, I can tell you.'

The words washed over Alethea. Men were odd, so keen to attack and fight and kill one another, often, it seemed with no personal animosity at all. Griffy had told her how terrible it would have been if Bonaparte had been allowed to hold sway over Europe, but it was all long ago and far away to her. She could not conceive of these fascinating waters being filled with the sound and fury of battle, not now with fishing boats and ferries and pleasure vessels moving to and fro in the cross breezes.

'We leave the Mediterranean here and cross into the Atlantic,' Titus told her.

'Yes, and I think we may run into a spot of nasty weather, judging by the way the mercury has been falling these last two watches,' said Coletree, coming back to the present.

Alethea turned appalled eyes on him. 'Worse than we have already suffered?'

He stared at her, amazed. 'We have had perfect weather since we left Livorno, sir, I never saw better.'

'But the motion of the waves was so extreme.'

He laughed. 'Oh, that is what those who are martyrs to seasickness always say. You are in good company, you know; Nelson himself was always prostrate for his first few days at sea. Those who are prone to it feel that a mill pond is a maelstrom, but don't be too alarmed. You are over your bout, you will find that if it comes on to blow, you will be quite unaffected. Only take care how you go, for it's easy enough to tumble down a companionway or be knocked out of your bunk, and a broken leg is far worse than the seasickness, let me tell you!'

Chapter Twenty-four

Blow it did, short, sharp and violent, and although the *Ariadne* was a most weatherly ship, by the time she limped up the Tagus, threading her way through the throng of pilots and fishing barques, she looked a sorry sight.

'Nothing that we can't repair pretty smartly,' Coletree said to Titus as the men looped the last coil of rope after dropping anchor in the great harbour. 'Not like in the Navy, when you had to go on your knees for a spar or a replacement for a ripped sail. I'm sorry for the delay, for we were making excellent time.'

Titus had asked the captain whether the repairs might not wait until they reached England, but Coletree had been unwilling to risk the vessel or the safety of the crew and passengers. 'Like as not it'll be smooth as glass all the way back, but then it might not, and we've some tricky waters to get through. If you don't mind, sir, I'd just as soon make all right before going any further.'

Alethea stood behind the men, not listening to their conversation, all her attention focused on the dazzling whiteness of the buildings, curve upon curve of them on the hills which rose so abruptly from the main quarter. The balconies, roofs and terraces were ablaze with flowers and shrubs in brilliant colours; it was so colourful, and the sun was so bright, and the scenes on shore looked so lively and picturesque that Alethea felt a wave of happiness; the first for many days.

Figgins's eyes were out on stalks, as she stared out at the people coming and going in the squares and open places on the northern side of the river. 'Those men aren't decent,' she said. 'Short trousers and bare arms and legs!'

'Never mind the bare flesh, look how dashing their red sashes are.'

'And those men walking up and down there, those swarthy fellows with teapots upon their heads, who are they?'

'They are Moorish porters,' said Titus, breaking away from his captain, amused by Figgins's artless remarks.

'And monks, look,' said Figgins, 'in dirty brown robes; we saw enough of those papists in Venice, and here they are again.'

'Worse,' said Titus gravely. 'For they have the Inquisition here in Portugal, you know, which keeps a close eye to make sure people's religious principles are sound.'

'I know about the Inquisition,' said Alethea. 'I read the most exciting book set in Spain, about a noblewoman who barely escapes the most awful tortures at the hands of the Inquisitors.'

'I gather you are a reader of Minerva novels,' said Titus.

'I am, and freely confess it, and you may look as disapproving as you choose, men always are so high-minded about novels, especially if they come in three volumes and have marbled covers.'

'You wrong me. I take great pleasure in a good three-volume novel, and I would sooner read even the worst of them than a collection of sermons or essays by some dull scholar at the University.'

'I am glad to hear it, you cannot be altogether at fault, then.'

He gave her a swift, intent, look. 'Am I generally at fault?'

'Oh, only as men are, you know. In wanting to have your own way, and sulking when your will is crossed and thinking you may interrupt anything that a woman is saying. Men are all alike in that way.'

'I never sulk.'

'You must examine your conscience and see who is the

better judge of that, you or those who have to endure your dark moods.' Her attention was caught again by activity on shore. 'Only look at that string of mules, I swear the front one knows the way all by himself. And a cart, pulled by bullocks. When can we go ashore? I long to explore. What are those dense groves of trees there, sir? And more of them, up there.' She pointed.

'Orange groves,' said Titus, after a moment's hesitation as to where her finger was directed.

'You're never going ashore,' cried Figgins.

'I am most certainly going ashore. Who knows when I may ever come to Lisbon again? I want to see as much as I possibly can while I am here.'

'Allow me to escort you,' said Titus. 'I intend to go ashore to stretch my legs, and I believe I remember enough of my time in Lisbon to be able to show you some of the sights.'

'Were you here before? How I envy you, owning this yacht and able to sail away and visit Lisbon or anywhere you want, whenever you feel like it.'

'Last time I was in Lisbon was some years ago, when I was serving in Wellington's army. Then, the town was full of soldiers, redcoats at every corner, and the harbour jammed with ships of the Royal Navy. There was no question of a yacht in those days.'

'How do we get ashore?' asked Alethea.

'We ask one of the men to summon a boat; the purpose of all these small boats with awnings is to ferry people to and fro, across the harbour or to the suburbs of the town.'

'It is odd,' said Alethea when they had duly been rowed ashore, 'not to understand one word of the language that is being spoken all around one. The Venetian dialect was very different from the Italian I had learned, but we could understand one another. There is a lemonade seller. I am thirsty and would love some lemonade. What do those curious-looking men have in those little barrels, do you know?'

'They are selling water. They are Spaniards, from Galicia. All the water sellers in Lisbon come from Galicia, I don't know why. Are you up to climbing these extremely steep streets after your ordeal at sea? There are always cooling breezes further up and one may have a splendid view of the city below and the river and harbour if you feel you can manage the ascent.'

Nothing would have stopped Alethea. She was getting her land legs back, and was eager to see everything she could.

'You speak the Portuguese,' she said, almost accusingly, as they walked up towards the church of San Roque, and Titus exchanged a few good-humoured words with one of the beggars stretched round the gateway to a palace.

'I learned it when I was here before. Most of us acquired some knowledge of Portuguese, and Spanish, too. To a military man, some acquaintance with the language of the country in which he is fighting is almost indispensable.' He stooped to drop a coin in the man's outstretched hand.

'Are they ill?' said Alethea.

'No, why should they be?'

'The way they just lie there, only think how beggars in London accost one.'

'They would not put themselves to so much trouble, and they don't need to importune us: giving alms is a way of life here. Besides, it is hot and easier just to stretch out in a patch of shade, and perhaps they have better manners than our London beggars.'

A service had just finished as they reached the church of San Roque, and the congregation was streaming out into the sunlight. Alethea was sorry not to have got there a few minutes earlier, so that she might have heard the music, but she was enchanted by the plump women with their regular, very white teeth who came chattering and laughing out of the church. No Sunday faces here, she thought, and she noticed, with a kind of sudden detachment, that many of the expressive eyes were turned in Titus's direction.

In the turmoil of her escape and the no man's land she felt herself to be in when she was travelling as Mr Aloysius Hawkins, she had never considered Titus primarily as a man seen through a woman's eyes, not as these women were looking at him.

He wasn't handsome in the way that Napier was, with regular features and chiselled mouth, nor of the corsair type like that unpleasant Mr Warren, but he had the advantage of a tall figure, and he certainly had an air. It was that masterful nose, no doubt. There was nothing of the rake about him, yet there was a touch of danger in his expression and promise of a more sensual nature in his well-formed mouth. It wasn't an ill-tempered face, for all the brusqueness and anger he had displayed in Switzerland and Italy, and she had to grant him a sense of humour which could also be read in his face. She wondered who the woman was whom he had gone to Venice to see. Had he found her? Another Emily Lessini, or perhaps a more dazzling Italian beauty.

'What are you thinking of?' he asked after a while. 'You look to be in another world.'

'Oh, nothing of consequence,' she said, colour rising to her cheeks. 'How sorry I shall be to return to our grey skies in England.'

'It is summer now, you may hope for as much sunshine as there is here.'

She leant against a low wall and looked out over the wide expanse of sea. 'No matter how much the sun shines, or how hot it is, it can never be the same as it is here. The air has a brightness to it that is quite different.'

She paused, and breathed in the air, fragrant with the scent of nearby almond flowers. 'I am not accustomed to notice my surroundings particularly. I believe some people experience the world through their eyes and others through what they hear; I am one of the latter. Here, however, I feel compelled to gaze and gaze at what is around me. I must store up every image that I can, to tell to Miss Griffin when I see her again.'

'A friend of yours?' he enquired.

'She was my governess. She is now quite a famous authoress, she has written several of those marble-covered novels, which have enjoyed considerable success.'

'And brought her an independence, I dare say. I have frequently felt that the lot of any governess is a hard one, and I confess that the mere thought of being in that position in the Darcy household, obliged to instruct and guide you and your sisters makes me tremble. Or perhaps your four sisters – it is four, is it not? – were all meek and good. Although Mrs Wytton has never struck me as being ideal governess fodder.'

'Meek and good? No, indeed!' Alethea thought of her older sisters, priggish Letitia, strong-minded Camilla, wild Georgina and wilful Belle and laughed. 'My eldest sister was considered to be excessively good, but in reality she was as obstinate as that mule down there which is refusing to turn the corner. She is pious, too, which is insufferable, or at least she pretends to be.'

Titus blinked. 'So much for sisterly affection!'

'I think we are as much attached to one another as most brothers and sisters are, but it is a mistake to imagine that one must always like one's siblings. And Letty would not listen to me when I—' She stopped abruptly, not willing to talk about Letty, nor about Georgina. 'Letty and Georgina are more concerned with the conventions than I am. Or than Camilla is.' She fell silent, and then, feeling she must make an effort, asked, 'Do you have brothers and sisters?'

'I have a sister and a brother.'

'Do you like them?'

'I like my sister – that is, I like her when she is not trying to interfere in my life and arrange my affairs for me.'

'Oh, that is a family characteristic, is it?'

The moments of easy camaraderie were at an end. He frowned, she retreated into her own thoughts and they didn't speak again until they had descended the hill and were seated outside a café in a little square. Alethea suspected that Titus had said he wished to stop there merely to allow her to rest, but in truth she was glad to sit down and there was so much to look at as they sat and drank coffee. Gulls wheeled in the azure sky, startlingly pink flowers glowed in the window boxes attached to every window, water trickled pleasingly from the open mouth of a sporting dolphin in the fountain.

Alethea gave a sigh of pure pleasure. 'I wish this moment could last for ever.'

One day, Titus hired horses and they rode to Alhandra, a small pretty town on the banks of the Tagus.

Titus had been pleasant, courteous and withdrawn ever since the day they had ascended to San Roque. He had accompanied her on one or two other expeditions, and although perfectly amiable, had stuck firmly to neutral topics of conversation. She had felt the veil of reserve, and regretted it, but could not but respect it. Even so, what he had to say was worth hearing, and she became aware of how long it was since she had spent time in the company of a clever man, and how much she appreciated it.

On other days, he had arranged for her and Figgins to be escorted wherever they wished by one or two of Coletree's men. She had gone to Cintra with Figgins in this way, a beautiful town, he had told her, but she had not enjoyed the day, returning fagged and complaining to Figgins of the headache.

He seemed anxious not to trespass on Alethea's sensibilities and to her surprise made no more remarks about her folly or what troubles might lie ahead of her, and for this she was grateful. He remained calm and contained, with no display of temper. His outbursts of anger didn't alarm her, in fact they rather amused her, but she was not in the mood for any kind of heightened emotion, and it was as though he sensed this.

Unless it was simply that the clear, bright light, the warmth of the sun and the friendliness of the people brought on a feeling of relaxation to him, as it did to her. She had an idea that this was a place where he had once been happy, and as they sat beside the horses in the shade of a spreading cork tree, eating a picnic lunch of bread and cheese and the local wine, which was light and pétillant and refreshing, she taxed him with it.

He lay back against the trunk of the tree, a kind of half-smile about his lips. 'I was happy, it is true. I had not at that time grown to hate the army, I found the life interesting and the companionship of my fellow officers agreeable. And I struck up a friendship with a charming Portuguese woman, I never knew anyone to laugh so much. What merry times we had together!'

Alethea tried to imagine how he must have looked then. Tall and dashing in his regimentals, she was sure, and that air of easy authority no doubt meant that he had been a good and successful officer. No wonder a Portuguese beauty had attached herself to him. Probably she attached herself to one or other of the officers whenever the army was in town.

Alethea had never had the least interest in the military life. She numbered various colonels and majors and captains among her acquaintance in London, but had always found any talk about army life tedious.

Now, however, she found herself eager to listen to Titus's account of his time in this country, keen to learn something of his past life.

'Our lines lay over there,' he said, pointing beyond extensive groves of orange trees. 'My brigade occupied Alhandra while the French were massing on the frontier. All the civilians had left, it was a deserted town when we arrived, very different from how it is today.' He stood up, and offered her a hand to help her up. 'I'll show you where we had our lodging, myself and a comrade.'

They rode back through the main street of the busy little town, and Titus stopped outside a church.

'A church?' said Alethea. 'How came you to lodge in the

church? I thought I had stayed in strange places these last few weeks, but we never resorted to a church.'

'We made ourselves snug in the sacristy,' said Titus, peering into the dark interior of the church. 'If there is no interfering priest about, I shall show you our quarters.'

There was a priest, but he was young and incurious, and a gift of alms caused him to shrug his shoulders in calm agreement when Titus said what he would be about, and he obligingly supplied them with a lamp, although such a dim one that Alethea thought it would be little use.

'What a gloomy room,' she whispered, as they stepped into the lofty chamber, a place of shadows in the faint glimmer of their light. 'Who are those dismal people in the niches in the walls?'

'Images of saints, I suppose.'

'Why are they dressed in black robes, like monks? I wish their eyes didn't glare so. Look how their garments stir in the draughts, what a creepy place it is, to be sure. How Griffy would love to see this, it is so exactly like a page out of one of her novels. Were you not dismayed to find you had to share your quarters with such depressing companions?'

'Not a bit. We were cheerful, hungry and tired, so we had neither time nor energy to spare for dead monks. Our watch-cloaks were very damp, I do remember that, and we were more concerned with trying to get ourselves warm and dry than with a few departed saints. Luckily for us, the priests hadn't taken their vestments with them so we each had armfuls of gaudy pontificals to use as bedding. We slept as soundly as anything, quite undisturbed by our surroundings or our companions up there in the walls.'

The brightness outside made Alethea blink. 'It is impossible to imagine what such a life must have been like. Do you not miss the excitement and the adventure of it all?'

'My fighting days? It was an occupation that belonged to that time of life, when I was young and filled with patriotic fervour. The romantic illusions of a youthful and heated folly, a friend of mine has called it. We did have some good times, some very good times, but then there is the sheer brutality of war that in the end wears down the spirit of any man who has half a heart or mind. And the loss of so many friends and companions, that sense of loss stays with one always, I suspect, although at the time one thought little of it, it was the daily lot of the profession of arms, and we had little time to grieve.'

'And there were compensations in the form of a shapely Portuguese miss.'

'Oh, as to that . . . Our horses are standing in the shade over there. We need to be starting back to Lisbon. Coletree hopes to catch the tide this evening.'

'So our time here is finished?'

'It is.'

Chapter Twenty-five

Southampton. Another harbour, but what a different scene, with low, angry clouds scudding across a rain-sodden sky. Alethea shivered, and Figgins went below to fetch her up her greatcoat.

Titus was talking to Coletree and the deck was alive with the sound of running feet and sharp orders as the *Ariadne* eased into her mooring place. He looked alert and quite oblivious of his wet hair and face. He came over to Alethea and bade her a good morning.

'We must take care how we arrange the final part of our journey. It will be best if we go directly to The Crown. It is the largest and busiest inn in Southampton, there is always a bustle there, so our arrival will not be remarked. Neither will our departure, for you must enter the inn as Mr Hawkins and valet and leave it as Mrs Napier and her maid.'

'You are very free with your musts,' said Alethea. 'I think I may make my own arrangements, I see no reason not to continue as I am until I am nearer Herefordshire. We shall have to spend at least one night on the road, and I am more comfortable travelling as Mr Hawkins.'

'Believe me, it is best that you do not spend any time in England as Mr Hawkins. Were you to be recognised, and that is more likely in England than abroad – and even there, heaven knows, you had to run into a cousin – then your situation, already difficult, would become impossible.'

Lady Hermione had advised Alethea to return to her proper identity the moment she stepped ashore, and Alethea had admitted the sense of her argument. That didn't mean she would let Mr Manningtree order her about in his customary way.

'I do not think it can be worse.'

'It can, believe me. This is the time of year when people of fashion and rank travel all over England, to their country seats, to stay with friends, on excursions and trips for pleasure. You are bound to run into some aunt or a girl you were at the seminary with, who won't be deceived by the trousers and the short hair. I assure you it is so.'

Figgins, who had openly listened to their exchange, settled matters. 'I'm shifting into my own clothes as soon as ever may be, and if you stay as Mr Hawkins, I shall ask Mr Manningtree to find a place for me on the Accommodation coach and I shall go directly to London. I heard what Lady Hermione said, and she's a lady with a head on her shoulders if ever I saw one. You aren't wishful to become Mrs Napier again, that's what it is, but Mrs Napier you are, like it or not, and will be so until Old Nick comes to claim his own and leaves you a respectable widow, able to marry again.'

'Oh, how I wish that might happen!' said Alethea.

'A divorce will set you free of your husband,' Titus said quietly.

'There can be no question of a divorce,' said Alethea. 'Are you acquainted with the Earl of Lullington? He is the head of our family, and although Papa does not pay much attention to what he says, he carries a great deal of influence generally. He is a man of narrow outlook and severe morals; he would regard the divorce of anyone connected with him as being quite unacceptable. No, a separation is the most I can hope for, and even that will not be easy.'

'We weren't put upon this earth to have things easy,' said Figgins.

Alethea knew these bracing moods, her maid's sharp tongue always covered her greatest anxiety. If Figgins thought she ought to become Mrs Napier as soon as they were ashore, then she was probably right.

'Very well,' she conceded, not noticing the concerned look on Titus's face at the dreariness of her tone. 'The Crown it is. How are we to proceed to Shillingford?'

'Post,' said Titus. 'I keep a carriage here in Southampton, since this is where *Ariadne* generally lies in England. I wish your journey to be as comfortable as may be.'

The Crown was indeed a-bustle, its yard full of horses and carriages awaiting passengers or discharging weary-looking travellers who would have time for no more than a quick swallow of coffee before they had to catch the tide.

No one noticed the four of them go into the inn. Bootle swiftly arranged for a private chamber, Mr Hawkins and manservant disappeared up the wooden stairs, and some fifteen minutes later, down came Alethea, in the dowdy gown, accompanied by her maid, to join Mr Manningtree in the parlour for breakfast.

'Figgins is distressed by my appearance,' Alethea told Titus as she made a hearty meal of ham and eggs and several slices of toast. 'I suspect she is more worried about my meeting some fashionable acquaintance in such a gown as this than she was about my disguise.'

'I hadn't thought of that,' said Titus, frowning. 'Of course, you will need clothes. You can hardly send to Tyrrwhit House for them; what is to be done?'

'There will be some of Camilla's clothes at Shillingford,' said Alethea. 'I am taller than she, but Figgins will contrive to make them wearable. I wish I may not incur her anger when she returns to find herself tripping over the hems of her favourite gowns.'

She spoke as though in an unreal dream. Clothes, Shillingford, Camilla: they would doubtless appear in her life in due course, but for now her life had narrowed to the immediate present, to this room in the inn, and, half an hour later, the interior of a well-sprung, well-appointed carriage.

'We shall lodge tonight at Oxford,' said Titus, as he

mounted his horse. 'And reach Shillingford sometime tomorrow night. It is a gruelling journey, but I think we need to travel as fast as ever we can.'

Alethea hadn't been to Shillingford Abbey since her sister Camilla's wedding. The newly married couple had gone abroad immediately after the ceremony, calling on Mr and Mrs Darcy in Constantinople before wintering in Egypt among the tombs and pyramids, an experience that Camilla had greatly enjoyed, judging by her ecstatic letters to Alethea.

The rain and her state of mind made the journey to Herefordshire one to be endured rather than enjoyed. How grey it was outside the windows of the carriage, rain-sodden fields, unhappy country folk trudging along with what protection from the elements they could contrive; even, in one village a bucket upturned over the head of a hurrying youth. That made her laugh, and laughter made her feel more cheerful.

'We are nearly there,' she said to Figgins, recognising the church in the village and the long, mellow brick wall that ran along the edge of that part of the grounds. The carriage made the sharp turn into the gate, and then they were bowling along beside the ha-ha, the abbey ahead of them, with a shaft of sunlight just breaking through the clouds, signalling that the worst of the summer storm might be over.

'There will be no problem with Mrs Burden, the housekeeper at Shillingford,' Lady Hermione had said. 'She will know you at once for Camilla's sister, she never forgets a face. And she may appear a trifle waspish, but no one who knows her can doubt the kindness of her heart. Titus will bear witness to that.'

'Yes, Mrs Burden and I have been friends these many years.'

Now the carriage was at the door, the butler was waiting, a footman in his country livery hurrying to open the carriage door and let down the steps. A groom came running from the direction of the stables to take the reins from Titus as he dismounted. 'Mr Manningtree, sir, I heard as you were in foreign parts, it's good to see you again. This'll be that mare from the King's Head in Hereford, I recognise her by that white sock. One of the boys will take her back when she's had a rest and a rub down.'

Mrs Burden was in the great hall, on to which the front door opened. Small and thin, she smiled when she saw Titus.

She welcomed Alethea, took in her stride the news that her sister's closet was to be raided for clothes for her to wear, and gave orders for her to be taken to her room.

'You will want to rest after your journey,' she said to Alethea. 'I shall send down to the kitchen directly with orders for a supper to be prepared for you, you may prefer to eat it in the small saloon, the dining room has been all closed up since Mr and Mrs Wytton are away. Mr Titus, will you not stay to eat?'

'No, no, I must away. I shall call in the morning, I dare say, to see how Mrs Napier does.'

And he was gone, before Alethea could thank him or say goodbye. She felt strangely bleak, but put it down to tiredness from rattling along in a carriage for so many miles. 'I think every tooth in my head has been shaken from its socket,' she told Mrs Burden as she followed her up the stone staircase to a bedchamber on the first floor.

She fell asleep as soon as Figgins had drawn the curtains round the old-fashioned four-poster bed, and woke to find cracks of sunlight peeping through the joins. She yawned and slipped out of bed to go to the window and drink in the landscape, a paradise of summer greens, a haze predicting a fine day, the countryside alive with the sound of birds. A cockerel crowed, late to his duty, and in one of the paddocks a horse whickered to its companion. It was all so peaceful. She heaved a deep sigh of pure pleasure and rang the bell for Figgins. How late was it? How she had slept, and how hungry she was!

Figgins had also slept, but not so long, and had found time to adjust one of Camilla's gowns so that it more or less fitted Alethea. 'Which it would be a better fit if you had more flesh on you, skin and bones still, though not as bad as you were.'

Alethea made a good breakfast, and then took herself off to the music room. Her brother-in-law had a good piano, she remembered, a Broadwood. She hoped it was in tune; a few chords reassured her and she began to search through the piles of music. How long it was since she had had the indulgence of playing so many of her favourite pieces.

Her fingers were woefully out of practice, and she settled down to some serious work. Absorbed in the music, she neither heard the sound of an approaching horseman nor the rapid footsteps approaching the music room. The door was flung open without ceremony.

'Of course you would be in here.'

'It is very early for a morning call, Mr Manningtree, you will shock the servants.'

'Never mind the servants. I had to come immediately I heard the news.'

'What news?'

'Only this, that Napier, your husband, is dead.'

Chapter Twenty-six

Incredulous, Alethea stared at Titus. 'Dead? He cannot be dead.'

'He is dead, I assure you, and has been dead this last week.'

Alethea looked down at her hands, still resting on the keys. 'Dead,' she repeated softly to herself. She couldn't take it in, the word meant nothing. Another word crept into her head. Widow. She was a widow.

She got up from the piano stool and went over to the window, looking out across the parkland with unseeing eyes. Then she spoke to Titus, reflected in the glass. 'I am glad of it. There, that is a monstrous thing to say of any being, is it not? It has the virtue, however, of being the truth.'

'You may not be so glad when you hear how he met his end,' said Titus drily.

'How was that?'

'He was murdered.'

'Murdered!' Now she felt some of the shock and alarm that might be considered natural to a young woman hearing of the death of her husband of less than a year.

'Who murdered him? In Italy, this was, I suppose, only how can the news have travelled so fast. Was he poisoned?'

'You do read too many novels, don't you? No, he was pistolled, and with one of his own guns.'

'Perhaps he killed himself.'

'Perhaps he did, if it weren't that he was shot in the back. And this event did not take place in Italy, but in London.'

'In London! How came he to be in London? We made sure he would still be hunting me in Italy.'

'Nevertheless, he arrived back in England last Tuesday, in perfect health and was found dead on Wednesday morning.'

'How did you hear this?'

'I had a letter this morning from my sister, who supposed I might be interested. It is also in the newspapers which I sent for at once: grave concern expressed that the killer has not been apprehended and brought to justice, our streets unsafe for decent citizens and so on and so forth.'

'A week ago!' While they had still been on the high seas, Napier had been breathing his last in London. 'I have never set foot in Napier's London house,' she said inconsequentially. 'He wouldn't let me visit London.'

'You may visit there as often as you please now, for I dare say the house is yours.'

Alethea blinked, surprised. 'I . . . that is, I have no idea how things are fixed. The lawyers – it was all arranged by the lawyers. I didn't consider it important, and of course my opinion on financial matters was never sought.'

'I should be most surprised if your own fortune at least was not secured upon you in the event of Napier's demise. As to the rest – however, that is not to be thought of at present. Now we have to consider what you are to do.'

'Must I play the grieving widow?' Then, as realisation of what had happened finally sank home, she sat down again.

'That's what the newspapers say you are, alone and desolated in Napier's country seat.'

'But the people at Tyrrwhit House will know I am not there.'

'Yes, and I dare say questions are already being asked as to your whereabouts. This happened only a week ago, it is not so very long. What would you prefer to do? My advice would be for you to go to London, my carriage is at your disposal, or you may order Wytton's to take you.'

Even amid the whirl of thoughts tumbling in her head, Alethea took in that Titus, for once, wasn't telling her what she should do. And, for once, she very much wished that he would. 'You advise me to go to London. What else can I do? Can I not stay here?'

'I think it best for you to be in London at this time; however, it is entirely your decision. You look quite pale, allow me to call Figgins to you.'

'It is just a shock, it is only now sinking in. Napier dead! Is it truly so? And in so terrible a fashion. Was there an intruder?'

Titus shook his head. 'According to the account in the newspaper, it seems that he had been dining with another person that evening. There were no signs of a forced entry.'

'Where were the servants? Perhaps one of them was the murderer, I cannot tell you how unpleasant his servants are. I should not be surprised to learn that any one of them had committed a crime.'

'Perhaps, but they can hardly all be potential murderers. I should not mention the servants, if I were you.' He paused, and spoke in a kinder voice. 'If you intend to go to London, I do not think you can go too quickly, you would do well to leave at once. You will stay with Lady Fanny, I assume?'

'Fanny? I hadn't thought – yes, yes; I had better go to Aubrey Square.'

Alethea took in nothing of the journey, heedless of a landscape that so shortly before had been desolate in the rain and was now aglow with summer. Her thoughts were all inward: her situation, her secrets – so many secrets – what would be required of her once she reached London.

The carriage turned into Aubrey Square, and there was Fanny at the door, holding out her arms and escorting her cousin indoors while issuing a volley of commands for wine, smelling salts, a doctor—

'Fanny, I'm not ill.'

'No, but you are so thin and pale. My dear' – with a cry of dismay – 'you are wearing yellow, it is positively indecent, where are your blacks?'

'Blacks?' said Alethea, as Fanny thrust her on to a sofa and instructed her to put up her feet. 'I've had no time to think of mourning.'

'No, not a word of protest, I can see how fagged you are from the journey. Dawson is bringing hot towels for your hands and face, and cologne. Oh, you are so young to be a widow, it is all so dreadful. And to die in such a way.'

'Fanny,' said Alethea, sitting up very straight, 'let us get one thing straight. I have to tell you that I feel no real grief at Napier's death.'

'It is shock; oh, Lord, I knew we should have sent for Dr Molloy.'

'It is not shock, it is sense. Ours was a terrible marriage – no, listen to me, Fanny, for I must speak before Cousin Fitzwilliam makes an appearance, he will die himself if he hears what I have to say.'

Fanny lifted her hands to her face. 'Alethea, you are not aware of what you say. And how come you to be so brown? Never tell me you have been outside without shading your face from the sun. How are you ever to get your complexion restored? And you are so thin, and I am sure you are grown another inch at least.'

'Only listen to me, Fanny. Quickly, now, while we are alone. Napier was not the man he seemed. He was unkind – no, brutal to me, he treated me as he would not have treated his dog.'

Fanny stared at her, aghast. Alethea could see that she was shaken to the core, but Fanny was no innocent, she had been out in the world long enough to know that not all marriages were happy.

'So charming a man, such exquisite manners, and a real love of music, we all thought, we hoped . . . only when you never came to London, I did wonder. I wrote to Letty, but she said Napier was the most doting of husbands, and Fitzwilliam said that you had always had a kick in your gallop and that you would settle down soon enough. And of course, when there is a child—'

'Thank God there are to be no children from my union with Napier.'

Alethea's words were so heartfelt that Fanny was silenced. 'Was it so very bad?'

Sympathy would undo her. She would not, must not cry. 'It could not have been worse.'

'Oh, good Lord, it is all too much for me, the murder, and you sitting there so calmly and telling me—'

'Napier was an innately cruel man, and selfish to the bone. He wished to destroy my soul and my music and my reason for living and that is why I'm not a grieving widow.'

'No, no, I quite see that. Only, Alethea, you must not say so. Within these four walls is one thing, but it must go no further. You have to wear black and be subdued if you cannot be tearful. Dignity will always be approved, and you will attract a deal of sympathy, young as you are.'

'Sympathy! That is the last thing I want.'

'I hope you said nothing at Tyrrwhit House that would reveal your feelings.'

'I wasn't there,' said Alethea, flushing despite herself. 'I have travelled up today from Shillingford.'

'Shillingford! Is Camilla returned? How comes this?'

'Camilla is still abroad, but her mother-in-law invited me to stay.'

'Then Lady Hermione is back, I had no idea.'

Alethea wondered whether to tell her that Lady Hermione Wytton was still in Italy, but decided it was best to keep a discreet silence. Dawson came in with a glass of wine and some macaroons. She greeted Alethea with a kind look, and said she was sorry to hear of her troubles, and that a supper was being laid for her downstairs.'

'I am sure Miss Alethea, Mrs Napier, I mean, is far too upset to eat.'

'On the contrary, thank you, Dawson.'

'Mr Fitzwilliam has been sent for to his club and is expected home directly,' Dawson said to Fanny.

Alethea's heart sank. Mr Fitzwilliam would disapprove of her yellow dress, of her having been at Shillingford, of her coming to London, of her lack of tears, of everything about her.

'Now, mind what I say, Alethea,' said Fanny as soon as Dawson left the room. 'Not a word to Fitzwilliam of how you feel. You must be a good girl, as I know you can be, and do just as people will expect. First and foremost, black clothes must be procured for you; Dawson will know how to go about finding something for you to wear at once, and then my dressmaker will come tomorrow and we can rig you out properly. Black, in June, and with your colouring, so unbecoming. Still, there is no help for it.'

Fortunately, the evening was got through more easily than Alethea had feared. The journey, the strain of putting on a front and her uneasiness at knowing how appalled her cousins would be if they had the least hint of where she had been these last few weeks brought on a genuine headache.

'Was there some estrangement between you and Napier?' Fitzwilliam asked as he tucked into a bowl of strawberries and cream. We heard from Georgina that you had been to Paris without your husband, although she gave no details . . .'

Thank God for that, at least.

'. . . then there have been rumours of Napier behaving rather oddly. People said he had gone to Vienna, to see Mr Darcy . . .'

'Papa is in Constantinople again, so that cannot be the case,' said Alethea, picking her words carefully. 'Napier was a man to act upon impulse.' That was true enough.

Fitzwilliam wiped his mouth and laid down his napkin. 'Any suggestion of a coolness between you and Napier must be denied. We cannot be too careful at a time like this.'

Alethea put her hand to her throbbing eyes.

'Alethea, you should go to bed, I can see how your head aches,' said Fanny. 'Figgins may bring you up a tisane, and in the morning, perhaps things will not seem so bad.'

The morning brought welcome activity: gowns, shoes, hats, all in unrelieved black, arrived at Aubrey Square, where Figgins and Dawson fell upon them, needles and scissors in hand, to make them fit for Alethea to wear. Madame Foutgibu arrived to measure and show patterns of more black clothes – 'For you will need to have everything black for now, there will have to be at least three months of the deepest mourning,' said Fanny.

Which prospect depressed Alethea's spirits still further. Scarcely a fortnight ago, she had been enjoying the brilliant colours of Lisbon; now her world had shrunk to a black nightmare.

'Surely I may leave off my blacks when I am here, within doors,' she said.

Fanny was adamant. 'Word would fly round London, you know how servants talk, or if we had callers, who caught sight of you – no, it is not to be thought of.'

And it was clad in black from head to foot that she sat with Fanny the next day, at the time of Napier's funeral and entombment in the family vault at Tyrrwhit. Mr Fitzwilliam had travelled down to represent the family; Fanny and Alethea read through the burial service at the appointed time.

'Amen,' said Alethea, shutting the Prayer Book and laying it down with a thump on the table. 'The End.'

'I know you did not, as things were, care for him,' said Fanny reprovingly, 'but this is not a time for levity.'

'He lived by violence and he died by violence,' said Alethea, but under her breath.

Free of him she might be, but freedom in any wider sense was not what life at Aubrey Square was about. Fanny had told Fitzwilliam that Napier had not treated Alethea well; he pursed his lips and looked grave and said that young women were not always the best judges of their husband's behaviour.

He expected Alethea to behave with excessive decorum, saying that any hint of frivolity at this difficult time was to be deplored.

Restless and bored, surrounded by domesticity and missing – although she refused to admit this to herself – Titus's clever and amusing company, Alethea grew more and more irritable. This worried Fanny, who had some understanding of her young cousin's turbulent nature, which in its turn made Alethea feel angry with herself and ungrateful and, in the end, even more irritable.

'Perhaps you should go down to Pemberley,' Fanny suggested.

No, Alethea didn't want to go to Derbyshire; memories of that happier world of childhood were too acute. 'I do not want to rusticate, thank you,' she said to Fanny.

Then Mr Fitzwilliam happened to mention Melville Place, where Napier's London house was situated. 'It is a good address,' he said. 'You will have no trouble finding a tenant in due course.'

'What,' said Alethea, 'a house where there has been a murder? Only a ghoul would want a lease on it.'

Mr Fitzwilliam looked surprised. 'Your husband was not killed in Melville Place,' he said. 'I thought you knew, he was murdered elsewhere.'

Chapter Twenty-seven

'Why need we go in at the back of the house?' Alethea asked Figgins, as she inserted the key into the lock of the small door that led into the mews of 17 Melville Place.

'When there's been a murder done, folk like to come and gawp.'

Once inside, with the door closed behind them, the sounds of busy London streets retreated. No heads looked out from the stalls, no familiar smell of horse and hay and leather hung on the air. A half door swung to and fro on a creaking hinge. A carriage, shafts up, stood in the coach house. Grass grew between the cobbles. It was all neglected, and the forlorn scene made Alethea wonder anew about her late husband.

She knew nothing of his London life, she had merely thanked God when he went to London for days or a week at a time. Although she had soon learned that the respite of her husband's absence was paid for when he returned to the country, his desire to control and destroy her intensified by his visit to London.

'Napier wasn't murdered here,' she said. 'I hadn't realised that until Mr Fitzwilliam started talking about this house.'

'It makes no difference. If that lot of gawkers get a glimpse of you, and know you for who you are, they'll be buzzing round like bluebottles. Best to go in this way and not give them the chance.'

'It looks so desolate without any horses or grooms or stablehands. Why is it all so unkempt, I wonder?'

'We'll find out soon enough.'

'He never liked this house,' Alethea said, as Figgins pushed open the door that led to the servants' quarters. 'Once, when he was drunk, he said that every time he stepped foot in it, he could hear his father's voice in his ears. I believe he and his father never got on together. His father disapproved of him. I dare say he was an estimable man.'

'As well for him,' said Figgins, as she led the way down a narrow, dark, odorous passage, 'for then he may be sitting up in heaven on a cloud, whereas Napier, if he has his just deserts, will be spinning on a hot spit turned by Old Nick himself.'

They found Watts, the caretaker, in the kitchen, a clay pipe in his hand, and a large tabby cat curled up on his wide lap. He turned bibulous red eyes on them and heaved himself up from his wooden seat, tucking the cat under a brawny arm.

'Here is Mrs Napier,' said Figgins briskly. 'So put that great animal down, and make yourself useful.'

The caretaker stared at Alethea. 'Mrs Napier? In the kitchen?'

'Yes, we came this way for convenience,' said Alethea. 'However, you may show us the way upstairs, if you please. It is very musty down here, I must say.'

Alethea wasn't at all perturbed to find herself in the regions of the house that most young ladies never ventured into. In her younger days, when she and Figgins had crept out of the Fitzwilliams' house in Aubrey Square, dressed as men so that Alethea could join her musician friends, they had frequently come and gone through the servants' entrance.

They passed through the doors that separated the two parts of the house and were in the hall. Dusty rays filtered through the fanlight over the door, otherwise it was as gloomy there as it had been below stairs.

'Not expecting company,' the caretaker said, 'me and Mrs Watts hadn't got any rooms ready.'

Alethea opened the nearest door and found herself in a dingy parlour, furnished in the fashion of the last century, with a faded Turkey rug upon the floor and shabby damask curtains hanging at the windows.

'Open them shutters, Watts,' Figgins said. 'Look lively, now.'

Alethea drew a squiggle of notes in the dust on an ornate commode, then regarded the grime on the fingers of her gloves with some astonishment.

'What do you expect if you go doing that?' said Figgins. 'The hem of your dress is quite thick with dust, too; black is terrible for showing dirt.' She turned back to Watts, who was trying to slide out of the room so that he could dive back to his chair in the kitchen. 'Did your master not care that his house was so ill kept? Where are the rest of the servants?'

'There aren't none. There was Mr Holbis here, from time to time, as looked after Mr Napier, his gentleman's gentleman he was, but he was sent off on half-wages while Mr Napier was away, and he ain't been back. Mr Napier never stayed in this house, although there are some of his clothes upstairs, what Mr Holbis says are out of fashion. He wasn't allowed to take them, which was wrong, for cast-offs belongs to a gentleman's gentleman, as everyone knows.'

'Holbis was a slimy creature,' Alethea said to Figgins. 'I am glad he is not here, he would be no use to us. However, if there are no maids, no footmen, no one in the kitchen, it will be impossible to stay here.'

'You will have to bustle about and see what you can do, you and Mrs Watts,' Figgins said to the caretaker.

He stared at her, aghast. 'There ain't no amount of bustling's going to get this house straight. In old Mr Napier's day we had a staff of twelve, not counting those out in the stable.'

'You leave the staff to me,' said Figgins, wrinkling her nose as she lifted a cushion. 'We don't need twelve, but we do need a cook and help in the kitchen, and maids, and someone to scrub. I'll get my brother Jack over, if it's all right with you, Miss Alethea, he's just come out of the Navy, where he was steward to a naval officer as has been made admiral and gone off to a shore post overseas. Jack didn't fancy any more overseas, he's had enough of foreigners to last him a lifetime, he says, so he'll be looking about for a position. He can come here meanwhile and give us a hand. Here, you, Watts, find a boy who'll take a note. Look sharp now, we haven't got all day.'

The sound of a bell pealed in the distance, followed by a brisk rapping at the front door.

'There now,' said Watts, visibly distressed. 'Who'd have thought it, callers and at this hour. Can't they see the knocker's off, meaning we ain't at home?'

'That'll be Griffy,' said Alethea, running into the hall. She threw her arms round the rather fierce-looking woman, dressed in expensive but unfashionable blue bombazine who stood in the hall, looking about her with some dismay. 'Oh, I'm so happy you've come, Griffy, we are in such a fix. Have you heard about Napier?'

'Is there anyone in London outside Bedlam who hasn't heard?' said Miss Griffin. 'Well, Figgins, I'm glad to see that you're back with Mrs Napier. Now, be careful with that portmanteau, it contains papers, and I don't want them fluttering all over the room, thank you. Alethea, what are you doing here? Why aren't you with Lady Fanny or the Gardiners?'

'I have been with the Fitzwilliams, and have been driven nearly mad, with nothing to do, and Fanny all solicitousness and my cousin full of disapproval, so I decided to come and stay here.'

'It is quite improper for you to be here alone, at such a time.'

'I have Figgins, and now I have you, Griffy dear.'

'I am not at all sure that I shall stay. Your message was so urgent that even though I am in the middle of the most exciting part of my tale, I felt obliged to put down my pen and come to Melville Place. However, it all looks to be in very poor order and I am not of a domestic turn of mind, as you know. '

'No, no, nothing domestic will be required of you, I promise. We shall find you a comfortable place for your writing and you may go on with your novel just as you would in your own house,' said Alethea. 'In the evening, you can read me what you've written, as you used to when I was in the schoolroom. And I shall tell you something of my travels – you will be interested to hear of the dangers we faced while crossing the Alps.'

'You have been abroad? I had no idea. Indeed, I haven't had a word from you since your marriage. You never wrote to me.'

'I did, indeed I did, but Napier made sure none of my letters was ever sent. I was so mistaken in his character, I can't tell you what a monster he turned out to be.'

'I dare say,' said Miss Griffin, with a significant look at Watts.

'Are you still here?' said Alethea. 'You may go, Watts, and you are to do just as Figgins tells you.'

He didn't look as though that was a prospect to bring him much pleasure, and he went grumbling off while Figgins began issuing a stream of instructions to his broad, resentful back.

'Why, here is a cat,' said Miss Griffin, who liked cats. 'A very handsome cat. Why do you laugh?'

'Oh, because Napier couldn't abide cats, and here is this creature lording it in his house. Although I don't know why I call it his house, for it seems he never lived here. I wonder where he stayed when he was in London.'

'I can tell you that, for it is in the newspapers. I don't suppose you have read them. He kept rooms a few streets from here, a handsome set of lodgings, apparently, done up in some style.' She gave Alethea a sharp look. 'That is where he was killed, did you know that much, at least?'

'I knew it was not here, and I am most grateful for it,

otherwise I could not have come. Griffy, ours was not' – she hesitated, searching for words – 'a happy marriage.'

'That's as may be, only you'd best mind your tongue when others are about, especially the servants. Figgins is to be trusted, of course, but you cannot be sure of anyone else. That Watts looks a thoroughly disagreeable fellow.'

She was removing her hat as she spoke, and Alethea gave a sigh of relief. 'You'll stay? Oh, thank goodness.'

'For the time being,' said Miss Griffin. 'Now, perhaps Figgins might be prevailed upon to make a pot of coffee. A strong cup of coffee, if you please.'

Figgins was as good as her word, and by midday her brother, in a footman's apron, was busy about the house. A friend of Mrs Figgins, who had once been in service, came round to oblige in the kitchen, bringing with her a sniffing waif of a granddaughter to lend a hand. Jack rustled up some old shipmates who were more than happy to earn a few shillings putting the house to rights in the nautical way, and Mrs Watts, fearing that she would be quite superseded if she let anyone else loose among her mops and buckets, set to with surprising energy, so that the house began to look much more the thing.

Not that Alethea cared much about it. She had found a harpsichord in the drawing room, its case slightly attacked by worm, but with the strings intact. She at once set about tuning it, causing Mrs Watts to cast scandalised looks in her direction and set up a muttering about widows, but Alethea took no notice.

Lost in her music as she was, she could still not shut out thoughts of her future. More than anything else, she needed to know how she stood, financially and legally. How could she find out? The family lawyer would know, but even if she summoned him, he would be shocked at being asked such a question, and probably be so full of contorted language that there would be no understanding a word of it.

Her father would tell her, or Mr Gardiner; they were

neither of them available to be asked. Mr Fitzwilliam might or might not know; either way, she could not trust him to tell her the exact truth. He would be so horrified, was already so horrified at a young woman's presuming to display any sense of independence, that he would hedge and fall into a temper and be no use at all.

Did Griffy have any views on the subject?

'None,' said that lady, when they were sitting together at the dining table. 'I have never had any chance of an inheritance; such money as I have and have ever had is what I have made by my labours. And since I never married, I have always managed my own affairs. It is different for you, there is property and a good deal of money, I dare say, and you have various members of your family to advise and guide you.'

'That's just it, I don't want to be guided. I want to be like you, and not have anyone telling me what I may and may not do.'

'That is your wild streak coming out, Alethea. I always warned you to take care how you let go of restraints, for there is no knowing where your actions may lead you.'

Figgins had come into the dining room to clear the table and set out the dessert. 'Ask that Mr Manningtree, Miss Alethea, that's my advice. He's bound to be a magistrate and all that, he will know what's what if anyone does.'

'Mr Manningtree?' said Miss Griffin. 'A clever, troubled man; I remember him from dear Camilla's wedding. I am sure he is knowledgeable about such things, but what has he to do with you?'

Alethea, thinking how much time she had spent in Titus Manningtree's company, and in what outrageous circumstances, had to consider before she answered. 'I have seen something of Lady Hermione, Alexander's mother, recently, and Mr Manningtree is a very good friend of hers, she is his godmother in fact. Figgins was greatly impressed by him.'

'Figgins is a good judge of character, but you can hardly be asking your forthright questions of a man whose connection with you is so remote. We are used to your ways, within the family, and even there your wildest schemes and pranks have all too often had to be smoothed over and kept from your nearest and dearest. A comparative stranger would be shocked to hear you talk the way you do.'

No, he wouldn't, Alethea said inwardly. During the companionable time they had spent in Lisbon, she had come to realise that, while Titus might not like or approve of what she had done, he had enough of the unconventional in his own make-up not to take the high moral ground over her actions. His concern was for risks she ran and the consequences of what she was doing, should it become known.

He didn't think any female should behave the way she did, that was clear, yet he had been kind to her, and she felt that he fully understood how difficult her marriage had been. She didn't think he would be startled or offended by her lack of sensibility in asking what she wanted to know; on the other hand, she had enough social sense to know that she would take a risk in asking him to call upon her, situated as she was – not without setting every tongue in London wagging. They might wag about her, already were, according to Cousin Fitzwilliam, but she was not going to give anyone cause to gossip about Titus; she owed him that, at least.

Titus read the note through once more. What a vile hand Alethea wrote, or perhaps it was scrawled in haste. Somehow, the flowing, lively, imperfect script brought her vividly before him, and it was with a smile on his lips that he folded the note and rang for Bootle.

'I am going out, Bootle. On foot, I feel a need to stretch my legs.'

'To the club, sir?'

'Yes, I shall be at the club later, and I shall dine there.'

He didn't tell Bootle that he would be going to the club after he had been to Melville Place. Bootle didn't need telling, however, that there was a lady in the case: otherwise why should his master have taken such unusual care about the tying of his neck cloth, or worn his new coat? Not for the club, oh, no, Mr Manningtree was far too casual in his ways for Bootle's taste, and more than happy to go to his club dressed with a carelessness that Bootle knew brought condemnation from his more dandified fellow members – condemnation of his, Bootle's skills, not his master's lack of interest in his appearance.

The message had stressed both urgency and secrecy, which was why, Titus supposed, he had to enter the house through the stables. Nothing with Alethea was done in the normal way; what was she up to now?

He was exact as to his time, and she was waiting for him by the kitchen door. 'Mr Watts is fast asleep,' she said in a whisper, by way of greeting, 'and Mrs Watts has gone off to visit her daughter in Sheep Lane. Not a word as we go through, however, for who knows how soundly he is asleep?'

Judging by the volume of snores, Titus thought nothing less than the last trump would awaken Mr Watts from his slumbers, but he obeyed his instructions, and they passed silently through the kitchen and up into the other part of the house.

Alethea gestured to him to go through a door, and he found himself in a parlour that had seen better days. He frowned. Napier must have been a poor kind of man to let his house get so run down; it wasn't in keeping with what he had heard of the man.

'Don't look disapproving, it is shabby, I know. Napier never came here, he didn't live here, you know, after his father died. They did not get on together. I have a great suspicion that old Mr Napier knew his son was not all that he should be.'

'Fathers generally do,' said Titus drily. 'Even though they are often reluctant to admit to themselves that their offspring have any faults.'

'Was that the case with your father? I am afraid my own papa has an excellent idea of all his children's failings. That is not to say he is a harsh parent, or does not delight in what we do well.'

'I am slightly acquainted with your father; everyone who knows him must admire such a man.'

He was surprised to see the pleasure his words gave her. Then she looked more serious. 'It is what makes it so hard, that I can't confide in him as I should. At least not until I have things sorted out for myself.'

There she went again, determined to tackle all her problems on her own. He longed to help her, to say, let me manage it all for you – but how could he? He was no relation, not a long-standing friend of the family, he had no position at all except what she might grant him. And he had no illusions about how little that would be. Yet she had asked him to call.

'You are not alone in the house?' he asked with sudden concern. 'You have Figgins with you?'

'Yes, Figgins takes excellent care of me, and also there is Miss Griffin, my former governess. She is upstairs, writing, she is the novelist I spoke of.'

'I dare say you help her with her plots, that is, if your ideas are not too fantastical.'

She gave him a quizzical look. 'Is that a criticism of what I do?'

'I assure you, it is not. I would not presume to criticise you.'

'Oh, this is very high all of a sudden, you have scolded and abused me across Europe and back, and now you say such a thing.'

'Some of your exploits may be criticised, that is not the same as passing judgement on you.'

'But you have passed judgement, frequently.'

Which was true, so how could he redeem himself? He couldn't say, your behaviour is outrageous, but I have come to admire you more than any woman I have ever known? Let alone tell her that she meant more to him than he had imagined any woman could. So much for his grand words to Harry, about being beyond the age of falling in love. He had an idea that even to say that would call down the mockery and retribution of the gods; well, it had certainly done so in this case.

'If I have done so, then I apologise. I had no right.'

She looked at him, astonished.

'Am I to meet this Miss Griffin?'

'She does not know you are here, I thought it better to keep your visit a secret. You will not want the polite world to know that you have been associating with a person whose name is in the newspapers.'

'As if I cared a damn for that.'

'You may not; I find that I do.'

He was startled, and it showed in his face.

'I may be heedless and feckless on my own account; there is no reason why I should drag others into my misfortune. My family cannot avoid the connection, you can.'

'I am at your service, please believe me.'

'I do, and that is why I sent for you. You are the very person who can answer a most important question. What is my position, in the eyes of the law, now that I am a widow? I am only eighteen, you know, so must I wait until I am twenty-one to have control of my fortune – and my life?'

'Why do you ask me? Surely your family has a legal adviser—'

'Yes, and he will merely advise me to wait until my father comes back to England, he will manage everything for me.'

'Don't you intend to return to your father's house? It is customary in these circumstances, with you being so young.'

'To Pemberley? No. It was the home of my childhood, and my childhood is gone. My marriage was an unhappy one, and it has changed me, as has my taste of freedom these last few weeks. I don't wish to set up as an eccentric, for it would upset my family, but I do wish to have my own establishment

– if it is in any way possible. Figgins said you were sure to be a magistrate, and I should have thought of it myself, naturally a man in your position will have a considerable knowledge of the law.'

'I would not risk an opinion on most legal questions, but this is one that I can answer. In the eyes of the law, you are of age. You may live how and where you choose. Whether your family will permit it, is another thing altogether. Moral pressure can be much stronger than all the laws in the land.'

'Thank you!' she said with real gratitude. 'I knew I could trust you to deal with me in a clear and reasonable manner.'

'That is, provided you have sufficient funds at your disposal to set up on your own, and that the money is not tied up in such a way that it imposes its own restrictions upon you.'

Her face fell. 'Oh, dear. If I cannot have any money free of ties, then I shall have to set about earning some.'

He felt a spurt of alarm. 'Alethea, I do hope you aren't thinking of opera, for although your voice is so very good, the life is such—'

'No, though I'm happy to think that I could engage in such an occupation if I were ever driven to it. I love the music, but the stage is not for me, I knew that very quickly. One has to have a flair for performing that I do not possess. No, there must be other ways in which an indigent female can earn a living. Griffy has always done so.'

'You are a Darcy, not a governess.'

'I was a Darcy, I'm not one any longer. My name, unfortunately, is now Napier and, thanks to my husband, it is a name that carries no honour.'

'You are young, you will marry again. You are free to choose your own husband, you need ask no one's permission.'

'I chose my own husband the first time, and look how that ended. No, I have done with matrimony, that is the one thing I am certain of.'

His heart missed a beat. She sounded so calm, so definite.

'Marriage to Napier has given me a poor opinion of the male half of mankind. They may go their way and I shall go mine.'

'We are not all such men as Napier!'

He spoke with unintended vehemence, and she looked surprised. 'I dare say you are not, but then Napier didn't seem to be what he was until after we were married. No, once bitten twice shy, as the saying goes. Not even for the satisfaction of losing the name of Napier would I venture into matrimony again. Now, I do not wish to seem rude, but I cannot count on Watts snoring away for much longer, so I think you had better go.'

Sir Humphrey was an urbane man, but with a look of shrewd intelligence in his chilly eyes. He was, he said, when he had made his bow, acquainted with Mrs Napier's father.

Which didn't cheer Alethea's spirits. Every time she thought of her father, and what he would have to say when she saw him again, she felt weak. Even with half the truth kept from him, there was enough in her behaviour to arouse one of his more caustic rebukes, a rebuke that would be made even more stinging by the knowledge that she had disappointed him.

'Are you alone?' Sir Humphrey said, looking around the room.

The door opened, and Miss Griffin came in. 'Figgins told me you desired me to be present,' she said, with a warning look at Alethea.

Alethea had expressed no such desire, Sir Humphrey's arrival had taken her quite by surprise. She had never met the man, and had no idea why he had called. More worldly wise, Miss Griffin knew exactly who he was, and why he must be here, and she had left her manuscript pages without hesitation when Figgins came running upstairs with the news of his arrival.

Sir Humphrey was introduced to Miss Griffin. Then, once

seated, he offered his condolences to Mrs Napier on the untimely loss of her husband, and without any further preamble he told them why he had come. He was a magistrate, and Napier's death had been a murder, and the murderer must be found and brought to justice. In the circumstances, Mrs Napier would forgive him for intruding on her grief, but it was his duty to discover if she had any information that might help them in apprehending the criminal.

Alethea was about to speak when Sir Humphrey raised a hand, and went on. 'If you could simply answer some questions, I believe that is all that will be required of you.'

The few extra seconds gave Alethea time to reflect. This man was not a Fitzwilliam, partisan and not always able to see beyond his convictions and prejudices. This was not a man to be easily deceived and hoodwinked. Nor was he likely to be taken in by tears and lamentations and expressions of woe at the loss of her husband; she had a notion that he had some idea of what kind of a man Napier was. Dignified restraint, a well-bred coolness and reserve were needed here, and a great deal of wariness. She nodded.

'You didn't accompany your husband to London.'

That was a statement, not a question. 'No.' Don't elaborate, she told herself; just give short, definite answers.

'Was this unusual?'

'I never accompanied my husband to London. He preferred me to remain in the country.'

'On this occasion also you stayed at Tyrrwhit House?'

There was a glint in his eye, and Alethea just prevented herself from falling into what might be a trap.

'No. I chose not to.'

'You were not, in fact, at Tyrrwhit when Mr Napier came to London. You had, I believe, gone to Paris.'

'My sister, Lady Mordaunt lives there.'

'Yes. Was there some estrangement between you and your husband, Mrs Napier? That recently married as you were, you chose to spend so much time apart?'

'I have always been close to my sisters.'

'You returned to this country when?'

Alethea decided it was time to make a venture of her own. 'If you wish to know where I was on the day when my husband was killed, all I can say is that I was, throughout that week, in company with persons who can vouch for my presence.'

'Their names?'

'I prefer not to say. You may take my word for it. Should suspicion fall on me, I would be able to name my companions. If you seek a murderess, you will have to look elsewhere. My husband was not altogether an amiable man; I dare say he made many enemies in his time.'

To her surprise, Sir Humphrey seemed to accept this. 'Mr Napier was a man of excellent reputation, but our enquiries have revealed some irregularities in his way of life that—'

'Pray say no more, I do not wish to know.'

'Can you tell me of any enemies of his that you know about?'

'No.'

Sir Humphrey gave her a penetrating look, but he had no further questions. Then, as he was about to take his leave, he said, 'I believe that you had a servant in your employ at Tyrrwhit, one Meg Jenkins.'

'My husband had such a servant, yes. I can tell you nothing about her, my husband and the housekeeper saw to all the hiring of staff. She was dismissed by my husband at Christmas.'

'Do you know why?'

'I suppose her work was unsatisfactory.'

'Like your answers,' said Mrs Griffin when Sir Humphrey had gone. 'Upon my word, Alethea, I never knew you could be so like your father, so haughty and controlled.'

Alethea collapsed on the sofa, landing with such force that little puffs of dust rose in the air. 'Was I haughty? I didn't mean to be.'

'I rather think it was the best thing you could have done, since it made your evasiveness sound like reserve and pride, that you did not like to admit that you had married a man not worthy of you.'

Alethea laughed. She found herself wishing that Titus had been there to see her playing that particular role – one she was sure he didn't think her capable of.

'It's what the soldiers say, isn't it, that one should get over rough ground lightly.'

'Were you in company? What kind of company, Alethea? I am very surprised that Sir Humphrey didn't press the point.'

'Oh, the best company, only it would not be quite convenient for me to name names at present.'

Miss Griffin's shrewd eyes were upon her, and Alethea found herself reddening. 'Do not look at me like that,' she said. 'I have done nothing wrong, nothing I am in the least ashamed of; however, I don't wish to drag others into this business. That man knows quite well I didn't murder Napier.'

'I think that is so, which is why he let you off so lightly.'

If that was lightly, heaven help the poor soul who came up against Sir Humphrey when he was in a more forceful mood. Alethea felt that she had brushed through as well as she could. 'It is odd about Meg Jenkins. I wonder why he asked about her.'

'A servant with a grudge is always going to be under suspicion.'

'I saw little of her – a fresh-faced country girl. Welsh, and shy and very young, she can't have been above fifteen.'

'A tasty morsel for a man of loose morals,' said Miss Griffin.

Alethea thought of her husband's mistress: the false, complacent Mrs Gillingham. 'I do not know that he was in the habit of molesting the female servants.'

'I think that there was a great deal about the man that you were unaware of,' was Miss Griffin's final word on the subject. 'Now, I wish to return to my writing, and I recommend you o put Sir Humphrey's visit out of your mind. A little music will restore your spirits, I am sure.'

Alethea didn't exactly feel unease, more a sense of curiosity. Who had hated Napier enough to kill him? Was the attack the result of a sudden argument, a mistake in the heat of the moment, or a contemplated crime of revenge or punishment? It occurred to her that she might never know, that her husband's death could become one of the many murders whose perpetrator was never brought to justice.

Figgins took a darker view. 'They'll hang some poor creature for such a crime, they always do.'

'What, an innocent man?'

'Or woman. Londoners like to see a woman hang.'

A sound night's sleep did much to lift the darkness that the visit from Sir Humphrey and Figgins's remarks had cast on her spirits, and she rose happily from her bed to look out on a London drenched in pale sunlight. She sang to herself as she drank her morning chocolate, and as Figgins helped her dress. 'How uncomfortable it is to wear black on such a day,' she said to Figgins who was trying to restore some order to her curling hair. 'Do you think I might not wear lighter colours within doors?'

Figgins gave her hair a forceful tug. 'What, with the likes of Sir Humphrey calling at every moment?'

'I am sure we shall have no more callers,' said Alethea confidently.

She was mistaken. An hour later, she was seated at the piano, practising assiduously, when there was the sound of loud knocking upon the front door.

She stopped playing, her hands rested on the keyboard as she listened.

Oh, no, surely that was Letty's voice. What was she doing in London? And another voice, just as familiar, that of Mr Fitzwilliam. Surely Figgins would have the sense to deny her – only it would take more than Figgins to keep Letty at bay.

The door opened. 'Upon my word, this is a fine time to b playing the piano,' said Mr Fitzwilliam. 'Here is Letitia, come with me to inform you of what has now happened, and to take you back with us to Aubrey Square.'

'I have told Figgins to pack up your things,' said Letty. 'I never was so shocked as when I heard you had taken yourself off to this house.'

'How are you, Letty? I hope that Figgins knows she takes her orders from me.'

'Hoity-toity, well, it is clear that you have not heard the latest news. I was never so ashamed of anything in my life as when Mr Fitzwilliam told me. To think that our name—'

'Oh, for heaven's sake, Letty, what news?'

'The worst imaginable,' said Mr Fitzwilliam.

Titus, being a Whig, didn't belong to Pinks, the Tory club, but patronised Benedict's, an establishment on the other side of St James's. He had taken a cup of coffee there, discussed new iniquities of the present government with his friends, and was sitting in a comfortable leather chair, idling through a newspaper, with his mind very much elsewhere, in the region of Melville Place, wishing that he might think of a reason for calling again at number seventeen.

A member he knew by sight as one Harvey Greendale was talking to a red-faced stranger in a blue coat. 'This will dent the Darcy pride,' Greendale was saying.

'It's a disgrace, and the girl is only eighteen, a pretty way to behave. I always said Darcy took too lenient a line with those girls of his. He should spend less time junketing off abroad and more time attending to his family.'

'Adultery and murder, pretty charges to be laid against his daughter. I warrant he'll be travelling back as fast as wheels will carry him. Do you suppose she'll have to stand her trial?'

'Bound to,' said blue coat. 'It's too big a crime and too much in the public eye for it all to be hushed up.'

'She had better be got out of the country if her family want to save her neck.'

'The question is, who is the man she ran off with? These young women have no discretion in their amours, that's the trouble with them. I suppose it's as likely to have been her lover who pulled the trigger, but they do say it was a woman who did it. Evidence of the servants, you can't get past that.'

'Now that it is all out in the open and in the newspapers, more witnesses will come forward, it's always the way.'

Titus had frozen at these words. He noticed now with a strange sense of distance that his hands were trembling slightly as he turned over the pages of the newspaper.

There it was, in the usual unctuous, insinuating words with which the writer announced to a censorious world some exciting tidbit of scandal. With how much regret the newspaper had learned that the authorities were eager to ascertain the whereabouts of Mrs N, widow of the tragically murdered Mr N, at the time of the said murder. There was some reason to believe, the paragraph continued, that all had not been well between the recently married couple, and that Mrs N had quitted her husband's roof in the company of one Mr H, a young man whose present whereabouts were unknown. The newspaper had it on the best authority that a woman was known to be the culprit, and that Mrs N was unable to provide convincing details of her own movements on the night when the terrible deed was perpetrated, beyond asserting that she had been in company all that time.

The editor of the newspaper concluded in a gush of morality that the grim outcome of the investigations might cause alarm to any female who was contemplating straying beyond the bounds of matrimony – and added that Mr D, Mrs N's father, was expected to return to these shores at the earliest possible moment.

A blast of rage shot through Titus as he screwed up the newspaper and hurled it into the fireplace, where, it being a warm June evening, no fire was presently burning. One or two members raised their voices in protest; most of them, after one glance at Titus's thunderous face, kept their opinions to themselves.

How had the newspaper got hold of their information? He had met Sir Humphrey, an old friend, at the club the previous evening, had ascertained that he had called upon Alethea, was perfectly satisfied with her answers, and was pursuing his enquiries among quite a different order of female: those connected with the more fashionable bagnios and bawdy houses.

'Was Napier killed by a whore?' Titus had asked.

Maybe not, Sir Humphrey said, for women were unaccustomed to pistols, but there was reason to believe that a woman of such a kind – dressed very fine, but certainly no lady – had visited Napier that evening, and Mrs Gillingham, who looked after the house where Napier lodged, admitted that he often had women come for the night. It seemed, Sir Humphrey said, with a kind of grim distaste, that such assignations were the purpose of Napier's visits to London. 'With his wife of only a few months left to languish in the country,' he added. Doubtless the whore who had visited Napier had a protector; he was probably the one who had fired the fatal shot.

Where, then, had the rumour in the newspaper originated? Titus asked himself. Somewhere or nowhere, like all such vicious pieces – and how had they got hold of Mr H?

He remembered that he had promised to attend a party at his sister's house. There he might pick up any gossip that was circulating, he told himself, and at least his sister wouldn't believe what she read in the newspapers. His faith in her good sense was dented, however, when he found Mrs Vineham among those present.

'So, you are back in England,' she cried as he bowed to her. 'I found Italy such a bore, Byron quite besotted with that dreadful Italian woman, Lord Lucius more than ordinarily tedious, and so I determined to make my way home as soon as ever I could. By the by, have you heard the shocking scandal concerning that young Mr Hawkins?'

'Mr Hawkins?' said Titus, his heart missing a beat.

'Why, yes, the young man you befriended, the nephew of Mr Darcy, only he turns out to be no such thing. I met a man in Venice, such a bore of a bishop I can't tell you, but he is closely connected with the family and assures me that no such nephew exists. Now it turns out that he was Mrs Napier's lover, that she ran off with him – it is incredible, I know, but perfectly true, I have heard it said by several people who know the parties concerned. So young, so rakish, we live in a wicked world, do we not, Mr Manningtree?' She gave him a dimpling smile, her eyes widening at him with a none-too-subtle invitation.

'If the young man were eloping with Mrs Napier, why was he travelling to Italy?'

'Oh, to escape from her family, they got wind of the affair and were determined to prevent their running off together. He would have had to fight a duel had he stayed in England, and I dare say he is no use at that kind of thing, why, he is hardly more than a boy. So he abandoned her, quite ran away, only when he reached Venice he must have been summoned by her for they say he quit the place in a monstrous hurry, and now it is all about town that he or she or both of them together did for poor Napier. Is it not shocking?'

'Is it not merely a sour rumour? I would beware, ma'am, of being so ready to blacken another's name; malicious gossip has a way of rebounding upon the rumour-mongers.'

'Upon my soul, you are very serious and moral tonight. I know what it is, you were taken in by Mr Hawkins; how men hate to be shown up as lacking in judgement.'

Annoyed beyond forbearance, Titus found his sister and took his leave. 'You cannot expect me to stay when you invite creatures like Mrs Vineham,' he said.

'Oh, that poisonous woman, I didn't invite her at all, she

came with the Durstons, and I could hardly turn her away at the door.'

'I advise you to do so next time, she doesn't belong in civilised company.'

'Pray do not let her chase you away, however – where are you off to in such a hurry?'

'To visit a whorehouse,' he said, leaving her speechless and indignant in the centre of her elegant hall.

'You have brought it all upon yourself,' Letty cried. 'Had you done your duty as a wife, none of this would have happened.'

'Duty? Had you been married to such a man, you would not speak of duty!'

'Alethea, that is quite enough,' said Mr Fitzwilliam. 'Letty has come from Yorkshire, travelling at the utmost speed and in great discomfort – only stopping for one night on the way – to be with you.'

'She might just as well have stayed at home. Who asked her to come to London, expressly to poke her nose into my affairs?'

She had gone too far. Letty's face was red with anger, Cousin Fitzwilliam's rigid with displeasure.

Her temper had got the better of her; try as she might, she couldn't keep back the words. 'Now you come running to my side, but what use were you when I travelled all the way to Yorkshire to tell you what kind of a man I had married?'

'You are young and inexperienced, as I told you at the time. It is the duty of a wife to submit to her husband, and—'

'And you agree with her, I dare say,' Alethea said to Mr Fitzwilliam, who took a step backwards.

'Such vehemence – of course, your sister is right. That is not to say that I don't appreciate that you and Napier were not entirely well-suited – however, a man is master in his own house and he expects his wife to show him respect and obedience.'

As Fanny does to you? Alethea said inwardly, a ray of

humour breaking through her anger as she thought how much, how very much, Mr Fitzwilliam was in Fanny's power.

The moment of amusement passed, and she addressed her cousin with cold civility. 'My late husband was a man who enjoyed using the whip. Upon his wife. I do not think that maidenly modesty was at the root of the hatred I felt towards my husband, nor that it was my duty as a wife to submit to such treatment.'

'Napier a flagellant!' cried Mr Fitzwilliam. 'I never heard anything so monstrous!'

'What are you saying?' said Letty. 'How can you invent such a thing?'

That was the difference between them. Mr Fitzwilliam, a kind, humane man, if one rather too fond of propriety, was still a man who lived in the world and knew that such inclinations existed.

Now he was reddening with anger. 'This is wholly unexpected. Do you tell me that he treated you, his wife – you are saying—'

'Yes.'

'Alethea,' said Letty, her mouth prim, 'you go too far, no well-bred woman—'

'Which is exactly the point,' said Mr Fitzwilliam. 'No well-bred woman should have to endure such treatment. If a man – there are women on the town who are willing – that is to say . . .' Speech failed him. 'It is a disgrace. Alethea, why did you not confide in Fanny?'

Alethea found she could bear Mr Fitzwilliam's disapprobation better than his concern. She bit her lip and shook her head, not trusting herself to speak.

'Or the Gardiners.'

'Alethea exaggerates, I am sure,' cried Letty.

'I think not,' said Mr Fitzwilliam, looking more severe than Alethea had ever seen him. 'This is not the kind of thing any young wife would invent. I just wish that Alethea had thought to consult an older woman, wiser in the way of the world than her sisters. It is understandable that they would have no knowledge of this particular vice.'

'Camilla would have understood and helped me,' said Alethea, reckless now. 'And Georgina knew precisely what I was talking of, only she chose to put her fingers in her ears and pretend she had not heard any of it. Letty isn't altogether to blame, she was taken in by Napier's apparent charm. He could make himself extremely agreeable: that was what misled me, when I agreed to become his wife.'

'I think there is no more to be said upon this subject.'

Letty was clearly prepared to argue, but Mr Fitzwilliam took no notice of her. 'Alethea, I trust that your maid will have put up what you need. We can leave at once.'

'I am grateful for your visit, sir, but I am not returning with you to Aubrey Square.'

'Nonsense,' cried Letty. 'It was always so, pig-headed in the extreme, no wish to listen to what older and wiser heads have to say upon any matter.'

'When it comes to pig-headedness—' Alethea broke off, there was no point in entering into an argument with Letty. That was the problem with her oldest sister, you could not argue with her, for she was right and you were in the wrong. 'I am staying here, at Melville Place,' she finished.

Mr Fitzwilliam said nothing, but held out a folded newspaper which he had brought with him. 'I think you should read this.'

Her eyes flew down the paragraphs, hardly grasping the sense of them, but understanding enough to know what she was being accused of.

Even so, rebukes, threats, appeals to her sense, her reason, her better nature, her decorum were all in vain. She remained adamant. 'Indeed, sir, I am as troubled as you are that our name has been dragged into the gutter by the press, but I do not think my presence in Aubrey Square will make a jot of difference. My name will be cleared when the murderer is found; until then, I am in the pillory and it will be better for me to remain here, within doors.'

'Alone, in a London house?' said Letty. 'It is not to be thought of.'

'She is not alone,' said a quiet voice at the door. 'I am sorry to intrude, Mrs Napier, but I thought you might be in need of some support.'

'Miss Griffin!' said Mr Fitzwilliam, in tones of high disapproval. 'Do you lend your countenance to this mad freak of Alethea's? Pray do not do so, for you will not want to be aiding her in her disobedience to the wishes of her family.'

'It is not in her power to disobey the commands of those in authority over her,' said Letty.

'Oh, be quiet, Letty,' said Alethea. 'You are not in authority over me, no, nor Mr Fitzwilliam. I am a widow, and in the eyes of the law, responsible for myself. I do not choose to go to Aubrey Square, and there is an end of it. Miss Griffin keeps me company, there is nothing in that for the evil tongues of society to cavil at, I believe.'

Chapter Twenty-eight

Ever since she had eavesdropped on Sir Humphrey's conversation with Alethea, Figgins had been turning things over in her mind. Now she whisked herself away from the door as Mrs Barcombe came storming out, a spot of colour on each cheek. Mr Fitzwilliam didn't look none too happy, neither; not surprising after those wicked words about Miss Alethea in the newspaper.

Miss Griffin had pointed them out to Figgins not half an hour ago. 'Do you know where Alethea was? Were you with her? Do you know the identity of Mr H?'

'I can only tell you what Miss Alethea will tell you herself, that she didn't run off with any man, and yes, I do know where she was, and it wasn't in London shooting her husband dead.'

'I never for a single moment thought it was. However, I fear that there is some reason for her to be so secretive about this, and that when the truth comes out, as it must, now, to clear her name of these shameful accusations, she is going to be plunged into an even deeper scandal.'

You don't know the half of it, Figgins said to herself.

'None of it need come out if they catch the murderer,' she said.

'Oh, in that case – but I wonder if there is any chance of it. Sir Humphrey clearly didn't suspect Alethea in the least. Small consolation, for the world will always believe the worst.'

'Meg Jenkins,' said Figgins. 'Why did Sir Humphrey mention Meg Jenkins?'

Miss Griffin gave her a sharp look. 'Did Miss Alethea tell you so?'

Figgins wasn't listening. Figgins had gone.

'Jack,' Figgins cried, bursting into the kitchen, where her brother was polishing a crystal decanter. 'Did a Meg Jenkins, turned off from Tyrrwhit House, ever tip up at Ma's, do you know?'

'Not that she spoke of to me.'

'I knew it,' said Figgins. 'I knew she'd come upon the town, a tasty morsel like she was didn't have a hope of a respectable job. Jack, I want you to find a whore for me.'

Jack stared at his sister. 'A whore? Don't you go talking like that. What do you want with a whore?'

'Not a whore, one particular whore. I reckon I know who that girl was who was with Mr Napier, the night he died.'

'Then if you do, you keep your trap shut and say not a word about it.'

'What, with the newspapers saying Miss Alethea did it?'

Jack had taken a great liking to Alethea, whom he found a very civil young lady, not one to come the nob, and with a smile and a please and a thank you when she wanted something done. And Martha thought the world of her, and Martha was a good judge of a character, almost as good as Ma. 'Tell me how you know.'

Figgins sat down at the table and told him all about Meg, and about Napier's nasty habits. He listened, unsurprised; he knew well enough about men who were keen on the whip. It was a vice prevalent in the Navy, he could name a dozen officers he knew, some of them very senior men in the service, who were inclined that way, and it would be the same ashore. 'If Sir Humphrey's looking for the girl, why trouble yourself about it? He'll find her, all right.'

'He doesn't know where to look. He's just looking for people who might have a grudge. It's me what's put two and two together.'

'And made five, if you ask me. If she did go into the trade, who's to say she had anything to do with Napier?'

'If we find her, we can ask her.'

'Looking for a whore in London is worse than needles in haystacks, there are thousands of them.'

'She was a pretty girl, she'll have been picked up for one of the high-class houses, you may be sure of it.'

Jack got up, removed his apron, and shrugged on his jacket. 'There's never a dull moment with you around, sis. Whore hunting, indeed, I hope Ma doesn't get to hear what you've been up to.'

Figgins brought her discoveries to her mistress.

'Meg Jenkins?' Alethea said. 'There was a serving girl of that name, at Tyrrwhit. How come you to think of her now? She was turned off, I don't know why, one of Napier's whims, I suppose.'

'Ah, there was more to it than that,' Figgins said, and told her of her encounter with the unfortunate Meg. 'I told her to go to Ma, but she never did. Anyhow, Jack's made a few enquiries, and a mate of his is chummy with a piece called Polly. On the game, she is, but she says there's a Meg Jenkins who works with her in a whorehouse – a very classy whorehouse, one of the King Street places.'

'King Street?' said Alethea, bemused. King Street to her meant Almacks.

'Yes, there's more kinds of dancing done in King Street than the nobs let on.'

Alethea frowned. 'Figgins, I'm sorry that any servant should come to such a place, but why do you come to me with this news? It is odd, however, that you should think of her just now, for Sir Humphrey asked me about her.'

'Yes, and I heard him do so, and that's what set me thinking. I reckon the law's looking for her, the reason being that she knows something about the murder.'

Alethea was now all attention. 'Indeed, you may be right.'

In which case, she thought rapidly, she would much rather she could talk to the girl herself, before any law officer got hold of her. 'Figgins, we're going out.'

'Titus! Good God, what does this mean?' Alethea exclaimed.

Titus, of all people, standing calmly on the back stairs of one of the most notorious houses in London, looking at her with a quizzical expression on his face. She had gone quite white, she knew; her own face must reveal her dismay and her sense of betrayal.

'What does this mean, indeed?' he said in a low, urgent voice. 'What in Christ's name are you doing here, in this of all places?'

'It is no more shameful for me to be here than you.'

This wasn't true. King Street belonged in a sphere adjacent to but quite beyond any respectable woman's circle. Only two kinds of women came into this house: ladies of the town and the servants who waited upon them and cleared up after them and their clients. For Alethea, such a place was outside her boundaries; a separate sphere that might be touched through the men of her rank who frequented these establishments, but into which she might never stray.

Except that she had. Dressed as a man once more – she and Figgins had raided Napier's wardrobe – she had intruded on forbidden ground, venturing into a place where desire was bought and sold and where the difference between the sexes showed at its most extreme.

Only to find Titus here, Titus of all people! The very last man she would have thought an habitué of bawdy houses, however fashionable. How wrong her judgement of him had been. Was she doomed never to fathom a man's character correctly?

Titus opened a door on his left, and, without ceremony, thrust her inside, leaving Figgins unregarded in the shadows on the landing.

'Let go of me this instant,' said Alethea.

'Be quiet, do you want to raise the house?'

'What room is this?' she said, as she took in the extraordinary opulence of the chamber. Silks and damasks, laces and even a shawl sparkling with gems, thrown carelessly over a screen, were all around her. There were two enormous gilt mirrors, each with a pair of pouting cupids at the top, and these reflected the light of dozens of candles in the crystal chandelier hanging in the centre of the room and in the various holders placed on what few empty surfaces remained. Her feet sank into the carpet, the overstuffed red velvet chairs and chaise-longue seemed to come towards her, huge and distorted. She shut her eyes and found herself swaying.

'Don't you dare faint,' said Titus. 'Not here. You are not to faint, do you hear me?'

There was a heavy scent in the air, musky and overpowering, that made Alethea's senses swim – that was until she took a deep breath and found herself sneezing uncontrollably.

'Must you do that? For heaven's sake, have my handkerchief.'

She buried her nose in it. It was clean and fresh and the mere feel of it gave her back some feeling of normality.

'What room is this?' she said again.

'It is the private chamber of Mrs Legrange, whose house this is.'

'Whose house – you mean she runs this house? The girls?'

'Oh, so you know what kind of a house it is?'

'Of course I do. I'm not a fool.'

'Forgive me, but of all places to come in that particular disguise, this has to be the most foolhardy.'

Alethea had recovered sufficiently from the effects of the perfume to dispense with the handkerchief, which she handed back to Titus. He folded it mechanically and thrust it into his pocket.

'They are Napier's clothes,' she said.

'They make a poor show, and I suppose that is Figgins out there, lurking, and doubtless listening at the keyhole.'

'Figgins would not do such a thing.'

'Would she not? Well, call her in, and we shall see how we can best get you out of here before you are discovered.'

'No one will discover us, that is why we are in this part of the house. Jack – that is, I understood this is where the girls live, when they are not . . . not on duty in the other part of the house. And I'm not leaving, I'm here for a purpose.'

'As am I, but you are certainly leaving, and immediately.'

'Anyone may guess what your purpose is, while I'm here to find out the truth,' she finished in a rush, aware that the look of fury on his face had given way to amusement.

'You think you can guess what my purpose is in coming here?'

'Why do men go to a whorehouse?'

'I'm sorry that you have such a low opinion of my morals.'

'I see how familiar you are with the house. Here we are in this dreadful chamber, and you know whose room it is, and what she is.'

'Mrs Legrange and I had some amorous dealings together many years ago. When I was only a little older than you are now. Strange to relate, although our paths have gone in very different directions, we have remained acquainted – as friends, not as seller and buyer, I do assure you.'

A likely story, Alethea said to herself, but what was it to her if Titus chose to spend time in the company of such insalubrious persons? 'Please let me pass, I wish to do what I came here for, and then I shall leave.'

'What have you come here for? Is it to talk to Marguerite Piercey?'

'No, it is not, I never heard of any Marguerite Piercey in my life.'

He was watching her closely. 'Formerly known as Meg Jenkins. Ah, I thought so. Then we have the same end in mind, only I do wonder how you came across her.'

'She was formerly in my husband's employ and was turned

off. She came to London to seek work, and Figgins's brother Jack found out that she had ended up here.'

'That's quite right. A common enough story, if a sad one.'

'And I can't imagine what you have to do with her. Or I can, perhaps.'

'You are wrong in your vulgar supposition. I, too, merely want to speak to Meg Jenkins.'

'Why?'

'Because I think she may know who killed Napier, and unless that is made clear, you will be left without a shred of reputation.'

'Is that any concern of yours?'

He looked down at her, his eyes unfathomable. 'Perhaps not, but I find it is.' He picked up a candlestick and opened the door before stretching out his hand and taking hold of hers. 'Let us go together, since you're here and will not heed my advice.'

'Do you expect me to?' she said, trying to keep her voice even, which was difficult when her heart was pounding and she found it hard to breathe. The touch of his hand unnerved her, she wanted to pull her own hand away, but found she could not do so.

'Next floor up,' whispered Figgins as they came out of Mrs Legrange's room.

'I can find my own way,' Alethea said to Titus. He took no notice, and instead drew her hand under his arm as they mounted the wide, shallow stairs.

A knock on the door on the next landing was greeted by silence.

Figgins bent her head to the lock, causing Alethea to choke back a laugh as she looked up and saw Titus in the candlelight, his face full of amusement.

Figgins gave the door handle a hefty rattle, and to Alethea's surprise, the door swung open.

What had she expected? Another boudoir, a plush bed, sumptuous hangings on every side? That was foolish, she told herself, looking around the sparsely furnished room. This was where Marguerite or Meg slept, not where she plied her trade. There were two narrow beds in the small room. On one of them lay a girl with the palest hair Alethea had ever seen, and huge blue eyes, rimmed with shadows. Like something out of a fairy tale, she told herself, but as a stream of abuse came from the rosebud mouth, she realised that this was the home of the wicked fairy, not the one with spangles and a wand.

Figgins was shocked. 'That's a fine way to talk, bet you scare the men off if you blaze away at them like that. Shut your gob, Polly, and let us talk to Meg.'

The rosebud mouth shut, and the girl stared at Figgins. 'How do you know my name? I never saw you before in my life.'

'Never mind how I know your name. Is that Meg?'

'Marguerite,' said the other girl. She had been brushing her hair and she swung its heavy darkness forward to catch the hairs at the back of it. She was wearing a not very clean gown over a shift and little else, and her opulent figure was very evident. Sloe eyes looked the three of them up and down, lingering longest on Titus.

'You're Meg Jenkins,' said Alethea. 'You were once employed at Tyrrwhit House, where you worked for my – for Mr Napier.'

The hairbrush was clenched in a tight fist as she slid from the bed to her feet. 'Polly, go and get Mikey, tell him there are men up here, tell him to come up and turn them out.'

'No, Polly, don't you do no such thing,' said Figgins. 'Or you'll wish you hadn't.'

Titus, meanwhile, had placed a hand over Meg's mouth to silence her shrieking. 'Sit down. I want some information, that's all, and I'm prepared to pay handsomely for it.'

'I don't know anything, anything at all,' said Meg, all the fight suddenly leaving her as she slumped down on the bed. She looked very young and frightened, and her eyes were those of a cornered animal. 'I've done nothing wrong.'

Alethea, filled with sudden sympathy, went over to the girl and knelt down beside her. She started to put her arm around her, but dropped it as Meg winced and let out a cry of pain.

Alethea stood up and stared down at her. 'Show me your back,' she said. 'Did he whip you?'

Tears were falling down Meg's cheeks and she rubbed at them with the back of her hand.

'He sent for me. I didn't know it was him, it was just another gent, I never heard his name, or I wouldn't have gone. I don't know how he found me, you see, I think it was by chance.'

Her voice had a definite country lilt to it; Alethea felt a pang of remorse at the realisation that the girl had not come from the kind of home where she would ever have expected to end up like this.

'He was full of wine, and there was wickedness in him. He said he would beat me until I died, and I knew he meant it.'

'That's all lies,' said Polly's sharp voice. 'She's making it all up. She goes with the ones who like the lash, that's why she's all cut up. Those marks will heal soon enough, and as for the rest of it, it's lies, like I said. I and Mrs L and all the girls will swear she never left the house all that evening. Mikey, too, that keeps the door, and some of our gentlemen regulars, we'll all swear. Now get out, you with your mincing ways and smooth talk, or I'll throw open the window and scream the place down.'

The journey back to Melville Place passed in a blur for Alethea. Her mind was a jumble of darting thoughts and memories, of Meg as she had been, of Napier when his black mood was upon him, of Mrs Legrange's chamber, of Titus, so threatening and yet a tower of strength.

They slipped in through the back, and Figgins, wiry, concerned and muttering reprehensible curses under her breath, helped Alethea upstairs. She brought up a hot bottle to warm the bed, and found her mistress already between the sheets, eyes closed, her face still taut and drained.

She roused her and made her drink the strong hot toddy she had brewed for her, and then blew out the candle before going, her mind buzzing with speculations, to her own room in the attic.

Alethea slept fitfully. Too tired at first to do anything but sleep, she woke in the dark hour before dawn and lay quite still, her mind clear, her thoughts grim. What had she done? What evil had she brought on herself, on her family?

She looked back to her life only a year before, and saw her younger self as a stranger.

How innocent she had been, how naïve! She had thought she knew all that she needed to know to take her place in the world, and she couldn't have been more wrong. She had blundered blindly from folly to folly, never listening to advice, concerned only with herself at any given moment.

She had ill repaid Fanny's kindness, had scorned the advice of her parents; oh, how much she wished she had listened to those warning voices, and had not rushed headlong into marriage. Pique and pride and hurt feelings had overcome reason and sense; she had cared more for what the world would say about her than she had for listening to the deeper dictates of her heart. She hadn't loved Napier, she had made a great mistake in marrying him. It had been a dishonest and a dishonourable action, to commit to a marriage where there was no real bond of love – had there even been much affection?

She had imagined, stupidly, that life could be lived on the surface, that if she couldn't be with Penrose for the rest of her life, then it didn't matter very much whom she lived with. What folly, and what a price she had paid for her error and for the betrayal of her own feelings.

Now, looking back, she realised how she had allowed herself to be overwhelmed by her passion for Penrose, how rashly she had let that attraction become all important to her.

Here she was, scarcely a year later, and Penrose meant no more to her than – than the casual friendship of a girlhood acquaintance.

Tears prickled in her eyes, but she was too overwrought to find release in a storm of weeping.

Thoughts crowded in on her. She had brought disgrace on herself, on her family, possibly on Titus – dear God, how was she going to find a way out of this wretched coil? What had possessed her, to dress up as a man and go off to Venice? Had living with Napier cost her her wits? It wasn't a scrape, it was a disaster, a scandal that would rock polite society to its foundations. She could never live in England again. What kind of a bleak future awaited her in some distant foreign place, where all she might hope for was that no one had heard of her name and the dreadful story attached to it?

It had all been unnecessary.

That was the cruellest rub of all. Letty might not understand or care what Napier was, but now it turned out that Fanny would have understood, at once, and would have known exactly what was to be done; yes, and Mr Fitzwilliam would have supported her, too.

She need have gone no further than Aubrey Square. So much for her pride in managing to reach Venice with only Figgins to accompany her. She had thought that a real achievement, and as it happened, she had been discovered the very first time she was in company with a group of her fellow countrymen. Not by all of them, it was true, only Titus, and it was absurd to suppose that you could deceive a man as acute as he was.

How much he must despise her. His sense of honour alone had led him to help her. She had been so shocked at finding him at that whorehouse, had at once attributed the worst motive for his being there and in that, too, she had wronged him, hitting out at him like that. When all he wanted was to clear her name, so that suspicion might be lifted from her without her having to reveal that she had been with him when Napier was killed.

How the newspaper editors would lick their lips over that story! Even if she hadn't fired the fatal shot, it was full as bad for her to have been with another man when her husband breathed his last. They would make Napier into a martyr, scorned by his wife, murdered under his own roof. Never mind that it was a far from respectable roof, and that he had been keeping very unrespectable company there. He was the injured party, she would be branded a shameless adulteress, and Titus would be condemned on all sides for his share in the intrigue.

Dawn, and the first murky light of a heavy summer's day, brought no relief from the turmoil in her mind. She dozed a little, in the end, and woke with a start as Figgins's face peered round the door at her.

'Visitors downstairs,' she hissed. 'It's Lady Hermione, and a very fine gent as I've never seen before. I let you sleep, seeing as how you've still got great dark rings under your eyes, only now you'd best get up as quick as you can.'

Alethea ran down the stairs, ignoring Figgins's appeals for her to wait so that she could brush her hair. Alethea didn't care that the cloud of dark curls wasn't brushed or pinned up, nor that her black dress was barely hooked up at the back: all she wanted was to see Lady Hermione.

'Good gracious,' was that lady's greeting. 'Alethea, my dear girl, how well you look in black. Allow me to present Mr Hellifield, who has escorted me from Venice. He is an old friend of Titus's and is eager to make your acquaintance.'

'I'm greatly honoured,' said Harry, bowing with grace over her hand. 'Forgive the intrusion, ma'am, but Lady Hermione said I might come. I have been longing to meet the woman who has so disturbed Titus.'

'Disturbed?' This was dreadful, here were his friends lining up to pour scorn on her.

'Why, yes, it was high time he was shaken out of his

complacent ways. He told me he was past the age of losing his heart to any woman, I am glad to have him proved wrong.'

Her face was burning. 'I have caused Mr Manningtree a good deal of trouble, and I am heartily sorry for it.'

'Nonsense,' said Lady Hermione.

Alethea blinked and turned her attention to Lady Hermione. She had been so delighted to hear that Lady Hermione was downstairs, that she hadn't stopped to wonder why she was there at all. 'How come you to be in London?' she asked. 'You were heading for the mountains, to escape from my cousin, the bishop.'

'Yes, but then word reached Harry, who has his own inimitable methods of receiving news from England more rapidly than anyone I know, that Napier had been murdered. He came to tell me of it, and I knew at once that this meant you were likely to be in some difficulty, so I made Harry accompany me back to this country.'

'Yes, and a devilish journey it was, too. Lady Hermione should have been a soldier, I never knew anyone travel faster or need less rest while on the road.'

'I have always been able to sleep in carriages,' said Lady Hermione briskly. 'I can't be doing with dawdling when one needs to be elsewhere.'

Alethea recalled her manners, and rang the bell for Figgins to bring refreshments.

'How pleased I am to see Figgins again,' said Lady Hermione. 'That girl is a treasure.'

'Not too sure about the butler, however,' said Harry. Alethea could see he was glancing about the room with a look of displeasure on his elegant countenance.

'The house was never lived in by my husband,' she said apologetically, 'and the staff was reduced to one old caretaker and his wife. The whole house is in a dreadfully shabby state, and the butler is Figgins's brother, who is more used to naval ways than smart London houses.'

'That explains it,' said Harry, seemingly satisfied. He drank a cup of coffee, rose, and took his leave of them with exquisite politeness. 'I, unlike Lady Hermione, am quite shattered by my journey and shall retire to a peaceful doze in a comfortable armchair at my club.'

'All so much talk,' said Lady Hermione, as the door closed on him. 'He may look no more than a dandy, but he was the toughest of soldiers and is not a whit worn out by the journey. He is off to find Titus, he is the most inquisitive man of my acquaintance, and he feels, quite rightly, that he has not had the whole story out of me. I doubt he'll get much out of Titus, who can be a clam when he wants. Now, my dear child, tell me exactly what has been going on, and how you came to be in such a fix.'

Try as she might, Alethea's account of her voyage back to England, the discovery of Napier's death, the surprising attitude of the Fitzwilliams, of the fix she was in, was incoherent and stumbling. Lady Hermione listened patiently, asking questions now and again, and finally summoning Figgins into the room. Figgins came in with Miss Griffin, rather to Alethea's surprise.

She could see Lady Hermione taking an immediate liking to the gaunt authoress, and in no time they had their heads together. With interpolations from Figgins, the narrative became clearer. Much of what was told was news to Griffy, and the colour flared into Alethea's cheeks as her ex-governess shook her head over her extraordinary exploits.

'Well, it is something to have sung in an Italian theatre as a castrato, and there is this to be said for it: no one will ever believe it.'

Gloom descended upon Alethea once more. It was kind of Lady Hermione to come back to England to help her, more than kind, but what could she do? What could anyone do?

Lady Hermione did not seem to have a defeatist bone in her body, however. 'I have it all straight in my head, now, and it is not so very bad. Titus will have dealt with this Meg

Jenkins, I can answer for that, so what we have to do is make your position unassailable.'

'That is more easily said than done.'

'It must be insupportable for you just at present. Harry and I noticed various unsavoury persons hanging about outside this house, and one of them was hawking a broadsheet about Napier's murder – how unpleasant it all is.'

'So what is to be done about it?' said Miss Griffin, who was obviously finding all this much more interesting than the most lurid plot she could contrive by her pen.

'Oh, as to that, it is quite simple. Now that I am in town, I shall simply inform everyone that you were with me.'

'With you, ma'am?' cried Alethea, astonished. 'But I wasn't.'

'Of course you weren't, you were busy being ill on Titus's yacht. What has that to do with it? You weren't in London murdering Napier, and that is the truth, and if one has to come at a truth sideways, from time to time, then so be it.'

'It would certainly stop all the gossip and remove suspicion from Alethea,' said Miss Griffin. 'Only, will it answer? Will you be believed?'

'Certainly I shall. I shall say that Alethea was with me in Paris. People seem to know that she was in Paris not so long ago – that will be thanks to your sister Georgina, who does not seem to know when she should hold her tongue,' she added. 'What could be more natural than that she was with me until – when was it that you reached these shores again? Monday of last week? Then you went, Alethea, at my invitation, to Shillingford, nothing more proper; it is her sister's house, after all.'

Titus couldn't believe his eyes. Harry, of all people, sitting in the club, a glass of wine at his elbow, looking completely at home. He strode across the room. 'Good God, Harry, what are you doing here? How glad I am to see you!'

Harry got to his feet. 'I imagine you'll be more glad to see

Lady Hermione, who whisked me from Italy as though on a magic carpet. We've come to sort out your little problems, Titus, that's all.'

'I'm obliged, but I believe I can manage my affairs for myself.'

'Your affairs, yes, but those of Alethea Darcy – no, Alethea Napier she is, of course, one forgets – are beyond your touch.'

'Keep your voice down, for heaven's sake. No one is aware that I am even acquainted with Mrs Napier, and it is best for her if it stays that way.'

'Not acquainted! When Lady H tells me you shared a cabin with her all the way back from Italy?' Harry said, quizzing his friend.

'I did no such thing,' said Titus, pulling at his neck cloth. 'Don't bandy her name about like that, it is most offensive.'

'Ah, touched a nerve, have I? Well, she's a widow now, and a rich one, so there's nothing standing in your way.'

'Nothing . . . I don't know where you got this maggot in your head, Harry, but you are on the wrong track entirely. I helped Alethea out of a difficult situation, at Lady Hermione's insistence, and that is all.'

'Not quite. There's the little matter of Cherubino, to begin with.'

'That was the difficult situation. Now, drop it, Harry, or you'll start to annoy me.'

Harry lifted a languid hand. 'I wouldn't do that for the world, knowing what a fire-eater you are. You'll be wanting to call upon Lady Hermione, I dare say. You'll find her at her house in Bruton Street, where she is no doubt writing letters to all her numerous acquaintance. London is rather thin of company now, of course, otherwise she'd be on a positive orgy of visits. I must say it's very good of her to take all that trouble to clear the girl's name. Of course, there is the family connection, she is very fond of Alexander's wife. However, no need to fret, my dear, Lady H will do the trick.

*

Alethea had thought she would feel uncomfortable to find herself in Titus's company again, but in the event, it was like greeting an old friend when Titus called on her that evening, bringing Lady Hermione into the house through the stables.

'How unconventional,' was Lady Hermione's only comment when she came through into the hall. 'I can quite see one wants to avoid attracting attention, although I think interest will die down very quickly.'

There was so much Alethea wanted to know. 'What is to become of Meg?' was her first question. 'She was defending herself against violence, she will surely not have to stand her trial.'

'There can be no question of a trial, that would be washing far too much dirty linen in public,' said Titus. 'And if Meg were to be arrested and tried, I very much fear she would hang, for all the swearing and perjury her friends say they will commit on her behalf. The courts never trust a woman of that kind, and the public like to see a murder end with a hanging.'

'You said that Sir Humphrey was on her track – good Lord, he has probably found her by now.'

'He will have found where she has been residing until recently, but I'm afraid the bird has flown the nest. Meg Jenkins is by now across the channel, where Mrs Legrange owns several establishments. I do not think she is suited to the work, however, and Mrs Legrange admits that she is likely to be too severely scarred to work in a fashionable house. So she is to have a new name and be given good references and a sum of money so that she can find more respectable work.'

Alethea's spirits rose; happy though she was to know that Lady Hermione had contrived to get her out of her own troubles, she had been deeply worried about Meg. 'I suppose it is all wrong, and the law should be upheld, but if that means she must hang for killing Napier, when he was going to kill her, then I have no time for the law.'

Scars, permanent scars on poor Meg's body; Napier must

indeed have been in a wild mood that night. She had suffered cuts and weals herself, but he had never attacked her with such viciousness, and she healed quickly. Such marks as remained would fade with time. Unlike the other scars that Napier had inflicted on her, she thought with momentary bitterness. And then, more philosophically, that she had been lucky. He might have stayed his hand with a new bride, but if he were capable of doing that to Meg, one day he would have attacked her with the same abandon, and she might not have had a pistol to hand.

'Think of it as a nightmare from which you have awakened,' said Titus, who had been watching her face.

'Yes,' she said.

'One remembers horrors, I think, for the rest of one's life, but memories do not always remain so sharp, and with time, and new circumstances, do not affect us so powerfully.'

He spoke like someone who had glimpsed his own hell and her mind flew back to the inn in Switzerland: the battle of Waterloo and its aftermath was his nightmare. As it must be for many others. It was easy to forget how much men might suffer, with the more adventurous lives they were able to lead, and on top of that, they had to endure the same domestic and family sadness and tragedies as their womenfolk.

Lady Hermione rose to her feet. 'You will be glad to be away from this house, Alethea, I never saw a more dusty, dreary place. Now, I shall leave you to your own devices for a few minutes, as I wish to talk to Miss Griffin. No, do not trouble to show me the way, Figgins may do that.'

There was a long silence after she had left the room. Alethea fingered the lace on her black dress; how she loathed having to wear widow's weeds. She didn't want to look at Titus, what was he thinking about, why did he say nothing?

'May I ask what your plans are?' he said at last. 'As Lady Hermione says, you will hardly wish to stay here.'

'I hadn't given it much thought,' Alethea said. 'The Fitzwilliams are urging me to go to them at Aubrey Square, or I could go down to Pemberley until my parents return. Or the Gardiners have asked me to stay.'

'There are your sisters.'

Alethea shook her head. 'I don't think I should be happy with any of them just at present.' Her face broke into a smile. 'Letty would insist on the strictest mourning, she is a stickler for that kind of thing, and Belle hardly wants a raven in the house when she is about to be delivered.'

'Go abroad. There you need not keep up the mourning, not even for the first three months. Return to Italy, where you may stay with the Wyttons.'

Alethea had a reason for not wanting to visit her sisters just yet, a reason she wasn't prepared to reveal to Titus. The prospect of being with happily married couples jarred on her, and there was no doubt that her four sisters were happy in their husbands and in their lives in a way she hadn't been, and had no prospect of being. She shook her head.

'Too much domestic bliss for you to stomach?' asked Titus.

He was shockingly acute, and his acuteness made her uncomfortable.

'Perhaps I should don my pantaloons and boots, and avoid wearing black that way,' she said with a wry smile.

'Alethea, don't you dare – ah, you are joking, I see.'

He was walking about the room as they were talking, he seemed ill at ease. He came a step closer to her, and was about to speak again, when the door opened and Lady Hermione came back in, with Miss Griffin on her heels.

'We have had a good chat,' Lady Hermione said. 'If you will allow yourself to be advised by us, you will pack up your bags once more, and brave the waves of the channel. No, you need not see your sister Georgina, or Camilla, or anyone you know at all. I'd like you to come and stay with me in Italy, spend the summer in the mountains, that will restore the roses to your cheeks. And in a place so remote from England, you know, you need not worry about mourning. Then, in the autumn, you can go to Vienna to join your parents.'

Her spirits rose instantly at the prospect of escaping from England to spend the summer with Lady Hermione. She turned to Miss Griffin. 'Griffy, do you think it is advisable?'

'I most strongly recommend it. You may place all your affairs in the capable hands of Mr Darcy's lawyer, and take yourself off until your health and spirits are quite restored. I am persuaded that it is just what Mr and Mrs Darcy would advise, since it is out of the question for you to travel to be with them in Constantinople, that is not at all the kind of place you need just now. And Lady Hermione has very kindly extended an invitation to me to come to Italy later in the year, when I have finished my book.'

Alethea gave her an impulsive hug, and then, after a moment's hesitation, another hug to Lady Hermione. 'You are all so kind to me.'

Titus looked rather as though he would have liked to be hugged, too, but he said nothing, and shortly afterwards took Lady Hermione away.

'I wish you will come, Figgins, but you need not if you don't wish it.'

'I told you before, where you go, I'll go, and I don't suppose it'll be as bad as that spa town you was on about. You aren't fit to be out on your own, if you want the truth of it. Abroad isn't what I fancy, I'll admit, and I've seen all the mountains I ever want to, but life isn't about what we want. Now, get to bed, and it's to be hoped you'll sleep less restless than last night. Calling out in your sleep, you were, and tossing and turning like demons were after you. Maybe now your mind's at rest you can sleep like a Christian.'

'I am tired,' Alethea said, with a huge yawn.

She didn't sleep, not at once. Instead she lay under the sheets, thinking about how extraordinary a day it had been, what a reversal of fortune it had brought. Then she remembered Harry's words about Titus being beyond the age of losing his heart. What had he meant by them? Anything, or nothing, and besides, what was age to do with it? Titus was a young man. Older than her, of course, but—

She turned over, giving the pillows a good thumping. He had seemed a little distant this evening, rather grave. It must go against the grain for him to be embroiled in her very shady affairs; how her stupidity had drawn in other people. There was Lady Hermione lying to save her reputation and Titus whisking Meg away from under the very nose of the authorities.

She smiled at that. He was the most decisive man, and more than a match for Sir Humphrey, for all that man's cleverness.

She would like being in Italy with Lady Hermione, but it was going to be a little lonely, perhaps. She wondered how Titus would spend the rest of the summer. At Beaumont, no doubt, busy, for a change, with his own affairs.

She fell asleep, thinking for the first time in many weeks more about someone else than about her own problems.

My dearest Hermione,

I was never more surprised when I got to town and heard your name on every lip; no one talks of anything except the Napier murder. That is mostly because London is as thin of scandals as it is of company; one really good crim. con. and the whole affair will be forgotten.

We dined with Sir Humphrey last night. He is mightily relieved, I fancy, that matters have turned out as they have, for whilst he would have liked to take the murderer into custody, he is well aware that a trial would bring to light all the shocking details, and just at this juncture the parading of Napier's vices for every Tom, Dick and Harry to hear about would please neither the government nor the authorities. Napier was too well-connected, as is his wife, for the tinder-box of public opinion not to be ignited at such revelations; Sir Humphrey spoke most feelingly of radicals and riots and so forth.

So it has all worked out for the best, and I hope that Alethea is at last finding some degree of contentment after such a troubled time. Do you think she will get over it? She has character, but even so, to be married to such a man, and then the murder – it is enough to distress even one of the most placid disposition, which she is not.

They say that the whore who was with Napier, whom he beat half to death – did you ever hear of such wickedness? – was known to him. Apparently, Mrs Gillingham, in whose house he had those lodgings, had come across her – I can imagine she is more than familiar with the inside of the bawdy house – and recognised her from when she was a servant at Napier's house. It seems that he had a fancy to have at her while she was at Tyrrwhit, only she would have none of it. So there was a strong element of revenge in Mrs G asking the abbess for her company for that evening. It was wrong of the woman to send her, for she has girls who are willing to be whipped, at a price, but this one was not one of them.

However it is, she is not to be found, and I for one wish her well. It is the way of the world that men will seduce or assault their servants, and that pretty serving wenches who go to London will end up in the bawdy house, but what Napier did was outside all bounds of acceptable behaviour.

Is it true, what they are saying, that Napier actually had Mrs Gillingham, who was his mistress – although I feel that is too polite a word to describe what she was – to stay at Tyrrwhit House on several occasions, obliging his wife to be in her company? I never heard anything more shocking, and, as you know, I hear everything.

I trust that the mountain air suits you, and provides a welcome relief from the heat of Venice. We are returned from Scotland, and are off to spend a week or so at the seaside; Freddie has been recommended sea bathing by his physician.

Pray write and tell me how Alethea does,

Your most affectionate friend,

Belinda

PART FIVE

Chapter Twenty-nine

From the moment Alethea set eyes on the Villa Serena, she knew she was going to be happy there. It wasn't a large or imposing building, but its mellow stone, blue shutters and brilliant flowers gave it great charm. Nothing could have been more different from London or the English countryside. Here were mountains shimmering in the morning light, high meadows speckled with flowers, a lake, silvery in the sunshine, and complete peace.

Alethea had never thought she would come to value peace and quiet. She had always longed for life and movement around her, had come to find the tranquillity of Pemberley a bore as she grew up, yet here she was, quite content to sit for hours on the terrace, her face shaded by a wide-brimmed straw hat, doing nothing but surveying her glorious surroundings.

In the cooler air of the evening, she found consolation in music, with long sessions at the pianoforte or playing on a flute that some guest had left behind.

'Not that I care much for the flute,' she told Lady Hermione. 'Although there was a time when I used to play it a lot. In London, when I was still in the schoolroom.'

'Now you look back and remember those days as being simple and uncomplicated, am I not right?' said Lady Hermione. 'Whereas, at the time, you chafed at the restrictions imposed on you, and resented the freedom and pleasures of the world allowed to your older sisters.'

'Not entirely, for although I did love to go about in London, I didn't envy them the demands of the season, the obligation to go to this ball and that rout, whether they wanted to or not. One has to be polite to everyone, you know, and that is a great bore.'

Lady Hermione laughed at that. 'You are just the same as your papa was in his younger days. He always had excellent manners, but it used to be obvious when he found a person tedious or without interest. He has learned to disguise his contempt for his fellow human beings, which is greatly to the credit of your mama. She taught him how to laugh.' And, after a pause, 'I dare say you will be pleased to see them both.'

Alethea considered the matter as she sipped cool, sweet white wine out of an exquisite long-stemmed glass. 'Yes, I shall be very glad to see them. Now that Papa has written so kindly and with such understanding, I feel I can face him without too much trepidation.'

She had been at first mortified and then thankful that her Cousin Fitzwilliam had taken it upon himself to write to Mr Darcy, and at the same time, unknown to her husband, Fanny had written a much franker letter to Mrs Darcy. Alethea was thus spared the embarrassment of relaying to two such interested parties the sorry tale of her disastrous marriage and its melodramatic ending.

Papa had written one of his forceful letters, condemning Napier, but also reminding her into what trouble her impetuousness and strong will could lead her, if she did not take care. She was now a rich, independent woman, not an easy situation for one of her youth, and would need to have all her wits and reason about her, but he trusted her good judgement and sense; her misfortune in encountering one – or should he say two – unworthy, dishonourable men should not, however, give a dislike of the sex.

'Very true,' cried Lady Hermione, when Alethea told her what Papa had written. 'At present you will be inclined to hate all men, but you will get over that.'

'It is not so much hating all men,' said Alethea after some reflection. 'It is more a matter of not trusting them.'

'Anyone who goes through life trusting people without making sure they are worthy of trust is a fool. Yet there are people who may be trusted, men as well as women. And short of casting yourself into a convent, which is hardly a practical way to spend the rest of your days, you will have to come to terms with men, who are not to be dismissed as a class, for there are as many differences in their natures as there are flowers in these meadows.'

'I could not like a bad-tempered or violent man, nor a weak or a stupid one.'

'That eliminates some ninety per cent of the male race, however it leaves a few to be considered worth knowing. All women become disillusioned with men, as I dare say all men do with women. When we are young, we make gods and goddesses of one another, then we soon come to realise that we are all merely human and imperfect. Some are more deeply flawed than others, some positively vicious, as you have learned the hard way, yet as time goes on, we learn to tolerate the flaws and appreciate the good qualities in those we love.'

'If they have good qualities. Napier seemed to have many good qualities. His liking for music, his attentiveness—' Alethea stopped, startled. She was speaking of Napier with detachment, how could this be?

'Men of his kind generally have a great deal of charm. Do not ask me why it should be so, but it is. Take heed of your experience, and be wary when you meet a man who makes you feel you are more interesting than anyone else in the world. He is sure to be up to no good.'

A few lines of Ben Jonson drifted into Alethea's mind. 'Love no man, trust no man, speak ill of no man to his face, nor ill of any man behind his back,' she quoted, rather sadly.

'Not a few of my acquaintance subscribe to that philosophy,' said Lady Hermione. 'Only going through life in that way is singularly joyless.' She paused, her eyes looking somewhere that Alethea could not see. 'I married a rake, that was my mistake. Alexander's father was a rake. He tried to be faithful to me, but in vain; an attractive woman would sooner or later come into his life, and he had no power to resist.'

Alethea felt a chill go down her spine. That, in its way, might be almost as much of a torture as having a flagellant for a husband.

'How did you manage?'

'As one does. I suffered a lot at first, then I had Alexander and the other children, which gave my life a different direction. And I was very fond of my husband. He made me laugh, and he had a clever mind; like you, I can't abide a fool. Over time, the strength of my feeling for him, and therefore my pain at his liaisons, faded. I found new interests for myself.'

Did she mean lovers? Alethea wondered. Judging by the mischievous smile hovering on Lady Hermione's lips, she did.

'Life doesn't turn out as we expect it to. When we come out into the world, our future seems as smooth and unmarred as virgin snow. It is an illusion, of course, and soon we weave a web of mistakes and failures as much as achievements and triumphs, and become used to walking on broken pavements rather than on paths of gold. It is what makes life so interesting, one quickly learns that one never knows what is going to happen next.'

'Oh, surely, ma'am, for most women, they know all too well what is going to happen next. There is hardly much variety within the domestic sphere where we are obliged to lead such little lives.'

'You'd be surprised how lively and wide-ranging those little lives may be.'

Conversations such as these gave Alethea much to ponder on. She had not before spent time in the company of a woman like Lady Hermione, shrewd, worldly wise, witty and serene. The older women she knew each had their virtues: Fanny's common sense and practicality; Miss Griffin's intelligence and dislike of cant, Mrs Gardiner's kindness and sense; her mother's warmth and humour and love.

None of them, however, had lived life to the full the way that Lady Hermione had, and Alethea liked the feeling her companion gave her, that life was an adventure, a journey to be savoured, both the good and bad parts, and, above all, enjoyed.

'We have been in solitude here long enough,' Lady Hermione announced one morning. 'You cannot live out of the world for ever, and we shall grow dull with only ourselves to talk to. Besides, the servants grow idle, and I can see that your Figgins is longing for you to wear some of the clothes that have been sent for you. The admirable Miss Griffin proposes to pay a visit to Venice in the autumn, so we cannot hope for her company, but I shall invite some other friends now that the weather grows cooler.

Alethea knew her duty and agreed, politely, but without enthusiasm. And now, as she looked down from the terrace to the winding road below, she saw a solitary horseman approaching. She hadn't asked whom Lady Hermione was inviting, and she was sure all her kind hostess's friends would be worth knowing; still, her heart sank at the prospect of an end to her summer idyll.

The figure became clearer as he approached. He was riding at an easy pace, glancing now and again up to the villa above him. He reined in his horse, shaded his eyes, then waved.

It was Titus.

Dear God, she thought, her heart pounding, he was the last person she expected, the last person she wanted to see. Not true, said a little voice inside her head. He was too much connected with those harrowing weeks, he was not an easy and relaxing person; no, she told the voice, she did not want to see him.

He was coming across the terrace to her, his hand extended. 'I am happy to see you looking so well.'

Titus had made up his mind not to visit Italy, not to try and see Alethea. He had news of her from an indirect source, Belinda Atcombe, whom he met at the Jerrolds' house in the country. Lady Hermione was rusticating, she said, with only the Darcy girl, Mrs Napier, who had been through such a terrible time, for company. Titus longed to hear if Lady Hermione had said anything more about Alethea, how she was, if she was happy, if she had been able to put the unhappiness of her marriage and her husband's death behind her.

His sister, who knew her brother better than he had any idea of, noted his moodiness and restlessness, and drew her own conclusions. 'You've fallen in love with Alethea Darcy, as was,' she said to him bluntly as they sat together in the drawing room one afternoon. 'No, don't frown at me or attempt to deny it, I have eyes in my head. She is too young for you, has far too fiery a temperament, will always be affected by what she went through with that odious Norris Napier, but there is no point in saying any of that to you.'

'It is what I tell myself.'

'Then you should also tell yourself that you are old enough to know that marriages are not made in heaven, and that no ordinary woman is ever going to satisfy you. Peaceful domesticity you cannot expect with a young woman of her ilk; do you give a jot for such a life? No, of course not. This time spent with Lady Hermione will restore her faith in herself and in others, I am sure of it, no one so capable as Lady Hermione for setting her on to a right way of thinking and feeling. She will not allow her to dwell on what is past, and will be kind or bracing as the need arises.'

Titus wasn't listening, he was lost in his own thoughts. 'Alethea finds me overbearing and conventional.'

'Then she must get to know you better so that she can discover you are no such thing.'

'Her treatment, first at the hands of that blockhead Penrose Youdall and then Napier, will have given her a lifelong dislike of men.'

'I never heard such nonsense,' said Lady Jerrold with great vigour. 'Alethea is a most courageous young woman; she is not one to turn her back on what life has to offer. Go to Italy – Lady Hermione will be delighted to see you – spend some time with her and with your Alethea. That will at least spare my carpets from being worn to a thread by your pacing up and down upon them.'

Titus had ignored her advice, returning to Beaumont, where he prowled about his estates, annoying his steward and bailiff and causing all his household to wish him elsewhere. 'Sitting in the library, gazing into the fire or watching the rain dashing against the windows, what use is that?' said Bootle, with strong disapproval.

He wasn't surprised when his master leapt out of bed one grey morning, shouting for coffee, his boots, his horse. He was off to Southampton, to the *Ariadne*, he was going to sail to Greece or America or anywhere where it wasn't raining and where he wouldn't be surrounded by fools.

Nor was Bootle surprised when the *Ariadne* slipped quietly into a mooring in Genoa, and Mr Manningtree told him that he was going on horseback to pay a visit to Lady Hermione Wytton at her villa in the mountains, with Bootle to follow on with his luggage in a chaise.

Titus's heart leapt when he saw Alethea on the terrace. Almost, he had persuaded himself that he would arrive to find her gone, to England, to Rome, to anywhere. Yet here she was, looking to his eyes more beautiful than any woman he had ever known, no longer wearing those wretched widow's weeds, inexpressibly dear to him, and laughing at him for jumping out of the way of a bee.

Alethea gave him her hand, but instead of shaking it, he took it between both of his, holding it, and looking full into her eyes for a brief, intense moment that seemed to last an eternity.

Cheeks aflame, she tried to force polite words of welcome to her lips; they would not come.

It was the physical presence of him that had thrown her off balance. He had been a presence in her mind these many weeks, for as she recovered from the bruising experience of the previous months, the memory of him, of his concern, his kindness and, yes, his high-handedness, came to her again and again.

His was a friendship she must always value, she told Lady Hermione, who gave one of her wicked, knowing laughs. Friendship between the sexes, her ladyship said with some astringency, was for children, fools and those of advanced years whom life had drained of feeling.

Surely, it weren't so, Alethea protested. There were men, she had met men in London, who wore breeches and carried themselves as men, but whom one knew instinctively had no interest in women. One could be friends with such men, could one not?

Lady Hermione had been ruthless in her dismissal of such an idea. 'Men like Lord Lucius, I suppose. They have nothing to do with the case. Besides, Titus Manningtree is none such.'

No, indeed he was not. Mr Manningtree was entirely masculine, there was nothing effete or pederastical about him. Yet he had a warmth and a quickness of understanding about him that was far removed from the make-up of such a man as Norris Napier.

Alethea had given a good deal of thought to her husband also, over these weeks. Her initial relief at his death had been tempered with an awareness that she didn't care to rejoice at the death of any man, even one who had wronged her so greatly. Yet perhaps it was better that he had died, for he would in the end have beaten some woman out of this world.

After the first excitement and scandal of the murder had died away, rumours had come creeping out about her late husband that appalled her. While he was alive, his fellow men had taken him at face value, rating him a well-bred, likeable man, a favourite with the ladies, and a pleasant companion at the club. Once dead, his victims found their voices: a servant here, a younger boy from his schooldays there. Even the liberal society of London, indulgent of male excesses, frowned at these revelations.

Napier still haunted her dreams, although less so as the days went past. She taught herself to wake when the dark shadows of those dreadful nights rose to torment her. She diminished him in her mind's eye, making him dwindle into a mere ineffectual puppet. Most of all, she strove to forgive him. The fault in his nature was inborn and undeniable. But there had been faults on her side as well. Had she not been on the rebound from Penrose, would she ever have considered marrying him?

She would not.

Penrose was different. Penrose she didn't forgive, because there was nothing to forgive. Their passions, both their passions, had been stronger than their morals or their duty, hers every bit as much as his. He might be blamed for coming to her as one with a free heart, when he had known all along that his family intended quite a different bride for him, but she did believe that he had genuinely fallen in love with her, it was not all pretence.

Penrose did not haunt her dreams, waking or sleeping. When she thought of him it was with indifference, not anguish. He belonged to another life, when she had been a different person.

And she had come to believe, during her time in Italy, that she was heart whole again, and would remain so. Her love affair and her marriage had inoculated her against love, and life would go on a great deal more easily because it was so.

Now, with Titus close beside her, disturbing her more than she would admit to herself, all her confidence and ease were blown to the wind. Titus, standing there, his hand now on the bridle as his horse sidled and tossed its head. It was a magnificent animal, sleek and powerful, with ears pricked forward, and dark, intelligent eyes roaming over his surroundings.

'From Harry's stable,' he said, looking down at her as though aware that some conversation was needed to smooth the awkwardness of the moment.

'I shall summon a man to take your horse,' she said, wanting suddenly to escape from him.

'If you mean Lady Hermione's groom, you will be unlucky,' he said, pointing down the hill to the meadow that lay spread beneath them. There was Antonio, walking beside his sweetheart, a pretty village girl. Arms round each other's waists, they were entirely absorbed in one another.

She averted her eyes, finding the couple's closeness unsettling. Titus was watching the pair with some amusement.

'Lady Hermione is away, and the mice are playing,' he observed.

'She is away for the day, but how do you know that?'

'I met her on my way. She told me that you would be here. And that you would be happy to see me,' he added, with another direct look.

It occurred to her that she had never had any closer contact with Titus than a handshake. They had never gone down the dance together, nor waltzed, nor sat together on sofas in polite drawing rooms. Their time together had been in very different circumstances, she thought, remembering Lisbon and the happy hours she had spent in his company.

'Alethea,' he said, and there was that in his voice that made her heart thud, a seriousness and warmth that sent a glow into her cheeks. 'I have come expressly to see you. I have stayed away as long as I could, for only a coxcomb would force his attentions on you while . . .' He hesitated, as though uncertain of his words.

'I must always be glad to see you,' she began with dreadful primness. What was she saying?

He looped the rein over his arm, as his horse shifted and stamped impatiently. He ran a soothing hand down the animal's nose, and blew at him, turning his head away so that he addressed the landscape rather than Alethea.

'If you are still – I know what you have suffered, and I dare say you have forsworn all men. Only I find I can wait no longer.'

He swung round to face her again. 'Indeed, Alethea, I am deep in love with you. I won't say I can't live without you, for those would be mere words, but—'

Alethea was overwhelmed by a surge of delight, mixed with fear and panic.

'No,' she said, her voice sounding husky and strange. 'Please do not say it. You are very kind – I am most sensible of the honour you do me – I cannot marry again.'

Silence between them. Then, at last, he spoke again. 'I was afraid it might be so, and truly, I can enter into your sentiments on this. Pray, listen, though. If the idea of matrimony is too distressing, if you feel reluctant to submit to the authority and control that the law gives a husband, then I will most happily share your life with you on any terms. Only tell me that you have some love for me, that you feel in time you may learn to—'

She put up a hand to stop him. She finally had to acknowledge the truth to herself, and, therefore, to him: she had fallen in love with him, unawares, almost from the moment she had met him.

His soul was in his eyes as he smiled down at her; it wasn't a triumphant nor a knowing smile, but a smile that sprang to his lips as he read what was in her heart.

'You mean you would live with me?'

'Yes. In every way as man and wife, and for me the ties between us would be as binding as any vows. But I would not have you fettered and dependent, against your inclination and at the cost of your contentment.'

She was amazed. What he was proposing meant his exile from his native land, the extinction of political ambitions, estrangement from his family and from many of his friends, exclusion from the world he had been born into. Was he really willing to make so great a sacrifice?

She was beyond words. Silently, she held out both her hands; he took them, pressing them close to him, then she was in his arms, her senses lost in a voluptuous darkness as he kissed her with a rising passion.

In the end, Alethea reflected, from within the rapturous comfort of his arms, there had been no awkwardness, no further words exchanged other than words of love. Her defences had tumbled down at the offer, at the look of glowing regard and love in his eyes.

Lady Hermione, on her return some hours later, looked at the couple with a knowing, satirical eye, and announced her intention of removing to Venice for a few days; she had some matters to attend to there, she said mendaciously.

Which left them alone for days of perfect happiness, loving, talking, laughing together as they climbed the slopes around the villa, cantered side by side across the meadows and spent enchanted hours sailing on the lake.

They arrived home hot and contented one afternoon, Alethea flushed and laughing from an argument they had had on their way back, to find that there was at least one visitor at the villa.

'The devil,' exclaimed Titus, 'it's that brother-in-law of yours, the clergyman.'

It was. Barleigh Barcombe was leaning on the stone balustrade at the edge of the terrace, watching them as they approached.

Alethea felt cold. Where Barleigh was, there surely was Letty, the most censorious of her sisters, the person she least wanted to see in all the world.

Barleigh greeted them with friendliness, underlain by a certain stiffness. Where, he enquired, was Lady Hermione?

'In Venice,' said Titus with perfect sang-froid.

'Letty?' Alethea managed to ask. 'Is she with you?'

Barleigh looked from one to the other of them with a widening smile.

'No, Alethea, she remains in England with the children.'

'Then are you permitted to come abroad alone?'

His smile was more rueful now. 'More instructed than permitted, Alethea. I am sent to bring you home.'

Titus gave a snort of derision. 'Sent by whom?'

'Letty and Lady Mordaunt, and also Lady Fanny, are greatly disturbed by rumours that have reached their ears, that you, Alethea, were not under the protection of Lady Hermione and that you were in the company of a man.'

'So she is,' said Titus, his humour restored. 'With me.'

'And Lady Hermione isn't here at all?'

'As I said, she is presently in Venice.'

'Ah.'

'Let me show you to your chamber,' said Alethea. 'Have you a man with you? If not, I am sure Bootle will attend to you.'

'Before you overwhelm me with hospitality,' said Barcombe, sounding rather weary, 'may I ask whether you will return to England with me?'

'No,' said Alethea. 'Come this way.'

Over dinner he came back to the subject: how bad it looked, her so recently widowed, her youth, the age difference between her and Titus, it would seem that he was taking advantage of her, the impropriety of her not wearing mourning—

Alethea and Titus listened, and held hands under the table, and waited for him to run out of steam.

He sat back and laid his napkin on the table with a sigh. 'Well, those are all the arguments I can muster. I have done my duty, now I can be comfortable.'

Alethea stared at him. 'Are you saying . . . ? Do you not mean all that you have preached to us?'

'Not a bit of it. As a clergyman, I have to tell you I find your morals shocking and depraved. As a human being, and at the risk of driving my dear wife into a frenzy, should she ever get to hear of it, I can only say that I wish you joy.'

'What a good fellow you are,' said Titus, leaping up and going round to grasp Barcombe's hand. 'And, with Alethea's permission, there is something you can do for us that will not perhaps assuage Letty's wrath, but that will strike a blow for your morality.'

'Married!' cried Lady Fanny as she opened her letters at the breakfast table. 'My love, they are married.'

'Who is married?' said Mr Fitzwilliam, buttering his third slice of toast.

'Why, Alethea and Titus Manningtree.' She scanned the rest of the letter. 'How generous he is, the control of her fortune is to remain with her, except for the Darcy money that is to be secured on their children.'

'Leave her in control of her fortune?' said Mr Fitzwilliam, choking on the mouthful of coffee he had just taken. 'I never heard of such a monstrous thing; the man's a Radical, that's what he is, a Whig, a Jacobin, a veritable free thinker!'

'And therefore just the man for Alethea,' said Fanny, with the utmost satisfaction.